A Cl

Pale canvas trousers housed ᴸᵒⁿᵍ ˡᵉᵍˢ ᵃⁿᵈ ʰᵘᵍᵉ ̲ . ̲ .ite cotton shirt, tucked neatly at his waist, seemed to cling to the breadth of his chest and shoulders. Sitting in dark contrast on the white collar of his shirt, was thick undulating chestnut hair. Wind tousled, it framed his face like a lion's mane. Clean-shaven, except for his moustache, which had been kissed by the sun to reflect shades of auburn and brass, his bronzed cheeks broke into deep creases as he laughed heartily at some comment from Pearl. Tiny wrinkles lit at the corners of his eyes, as well. His eyes, how could she have not noticed them before? They were the most intriguing color. A greenish blue or was it bluish green? She couldn't be sure. But they were bright and clear—and they seemed to be looking right through her. Oh biscuits! Jolian paled. He was looking *at* her not through her. He'd caught her staring. How would she explain?

What They Are Saying About
A Claim On Her Heart

"...This is a masterfully written tale. Characters are true to form but not the form that is expected. The constant of bringing the reader to the brink of understanding then turning it about keeps you turning the pages. Whatever will happen next?

This is a book that I highly recommend to anyone who is sick of formula romances. *A Claim On Her Heart* marches to the beat of its own drum. On my surprise reading scale this rates—five ! ! ! ! !"

Wings

A Claim On Her Heart

by

Camille Cavanagh

A Wings ePress, Inc.

Historical Romance Novel

Wings ePress, Inc.

Edited by: Lorraine Stephens
Copy Edited by: Leslie Hodges
Senior Editor: Leslie Hodges
Executive Editor: Lorraine Stephens
Cover Artist: Richard Stroud

Wings ePress Books
http://www.wings-press.com

Copyright © 2007 by Camille Netherton
ISBN 978-1-59705-890-2

Published In the United States Of America

April 2007

Wings ePress Inc.
403 Wallace Court
Richmond, KY 40475

Dedication

There would be no story had you not encouraged me to find my voice.

There would be no truth if you had not accompanied me to the Cariboo, pardoning my need to wander through cemeteries and study in the archives and there would be no book had you not begun that silly competition...I love you Scott.

(p.s. neener neener, neener)

Acknowledgements

The Author would like to gratefully acknowledge and thank those who helped with the production of this novel. They include: Marlene Ablitt, for reading everything I write and for always being my number one fan, Emerald Hodges, Valerie Hodges, Margaret Netherton, Rosemarie Hirtreiter and Correna Schwab for their dedicated readings, encouragement and suggestions; Sean Netherton for his wonderful recommendations for Native names; and a special thank you to my critique partner and fellow author Lissa Larer, who, with her positive guidance and constant esteem building advice allowed me to trust email and myself, and proved to be a driving force in my ability to find "the end".

One

January 1863, colony of British Columbia

"Hurry up, Jo, this is your second stop today!" Jakeb's booted foot crunched the frozen white path. Jolian glanced between the snow-laden branches to the trail above her and saw her brother hop from one shabby leather sole to the other. His red cheeks were stiff from the cold and Jo saw his next words huffed out in front of him.

"Jo... Ma and Pa are getting too far ahead!"

"I'm coming!" Her frozen fingers fumbled with the buttons on her union suit. She'd waited as long as she could to relieve herself. Did Jakeb honestly believe she wanted to expose her bare skin to the raw Cariboo air for any extended period of time? She yanked homespun trousers over woolen-covered thighs, tucking the flannel shirt tight at her waist.

Her second stop today, ha! Didn't he welcome the break from the non-stop walking? Their last break had been more than two hours ago with only enough time to nibble cold biscuits and down stale coffee. Her belly growled in response to the memory of the false nooning. She shook her blanket coat free of a dusting of snow and then slipped her arms into the heaviness of its sleeves. Would she ever feel warm again? Even the thickness of her clothing couldn't stop her teeth from chattering. Time to walk again. At least it might take her mind off the temperature. For the fiftieth time today she cursed the weight of her canvas pack as it settled into place on her shoulder. The curse echoed in the hollow of her belly and sent back the ringing of her second favorite grumble: the fact that the entire miserable situation was of her own making.

1

With the toe of her oversized boots she covered the hole she'd made in the snow. No sense attracting unwelcome animals. A flutter of an entirely different kind, twinged in her belly. Who knew what creatures lingered behind the surrounding ancient pines and cedars? A barely audible prayer whispered from her lips. Shelter, or any thing resembling shelter, would be more than appreciated. The old map her father was following had been pretty accurate thus far, allowing them to find abandoned roadhouses and trappers' cabins along their route. Maybe they'd get lucky again soon.

"Jo-li-an!"

"All right, I'm finished!" She waded through thigh-high powder until she found the branch she'd clung to when she'd left the trail. Mittens slipped on the wet pine needles as she heaved herself up the branch, hand over hand. Her breath came out in white puffs and a very unladylike sound grunted from her throat. Jakeb reached out a hand to pull her back up onto the trail while keeping his eyes focused on the direction their parents had taken.

"Can you still see them?" She fiddled with her glove trying to right the fingers.

"They just rounded that bend yonder." Jakeb motioned with a glove-covered hand. "I think they're—"

The sound of the gunshot stopped him mid-sentence. The echo hung between them and it felt as though time suddenly began to move with minutes between each second.

"Maybe pa saw a rabbit," Jakeb muttered as they stared in the direction their parents had gone. His astonishment rooted him to the spot.

"Run!" Jolian's mind screamed, but she remained inert. Then Jolian heard a sound she knew she'd remember for the rest of her days. Her mother's scream bounced off the canyon walls and reverberated in Jolian's bones. Almost drowning out the sound of the second shot... almost.

Time sped for a moment as Jakeb removed his pack and tossed it off the trail into the trees. He lifted her up, pack and all, and then half threw her into the trees as well.

"Stay there," he whispered. "Don't make a sound. Stay right there until I get back. D'ya hear?"

Jolian half nodded and bit down hard on her lip to hold in her own scream. Blinking back tears, she tried to focus her eyes on Jakeb, as he turned from her. She supposed he was running, but he seemed to be moving at half speed instead. She crouched lower in her hiding spot, willing the snow-burdened evergreens and the mounds of soft powder to conceal her. Heart hammering in her chest, she fumbled for Jakeb's pack. She grabbed the shoulder strap, and pulled it close, trying to quell the shaking that threatened to overtake her entire body.

She should be running too, with her brother. She shouldn't be crouching lower and lower, frozen with fear. Her parents... Her parents! What should she do? Should she follow Jakeb? What if he needed her help? Should she just stay put as he told her? Her parents... Jakeb!

Through the evergreens, she had a partial view of the trail before her. She fixed her gaze there and pleaded with her mind to go blank. Her muscles tensed and the hair on the back of her neck stood up as she thought she heard her brother shouting in the distance. Then silence. She couldn't move and her breathing became quick and shallow. Jolian summoned the will to lean forward and strained to see more of the path. Minutes passed, she commanded her ears to hear something, anything. Then it was there... the sound of hooves crunching the snow on the path above her. Her instincts took over and she scrunched her eyes closed and pursed her lips. Blood rushed through her head; making her feel woozy and she had to open one eye to maintain her balance. She turned her one, obligatory eye towards the sound of the ever-nearing hooves.

A horse came into her sight. It's rider had a bushy black beard sticking out between his shabby felt hat and his gray overcoat. He was leading their two mules, burdened with their belongings. There was a pounding like drums in her ears and she held her breath as the man approached her hideaway. An odd sound reached her.

Laughter. He was laughing! Surely he could see her footsteps in the snow. They'd lead him to her... he was going to shoot her, too! Tremors engulfed her heart and lungs. She had to move, but couldn't. It was as if the frozen ground held her in its glacial grip. Her eyes were locked on the man before her, burning his face into her memory. His laughter rebounded throughout the gorge, mixing with the pounding in her ears until her vision blurred and narrowed.

Jolian forced herself to breathe in slow, measured breaths. She couldn't afford to lose consciousness now! His horse snorted and blew dual white puffs of breath through its nostrils. Its hooves carried the man closer and closer to where she

3

trembled. Behind the horse, the mules brayed their protest and the man's laughter was their response. He was almost upon her! She could see his eyes staring at her through the bush. He'd seen her! She should run! She couldn't move! Only her thoughts and pulse were racing.

He was directly in front of her now. Jolian closed her eyes again and began to pray. *Our father who art in heaven, hallowed be thy name...* had she heard that or just imagined it? She opened one eye and saw the man pass her by. She watched as he shifted his weight in the saddle and spit a stream of brown juice out into the snow. The mules, carrying all of their belongings, passed her too and she could only sit, staring, reciting the prayer over and over. It took her several seconds to realize the man hadn't seen her after all. He'd passed her by.

The man and their mules disappeared into the distance, but she sat petrified, unable to make her body obey the will of her mind. She had to move! She had to get to her family. Finally, she managed to wiggle her fingers. She loosened her hold on the strap of the pack and tightened it again. Rising to her full height, she paused and let her body adjust to its own weight. She squeezed the strap of the pack once more, trying desperately to connect with the present, and then slung the pack over her shoulder. Somehow she carried both packs and herself to the trail.

Move legs! She forced them to walk her closer to the bend in the trail where her parents and then Jakeb had headed. Despite the cold, a drop of perspiration trickled from her temple to her chin. *Keep moving legs, keep moving.* If she could focus on that. A cramp gripped her stomach, the snow crunched beneath her feet. Bitter cold stung her nostrils. She could feel the dampness of perspiration on her scalp as the icy wind passed through the curls on the back of her neck, below the band of her cap.

She'd have to light a fire soon. Such an inane thought. She tried to keep her mind blank as she reached the bend and closed her eyes. If her family were okay, they would have come back for her. She couldn't look; she didn't want to know... she couldn't bear this, not this! It couldn't really be happening.

Jolian opened her eyes and focused them on her feet as she rounded the bend in the trail. *Step, step, one foot in front of the other*—boots. She saw booted feet in front of her own. *Whose boots?* She made her eyes move up the body that lay before her.

She knew her father's stocky build, even though her brain refused to register that it was him. She saw his Hudson's Bay blanket coat, the one he'd purchased at Fort Yale... he'd been so proud. Her gaze moved up to the beard he'd grown on the trip. Thick blond whiskers interspersed with ribbons of gray. Her mother had said it made him look woodsy. His mustached mouth was open, as if he was trying to speak, but no sound escaped.

His eyes stared vacantly up at her. So many times they'd twinkled with laughter as he spun a good yarn, or looked sleepy and hazy when he'd had too much whiskey. Wonder, sorrow, love. She'd seen all of those in his eyes. They held nothing now, nothing. Above his right eyebrow was a hole, a tiny hole in his head. Blond curls framed his head and a halo of blood framed his hair. Blood, so red on the white snow.

Jolian dropped the packs she carried, and lifted her eyes to take the whole scene in at once. Three bodies scattered the clearing, her father's in front of her, her mother a few feet ahead and Jakeb to the left of her.

Three bodies, and blood. Jolian felt as though she was watching herself discover the horrific scene. As if she was separate from the person who stepped over the lifeless body of her father. *Careful, avoid the blood. If you don't touch it, it can't touch you.* The eerie absence of sound assaulted her, pounded her chest like a hammer. No animals, no wind, even her own footfalls fell soundless.

Jolian walked toward the body of her mother, lying face down in the snow. There was much more blood here—much more—very red, against the stark snow. She must be dead, no reason to look. There was a bullet hole between her mother's shoulder blades.

He shot her in the back! She must have tried to run. But why was there so much blood? *Careful, don't touch it!* Jolian knelt beside her mother's body, and picked up her hand. *Cold. It's the snow; the snow's made her cold.* She put her mother's hand down gently in a clean patch of white.

She reached her own hand down to smooth her mother's skirts. They must have lifted as she fell. She wouldn't approve of having her stocking-clad legs exposed. It wasn't proper. She pulled and tugged until her mother's legs were discreetly hidden. Her eyes focused in on the hem of her mother's dress. The satin ribbon that edged the hem hung in shreds. Its brilliant blue faded to only a distant memory of its former self. If she closed her eyes, she could picture her mother's hands, lovingly stitching the ribbon onto that dress. The determination and pride in her eyes as she sewed the tiny, almost unseen, uniform stitches... inch by inch by inch. Jolian fingered the tattered satin as she let the happier thought cement in her memory. There had been a hairpin to match, with blue satin ribbon roses...

She moved up her mother's side, avoided a large patch of blood and placed a hand on her shoulder. Why was there so much more blood here? She lifted her mother's shoulder to roll her body over and she had her answer then, the reason for all the blood. He'd cut her throat! He'd more than cut—Oh dear God! Jolian tasted bile. She gagged and retched until her body began to shake with emptiness. It was so horrid! It was all so horrid!

What was that? She'd heard a noise! Jolian stood and snapped her head in the direction she'd come. Was it him? Coming back? Icicles of terror formed on her spine. Again the sound.

Moaning, it was a moaning. *Could someone be alive in all of this? How could...? Jakeb!* She saw movement, rushed to him and knelt beside the body of her brother. The hair on the left side of his head was matted and sticky looking.

"Jakeb?" Her own voice sounded distant to her. "Jakeb, its Jolian. Can you hear me? Are you shot, Jakeb? I can't see a bullet hole." She quickly scanned his body but could not see any other injuries. Why hadn't Jakeb been shot? "Where is your bullet hole?" Maybe she just couldn't see it.

Jakeb tried to sit up and collapsed back down again. What should she do? She didn't know what to do! Why hadn't she learned nursing or something useful? Cooking, she'd studied cooking! How incredibly naïve. As if cooking would help now.

Get a hold of yourself! Build a fire, boil some water, clean and bandage his wound. Yes, there was her plan of action. She could cope with this, she could. Jakeb seemed to have fainted. Jolian ran back for the packs she'd dropped, making sure her eyes never focused on the bodies of her parents. She couldn't think of them now. She must think of Jakeb; she had to help her brother.

"It will be fine, just fine Jacob. I'm going to build a fire and you'll be as good as new in no time at all." She called to him as she grabbed both packs, then rushed back to Jakeb's side and fumbled through her belongings for her flint box. At least she knew how to start a fire. She found the box and began to search for some dry twigs.

Everything was wet with snow. What good was knowing how to build a fire if there was nothing to build it with? *Calm down! Yes, think rationally.* In her pack were books, her precious books of recipes. She'd had to bring them, even though she'd cursed herself daily for it. They'd been so heavy after a mile or two. How strange that they'd be the first things she thought of burning, after carrying them all this way.

She pulled two books from her pack and cleared the snow, as best she could, in a circle about two feet across. Gathering the driest branches and twigs available, she laid them crisscrossed in the circle and hoped the books would burn hot enough to catch the fire.

She picked up the first book; the one she'd painstakingly compiled with her tutor Jean Pierre. Filled to bursting with all the recipes they practiced and perfected over the years. Without a second thought she began to tear the pages from it. They're only pages; the recipes they held were recorded in her mind. The first book torn and ready for the fire she turned her attention on the second, her mother's recipe book. She picked it up, opened the first page and closed it again. The fire would have to start without this book; she couldn't burn it, not now.

Jakeb stirred and Jolian focused her mind on the task at hand. Foolish girl, letting your thoughts dwell on sentimentality while your brother...

She left Jakeb and ran into the surrounding grove of trees. The snow was deeper here, thigh high in some places. Reaching a giant pine, she dropped to her knees. The ground was barren beneath the tree, as its heavy branches had helped keep the snow at bay. She crawled under its snow-covered arms with ease now and reached up the trunk. There, as in many of the surrounding trees, lay sphagnum, a highly absorbent dry moss that would be just the accelerant she needed for her fire.

She returned to her fire pit and had to strike the flint several times before she created a spark that ignited the moss. Moss glowing, she lay it upon the pages and then blew gently until she could see a tiny flame. The fire caught, and she added more and more pages until only the binding of the book remained. The flames began to catch the twigs. She dug in her pack for her gold pan. Filled with snow, she set it on top of two of the sturdier looking branches. *Careful*, that would be all she needed, to tip the pan and have the melted snow extinguish her fire!

In her pack, she found the cloth she used for washing and placed it in the pan of melted snow, which began to boil. She used the Bowie knife from her belt to stir the cloth about in the boiling water and then to lift it out. Steam from the cloth mixed with the smoke from the fire, as Jolian waved the wet cloth back and forth in an attempt to cool it enough to handle.

When she could finally manage it, Jolian wrung the excess water from the cloth and gently placed it on Jakeb's head wound. He winced as she touched him. She was careful to only allow the hot cloth to touch him and not her fingers.

"It's all right, Jakeb." Jolian tried to sound reassuring. She'd refuse to let anything but positive thoughts into her mind. "It's all right, everything will be just fine, you'll see. I'll wash you up a bit. Don't you worry. We'll be back on our way in no time, no time at all."

Jolian felt as though she moved in a dream. She couldn't seem to put her thoughts together cohesively anymore. They skipped from one thing to the next. She knew she rambled, but better to ramble than face the reality around her. She thought of a bath, a lovely warm bath in her uncle's hotel back in San Francisco... she could almost smell the lilac scented water. Or the cheese soufflé baking in the oven on Sunday mornings. An image of her uncle flashed before her and she shook back to reality.

Shirttail covering her hand, she took the pan from the fire. It sizzled as she set it in the snow. Darkness was coming. The smell of the fire was in her nostrils. Smell! What about the smell of the blood? Surely wild animals could smell all this blood! Last night she'd heard wolves. She'd felt afraid, even in the roadhouse. Now she was among them in the wild, and surrounded by blood and death... practically alone... She couldn't think of it. She wouldn't.

She dropped the cloth into the pan, and instantly the water darkened. Jolian gagged as she stirred the cloth with her knife. She lifted the cloth as before, waved it about, to cool it, then put knife back in its sheath in her belt and wrung out the cloth. This time as she squeezed the cloth, blood oozed through her fingers.

She screamed. She screamed for the horror of everything around her. For the hole above her father's right eyebrow. For her mother's nearly severed head. She

8

screamed because her brother's blood was running down her arms—He would die, too—she couldn't stop it. His blood had touched her and made everything real. This wasn't a nightmare from which she'd awaken. There'd be no parents to comfort her—to stop her screams. Screams in the dark—darkness was coming...was here. She screamed to fill the emptiness—She screamed to hold on to what was left of her sanity.

Two

Cooper Holt swore under his breath. Damn! It was cold! For the second time in as many days, he questioned his judgment in accepting the job Guy had offered him. Surveying gold claims in Barkerville, the latest town to strike it rich in the colony, had appealed to the adventurer in him. Of course, he'd been dead drunk at the time Guy had suggested it... Still, there was something about the word "gold" that made a man's heart beat faster.

Not that he was going to have much time for prospecting by the sounds of it. The Lieutenant at Fort Kamloops figured the real rush of miners would arrive with the spring thaw. The colony had a strict miner's code in place, and much of the 'keeping of the peace' would be dependent upon the survey work Cooper and Guy's newly formed company had just won the right to complete.

Cooper reached for the flask in his left breast pocket but came up empty. Second stupid thing he'd done, agreeing to stay sober for the duration of the project. Although, if he was honest with himself, he knew the whiskey had to go. He couldn't keep living like he had been. He wouldn't keep living if he didn't stop drinking and the promise of gold in the hills gave him good reason to keep going.

"Hey, *mon ami*, d'you hear something as well?" Guy reined his horse beside his longtime friend.

"Hmmm, hey?" Cooper licked his dry lips and focused on his friend. "What's that you said?"

"Ts'kaw's been riding just ahead of me and motioned he heard a sound. I was wondering if you heard anything back 'ere?"

"Nope. But then again, I was thinking on something and not really... Say there's Ts'kaw, he's motioning us to come ahead."

Cooper urged his mount to a trot behind Guy's horse on the old Indian trail. Then he heard what must have alerted Ts'kaw. The most unusual sound. A mewing? No, more like the sound of an injured animal. What the...? His horse rounded a bend in the trail, which lead to a clearing of sorts. Cooper blinked his eyes in disbelief. There had been some kind of slaughter here!

Three bodies, wait—there was another it seemed. Ts'kaw moved towards what appeared to be a small child, no, a young boy, curled into a ball beside the fire. Even in the darkness, Cooper could see the patches of blood seeping into the light of the snow, around at least two of the bodies. *Who on Earth... What could have possibly gone on here?*

Cooper dismounted and tied the reins to a tree branch. "Easy, Storm." He reassured his horse when he balked at the smell of the blood. Cooper hurried to the spot by the fire where Guy and Ts'kaw stood.

"What the hell happened here?"

Ts'kaw bent and examined the crumpled mess of blood stained clothing, which was the boy by the fire pit. Other than the whimpering, no sound of protest or acknowledgement could be heard. Ts'kaw moved to examine the other body lying by the fire. He spoke in his native tongue to Guy and then moved away toward the other two bodies.

"Ts'kaw's village is not far now," Guy explained. "He says for us to make a litter for ze boy... ze one lying by ze fire who is also alive. Ze one who sits crying by ze pit can be carried by horseback. Ts'kaw's people will come for ze others." Guy placed his hand on his friend's shoulder when Cooper began to speak. "I know, we have all seen too much of death. It is best for us to do as Ts'kaw asks. This is his milieu; he is ze one of expertise for these things. You and I, our job is to forget this 'orrible scene. We must do ze job of keeping ze living alive now."

Cooper nodded. He knew his friend was right. They were on Ts'kaw's people's land; the Carriers would know best. He retrieved his machete from his saddlebags and began to cut and strip branches for a litter. He'd been surprised to hear another lived amongst the carnage. Two out of four, they'd been luckier than most.

~ * ~

In the end, they decided Cooper would carry the whimpering boy with him on his horse. Storm was more used to carrying passengers than the other horses. Cooper's heart went out to the lad the moment he'd lifted his slouched shoulders onto his horse. He knew what it was like to lose someone you cared about.

Ts'kaw pulled the other boy on the litter behind his horse and they followed him to the village of his people. Pitch-blackness engulfed him as Cooper and his party came upon the village of the Carriers. Even the white of the snow covered ground offered little light to the darkness. If not for Ts'kaw they would never have found their way. A small fire in the centre of the village illuminated their path and cast shadows upon wooden homes built in a semi-circular pattern. The quiet was palpable.

Ts'kaw dismounted and spoke to a tall man who seemed to appear from nowhere. The man called out, and at once the entire village came alive. People rushed about carrying blankets and food. An obviously pregnant woman approached Cooper and removed the boy from in front of him. Cooper gratefully let go of his burden. The boy had seemed a mere slip of a thing at the outset, but as their ride had lengthened he'd become much heavier.

Responsibility for the lad gone, Cooper shifted his weight in the saddle and focused on the village around him. Among the bustle of the natives roamed numerous dogs, too many to count. They strayed near the frozen river and some roamed in pairs between the dwellings. The houses themselves varied in size and shape, most being square, fairly large and made of what looked to be bark wrapped about branches, pounded vertically into the ground. Roofs consisted of bark as well and had holes at the top, which upon closer inspection, emitted smoke, most likely from a central fire. While Cooper had spent most of his life in the colony of British Columbia with his longtime friend Ts'kaw, he could not remember ever having seen a winter village of the Carrier people.

Ts'kaw most often wintered with the Holt family in Victoria. Cooper's father, a Royal Engineer, had taken upon himself, the role of formally educating the young native. Ts'kaw had taken to surveying like a fish to water, which pleased his father and Cooper could now admit, caused some ruffled feathers on his part.

"Competition is a healthy part of a any young man's life." His father's voice boomed in his memory. Cooper smiled and shook his head letting the sound of ice cracking on a nearby waterway invade his thoughts. Ice fishing most likely, as dawn approached. A hunched-back village elder strode towards Ts'kaw, and Cooper tried to make out what he said.

He felt confident in his command of Chinook, the trading language, but his knowledge of the Carrier language was limited. He sat atop his horse, waiting for Ts'kaw to finish speaking with the old man. It was only respectful to wait to be invited into the village. Ts'kaw motioned for him to dismount and he did so. His friend spoke in Chinook, that odd mixture of Native and French, adding in the occasional English word when he could.

"*Tyee say tenass man wake skookum la tate, Tamanass man make skookum again, lay lay. Tenass klootchman quass waw waw, yaka sick tum tum. Yaka tikke le Job clatawa. Tamanass man no iscum le Job, only tenass klotchman kopet le Job tum tum.*"

Copper understood full well what Ts'kaw said: the one boy was injured in the head and the doctor could make it well after a while. The other one, that Ts'kaw called tenass klootchman, was sick with grief in *her* heart and only *she* could make it go. Ts'kaw must be mistaken. Surely that was not a *girl* they had found whimpering by the fire. He'd carried the child in front of him all this way. If the boy were a girl, he would know it!

It was very late and they were all tired. After everything they had been through this evening, Cooper knew he should just let it lie. Yet something in the way Ts'kaw had spoken to him... "I am insulted you think me so stupid, Ts'kaw." He was tired of Ts'kaw's arrogance. "You know, if you can't tell the difference between a boy and a girl, its no wonder you're not yet married."

Ts'kaw flushed under his dark skin, turned and spoke to their mutual friend Guy, in Carrier. He seemed quite adamant in his speech though his body remained calm. When he finished, Ts'kaw turned back and muttered a comment to Cooper in Carrier as well, knowing full well Cooper couldn't follow what he said.

"What did he say now?" Cooper demanded of Guy.

"Ts'kaw says Mutsikanutlo, the curly haired one, is most definitely a *sak'usda*, a sitter on moon. He says you can believe her to be a boy if you wish, because she wants you to believe it. Either way, he will not, as a single man, share his home with her. The Elders would not approve of a Carrier man having a *sak'usda* in his home without a married woman present. You and I, however, can share our space for the night with whomever we choose and no questions will be asked."

"And what was the rest of it he muttered to me?"

"I didn't hear..."

"Don't lie to me, Guy. Your Carrier is as good as your French." Cooper watched his friend shift uneasily in his saddle.

"You don't want to know."

"I *do* want to know damn it!"

"We are all tired and it's—"

"Tell me!"

"He said," Guy began hesitantly, "if you cannot tell a girl from a boy, it is no wonder that you cannot *keep* a wife."

Cooper's laughter startled his friend. "I guess I deserve that much. If anyone else said it I'd knock them flat out." Cooper saw Guy nod willingly as he dismounted from his horse. "But coming from him, well I did deserve it." He draped his arm across his friend's shoulders and ushered him towards a wooden hut. "Let's go get some of that salmon I smell."

~ * ~

Jolian's eyes opened involuntarily. She groaned and closed them again. She didn't care where she was. Wherever she was she hadn't had nearly enough sleep to face it. Too late, the woman sitting across from her had taken advantage of that split second to glare at her. Jolian crumpled her brows and rolled over. She didn't care whom the glaring woman was any more than she cared about her situation.

Her ribs ached as she moved. Why was that? Damn! She began to wake up and the memories flooded her mind. Anything would be better than *that*. She took a deep breath and again felt the stabbing pain. Inch by inch she lifted her torso and the hide that covered her slipped to her waist. At least they, whoever *they* were, hadn't undressed her. She still wore her woolen unionsuit and she knew it covered her too-tightly-bound breasts as well as every other part of her body from neck to ankle.

"Where are my clothes?" the words crackled out of her dry throat.

"Good day to you. I am happy you wake now. Your clothes are clean now and near the fire to dry."

Immediately, Jolian felt sorry for her snippish tone. Who ever this woman was, she had obviously taken care of her and she knew she should express her gratitude. She tried to smile and nodded her thanks.

"I am Aklu'ut, sister to Ts'kaw, and you are in my home now *moosum* two days."

"Two days! What the—?"

"You very tired. Tamanass man leave me watch you, fix you drink. I am dress and undress you. I keep cloth on you. No worry on that. No man come here. My man even not come."

Jolian felt stunned. *Two days had passed?* She wasn't sure what *moosum* meant, but assumed it meant some kind of sleep, as she had no knowledge of the time passing. She didn't even feel like she'd had one decent nights' sleep since... she could feel the bile rising in her throat and looked about frantically for a place to vomit. Aklu'ut seemed to sense her need and as if by magic produced a basket for her and stayed right beside her as her stomach heaved. The kind woman mopped her brow with a damp cloth and whispered foreign phrases in her ear.

"Thank you." Jolian held on to Aklu'ut's hand as she reached to remove the basket. Her voice came out in a dry hoarse whisper. "You have obviously taken very good care of me for a good many days. I truly thank you, Aklu'ut."

The native woman just smiled and patted Jolian's hand. As she stood to remove the basket, Jolian realized that Aklu'ut was noticeably pregnant. Jolian's admiration for the woman increased.

"I know sick *tum tum kokwa.*" Aklu'ut returned and tested the clothes by the fire and then handed Jolian a dipper of water from a nearby basket.

Jolian drank gratefully. She thought she understood the woman's words and mimed her own hands to help Aklu'ut understand her. "Yes, being pregnant, ah with the baby, you would be vomiting as well."

"No vomit. Sick *tum tum. Kokwa,* I same like you. I sick in heart. Month you say July, small pox come. My family and all village die. I then in village of husband with Ts'kaw and Zaxsa. I have now only husband, Ts'kaw and Zaxsa. Zaxsa be father of my father. Ts'kaw, he be Tyee, chief, in month we canoe half of it in. Now no village to be Tyee for."

Jolian could only nod her head in understanding. She could barely wrap her mind around the death of her parents. How did one go about mourning the death of an entire village? She couldn't fathom that. And Jakeb, what had become of her brother?

As if reading her mind, Aklu'ut handed her the clothes from the fire. "You brother wake *skookum*."

Jolian blinked "Jakeb? I don't understand."

"*Skookum*." Aklu'ut mimed a strong person by stomping a bent leg and raising a bent arm with her hand clenched to a fist. Next, she made her arms and legs appear limp and fragile. "Wake *Skookum*."

"Weak?"

"Yes. You brother weak. I make all right you see him?" The woman smiled and her broad flat face exuded reassurance, warmth and concern. Despite the heaviness of her heart, Joilan felt a flicker of kinship and forced a smile.

"Yes, yes please, Aklu'ut. I want to see my brother."

~ * ~

There was no passage of time in the Carrier village. Everyday held brilliant sunshine and sub-zero temperatures. Jolian visited Jakeb and found the wound to his head healing, though painfully slow. When he had regained consciousness, her brother told her he'd been kicked by one of their mules. Jolian thanked heaven above the murderer had not seen fit to shoot Jakeb anyway.

While she felt quite comfortable in Aklu'ut's presence, she decided to maintain her mother's wish and continue to masquerade as a boy. Only Aklu'ut and Zaxsa, Jakeb's caregiver, knew the truth. Her mother had been so concerned for her safety and had sworn, "Not even a man's eyes will touch you on this journey." Safety. The irony of it all stung in her eyes. She decided her best course of action was to keep to herself and keep her disguise.

Once her own strength returned, Jolian insisted on pulling her weight in Aklu'ut's home. Other than her visits to Jakeb each day, Jo worked from the time she woke in the morning until the time she fell onto her hide to sleep. She remained tucked away in Aklu'ut's tiny wooden home seeing only her brother, Aklu'ut and Zaxsa. All the days melted together. Day passed to week and week to month.

She hoped she made things a bit easier for the pregnant Aklu'ut, but her motives were selfish as well. Aklu'ut was one of the women in charge of cooking, for most of the village it seemed, and Jolian knew cooking inside and out. She welcomed the change of cooking something other than the endless meals of beans and bacon she'd made for her family on the trail. "Miner's staples" her pa had called them. Her throat constricted and she turned her mind back to the simple Native recipes. Cooking was a mind-numbing experience for her.

She couldn't bring herself to think about her parents' death, but she also couldn't move beyond the fact of being orphaned. She didn't know what to do or where she would go when it came time to leave this haven. Would Jakeb ever be the same or would her life be spent caring for him? So many thoughts rumbled about in her head as she prepared meals morning, noon and night, she began to think she might be losing her mind.

One thought in particular chanted in her head as she prepared the day's breakfast—giving her no peace, no serenity. It was her fault, the entire thing. Sure, her father had been the one to spin the yarns, knitting the family closer, making them believe their fortune lay "just around the next bend" ...but they had bought into it, too. Why hadn't they heeded the warnings? Why hadn't they waited until spring? They had to be first... they had to stake the best claim. He wasn't going to wait and make the same mistakes he'd made in '49.

They hadn't wanted to go, not at first. But Joseph Grayson could talk a beggar out of his last nickel. Her father had wanted it, more than anything and being a rather selfish man, it soon became what her mother wanted, too. Jolian hated that her mother never had one dream of her own. Because of that, Jolian had decided she'd never live *her* life in anyone's shadow and if that meant a life of spinsterhood, she'd actively pursue it! Determination to choose her own path in life eventually sealed her decision to join the family trek. And while she hated to admit it, her parents' promises of gold-paved streets leading to her very own restaurant had swayed her decision as well. Eventually, promises lead to dreams and dreams to plans and she'd finally given into the "fever". She had no one to blame but herself. Well, herself and the self-serving attitude that consumed miners in general. Sorry lot, the bunch of them!

Aklu'ut's soft-spoken words interrupted her thoughts. "You *capeau*, ah... cook all sun, many sun. Still sick *tum tum*. Cook is *muck a muck* for my people but *masatchy* for you. You *kopet* cook! You try *chee*."

Jolian was beginning to understand the language Aklu'ut spoke to her. Aklu'ut said her people appreciated her cooking, but it did her no good personally. Aklu'ut wanted her to try something new. Aklu'ut went on to say that cooking would serve her well in the future, but for now she needed "a challenge for her mind as well as her body".

The wise Aklu'ut had once again assessed, diagnosed and prescribed the much-needed tonic, this time in the form of weaving. Jolian had seen and used the beautiful baskets the Carrier women handled. It hadn't occurred to her that, of course, they would make them right here in the village. She'd noted how the baskets swelled when they were immersed in water, which made the layers of weaving seal watertight, and she wondered what substance they were made from. She couldn't believe it when Aklu'ut told her it was cedar bark!

The bark was stripped and worked until it was as soft as cloth and easy to weave. As she watched Aklu'ut's hands work, Jolian felt truly amazed at her dexterity and precision. The baskets were not only functional but also a work of art and a labor of love.

As she watched her own hands beginning to weave, Jolian began to welcome the rhythm of motion. She had to concentrate on the pattern and the design, leaving no room for self-pitying thoughts. She began to see that her hands were creating. She was creating. For the first time in a long time Jolian felt a spark of life. The basket she was making became a symbol of life to Jolian. If she could create this, why not a new life for herself?

She decided when her basket was finished, she would present it to Aklu'ut as a gift for her unborn child. Everyday, she thought about the baby and its new innocent life and slowly she could feel the pain in her heart beginning to ease. Each time she finished a layer of the basket, Jo made herself think of a wish for the baby's future. The baby would sleep in her basket of wishes, and that one thought chased away the last of her mournful spirit. The death of her parents still caused her pain, but now, she could at least view it from a distance.

Jakeb began to show improvement as well. He walked with a limp and his speech was off a bit, but Jolian thanked the powers that be for sparing the life of her brother.

As her spirit began to heal, Jolian felt renewing energy serge throughout her body. She wanted to show her appreciation to Aklu'ut for all she and her people had done for her and Jakeb. She insisted on resuming her role of cook but didn't wallow in it as she had previously. Each morning she would rise with the sun and Aklu'ut, to prepare a meal for the tribe. Midmorning was spent gathering what little food could be found in their snow covered surroundings.

Jolian thought it a complete waste of time and energy to leave the warmth of Aklu'ut's home, bundle themselves in firs and forage for food. The village had stockpiles of dried and well-preserved food, everything from berries to jerked moose meat. Aklu'ut told her while it may appear they had plenty to last until the spring, it was always wise to spend a portion of the daylight hours searching. If they did not, spring may decide they were too portentous and then she would be sure to stay away and starve them all. Besides, there were valuable branches that could be gathered now if one just knew where to look.

At first, Jolian wanted to laugh at the naïveté of Aklu'ut's people. "Spring comes when it comes, not because you are prepared or unprepared, and certainly not because you possessed any specific personality traits, such as arrogance." She spoke in her mother's voice. Aklu'ut just smiled and continued foraging for bark and mushrooms. Patience was a virtue she would do well to learn from her new friend.

Jolian thought of her own family's preparations for their trek North. How ill-prepared they'd been! Who was she to comment on the rituals of Aklu'ut's people? Aklu'ut's family had been doing this for generations. She should shut her mouth and give them the respect they deserved. Gathering food when it could be found wasn't foolish but rather a wise thing to do, regardless of your reasons for doing it. Jolian decided to learn all she could from Aklu'ut's vast knowledge. Never again would she be caught unprepared!

Thus, Jolian bundled herself up each day after the morning meal and set out in the vast, chilly sunshine and followed Aklu'ut's snow shoe prints. They'd dig in the snow for certain barks and branches. Jolian learned more about edible plants and non-edible plants than she could ever possibly use in her lifetime. Aklu'ut explained which plants could be used for salves, tonics and ailments. Which barks should be boiled or ground and which made into a tea or paste, this filled their conversation from morning till night.

Just when Jolian thought she had mastered the native vegetation, she'd learn something new. Jolian watched as Aklu'ut examined a branch, broke it open and sniffed at the inner flesh. She used a tiny bowl-shaped tool to extract the soft insides and then showed Jolian how to use the substance to make a decoction for constipation.

"I had always believed there could never be a more patient soul than my mother, until I met you Aklu'ut." Jolian smiled and squeezed the hand of her friend.

Aklu'ut's face beamed with the compliment.

~ * ~

With pride in all she had accomplished, Jolian finished her basket and set it aside. Aklu'ut did not seem herself these past few days. She appeared restless and cleaned constantly. Jolian could not imagine the joy and apprehension her friend must be feeling. She wondered, as she had many times in recent days, if she would ever be in Aklu'ut's shoes. That a woman, disguised as a man, who had sworn off men to actively pursue spinsterhood, could even be thinking about the state of pregnancy was suddenly hilarious to Jolian. How did she ever come up with such thoughts!

Aklu'ut looked at her with curiosity and Jo let her in on her private joke.

"I do not see laughing in words." Aklu'ut shook her head. "Watching belly swell from child is most joy, most wonder. I am knowing the "one on high" one day make a baby for Jo."

Aklu'ut's voice filled with concern as she told Jo, "You no imagine future because one on high is not yet to reveal your destiny. You must think about future everyday. You think and ask one on high to think also. You welcome with Aklu'ut, but Aklu'ut is not Jo's destiny. This time for Aklu'ut and Jo is waiting time. Jo stay until the waiting time over. Then living time begin again."

Aklu'ut said her husband would be moving back to their home after the birth of their child and Jo would have a hard time keeping her identity hidden if she lived with the couple.

"Many days I spend in my mind. I think and think about baby. I think what I want for baby in world. I think how I can change world for baby. What I change to make good for baby now."

Jo was about to respond when Aklu'ut's face began to distort in pain. Jolian felt panic begin to rise in her. She didn't know what to do to bring a baby into the world!

"You be alone for two days now." Aklu'ut seemed to sense her discomfort, but mistook the reason. "I go to sister of husband. You be alone is good?"

Jo breathed a deep sigh of relief. How silly of her! Of course Aklu'ut would be taken care of by her people. Jolian had been secluded with Aklu'ut for so long she had momentarily forgotten the bustling village around her. Once again the selflessness of her new friend astounded her. About to deliver a baby and Aklu'ut was worried about *her* welfare? Jo hoped her words conveyed her heartfelt thanks and friendship.

"I will be fine Aklu'ut. You have seen to that. I have many things to thank you for but now is not the time! What can I do to help?"

"I go home of Guzzie. You walk with me?"

"Of course."

~ * ~

Jolian left Aklu'ut in Guzzie's capable hands and rushed back to her own abode. Once inside their tiny home, she found her pack and fished inside. She grasped the item tightly and half ran to the dwelling where Jakeb convalesced. Aklu'ut's elderly grandfather, Zaxsa, was, as always, sitting by a circular rock-lined fire as Jolian entered his home.

"Mutsikanutlo, come see *Ou*?"

"No, I have not come to see Jakeb today. Today I come to speak with you." Jo smiled at the nickname Mutsikanutlo, curly haired one. 'Jo' was so much easier to say!

Skin as tough as leather broke into deep wrinkles as he smiled, stared into the fire and spoke in a gnarled voice. "Ou, Jakeb *skookum* now. Jakeb *momock chaco muck a muck*."

"I am glad that Jakeb is strong and can leave the house to bring you good things to eat. He should be doing everything he can to repay you..."

Zaxsa stared into the fire as if she'd not even spoken. Jolian searched her mind for the right words and hoped she wasn't calling him a name or speaking gibberish.

"I come to speak with you... *Nika waw waw mika*."

Zaxsa turned and looked her directly in the eye. His face wrinkled again and she continued. "*Nika hooey hooey mika...* I want to trade, to exchange with you."

Zaxsa stared at her, the firelight reflecting a glint in his eye. He bent his head down slowly and raised it again.

"I want fabric... *Nika tikke...* ah, ah..." Great, she didn't know the word for fabric. *Now what?* Jolian's eyes searched the room until they found the desired object. She moved over to the shelf where Zaxsa kept his clothing. She held up fabric of all different kinds and mimed her pregnant friend and then the baby.

"What do you want in exchange? I have this knife—" Jo spoke in the elder's language and held her bowie knife forward for him to examine it. It was a good quality knife in a leather sheath.

"*Ikta mika tikke klale, de crème, pe chuck, pill, te kope?*"

Did she want black, cream, green, red, or white? Ha ha! She silently thanked Aklu'ut for teaching her how to weave. She would have never known half of the language or any of the colors if it weren't for Aklu'ut.

"*Nika tikke de crème, te kope, Marcie.*"

"*Mika midlight. Nika momok chaco six.*"

She should sit and Zaxsa would bring a friend. He took her knife and was gone like a summer's breeze. Jolian shook her head in awe that such an elderly man could move with such speed, silence and agility.

With nothing else to do, she sat by Zaxsa's fire, took Aklu'ut's advice and began to think about her future. What was her destiny? The Carriers had been more than kind to her and Jakeb, but Aklu'ut was right, she didn't feel like she belonged here, not forever. It was just a waiting place, and she felt as though her wait was almost over. *Where to then?* She didn't have the money to return home and she didn't have the desire to continue on to the goldfields.

Jolian stared into the fire and watched as the flames turned from yellow to red to blue and back to yellow again. The fire danced and kicked and sputtered. It died low and caught again. It twisted and turned as if it were alive. It was alive, in many ways more alive than she. She felt determined to have the life she wanted and it wasn't going to be found sitting, waiting. But how? Where? Did she have that kind of courage? Jolian stared and stared, trying to find truth, seeking a wisdom she didn't yet possess.

~ * ~

As it happened, Cooper didn't have to make a decision regarding the boy he'd carried in on his horse. Ts'kaw's sister took in the lad and cared for him for the duration of their stay. Life in the Carrier village felt easy and relaxed for Cooper. He had nothing to do each day, other than the usual chores expected of a guest.

They had been heading to the village when they'd discovered the horrible murder on the trail. Cooper and Guy had left the village the day after they'd arrived with the boys. They traveled to the closest Fort, Alexandria, and reported the crime. There, they'd given as much information as possible and then returned to the Carrier village to wait. Cooper and Guy availed themselves of Ts'kaw's hospitality, while the days rolled slowly into a month.

Cooper hardly saw anything of the two boys they'd helped. Though that didn't really surprise him. He knew the one boy stayed with Zaxsa, as his dwelling was used like a hospital during the winter months. While most of the Carriers grouped themselves together during the long cold months, Cooper knew that Ts'kaw's sister lived with only her husband but that he had gone to live with Zaxsa too, while the other boy stayed Aklu'ut. Aklu'ut and her husband had only recently joined the village and with Ts'kaw away much of the time, had probably kept to themselves.

With the formation of their surveying company, Guy had offered Ts'kaw a position surveying the claims in the goldfields. Ts'kaw had agreed to help with Cooper and Guy's new business, but only on the condition he could stay with his sister until her baby was safely delivered. An amicable plan for everyone as no surveying could be done until the spring thaw, and Aklu'ut's baby would arrive in early March.

Then on the day the Tamanass man pronounced the older boy, Jakeb, fit to travel, Aklu'ut gave birth to a strong baby boy. Everyone in the village celebrated. Everyone, except Cooper. He wished Aklu'ut well and hoped he effectively hid his pain. Back at his dwelling he began to gather his belongings. It would only be a short time now until they'd be on their way.

The valley cradling the Carrier village began to show signs of an early spring. Trees were budding and grass shot through the snow. The river flowed strongly as it freed itself from its frozen overcoat. Better to take notice of these things than to think about Aklu'ut, Cooper decided. Ts'kaw's sister and her baby brought back too much of his past. Only just beginning to embrace his soberness, he didn't need to have all that hurt dredged up again.

Cooper found his saddlebags and began to pack some items away. Knocking interrupted his solitude. He turned to see the younger of the two brothers, the one Ts'kaw had mistaken for a girl, poking his head in through the doorway. A bit of an odd way of entering a room, but Cooper let it slide. His mind wandered back to the past, despite his own protests, and focusing in on the boy's words became difficult.

"I hope I'm not disturbing you."

"You aren't." Cooper made his voice acknowledge the disturbance even as his words dispelled it.

"Zaxsa said I would find one of you here. Ts'kaw is busy with Aklu'ut's new boy. Have you seen him? He's quite lovely." The boy looked him straight in the eye for a few seconds but then his cheeks reddened and he lowered his gaze and continued. "So sorry. It's Jo, Jo Grayson. I've come to thank you for saving my life and the life of my brother." The boy entered the dwelling and extended his hand.

Kind of an odd lad but Cooper shook his hand and made some self-effacing remark.

"I am sorry not to have come sooner, to give all of you my proper thanks. I was... It has been a difficult time. I hope you'll understand."

"No apologies necessary. A horrendous tragedy, really quite disturbing. We are all grateful to have helped." Cooper noticed the boy still wore a black band on his arm and he rubbed his own arm in memory. He wanted to be off of this subject of the past as soon as possible. "Much better that we think to the future now."

"Yes, the future. That's the other reason I wanted to see you."

"Yes?" Cooper had half turned his back to the boy to signal his wish to end the conversation. He could use a drink. Damn his oath! He settled for a mug of water and turned to offer one to the boy. The lad had been talking and he'd missed it. He'd use his old 'I've been listening' trick from his drinking days. He stared into the boy's eyes and repeated the last thing he said.

"So, for all of those reasons, you wonder if we'd consider taking you to the goldfields with us?"

"Exactly."

"Well, I'll have to discuss it with my partners and get back to you, son."

"Thank you, Mr. Holt." The boy stretched his hand out again and Cooper gave it a firm shake. He placed his hand on the boys' shoulder and led him towards the door.

"I'll wait on your answer then."

He nodded, gave his best attempt at a smile and watched as the boy practically tripped over his eagerness to leave. Cooper was grateful. He needed to be alone with his thoughts for a while. He walked across the dirt-packed floor, picked up his tin mug, drained the water and then refilled it. He felt restless but at the same time hesitant, to get on with their journey. The trail held so many memories, too many. Guilt was a sneaky predator. It crept in while you least expected it and wound its rope about your neck. He shrugged it off with a raise of his shoulders. People live, people die and life goes on. He began to drain his second mug of water and then paused mid way through. Something nagged at the back of his brain, like he'd just agreed to do something without thinking it through.

~ * ~

Jolian moved as fast as her feet would carry her without actually running. Reaching the back of Aklu'ut's dwelling, she paused to catch her breath. She leaned her back against the side of the building and let her eyes search the sky. Her heart hammered hard in her chest as if she'd run the distance instead of walking. She felt giddy and lightheaded and she couldn't put her finger on the cause.

Focusing on slowly breathing in and out seemed to help. She concentrated on a single white cloud, meandering across the sky, until her breathing returned to normal. Why did she feel so panicked? She'd weighed all of her choices and made her decision. She was pleased with her choice, so what caused these feelings? Probably, the apprehension of being back on the trail again. Yes, that would surely make anyone feel nervous.

~ * ~

Cooper helped himself to a healthy portion of the meal in front of him. Couldn't be certain of all the ingredients, salmon, nuts, greens of some kind all mixed with what looked to be a mashed yam. Whatever it was, it smelled wonderful and his stomach rumbled at the scent. It felt good to have an appetite again.

His mother had always said he must have a hollow leg to be able to pack away the large quantities he did and still look fit and trim. His father teased it would catch up with him sooner or later as he'd rub his own protruding orb. His friends' wives were always willing to invite him for a meal, as if they felt complimented by his appetite. Cooper smiled to himself as he loaded an extra spoonful of the salmon mixture onto his woven bark plate.

Just then, Guy entered the eating area of the house, practically poking his nose into Cooper's mound of food. "*Sacre blue!* Save some of ze food for ze other people in ze village that wish to eat, *Mon ami*!"

Cooper gave his friend a fake laugh with a full mouth. "This is too good to share," he teased, "but seriously, you'd better help yourself before I start on seconds."

Guy chuckled as he did Cooper's bidding. "Lorna was not mistaking when she accused you of eating her house up."

Cooper felt himself recoil at the mention of Lorna. "She accused me of eating her out of house and home." Annoyance at discussing her was evident in his voice as he corrected Guy and quickly changed the subject to matters more pressing.

"What do you think we should do about the two boys, Guy? The Tamanass man says the elder one is fit to travel, and we really have imposed on the Carriers long enough, don't you think?"

Guy nodded his response as he chewed and swallowed a mouthful of food. "We cannot ask for them to remain here, that is certain. I think our only choice is to take them with us to ze goldfields."

Whew, he'd hoped that Guy would suggest that. It would get him off the hook for the promise he'd made to the Grayson kid.

"That was my thought as well. That's probably where their family was heading anyway. Although, why they didn't wait until the spring thaw is beyond me. If Billy Barker himself can winter in Victoria, why couldn't they?"

"Many foolish decisions are made when gold is involved, *Mon ami*."

"That, I am sure of," Cooper agreed. Ts'kaw entered then and helped himself to the meal. Cooper filled him in on the conversation. "I suppose we could take them to your place?" He directed his question to Guy.

"*Non!* Po would not forgive me."

"Ah yes, good old Po!" Cooper smiled "How is that cantankerous old maid anyway?'

"She would not be so fond to hear you call her ze old maid." Guy laughed. "But, I suggest you ask Ts'kaw if you wish to know Po's keeping's. He has seen more of her than I, as of late."

"Ts'kaw, you sly dog!" Cooper faked a punch to his friend's shoulder. "I'll admit she's a looker, even if she is the meanest woman this side of the Rockies... But Po? What could she possibly see in a dried up, ugly, old brave like you?" Cooper couldn't resist needling his friend about his good looks. Even the most 'respectable' of women he knew in Victoria stared in awe and even blushed whenever the handsome native passed them on the street. Someone who had that kind of effect on woman deserved to be ribbed about it. But Ts'kaw took it all in stride. He spoke instead of what they would do with their wards once they reached the goldfields. Guy had a suggestion.

"My friend Pearl would be pleased to take them in. Most of all, ze young one, as I am told he can cook. Ze last time I was home, I spoke with her and she mentioned needing someone to feed her girls. I think she was round about asking me to get Po to cook for her, but we all know what Po would think of that."

Cooper chuckled out loud at the thought of Po working for Pearl. Although it had been awhile since Cooper had seen either one of them, the thought of the two stubborn women in the same room made for a good laugh.

"Pearl needs help and the boys will need work, it sounds perfect." Cooper looked at Guy as he spoke. For some reason he couldn't seem to look Ts'kaw in the eye right now. Maybe it was the guilt he felt at dumping the Grayson kids off on Pearl. He felt responsible for them but he had work to do, too. No, the arrangement with Pearl was the best for all concerned.

"Pearl also has that old cabin out behind of her new place." Guy turned to face Ts'kaw. "I am sure that ze boys could stay there as well."

Although he never spoke above a whisper, Ts'kaw's voice thundered in the wooden home. "I no longer hold my tongue. I know Pearl to be a kind woman with a generous heart but I do not think the place for the wards is in the home of a whore."

~ * ~

Jolian lifted her eyes to the sky and whispered a prayer to the Heavens. She let her gaze drop and rest upon the wooden structure high above her. It housed two canoes, filled with the bodies of her deceased parents. Despite the appearance of spring, the ground was frozen solid and graves could not be dug. She couldn't endure the thought of the cremation ceremony the Frenchman had suggested, even though in her heart she knew the bodies that lay above her were only the shells of her parents. Their souls were long gone, in a far better place she hoped, she believed. She'd return here someday soon and see her parents buried in proper graves, but for now she'd just say her goodbyes.

Why hadn't they heeded the advice of the Scotsman who ran the fort in Yale? The gold—the damn gold! She hated it now, even the thought of it. But where else could she go? Why, Pa? Why did you have to go? Ma, so beautiful, the true strength of their family, yet always so willing to cave in to her husband's crazy ideas and fondest desires... Oh, Ma, you are truly missed, missed so much...

She wiped at her eyes with the sleeve of her blanket coat. It wouldn't do to be seen crying. She was, after all, supposed to be a boy, an orphaned boy. Her parents were just so alone, so separated from everything out here. Jakeb hadn't even been by to see them. She supposed everyone had to grieve in his own manner.

She breathed in the fresh scent of pine and snow and turned back for the heart of the village. Movement in her peripheral vision stopped her in her tracks.

Slowly she turned her head to see a doe emerge from the bush and cautiously walk to a patch of grass that poked its tender new shoots through the snow. The promise of spring. Rebirth, re-growth, renewal. She should take her lessons from Aklu'ut and Mother Nature. She would have to find the courage to begin anew. She would have a fresh start in the goldfields, if she could find a way to convince herself of it.

~ * ~

Jolian tucked the soft cream-colored cloth around the baby. It had been a good trade, her knife for the fabric. She'd lined the basket she made for Aklu'ut's son with the soft spun cotton. She'd sewn by daylight and candlelight for the past three days and had a baby size quilt to match. He was so beautiful, just so beautiful. Aklu'ut was very lucky to have such a perfect baby boy.

"*Marcie,* Jo."

"My pleasure Aklu'ut. Although with the amount he wants to eat I have my doubts as to how long that quilt will serve him!" The women laughed together as the child whimpered and Aklu'ut put him to her breast. It amazed her to watch the child

28

latch on and begin to suckle. The beginning of life was such a miracle. Jolian knew well the look in Aklu'ut's eyes. She'd seen the same one in her own mother's eyes so often, that to see it again made her own eyes well with tears.

"You sick *tum tum*?"

"I am just so pleased for you." Jo placed her hand on her friend's arm. "I am sad to leave, but I know I must."

"Waiting time finished for you. Now go to find living time."

"How did you ever get so wise Aklu'ut?"

Her friend smiled and looked down at the child at her breast. "I know nothing now." Aklu'ut spoke in her own language that her heart was bursting with wishes for her child. She felt all she ever knew would not be enough to give her child the life she wished for him. She said if there was one thing she did know for certain, it was a mother's love for her child is everlasting, the kind of love that transcends this life. The child would never be alone; for her love was planted in his heart and he need only to open his soul to feel it.

Jolian could feel the tears falling from her cheek. It was pure love, and she had it in her heart, too. At that moment Jo felt the courage to go on and face her future. *She was never alone as long as she let herself feel the love in her heart*, what a comforting thought. She kissed Aklu'ut's cheek and the cheek of the babe.

"I won't say goodbye."

Aklu'ut nodded and Jo turned to leave. She felt scared and excited and could not imagine what her future might hold. Yet what ever it was, she was ready to face it head on.

Three

Sheer determination to face her future was wavering badly and she had only been away from the village for three days. Jolian hadn't given much thought as to how she would get to the goldfields, only that she *would* get there. She had been riding horseback non-stop and her behind, aching last night, was stone cold numb today. She had only ever ridden sidesaddle and only once before at that! But of course she couldn't tell the men, not if she wanted to keep up her disguise. So, she had been riding astride for the past two days.

That was the other thing; keeping up her disguise was nearly impossible while living non-stop with men. Although she didn't really have to worry about Ts'kaw as she hardly ever saw him, especially at night. Her one saving grace was Jakeb. He had decided to accompany her to the goldfields and the three men gave the two 'boys' some time on their own each day.

She had discussed her disguise with Jakeb and they had decided it would be best for her to continue, as her mother had first demanded, for safety's sake. Jolian hated the dishonesty, but she hated the idea of fighting off unwelcome advances even more. Not that she felt threatened by any of the three men who'd rescued her, they all seemed decent enough but once they reached the goldfields who knew what she might be facing. The fewer people who had her secret to keep, the better.

Still, she had never thought keeping her masquerade would be so difficult. When she had started her disguise, traveling with her parents, she could be herself in private. The same had held true when she stayed with Aklu'ut. Pretending to be a boy for part of the time was much easier than pretending all of the time. Simple things, like relieving one's water, were more, well, easier said than done.

She hoped the three men didn't think it odd that she always disappeared into the bushes whenever someone relieved himself or when she had to 'go'. Actually, it seemed the men hardly noticed her at all. Maybe they simply felt she was one of the boys. They hadn't even asked her to cook for them, which was a bit odd. Usually, as soon as someone found out that you could boil water you were given the chore of cooking.

"We'll make camp here for the night." The Frenchman, she wasn't sure of his name, had ridden his horse along side and spoke to her. "There's an old trapper's cabin through those trees over d'ere. Ts'kaw has caught and skinned a rabbit, and as we hear you are good with ze cooking..."

"I'd be happy to prepare the meal." Jolian smiled. She might have known... It was the least she could do for these men. After all, she did owe them her life. It gave her nightmares to think about what might have become of her if these men had not found her when they did. She knew that Jakeb would not be here now either, although he didn't seem to be showing his gratitude in quite the manner she'd expected. She wondered if the Frenchman, ah yes, Renault, that was his name. She wondered if Mr. Renault felt the same way, because as her brother rode up he turned and rode off in the opposite direction.

"All right! I was wondering when we were going to sssstop." Jakeb said as he reined his horse next to hers and tethered it to a tree branch. "These guys ride like the devil's nipping at their heels, hey?"

"I am sure they are anxious to get to the goldfields. After all, we did delay their trip by several months."

"Don't blame yourself for anything, Jo! Those guys wouldn't have waited around for us if hadn't sssuited their needs."

"Jakeb! How can you be so callused? Those men saved your life! I could never have kept you alive in the dark, with the wolves..."

"Hey, don't go and get yourself all worked up about it. I am not ungrateful, I'm just sssaying you shouldn't feel so indebted to them either. Who knows what kind of deal they've cooked up for themselves by bringing us with them? They're probably getting some kind of pay off for finding two gullible workers."

Jolian focused her best 'How can you be so ungrateful?' stare at her brother but it had little effect. Her brother had always felt the world owed him more than he'd been born with, and he was becoming an expert at voicing his opinion.

"I can't believe I've agreed to that job in the mercantile." Jakeb shook his head with distaste. "I mean, who the hell goes to a gold rush town without intending to mine? I tell you, Jo, the first chance I get I'm ssstaking myself a claim." Jakeb ground his hands into his hips.

Jolian heaved a sigh and let it go. She let her brother ramble on and on as she gathered twigs, lit the fire and fed it until she thought it hot enough for cooking. Better that he let his demons out on her than upon those who were aiding them.

Ts'kaw brought the rabbit meat, skewered and ready for cooking, and handed it to her. If he took notice of Jakeb's raging, he didn't appear to show it. The two other men arrived shortly after and still Jakeb rambled. Jo felt embarrassed with the lack of thankfulness her brother displayed. She could feel the shame glowing in her cheeks and turned toward the fire to hide it from the men. Their lives had been turned completely upside down. Nothing, it seemed, would ever be the same again, except Jakeb.

~ * ~

Jolian prepared pan-fried yams and coffee to go with the rabbit. After the long day of riding anything would have tasted good, but her earlier conversation with Jakeb had left a sour taste in her mouth. She thought about it as she unrolled her bedding by the fire in the tiny, log cabin. Scooting down in her blankets as far as possible without poking her toes out, she pulled her bedding up around her chin and tried to sleep. Her indigestion came from not only Jakeb's ungratefulness but also his determination to mine . Despite her willingness to go to the goldfields, she felt certain she wanted nothing to do with miners. Miners and their silly dreams ruined everything. She just wanted to get to the closest town and make enough money to get back home.

Mr. Renault had told her about his friend Pearl who lived within a half-hour's ride of the goldfields. He said the last time he'd spoke with her she'd mentioned needing a cook and he felt sure Jo would be able to find not only employment, but lodging with her as well. Jo hoped the woman was still in need of help and wondered what kind of business she ran.

Not that it mattered, really. Jo would take any work offered. She had a plan. Work like the devil and save every penny she made. She'd heard the men talking about a new road, "the Cariboo Wagon Road", being constructed to get miners and goods to the goldfields in Barkerville. Apparently men would be working on it around the clock and would have it ready within the year. She hoped by that time, she would have saved enough money for stage tickets for herself and Jakeb.

From her eavesdropping she knew the road would run from the town of Barkerville back to where they'd begun in Yale. From Yale she could get passage on a sternwheeler back to San Francisco. Maybe back home she could put this horrible journey behind her. Maybe there she could truly begin to live again. Jolian snuggled lower in her blankets and allowed the heavy pull of sleep to consume her weary body.

~ * ~

The smell of bacon frying stirred Jolian's senses. She could see her mother standing by the fire turning the pieces with a fork. She heard the pop! as the fat sizzled in the pan. It had all been a dream, just an unspeakably atrocious figment of her imagination! What a horrible person she must be to imagine such unspeakable atrocities could have happened to her family!

She opened her eyes to see Mr. Renault crouching by the fire. It was real, all of it. Reality sank into her bones with the damp of the morning. She rolled over onto her belly with a groan, rubbed her eyes and tried to shake the sleep from her body. She needed a bath and some time alone. Her breasts had been bound since they'd left the Carrier's village and the binding felt worse than her old corset.

"*Bonjour.*" The Frenchman's voice rang out cheerfully in her direction as she searched the ground for her shako cap. She found it, crammed it down on her head and mumbled a barely audible reply. The cap was filthy and needed washing but then again, so did her hair.

She rolled her blankets and tied them with twine. She'd had a nasty night's sleep, tossing and turning and practically freezing to death. Grumpiness invaded her and she didn't care who knew it.

"The day promises to be good, no?"

Jo grunted and headed out of the cabin and into the bushes. Why hadn't she just stayed in the Carrier's village? Surely one of the natives would have traveled back to

Yale eventually. She should have stayed where there were at least a few comforts of modern society. Living on the trail was not fit for man or beast! That thought brought a smile to her lips. Of course, living in the wild was fit for beasts! She felt her grumpiness beginning to melt away, somewhat.

"Jo, time to hit the trail!" Jakeb called to her from somewhere near the cabin. *Hit the trail?* She'd only just woke up! Her grumpiness returned wholly and then some. She hadn't even had time to wipe her teeth. Maybe a man could roll out of bed and hit the trail, but she couldn't... she wouldn't! She had a mind to march back to the cabin and tell them... tell them what? That she needed more time with her toilette? That would never do. Jolian sighed so hard she could see her own breath before her. She abandoned her anger along with her wish to be cleaner and returned to the trail.

There they were, all four of them, sitting atop their horses waiting for her. Despite her filthy shako cap, short hair, and men's clothing, she suddenly felt all woman. How many times had she prepared to go out, in what she thought was a hurry, only to find her father and brother waiting impatiently for her, like the men were waiting now?

Jakeb had fastened her bedding and pack to the saddle of her horse. *Probably just to hurry me along,* an ungrateful thought told her. She mounted her horse and nudged it onto the trail. Her muscles screamed in protest, but she never let out a whimper. She wasn't going to blow her charade now, not after coming this far. She'd make it safely to those damned goldfields if it was the last thing she ever did on this earth!

~ * ~

They rode through the nooning only nibbling on jerky and hard tack. She hoped they were going to stop soon as she needed to fill her canteen and she'd developed a cramp in her lower abdomen that wouldn't seem to subside.

The cramp... Dear Lord! Suddenly she realized the reason for her grumpy mood earlier. Her monthly was here! Jolian could feel a trembling begin to rise in her throat. She'd made it through so much and resolved herself to keep going, and now her own body was going to betray her?

Her eyes searched about frantically. Maybe she could accidentally fall into a stream to wash the stains she was sure were soaking through her clothing. Or maybe she could cut herself on something, just a minor cut. How ludicrous! Were they never going to stop? Her head began to pound with the anticipation of her inevitable detection. What should she do? What should she do?

"Are you feeling a bit anxious?"

"What?" She snapped her head to see that Mr. Holt had ridden along side of her.

"I said are you feeling a bit anxious to meet your new employer and settle into your new home?"

"I... ah, no, I am actually looking forward to it." *And some of the comforts that privacy will allow,* she added to herself. She could hardly wait to soak in a bath, to be out of her boy's disguise, even if only temporarily. Jolian felt a warmth begin to penetrate her cheeks. She shouldn't be thinking about feminine things whilst maintaining a conversation with a man! While her thoughts couldn't give her away, her blushing at them might. She should be more careful!

Mr. Holt poked the brim of his hat up with his index finger and eased forward a bit on his saddle. "I'll ride ahead with Guy and inform Pearl of your arrival then. We should be coming upon Pearl's Place any time now."

Jolian nodded her response but the man had already ridden on ahead. She realized they'd been climbing in elevation for some time, but she had no idea they were so close to their final destination. Her panic about the situation eased slightly. Maybe she could find a way to keep her problem hidden until she could make other arrangements. Maybe she'd have to confide in her new employer after all. Her heart began to pound harder in eagerness of the meeting and the new beginning awaiting her.

Jolian gazed around the thick-forested path and snow capped peaks in the distance. So this was Richfield Mountain. Breathtakingly beautiful landscape surrounded her. Everywhere as far as her eyes could see, lush green mountainside and clear blue sky abounded. Jolian had to stop glancing about and pay close attention to Jakeb's horse in front of her, lest she loose sight of the path.

The trail was not well marked in this area and obviously must not be traveled on a regular basis. Pearl must own some type of restaurant or general store. A place that offered goods you couldn't get in town. Otherwise why would the miners travel the extra distance, on an ill-marked trail to come here? Jolian suddenly felt quite foolish for not asking more about her employer.

Another cramp besieged her lower abdomen and Jolian winced involuntarily. What was she going to do? Then, before she had a chance to dwell on the matter, the trail gave way to a clearing. They were staring at a long road wide enough to accommodate two carriages traveling abreast. At the end of the road was a modern day house with all of the trimmings. The two-story building was ox-blood in color, with royal blue trim and white gingerbread. As they approached, Jolian could see that not only were there glass windows but some of them were even stained! A wide front porch with white banisters and spindles wrapped around to the right and ran the length of the house on that side. To the left of the porch the building was rounded and boasted a turret.

What an extraordinary home in the middle of nowhere! Jolian loved it immediately. It reminded her so much of San Francisco, her eyes began to tear in response. She saw Messrs. Holt and Renault walking up from what appeared to be the barn. With them was one of the largest women Jolian had ever seen. The walk was obviously tiresome for her as she kept mopping her brow with a lace handkerchief.

"Jakeb, Joe, I wish to introduce you to my friend Pearl Tuttle. Pearl, these are ze two boys I mentioned in my letter." Guy Renault gestured towards them with a funny little formal bow.

"Pleased to meet you, Ma'am." Jakeb had suddenly come down with an attack of politeness. He hopped from his horse, shook the woman's hand and spoke so sweetly you could have knocked Jolian off of her horse with a feather!

Instead she smiled and said, "We surely do appreciate your hospitality, Ma'am."

"It's Pearl. No Ma'am or Missus, just Pearl. We ain't much on formalities 'round here. Guy tells me that you boys are in need of a place to stay and that one of ya kin cook the snout off a pig."

"That would be me." Jolian smiled. What a wonderful woman! She instantly felt welcomed.

Mr. Holt tipped his hat to the woman, "We are sorry to be off so quickly, Pearl, but if we want to reach Guy's place before dark we'd best be on our way."

"Are ya sure, Coop? Y'all ain't been by fer so long. I'm sure Doralynn would be more'n happy ta put ya up fer the night, Guy." Pearl swayed her body close to the men. If she wasn't mistaken, Jolian could have sworn Pearl was flirting with them!

And indeed it sounded like *he* was flirting as the Frenchman flashed a charmer's grin, "Ah, you are za devil, Pearl. You know I would love to spend a relaxing evening with her but we have promised Ts'kaw he will see Po before nightfall."

Aklu'ut's brother threw the Frenchman a murderous look, but he only laughed.

"Po? Ts'kaw, ya gorgeous hunk of man. Ya ain't gone and attached yoreself ta that dried up old hag have ya? I thoughts ya had more sense than a horse's arse, boy." Pearl shook her head as she spoke and continued to mop her brow with the handkerchief. Jolian glanced at Ts'kaw. The man who always stood proud and sure of himself, looked as though he may actually be blushing under his copper skin.

Pearl said her colorful goodbyes to each of the men in turn. They must be very close as each of the men received a kiss full on the lips! Although, Ts'kaw appeared quite reluctant at the woman's advances, the other men just laughed and waved as they rode off in a swirl of trail dust. Jakeb took his horse into the barn, leaving Jolian still sitting atop her horse wondering what to do. Those men, while she felt she hardly knew them, had been the difference between life and death for her. She should have done more, thanked them somehow. Or at least made arrangements to see them again in the future, when she'd be able to offer something financially.

Pearl stood with her hands on her hips, her back to Jolian until the men were out of sight. She turned to face Jo and looked her up and down. "If ya ain't stayin' ya better gets riding or ya ain't gonna catch them. Those fellers always ride like the wind."

"Oh, I'm planning to stay." Jolian wiggled uncomfortably atop her horse.

"Then ain't ya better get down off yer horse?"

Jolian made a quick decision. "Pearl? I have a confession to make..."

"Well I am far from being a preacher, sonny-boy, but I reckon I cain hear ya out."

Jolian confided her true identity, and current problem, to her new acquaintance and felt immediately grateful.

"Yore a woman? Spit and polish! Get yoreself off of that horse and get into my kitchen! The boys filled me in on a bit of yore past and I reckoned it'd be a tough row to hoe for two lads, but a woman... She-oot!" Pearl mopped her brow with her handkerchief while Jo dismounted.

"Have ya gots the necessaries fer yer monthly?" Pearl looked about as she whispered in an animated fashion.

"Yes, if I could just be shown the outhouse—"

"It's out back a the kitchen. I'll take yer horse ta the barn fer yer brother ta deal with and ya kin meet me and him in the kitchen when yer through."

Jolian nodded her thanks, removed the saddlebags from her horse and handed the reins to Pearl.

~ * ~

Jolian let herself into the house from a door on the back porch. The kitchen was modern with a wood burning stove and everything! Relief wrapped her body like a security blanket. She could see herself working here. Steam billowed from a huge cast iron pot on the stove. As she moved a step forward she could see the pantry through an open door off to the right of the work area. The shelves appeared well stocked and organized. Of course there'd be a few things she'd have to change...

A long pine table sat just through a doublewide archway, which Jo assumed was the eating area. Pearl's cumbersome form appeared in the arch, filling most of it. She gestured backwards with her arm as she spoke.

"Y'all just set yoreself down at the table here. I've set the water ta boilin' fer a bath. I gots myself a real nice tub in that room off the kitchen there. Course, you'll be having to fight off my girls fer time in it."

Jolian did as she was bid. "How many girls do you have?"

"Currently, there's five. Doralynn, she's my newest, been with me just over a year. Then there's Gracie-Rose, Harriet, Elspeth and Vera. You ortta watch out fer her. She'll chase anythin' in pants!"

Jolian couldn't help but wonder again what kind of a business Pearl ran. When she'd spoke of her 'girls', she'd said it with such fondness that Jo thought she'd meant daughters. Then when she'd used the word 'currently', Jo thought maybe a boarding house. But now she was beginning to think...

"Pearl, may I ask what kind of business I'll be cooking for?"

"Ya mean they ain't told ya yet?"

Jolian shook her head as Jakeb entered the kitchen and sat down beside her at the table. He took the cup of coffee that Pearl offered and stretched out his legs as if he owned the place.

"You are sittin' in the kitchen of the finest house north of San Francisco and east of Chicago!" Peal puffed her cheeks and looked proud as a peacock. "My girls are clean and skilled in the art of pleasin' a man. Shore, they're gonna cost ya a mite more than them trashy ones in town, but you won't be wakin' up with the 'itch' either!" She laughed heartily at herself and turned to look at the two siblings. Her brows pinched together as she looked at Jakeb.

"I knows what yore thinkin'." Pearl stuck a chubby finger in Jakeb's face. "I gots me several rifles and my own personal pistol and I cain hit the dung off a fly. So, don't get no idears in yore head 'bout getting any free-bees. Cause it ain't gonna happen... Ya hear?" Jakeb nodded and Pearl continued. "If I so much as catch you sniffin' my girls without my say so, yule find yoreself more like a girl than yore sister here."

Jakeb turned to Jolian and raised a quizzical brow, "You told her?"

"It's a long story... I..."

"I wants ta know if we gots ourselves an understandin'?" Pearl huffed. "Yore sister'll be working fer me, and I'll pay ya a fair wage, deducting room and board, a course." She looked from Jakeb to Jo and back again. "But you, you gots ta give me yore word, if I lets ya live in my cabin out back that yore gonna keep yore eyes and everything else off my girls."

"Pearl I don't think my—" Jolian wanted to defend her brother against such accusations but was cut off mid-sentence as Pearl aimed a chubby finger at Jakeb's nose.

"Swear it, boy, or the deals off."

"I won't touch your girls, Ma'am, I swear." Jakeb spoke, palm in air.

"Good, it's settled then." Pearl reached out her hand and shook each of the siblings' hands in turn. She made her way from the table to the stove and then gestured with her arm as she spoke to Jolian.

"This here's the bath I told ya 'bout. The girls are napping, like I makes 'em do every day after the noonin'. And nobody else comes up here til dark, so it ain't likely you'd be disturbed, but you'd be wise to drop the bolt on the door just in case."

"There's one other thing that I believe needs to be settled before we can agree to live here." Jakeb sounded so business like that Jolian was intrigued. "I understand my sister has let you in on her 'secret'. But I must insist that if she is going to be working in a... a house of... ah... here, then I insist she continue with her disguise as a boy. I am the one who's responsible for her welfare and she'd be better off being mistaken for my younger brother."

Jolian couldn't help but smile at her brother's awkward attempt to be the 'head' of their family and take her well being into consideration.

Pearl focused a steady gaze on Jolian. Slowly, she moved her eyes from Jo's feet to the top of her head and then turned to look at Jakeb. Jolian felt like an animal at auction.

"Shore, I'll keep yer secret. But I thinks yore gonna have a hard time finding a husband fer this one. Men around here like fer their women ta have titties."

Jolian couldn't hide her gasp. She'd never heard someone speak about her in such a way! She had breasts, nice breasts. They were bound on purpose, for her ruse. She opened her mouth to speak but Jakeb spoke first.

"I've heard women are pretty scarce around these parts." If Jakeb was trying to come to her defense he was doing a poor job of it!

"Yore right about that. I guess some of my customers might take a fancy to a skinny young'un. Ya have my word, no one'll know but us three."

Jolian had never felt so insulted in all of her life. First by Pearl and then by her own brother! She could get a man if she wanted. She had been the one to decide she didn't want a man. Well, that she didn't want to be married, at least. Jolian could feel the temperature rising in her cheeks. Nothing would be more embarrassing now than for her to blush. She quickly turned on her heel, nearly loosing her balance but catching herself by grabbing on to the side of the stove. She left the two of them discussing Heaven knows what and took the heated water into the windowless room with the bath.

Jolian let the heavy bar fall across the door before she began to remove her clothes. *No breasts, hah!* She'd show them breasts. Well, not really. She managed a little laugh at her vexation and felt her anger dissipate. One wall of the room was lined with several wooden shelves, which held numerous toiletries and cloths. She picked out a bottle, popped the lid open and inhaled deeply. Lavender, oh what a magnificent scent. She stripped off the rest of her clothing in anticipation.

Lying in her hot scented bath, Jolian wasn't sure whether it was insanity or the glorious steam but she decided to stay and work for Pearl. She knew it was *that* decision which would seal her fate as a spinster, not the size of her breasts, as Pearl had so cruelly suggested. Choosing to work in this place was like saying she never wanted a decent man to take notice of her again.

When it came right down to it, she really didn't have much of a choice. She could stay and cook for Pearl and her girls, or she could leave. And right now the lavender bubbles were saying stay, stay. Jolian bent her knees and let her shoulders sink below the surface. Ah, such luxury!

She couldn't remember the last time she felt this relaxed. She silenced the voice sounding the alarm bells in her head. She would keep her disguise as a boy and not because Jakeb thought she should. It would be extra insurance to ward off any unwanted trouble. Pearl said she rarely had any customers come by her place before dark. Jo should have plenty of time to complete the daily chores and be back at her cabin before nightfall.

She didn't want to think about the fact that she had just decided to work in a house of prostitution. She just wouldn't think about the 'business' that went on after she left for the day and she'd be fine. She'd just think of this as another hotel, one where she cooked for the employees rather than the guests. The surroundings weren't quite as well appointed as her Uncle's hotel, but she could never remember having a bath there, which felt as good as this one did.

Jolian closed her eyes and let her head slip under the water. She'd start work, as a boy, for Pearl tomorrow; however, right now, in her bath, she was all woman.

Four

"How can you call 'em hotcakes when there're shiverin' cold?" Vera spat her mouthful of half-chewed food back onto the chipped, red china plate. With a loud "Harrumph" she pushed the plate way and leaned back in her chair. "Howse a workin' girl s'posed ta keep her strength up with slop like this?"

"Shut yore trap, Vera!" Pearl said as she bustled her ample form around the wooden table retrieving dishes. "It was hot when you was called fer it. Now eat up! Jo ain't fixin' nothing special fer ya, jist cause you cain't haul yore sorry butt outta bed."

Jolian listened to the familiar exchange from her usual spot in the kitchen. Her arms were elbow-deep in hot soapy dishwater and she felt a smile tugging at the corners of her lips. Even with her back to the eating area, Jo could picture Vera in her mind's eye. Vera, the feistiest of Pearl's girls, would be sitting at the table in her underclothes. Her enormous breasts pushed up so close to her chin, that they looked like rocks on the edge of some gaudily painted garden.

Jo turned as Pearl made her way into the kitchen and lowered an armful of dirty dishes into her bucket.

"D'ya hear her?" Pearl spoke loudly enough for the girls in the eating area to hear.

Jo smiled to herself. "Um-hmm."

"Always goin' on 'bout somethin'. If it ain't one thin' it's another with Vera. She ortta jist pack up 'n go. That's it all right. I ortta send her packin'. I don't need her whining and complainin'..."

"Missed one." Vera interrupted as she handed Pearl her plate, now void of food.

"I thought you weren't eatin' 'em." Pearl placed her hands on her hips. Vera shrugged, licked a finger saucily and swayed her way past Jo and into the parlor to join the other girls.

"I swear..." Pearl half muttered under her breath. Pearl turned to Jo and looked her up and down. "Now, Jo, don't you be stayin' in this kitchen all day. Hell, ya bin in here since afore the rooster cawed I'm sure. You ortta finish up and go and get some sun or somethin'. I knows ya ain't gonna put color in your cheeks no other way. You look paler than what's natural, and I ain't wantin' folks ta be saying Pearl don't know how ta treat her girls."

Pearl took a breath, looked around the empty kitchen and added more quietly "That's if they knowed ya was a girl." She laughed heartily at her own joke and waved a chubby finger close to Jo's nose. "Now mind me, child. Don't you be settin' a foot in this house again 'til supper."

Jo hoped her smile conveyed her gratefulness for the suggestion. Pearl returned her smile and patted her on the behind. Then in a voice loud enough for the girls in the parlor to hear, she said "And eat something, *son*. Landsakes, but you are as skinny as a broom!" Pearl turned towards the parlor and in a voice that nearly shook the walls she hollered "Vera! I wanna talk to you 'bout putting on some clothes while yore under my roof..."

Jo smiled and shook her head as she finished washing and wiping the dishes. She had long since forgiven Pearl for her comments about her skinny body. Over the past few months she'd come to understand and appreciate Pearl's unique sense of humor. She was proud to admit that the owner of the house was now a dear friend.

She'd never imagined she would ever meet people like Pearl and Vera at all, let alone work with them. Back before her Pa had heard the word 'gold' she didn't even know what a house of prostitution was and she certainly had no idea of what went on inside of one. But, that was a lifetime ago. Before she'd known gold fever couldn't keep you warm in the Cariboo in January, and that her parents were just people with dreams, too. People who lived to make her world richer and who died for no better reason than another man's greed.

Jolian swiped at her eyes with her shirttail and quietly let herself out the back door. She took a deep breath and filled her lungs with the scent of wildflowers and pine. Hands in her pockets, she sauntered through the tall grass that filled in the mile or so between Pearl's back door and the edge of the woods. The breeze promised summer as it toyed with the curls on her neck.

Tucked neatly between two tall cedars was the tiny log cabin Jo shared with her brother. Again, as she did every time she thought of her brother lately, Jo said a little prayer. Jakeb had a lot on his shoulders these days and Jolian couldn't help but wish for the carefree brother she'd admonished him for being in San Francisco. Then again, she felt as if she were a different person too, from the one who lived back in California. She was different from the girl who wore a corset and skirts, not just because of her trousers and flannel shirt. She was changed forever in so many ways; it was hard to believe they had only left San Francisco a year ago.

In the past few months she'd settled down to working at Pearl's, and as it had been with Aklu'ut, Jolian found the chores kept her feeling alive. Pearl paid her a fair wage for cooking three meals a day for her girls. She and Jakeb were welcome to have any of the food she prepared, once the girls had been served.

Pearl had a maid of all work who came in three times a week and the girls were responsible for keeping their own rooms tidy. Still, the cooking and occasional washing up took up most of her day. Responsibility for going into town to purchase any needed victuals was the part of her job Jolian least enjoyed. She had been in the nearby town of Richfield and found it useless for any type of shopping at all. Even though the seat of the Cariboo's government was fixed there, Richfield was more of the type of town one would pass through on his way to Barkerville.

Jolian swatted at a pesky mosquito. As the current hotbed for mining, Barkerville teamed with people whom Jolian felt certain would see through her simple disguise and she could hardly stand to be within five miles of the town. She half wished she'd never agreed to continue with her disguise for it only complicated her life. She swatted at the bug again, squashed it firmly against her neck and scrunched her nose in distaste.

Fortunately, with Jakeb working at the mercantile, she could often present him with a list of supplies and avoid the town altogether.

God bless Jakeb and keep him safe. The standard prayer ran through her thoughts like clockwork. She felt thankful too that Jakeb shared her cabin. It made her feel safe and there were times when it almost felt like a home. At the moment though, she was grateful he was at work and she could enjoy a few moments alone.

Jo stepped into the coolness of her two-room cabin, took the shako cap off her head and ran her fingers through her sweat soaked hair. Her hair would need cutting again soon. She would have loved to spend some time in Pearl's bath but it seemed to be getting harder and harder these days to find a time when the tub wasn't in use.

The past few weeks had seen the daytime temperature rise considerably, and any time the 'girls' weren't working, they seemed to spend in the tub. Besides, she was beginning to get odd looks from the girls for smelling like lavender. But no way would she give it up, it was the only decent thing, to her knowledge, that kept the bugs away.

With the rise in temperature came the mosquitoes. Extremely aggressive, unless she was completely doused in lavender, they would fly right into her face. Jakeb used bear grease to rid himself of the nuisance. She shuddered at the thought of putting the slimy, smelly lard on her body again. She'd have to ask Pearl if there was anything else. Something less feminine than lavender, but a whole lot less manly than bear grease!

She walked through the tiny living area that doubled as a kitchen and entered the bedroom. The porch off the back of the bedroom was almost as large as the house itself and served as a wash area. Jolian felt drawn to the porch and leaned against the rough railing, staring into the woods. Thought of the cool lake, a scant half-mile away, swam in her mind. She would love to go there, but simply couldn't bring herself to bathe outdoors in the middle of the day. They were relatively secluded on Richfield Mountain, but still, it felt too risky.

Her eyes rested on the bowl and pitcher atop of the chest of drawers as she walked back into her bedroom. A cloth bath would at least wash off the squashed mosquito. Sighing audibly, she crossed to the dresser and took down the pitcher. Not much water, but it would have to do. Jolian poured the water into the bowl and set it on the lower dresser. She turned to her bed, which was separated from Jakeb's by a blanket strung across the room.

Hooking a thumb under each suspender, she slid them off her shoulders and then unbuttoned the heavy flannel of her shirt.

"Ahh." She sighed aloud as she undid the scratchy woolen trousers and let them slide down the drawers on her legs. The thought of the cool cabin air on her bare, hot skin sped up her fingers as she unfastened the buttons of her union suit. She needed to invest in some summer clothes soon. Maybe Jakeb could buy her something suitable.

Socks off and Jolian stood naked save for the cloth that bound her breasts to her body. Layer by layer, she unwrapped the muslin, took a deep breath and turned to see herself in the round mirror above the dresser. A faded tapestry ottoman held her naked buttocks as she sat and studied her face carefully. Pearl was right. She had become thin and pale. Her eyes seemed lighter and larger in this version of her face. *No wonder people have no questions about me being a boy*, she thought.

Jolian picked up a cloth, dipped it into the lukewarm water and wrung out the excess. She lay the cloth on her face and let her skin drink in its moisture. Slowly, she moved the cloth to the nape of her neck and down each shoulder. Freshened with the remainder of the water; she ran the cloth gingerly over each breast. Wrapped in muslin all day they were sensitive to everything that touched them. They responded to the coolness by rising upwards, their tips hardening to rose-colored buds. She moved the cloth down her ribs, her stomach, then lower, to the hollow between her hipbones and then down the length of each leg.

She felt cool and alive again. What had begun as an early spring had quickly changed back into winter. Then just as suddenly, the snow seemed to have melted into summer. Jolian reached for her discarded clothing and then decided against it. Who would see her naked inside her cabin? Besides, she felt like being a woman for a while.

She cupped her hands in the basin of remaining water and brought them up to her short-cropped curls. Though it had been almost a year since she'd shorn her locks, it still took some getting used to when she passed a mirror. She massaged the wetness through to her scalp, picked up her hairbrush, then brushed and fingered the curls until they were soft waves hugging her face. She pinched her cheeks to add some color and moistened her lips with her tongue. Amazing! The hollowed out boy face that had stared at her only moments before, took on a softness that could only be described as feminine.

"I wonder if a man would like this face?" Jolian thought aloud.

~ * ~

Jolian let herself in the back door of Pearl's place. She'd folded up the front of her shirt to make a sack for the sweet fennel she'd harvested. While summer appeared to be upon them, Richfield Mountain was so high in elevation they were still waking up to frost some mornings. Frost in the mornings and scorching by noon, she laughed at the absurdity. It made gardening quite a challenge to say the least. Thanks to Aklu'ut, she had some knowledge of vegetation, which made their meals a lot more interesting, and her forages to the woods more profitable. Balancing her berry filled cap with one hand and straightening out her shirt with the other, she let the fennel bulbs fall on to the wooden counter top, just as Pearl bustled her way into the kitchen.

"Well, don't ya look like the cat that up'n swallowed the bird!" Pearl sauced. "What's ya gots there?"

"Look what I found, Pearl!" Jo beamed as she thrust the contents of her upside down cap at the woman. "They're raspberries, and they're good!"

"I kin tell ya've been samplin' them by the stain round yore mouth." Pearl nodded.

"I thought the girls would like them with cream for dessert," Jo explained wiping her mouth with the back of her free hand. From the look on Pearl's face she knew that her attempt at cleanliness only amounted to a minglement of berry juice and dirt smeared about her face.

"I reckon they would at that. I was jist comin' ta fetch ya, Jo. Ya gots a visitor."

"A visitor? Who?" Truly puzzled, she dumped the raspberries into a bowl and quickly put the cap back on her head. Everyone she knew lived here.

"One of the ones that brung ya to me. He's waiting in the parlor."

Jo pulled the shako cap lower on her forehead and followed Pearl out of the kitchen. She had to shuffle in her oversized boots to keep from slipping on the highly polished parlor floor. She concentrated on her boots and was ill prepared for the sight awaiting her.

"Jo," Pearl stopped and looked behind her as she reached the parlor. She stepped to one side as she motioned to the man rising from the settee. "I'm shore you remember Cooper Holt, the man I tole ya'bout."

Jo cleared her throat to hide her startled intake of breath. She'd never met this man before, had she? She would have remembered someone like him. Of course, she'd been out of her mind with grief at the time... but surely... Cooper Holt? She had spoken with a Cooper Holt about bringing her to the goldfields. Hadn't that been the name of one of her three rescuers? She supposed it could be the same man...

"How do you do, sir?" Jo mumbled stretching out her hand to shake his.

"I'm fine, Joe, thanks." His husky voice stirred her insides and the firmness of his grip on her hand made her knees weaken. "I trust Pearl's been keeping you well and out of trouble." He chuckled, a deep throaty sound. Not trusting her voice, Jo nodded her reply.

"Good. Well... I wish I was here under more pleasant circumstances but ah, Guy Renault and I have just returned form Fort Kamloops. We stopped at the Carrier's village on the way back. I know you stayed with Ts'kaw's sister and I thought I'd let you know that all is well with her and her son." He put his fist to his mouth, cleared his throat and continued. "The ground was soft enough to dig deep graves and so we buried your folks. I know when we left the village you'd indicated to Aklu'ut you wanted to be present... it's just that the summer's come up quite quickly and preserving the bodies any longer would be... ah—The spot's a fine one overlooking the valley, I think you'd find it suitable. I... ah... well I just wanted to let you and your brother know."

The mention of her parents made her throat suddenly constrict. "Thank you, sir." Jo managed to squeak out. She couldn't think of this now—it wouldn't do for a boy to cry in this situation—she swallowed hard and shoved her feelings down. She needed to concentrate on something else to keep her composure. Her gaze focused on the man before her. He looked from Jo to Pearl and then to a bottle of amber colored liquid on the table beside the settee.

"Shore I cain't fix ya a glass?" Pearl questioned him.

"I think I'll take you up on that lemonade you offered." Cooper flashed an even white smile at Pearl as she turned and swayed her substantial form back toward the kitchen.

He turned his gaze on Jo, pulled his lips into a straight line and nodded. "Guy and I are heading down to Fort Alexandria for about a week on business. Once we're back I could make arrangements for you and Jakeb to go and visit the grave sight, if you wanted."

Jo met his gaze and spoke clearly this time. "I'm obliged to you, Mr. Holt. I'm sure we would, if we can get away. I'd like to see about making arrangements for a marker."

"That's fine." Cooper gave her a look of condolence and patted her shoulder.

Focus on him, on his hand on your shoulder. Jolian could feel the warmth of his hand through her clothes to her skin. She felt the heat flow through her veins and begin to flood her cheeks. She quickly dropped her head in an attempt to hide the effect of his touch.

She breathed a sigh of relief as Mr. Holt changed the subject. "How's your brother faring? Pearl mentioned he's still working for old Elijah Duke at the mercantile in Barkerville and that he's got himself a partner in a claim on back street as well."

"Um-hmm. He's doing fine." Jo kept her eyes on her boots and hoped she wasn't appearing rude. Maybe focusing on Cooper Holt wasn't such a good idea. "Jakeb still has a bit of a limp, but all in all he's well. His claim hasn't amounted to much yet—but he's eternally hopeful, Jakeb is." She tried to make her voice sound manly and low, but her eyes had a will of their own.

Pearl returned with the man's lemonade and engaged him in conversation. Jolian seized the opportunity to scrutinize him freely.

Pale canvas trousers housed long legs and hugged slim hips. A plain white cotton shirt, tucked neatly at his waist, seemed to cling to the breadth of his chest and shoulders. Sitting in dark contrast on the white collar of his shirt, was thick undulating chestnut hair. Wind tousled, it framed his face like a lion's mane. Clean-shaven, except for his moustache, which had been kissed by the sun to reflect shades of auburn and brass, his bronzed cheeks broke into deep creases as he laughed heartily at some comment from Pearl. Tiny wrinkles lit at the corners of his eyes, as well. His eyes, how could she have not noticed them before? They were the most intriguing color. A greenish blue or was it bluish green? She couldn't be sure. But they were bright and clear—and they seemed to be looking right through her. Oh biscuits! Jolian paled. He was looking *at* her not through her. He'd caught her staring. How would she explain?

"Joe? Joe, are you all right? I think you're bleeding!" He moved toward her, a genuine concern glowing in those incredible eyes. A spark of fire ran through her as his fingertips brushed over her left eyebrow.

He was so close Jolian could feel his breath warm on her cheek. She closed her eyes and parted her lips and felt as though she would swoon dead away.

Pearl broke the spell by pressing a lace handkerchief firmly to Jo's brow. She sniffed the cloth and huffed "Landsakes, Jo! You ortta start taking a bowl with ya when you pick berries!"

Jo reached her own hand up and gingerly touched the sticky trail of raspberry juice. Cooper laughed, that deep throaty sound again. Pearl guffawed along as well. Jolian thought she'd just expire of embarrassment right then and there.

"I'd better see about the meal," Jo mumbled. She stretched her hand out to Cooper Holt. "I thank you again for all you've done for me and my family, ah, Mr. Holt, sir."

"You're welcome and it's Cooper, son. About a week then and I'll see you again." Laughter still rang in his voice as he shook her hand with steady firmness.

"Mmm-hmm," Jolian nodded and hurried back to the safety of the kitchen. Arms bracing her body, she leaned against the stove, her head down. A tide of emotions rolled back and forth through her. His touch, on her shoulder and above her eye had stirred something deep inside her—a feeling so strong, almost primitive. She wasn't sure what it was, but it had moved her, changed her somehow.

Those were not the thoughts of a woman who was actively pursuing spinsterhood. She busied herself with preparing the meal and tried unsuccessfully to keep her mind on her task. She must have had too much sun today. Surely that was the cause of the strange feelings, the warmth that flooded her; yes it must be the sun.

Jo took a deep breath and unconsciously focused her eyes out the small kitchen window and on the trail that lead to town. When she saw Cooper riding away, she stopped separating the feathery fennel leaves from their stalks and stood staring. As hard as she tried to convince herself, she knew it was more than too much sun that caused the feeling of warmth flowing through her body. Maybe she'd re-think spinsterhood, maybe.

I wonder what he thinks of me? She thought idly. *He thinks you're a boy!* Came the answer. Of course he does. *All he's thinking of, quite rightly, is the two brothers who lost their parents and all I should be thinking about is dinner. Besides, if he's up here he's most certainly a miner, and that, foolish girl, settles that.*

Jolian silenced her inner voices by sticking her bottom lip out to one side and blowing a puff of a breath at a stray curl on her forehead. She'd not give up her pledge for some miner! Why surely she'd spend the rest of her days, following him to the ends of the earth in search of gold. That was not the life for her! Her life would be her own, even if society gave her chastity and solitude as punishment for her choice.

~ * ~

Jolian made a quick salad of thinly sliced fennel bulbs, its feathery greens, walnuts and apples to go with the stew. As she was laying it out on the table, the first of Pearl's girls came down to dinner. The girls, five in all, didn't pay much mind to their cook. Except for Vera, who, thinking Jo *was* a boy, would sometimes tease her about spending her pay 'upstairs'. Jo usually kept her head down, continued her work and Vera would eventually leave her alone. Tonight though, Vera seemed to have a bee in her bonnet.

"Oh, Joe honey," she drawled sweetly, "how's about comin' up ta visit me after dinner?"

Jo began to wipe the wooden countertop and tried to ignore Vera's advancing half-dressed form.

"Leave him alone, Vera," the voluptuous blonde named Elspeth said. "He's just a sweet kid and he don't need you ta corrupt him."

"Corrupt him?" Vera half yelled at Elspeth, then turned back to Jo, her voice as sweet as maple sap in March. "I ain't gonna corrupt him. I's gonna change his life. Wake him up and show him the ways of a woman."

Vera sauntered into the cooking area and moving closer and closer to Jo. As usual, undergarments were her clothing of choice. Jo had to bite her lip to keep from laughing as Vera leaned on the counter and her breasts nearly popped out onto Jo's cutting board.

"Do ya knows about women, Joe? Doose ya? Do ya know what a woman like me could do to a thin' like you? Ya know I fancy you. I'd even be willin' ta 'help ya out', so ta speak, free of charge." Vera walked her fingers up Jo's arm and pressed her body closer.

Jo tried to move away, but the stove blocked her retreat. This wasn't funny anymore! She had to think of something before Vera got any closer and discovered the truth. Jo turned her back as Vera pressed her body right up to her. Vera reached out her hand and grabbed Jo's behind.

"Ooh!" Vera spoke loud enough for the girls in the eating area to hear. "I wonder if yore this hard all over." Then she whispered in Jo's ear. "I bet one part of ya is anyway".

"Vera!"

Vera startled and moved abruptly from Jo. "I told ya to leave the help alone!" Pearl bellowed as she quickly moved to put herself between Jo and the whore. "I don't care how long you've been with me, Vera. I swear if I ever catch ya in here again, doin' what—I knows you were thinkin it, don't open yore mouth ta me! I say if ya bother Jo again yore through, ya hear!"

There was no friendly banter or teasing in Pearl's voice. Jo had never seen this side of her. But Vera obviously had, as she seemed to sense danger and hurried out of Pearl's way.

Alone with Pearl in the kitchen, Jolian tried to create an aura of normalcy again. "I'm sorry, Pearl," Jo mumbled "I tried to avoid her."

"I knows it, and ya ain't got nothin ta be sorry fer. Vera don't mean ya no real harm, she's just a flirt, always has been. Makes her damn good at her job, but a pain in the patoot ta be around just the same." Then in a whispering voice Pearl added, "I'd love ta see her face if she ever found out yore secret though, ooh!"

Jo smiled and Pearl continued to whisper. "Ya feelin up ta servin the meal?"

With a nod from Jo, Pearl moved to the eating area and hollered, "Come 'n git it!"

~ * ~

Vera was back to her usual self by the end of the meal, but she kept her distance from Jo. After the girls had eaten and gone upstairs to get ready for 'work', Jo sat down at the table with her own plate of stew and biscuits. A knot the size of her fist clenched in the muscles between her shoulder blades and she felt as though she could jump out of her skin at the slightest noise. It wasn't just Vera's teasing, but all the events of her day. She'd barely had a chance to think about the news Cooper Holt had brought her.

The fact that her parents now had graves seemed to ease her pain. She was actually grateful Cooper and his friends had taken it upon themselves to bury her folks. Maybe by visiting the spot and saying goodbye she could finally let her memories of them rest peacefully.

Jo finished eating and tidied the rest of the kitchen. It would be dark in a few hours. With nightfall came the customers the girls awaited and Jo avoided. She always made sure she was safely secured in her cabin before the first horse came trotting up the path. Now that the long days of summer were upon them, she had more time to relax between her evening meal and the trot to seclusion.

Lately, Jakeb had taken up the habit of meeting her at Pearl's on his way home from work. It was a nice time for them. Growing up, Jolian and Jakeb had enjoyed a close relationship. Jakeb had always been a bit of a talker and had taken advantage of Jolian's naïveté on countless occasions, to spin a good yarn. They'd drifted apart in their teen years, each working their way toward adulthood, pursuing their own individual goals. The family trek for gold had re-united them and their parents' death had forged a new bond. She felt like she was getting to know her brother all over again.

Jolian put the remainder of the food into two blue enameled pots and grabbed the bowl of berries to take back to the cabin with her. Jakeb entered through the back door just as she was leaving.

"All ssset to go?" He asked as he took the pots from his sister's arms.

As the late afternoon sun shone in all its glory, the siblings walked through the tall grass towards their cabin. The path was becoming as familiar as their new friendship and Jolian spoke about Cooper's earlier visit.

"He said they'd be back in a week and we can make arrangements to see Ma and Pa's grave."

"Sssounds fine to me." Jakeb's face contorted as he tried to get out certain sounds. "I'm sssure Elijah can spare me for a ssspell. It's good to know our folks have graves to rest in now. I never liked the idea of them Indians preserving their bodies till spring. You just never know with those primitive cultures, if they're gonna do as they sssay. You know, if you can trust 'em."

"Jakeb, I don't think I need to remind you that you owe your life to those people! I hate it when you talk about them like they are less than we are." Jolian poked a lock of hair into her cap.

"Yeah, yeah." Jakeb rolled his eyes. "You ssssound like Ma when you go ssssspouting off like that. I'm not ssssaying I don't appreciate what they've done; I just mean their ways aren't our ways. You got to be careful, that's all. I'm just glad to hear Ma and Pa got their graves."

Jo decided to avoid the argument. "Yes, it does seem to help a bit doesn't it?" The siblings stayed lost in their own thoughts for the rest of their walk. In the comfort of their own tiny kitchen, Jolian dished the stew onto a plate for Jakeb and filled him in on the rest of the events of her day. It was good to have a confidant again. Although Jakeb could never take the place of her mother, to whom Jolian used to tell everything, he appeared, at least, to be interested in her ramblings. Sometimes he reverted to his old tricks of teasing and taunting her but for the most part, he listened and advised her when she needed it.

Jolian hoped she could rely on their new, more mature relationship. She didn't want teasing, she wanted answers. She'd decided to keep her new strange feelings for Cooper Holt to herself for the time being but the episode with Vera had left her puzzled about something. She explained it to Jakeb.

"And then she grabbed my behind and said something about me being hard all over or at least in one part."

Jakeb was laughing so hard, Jolian thought he might choke on his stew. He stopped suddenly though, when Jolian asked, "What part did she mean Jakeb?"

Jakeb swallowed hard and took another big mouthful of his biscuits and gravy.

"Jakeb?"

He seemed embarrassed and Jolian felt confused. Was this some kind of ploy to make her believe a story?

"C'mon Jakeb, tell me what she meant, honestly. I know what it has to do with, but I don't understand what she said."

Jakeb finished his stew and wiped his mouth with the back of his sleeve.

"Wwwell," he began slowly. He looked at her and Jolian couldn't tell if he was sizing her up to tell her a big secret or getting ready to tell her a whopper. "You know about when a man and a woman are together—"

"Yes." She interrupted and then continued in a whisper. An inherited trait from her mother, Jolian often whispered when she was repeating something she shouldn't know or something that might be a bit scandalous. "Ma told me when you marry a man you share a special time called lovemaking and that's how you make your children. You know you've made a child when your monthly stops coming. She told me some women like this lovemaking and others don't, and I guess men always like it cause they go to places like Pearl's to pay for it. Either way, Ma said you don't do it until you're married."

"I think you've got the gist of it." Jakeb smiled at her and tried to change the subject. He looked like he was stifling a laugh. Was this all a big tease to make her believe something?

He cleared his throat and said, "This is a fine tasting salad. What are the leaves with this apple? They taste kind of like licorice."

"I'm still confused Jakeb. What did Vera mean about being hard? Or that one part of me was hard?"

"It's not part of you," Jakeb sighed, but was still smiling as he said, "Remember, Vera thinks you're a man."

"Oh." Jolian swallowed hard and decided she needed the information. "So what exactly do you do when you do lovemaking, Jakeb?"

"Its called making love." He explained the specifics with a slightly reddened face.

"I don't think I'd like that," Was all she could say when he finished.

"Well, no one's going to ask you to do it if you look at him like that!" Jakeb laughed and she softened the expression on her face. " But honestly, Jolian, you'll know it when the time is right and if it's with someone you care about, I'm sure you'll like it just fine."

"Did you ever do lovemaking?"

"Yup."

Her eyebrows raised in surprise. "With who?"

"Sally Redmont"

"Sally Redmont!" Now it was her turn to laugh. "If her Pa had found out he would have killed you! Did you like it, Jakeb?"

"Sssure, ssure I did."

"Did Sally Redmont?"

"Yup."

"How do you know she liked it? Did she say 'I like this', or did you ask her—"

"I jjjust know she did." Jakeb puffed up his chest, tilted his head sideways and winked at his sister. "A man knows when he's pleased a woman."

Jolian smiled at her brother's attempt to appear so manly. She tried to stifle a giggle as she thought about her brother and that pinched faced Sally Redmont. Sally Redmont had always seemed such a prude! She must have cared for Jakeb if she'd let him get so intimate. Jolian wondered if she'd ever have those kinds of feelings for a man. Maybe one like Cooper Holt... "Thanks, Jakeb, for telling me."

"You're welcome."

Jolian crossed the room and entered the bedroom. She picked a nightshirt out of the bureau and took a cloth, blanket and soap from the washstand. Re-entering the kitchen, she called to Jakeb, "I'm off to bathe in the lake." He nodded his reply, not taking his eyes from the bowl of berries beside him.

Must still be thinking about Sally Redmont, Jolian giggled to herself again. She stepped off the back porch of her cabin and as usual, took a few minutes to watch the surrounding woods before she started on the path to the lake. A silly ritual really. Pearl's customers never ventured into the woods, let alone anywhere near her cabin. *We really are in the middle of nowhere*, she thought as she fingered the revolver in her pocket.

Pearl had given her the Colt just after they'd moved into the cabin. She had taught her how to use it and Jolian had practiced shooting tin cans and an old stump until she felt reasonably certain she could hit whatever she aimed at, and not her own foot. She had sworn she'd never handle a gun but then she'd never imagined herself living the life she had now. Her fingers touched the cool metal in her pocket and a chill ran through her. She hoped she would never have to aim it at a human with the intent to fire. No one *ever* strayed past Pearl's, she reminded herself. But safety was something she would never take for granted again.

Just carrying the gun gave her the sense of security she needed to walk alone. She'd sewn a special section into the pocket of her trousers where the heavy gun could hide. Her trousers were so baggy she could keep the gun with her always, without anyone ever knowing. In fact, it had become such a fixture in her wardrobe she hardly felt the extra weigh of it at all.

Jolian hugged her bundle of belongings in front of her as she walked. She felt a lightness in her step that had been sorely lacking for some time. An urge to start skipping down the path or to twirl in circles almost overwhelmed her. Genuine happiness filled her from head to toe. It must be the beauty of the evening that set her soul so free. The sky became truly inspiring as the sun made itself ready for bed. She would have to get moving! Once the sun set, she had only a half hour or so before dark. She may be able to walk alone in the woods at dusk but in the night, well, that was another matter altogether. She hurried her steps until her bathing spot came into view.

As usual, Jolian stopped at the edge of the woods and inspected the clearing and picturesque lake. Lakes really, she supposed. Three lakes, each contributing to the lake below as the mountainside gave way to cliff after cliff. Her gaze traversed the middle lake where she bathed. Everything was still. Not even a breeze to ruffle the grasses.

From time to time she would see a moose, caribou or even a bear at the upper creek bed, which was about a hundred feet up from the spot where she bathed. They'd keep their eyes on her as they drank, and she'd keep her finger on the trigger. Dense woods surrounded the creek bed above her, and as soon as the animals had drunk their fill, they'd disappear into its darkness. A trickle of water fell from that upper bed down into her bathing spot. Rocks, shrubs and grass bordered her lake. Jolian had never seen anything more than a jackrabbit or raccoon sipping from its shores.

Her bathing spot had it's own natural drain, too. The far end of the lake, close to a half-mile away narrowed into a full-fledged waterfall, which fell to the lower creek. Jolian often felt small and insignificant here. Like she was a tiny bug on some giant's staircase of water.

While she loved her scented baths, Jolian had come to enjoy bathing in the lake. It was her time to be free and unencumbered. A place where her defenses could dissolve and her spirit could rejuvenate.

Jolian ventured out of the woods to the lake's edge. The elongated pool of black water reflected the surrounding cedars and snow capped mountain peaks. Placing her toiletries on a large flat rock which jutted part way out into the lake, she lay her gun carefully, just where the rock met the water, so she could get at it if need be. She discarded her clothes carelessly, like a child and then ventured into the chilly water, its coolness welcomed after the intense heat of the day.

Within seconds she was waist deep in the mountain spring. Jolian took a deep breath and dove forward. Acclimated, she let her body float noiselessly in the blue-black basin. She lay on her back and gazed at the afternoon sky. The sun's golden eye winked at her from a pillow of billowy clouds. She laughed a little and winked back. She floated for ages, occasionally adding a finger or toe splash to the chirping of the crickets and the gentle breath of breeze in the trees. Inhaling deeply, she expanded her lungs with the scent of pine and cedar.

Reluctantly, Jolian rolled onto her belly and swam back to the rock from which she'd drifted. The sun slipped lower on the horizon as she reached a prune-shriveled hand for her soap and cloth and rubbed them together. Slowly, she washed. Luxuriating in the freshness of the water and the freedom of being completely herself. She felt thoroughly relaxed and began to sing a lullaby from her childhood. She couldn't remember all of the words, but the tune haunted her.

She loved to sing and missed it sorely. During the day, always surrounded by people, she had a hard enough time talking like a boy let alone singing like one. Alone, in the fast fading daylight she felt no inhibitions or self-consciousness. She was all woman as she let her voice echo throughout the vibrant sky.

"Still, now, and hear my singing. Sleep through the night, my darling. We have a tiny daughter, thanks be to God who sent her..."

As the sun began to sink toward the horizon, it lit the clouds from underneath. She sped her bathing, singing with vigor as if to calm herself. Most people would have stopped to reflect upon the day's beauty but not Jolian. Sudden colour, more vivid than an artist's pallet washed the sky and soaked her with ominous dread. Salmons and magentas swirled with plums and lobsters. The colours crept up her spine like cold fingers. Scallops of indigo and steel edged clouds eddied with waves of rose and daffodil. But to Jolian it was gun steel and blood red and apprehension churned in her stomach.

Five

Remnants of daylight guided his path as Cooper Holt urged his horse along the overgrown trail. It'd been a while since he'd ridden here and he was beginning to think he'd made a wrong turn. He moved his mount cautiously through the blue spruce and pine until he came, finally, to the giant cedar.

"This way, Storm," he said with more sureness than he'd felt in the last half-hour. "Just over this rise and we'll get you a drink."

He'd been riding since he'd left Pearl's Place this morning, hadn't eaten since noon and both he and his horse were tired and hungry. Cooper had gone through the towns of Richfield, Barkerville and Cameronton, all within a few miles of each other. In fact the three towns shared a common main street of sorts. Odd the way these mining towns sprung up along the creeks. Rough log cabins, false front buildings and tents seemed to appear overnight, whenever the word Eureka! was heard.

He'd renewed a few acquaintances at the government offices in Richfield, then he'd stopped for bannock and coffee at 'Wake up Jake's' in Barkerville. Where folks got some of the names for their establishments, he couldn't figure. Of course he knew the story behind the name of the town Barkerville. Who hadn't heard about old English Bill who'd struck paydirt on the lower portion of William's creek? He'd sunk a shaft fifty-two feet down before he'd hit bedrock. He must be one determined man, Cooper reasoned, as the miners in Richfield hit bedrock around fifteen feet. Amazing the length and depth some folks would go in search of Cariboo gold. Cooper figured at the rate Barkerville was growing, it would either burn itself out, or it would soon overshadow the surrounding towns.

After his lunch, Cooper wound around the Jack of Clubs Lake where he'd met up with Ts'kaw and surveyed five new claims, which had been staked in the past week. He'd checked in on an old trapper friend who lived past Pinkerton creek and had been suffering from influenza. Cooper had fixed the old timer a hot toddy and a pot of stew and the man was up an about before he'd left. By dinnertime he'd traveled full circle up Pinkerton Mountain to Guy's house, which was only an hour, as the crow flies, from Pearl's place.

Cooper and Guy had decided to leave for Fort Alexandria in the morning. Though only a day's ride from the Carrier village, that made it fours days ride from here. Cooper and Guy hoped to push their luck and their horses and make the round trip in seven days. Claims were popping up in town faster than they could survey them. Ts'kaw would stay behind and attend to some note taking but still the work would pile up fast. They'd been working long and hard these past few months and Cooper looked forward to the break, even if it was only a trip for business.

Guy had offered him a bed when he'd arrived at his homestead, but Cooper had declined. It was such a beautiful July evening, he'd told Guy he'd rather sleep under the stars at the 'Giant Steps', the name they'd fondly given the spot he was looking for now. Guy would meet him there tomorrow at daybreak, and they'd be on their way from there.

Cooper couldn't help but smile when he thought of his meeting with the Grayson boy. The boy seemed so awkward and unsure of himself, rather like he had been at that age. Now that he'd seen the lad again, he had no doubt as to the truth of his gender. He'd have to really rub it in next time he saw Ts'kaw, too. Imagine, insisting Joe was a girl! Ts'kaw was very wise about a good many things, and he often displayed the ego to go along with his knowledge. Cooper felt it was his duty, as a true friend, to show Ts'kaw the error of his ways. Yup, it'd feel real good to watch Ts'kaw eat a little humble pie!

The surrounding cover of trees ended abruptly, as Storm and his rider came upon the little piece of heaven they'd been looking for. Suddenly, the horse stopped moving and pricked up his ears.

"I hear it too, boy," Cooper whispered as he dismounted and quickly surveyed the area. A woman's voice echoed in the distance. He couldn't make out the words, but it sounded as though she was singing.

"It's all right, all right, Storm," Cooper reassured him. "Wherever she is, she's a ways from us."

He left his horse to drink his fill and silently moved to the cliff, where the water trickled down to a pool below. Cooper felt his breath catch in his throat, and he held it there, lest he make any noise that would distract the sight, which met his eyes.

Floating in a puddle of sunset beneath him was an exquisitely carved, naked woman. Cooper blinked hard and refocused his eyes, thinking he must be dreaming, but he knew she was real. From her lips to his ears, the breeze carried the haunting melody he'd heard earlier. Cooper let his breath out slowly in a long silent whistle. The fact that she was naked told the gentleman in him to avert his eyes, but that same fact that kept him rooted to the spot captivated by her every move.

The sun sank lower on the horizon and Cooper watched, mesmerized, as the mermaid emerged from the water. She reached for a blanket and Cooper quickly took in every inch of her as she dried her tiny form. Her damp hair clung to her head and seemed to form ringlets around her face. The sinking sun turned tiny droplets of water into glistening diamonds on her skin. She rubbed her arms with a blanket and Cooper felt pressure in his groin. It had been a long time since any woman had caused that kind of response in him. She hurried, rubbing the blanket down each shapely leg and he willed her to go slower, to take her time.

As the setting sun breathed its last breath it cast a golden aura around her. His gaze traveled down her neck to her breasts and on downward, past the curve of her hips, to the pale triangle between her slender yet well formed legs. She dried each body part quickly, though thoroughly and Cooper began to envy the blanket; it touched her everywhere he wanted to touch her.

His breath was raspy and short and he knew he couldn't look much longer. She pulled a nightshift over her head, gathered her belongings and started down the path towards Pearl's Place. Cooper watched as she disappeared into what was fast becoming the night, and then he inhaled deeply, letting his breath fill his cheeks as he exhaled.

Now that he could no longer see her, he began to wonder if he had imagined the whole episode. What would a woman like that, be doing bathing in the lake, alone? She'd headed towards Pearl's, but she couldn't be one of the 'girls'. Cooper had nothing against whores, but he knew enough about them to know with night falling they wouldn't be out bathing. She also couldn't be someone's wife or daughter, for no man in his right mind would let her wander alone in the wilderness. Women were scarce in this country, and once you found one, you protected her more fiercely than your gold claim.

An image of Lorna flashed before him. *You did your best to protect them; you did your best.* Cooper shook his head slightly as if to shake the dark haired image of Lorna from his mind. He refocused his eyes on the lake and surrounding woods below. If the angel wasn't a whore and she wasn't married, she had to be a figment of his imagination. Still, the hard pressure between his thighs was a bittersweet reminder that the vision had been real. Too damn real.

This was a puzzle, and Cooper felt determined to fit all the pieces together. For now though, he'd have to be content with letting his mind work on the problem. There was no trail that he knew of that led to the lower creek bed. From his lookout point the only way to the lower lake was back down and around, the way he'd come. Both he and his horse were too tired to make that journey again tonight.

He began to unroll his bedding. *She'd headed towards Pearl's... Who was she?* He knew for certain the only help Pearl had hired in the last year were the two boys that he'd brought to her. Pearl had been complaining to him earlier and he kicked himself now for his waning attention. What had she been going on about? Something about her maid of all work? Yes, that was it. Now, what had she said? Had she hired a new girl? No... No, she'd been complaining. Ah yes, her maid couldn't come more than three times a week and it was nearly impossible to find female help this far north. That's what Pearl had said earlier. He had been listening after all.

Pearl couldn't have found someone new since he'd left this morning. That seemed highly improbable. Still, the only thing between the lake and Pearl's place was Pearl's old cabin, home now to the Grayson boys. *Jakeb and Joe. Jakeb and Joe... Joe had blonde curls.* No! Joe was a boy! Hadn't he just confirmed his perceptiveness this morning? Still, the curls... and Ts'kaw had been adamant...

He began to have a vision creep into his brain, one he didn't want to acknowledge. The thought that he may already know his sunset angel broke through into his consciousness anyway. Cooper swore under his breath at the thought of having to admit Ts'kaw was right.

62

He turned his mind back on the image of the angel in the lake as he stripped off his trail worn clothes. Without a thought to temperature, he dove into the icy lake hoping to relieve the pressure of his throbbing memory.

~ * ~

Jolian stumbled, turning her ankle as she tried to keep herself upright. It was getting darker. The roots and tufts of grass on the narrow path were in her way. Her chest felt tight. She had to raise her shoulders to let in even the tiniest bit of air. Uneasiness crept up her spine. Shifting her belongings to one hand, Jolian fished her gun out from her pile of toiletries. She dared only one glance behind her, then held her finger on the trigger and the gun straight ahead as she ran as fast as she dared, to her cabin door.

She reached the door out of breath, and paused to calm herself. She couldn't shake the feeling of being watched. She was acting absurd! No one knew she was here, no one could find her. Everyone thought she was a boy, Jakeb's little brother. She was safe here. Despite all of the terrible things that had happened in the last year, there was one thing she could tell herself over and over. She was safe here. And she had Cooper Holt to thank for that.

Her heart calmed instantly at the thought of him. Jolian took a deep breath and let herself in the cabin door. Jakeb, bless his heart, had left a lantern burning for her and she could hear a gentle snoring coming from his bed. She licked her fingers, put out the wick and crept silently into the bedroom. She pushed passed the curtain separating her bed from Jakeb's and placed her toiletries on the lower dresser. Her bed looked fresh and inviting puddled in the shaft of moonlight streaming through the open curtain. She moved to draw them and then decided to leave them partly open.

The night felt welcoming again, now that her calmness had returned. Impulsively she stripped herself naked and crawled between the sheets. She wanted to think about Cooper, and somehow it only felt right to think of him when she was feeling like a woman. Lying naked in her bed allowed the wind-dried flannel sheets to brush roughly on the usually unexposed parts of her flesh. The sensation was new and exciting. Jolian stretched in the moonlight like a cat on a rug. She felt relaxed enough to purr. She lay on her back and stretched again, right down to her toes.

She imagined the roughness of the sheets was Cooper's hands on her body. Running up and down the length of her, pausing here, and there, yes she'd like him to touch her there. She felt wicked and thrilled, curious and scared all at the same time. These were not the thoughts of a spinster; she really should try to think of something more chaste. Still, they were only thoughts; no one knew she was thinking them. And it felt so, so delicious to have this exciting fantasy playing out in her mind. It couldn't do any harm. There, she'd talked herself right out of the guilt she felt for her wickedness. She closed her eyes and let her fantasies melt into dreams.

~ * ~

By the time Pearl bustled her way into the kitchen, Jolian had been up and working for hours. Pearl poured herself a cup of coffee from the simmering pot on the stove and grimaced, as she tasted the steaming brew.

"Land sakes, Jo!" she teased. "This stuff's strong enough ta burn a hole right through me!"

Jo smiled at the comment and flipped the eggs in her skillet. Jakeb used to say "holy cow!" every time he sipped her coffee and her mother would remind him, "only God is holy". A few more stirs and the eggs were perfect. She lifted them out onto a plate and added two thick slices of cornbread. Placing the eggs in front of her employer, Jolian turned back to lift down a pan of sourdough she'd left to rise on the kitchen windowsill. Gently she prodded the dough out of the pan and punched the soft mixture down with her fists. Satisfied with the consistency, she began to form round loaves.

"Yore about the best cook I've known, Jo, but yore coffee shore leaves a person wantin'—fer a stomach tonic!" Pearl laughed heartily at her own joke. "Put that dough down fer a bit and sit with me. I got myself some mighty fine news last night and I'm wanting ta share it with someone."

Jo did Pearl's bidding but rather than just seat herself at the long pine table she brought a basket of apples and a paring knife to peel them. She could peel apples in her sleep she'd done it so often!

"Last night we was busier than usual. Me and the girls was purt near hoppin' ta make shore everyone was happy and gettin' their monies worth, so ta speak. Then who do ya think should come in, but old JP Dillon." Pearl looked eagerly at Jolian and Jo stared back expectantly. "JP Dillon, ain't ya heard a him?"

Jo assured her, she hadn't.

"You ortta get yoreself into town more often, Jo. He's the one who struck a big lead last summer with Billy Barker." Pearl's small brown eyes and painted brows looked questioningly at Jolian. "Lordy, ya must a heard of him!" Jolian nodded in agreement as she sliced an apple into a pie plate. "Well Billy's what ya might call a handsome devil, and a good friend a mine, I don't mind tellin' ya. He proposed to me, as a matter-of-fact, right after his claim hit last summer. Course, he was purty liquored up at the time, so I tole him I'd wait fer a sober proposal. He tole me 'Pearl, yore purty smart, an' purty, too!' I swear them were his exact words!"

Jolian smiled at the woman across the table from her. She was so alive and feisty; Jolian believed every word she spoke. "I'm sure you're quite right." And couldn't help but think of a certain miner *she* would like to hear sweet words from. A smile played at the corner of her lips.

"Course I is." Pearl nodded as she reached for a pot of strawberry preserves and spread an ample layer on her cornbread. "Anyways, last night JP told me that my Billy's coming back to town. He spent the winter in Victoria, ya know like all of them miners does. They kin work night an day diggin fer their gold but come an itsy bit a snow and, poof! they's gone like the devil on Sunday! Anyways, JP says he gots a letter from Billy what says he's coming back this July and he's got a big surprise fer everyone. Don't ya see? I just know it's my sober proposal, the one I tole him I'd wait fer. Won't that be the biggest surprise! An ol' whore like me, up'n marryin' the likes of Billy Barker! Folks'll be shocked outta their drawers!"

Pearl seemed lost in her own thoughts, and Jo didn't want to spoil her happiness. If she couldn't see the flaw in her way of thinking, then Jolian didn't want to be the one to burst her bubble. Granted, Pearl probably knew more about men then she would ever know, but it seemed to her, if a man was planning to ask you to marry him he'd write *you* the letter, not his partner.

"The timing of it couldn't be better," Pearl said.

"What's that?" Jo asked, realizing she'd not really been listening.

"My retirement," Pearl repeated. "I say the timing couldn't be better. What with Barkerville growin' and growin'. When I first opened, this here was the perfect spot.

Close enough to the trail, and far enough from the competition. I heard they're buildin' two more "houses" right on the main street in Barkerville! Ain't no miner gonna travel up here if'n they can get it right in town. Yup—perfect timin' fer me ta ree-tire." Pearl lowered her voice to a whisper and leaned closer to Jo, winking as she spoke. "'Course, I'd be obliged to ya if ya kept yore mouth shut 'bout all this. I wouldn't want ta scare off my girls."

"Your news is safe with me."

"JP let me in on some more news, too!" Pearl laughed as she finished the last bite of her bread. "He said with more 'n more miners arrivin' every day, he's heard folks is starting to call Barkerville "the gold capital of the world". I bin saving up ta build me a proper business, respectable, ya know, if I ever got the notion. Well I guess I gots it now! I'm gonna build my place right in town. Hell, as "Mrs. Barker" I could build purt near anythin' I wanted in Barkerville! I'll cash in on all them miners' good fortune. I was thinkin' about a boarding house, or maybe a dinin' establishment, y'all could still work fer me there couldn't ya? But like I said, lets keep it between us fer now."

"I will," Jo agreed, her mind whirling. Boy, could Pearl talk once she got going. It made her feel dizzy trying to keep up with the conversation. Not that she ever really got more than a few words out anyway, where Pearl was concerned.

"I've got a whole lot ta be plannin' and I'll leave you to yore work," Pearl hollered as she left the kitchen. "See ya at the noonin'."

Apples peeled, cored and sliced, Jo went back to her bread dough and put it in to bake. Then she was out to the chicken coop to collect more of the eggs for breakfast. Once the girls had eaten and the dishes were done, Jo wandered out to the garden to snip some early chives and look for some more sweet fennel or maybe some wild carrot. Pearl's girls often collected wild carrot when they went into town. It usually grew in the lower areas and they used the flowering heads as living lace on their gowns. Jolian really didn't expect to find it growing this far up the mountainside but the alpine climate of Richfield Mountain made the abnormal, normal. Plants of the carrot variety were often poisonous and she had to call upon everything she'd learned from Aklu'ut whenever she stumbled upon them.

While she was in the woods she spied a customer stopping by Pearl's. She knew the man. A trapper named Gunderson and the only customer that Pearl allowed to visit during daylight hours. Jo stood still as a cedar and watched as the man lifted a hind and leg of an animal out of his wagon. By the size and coloring, Jo judged it was probably a piece of moose. It was how the man paid his bill at Pearl's and she supposed the arrangement was suitable for all.

Either Pearl's place is pretty expensive, or he's a frequent nighttime customer, too. The same man was by once a week with a cut of deer or pheasant or rabbit. *What time he doesn't spend here must all be spent hunting.* Jo tried to suppress a giggle. *He'd have a lot more time if he just found himself a wife.* This thought made her giggles overflow and Jo ducked lower in the surrounding alders to keep herself from the customer's view. Paying more attention to hiding than her footing caused her to trip on a root. Her vegetables spilled onto the ground and she knelt to recover them, still giggling to herself.

"What's sso funny?"

Jo spun around on the ground. "Oh, Jakeb, you startled me. I guess I was too lost in my thoughts to hear you."

Jakeb picked up a carrot rubbed it on his shirt and bit the end off, munching loudly. "What had you so amused?"

"You men. I just can't figure you out."

"Us men! We're sssimple compared to you!" Jakeb snorted and scrunched his nose. He finished his carrot and tossed the top greens into the surrounding bush.

"Umm, I suppose." Jolian changed the subject. "What are you doing up here this time of day, Jakeb? Won't Mr. Duke be missing you at the store?"

Jakeb shrugged his shoulders and watched as his sister finished retrieving the vegetables. "I went into town early but it was pretty ssslow. Elijah figures tonight's going to be busy and he wants me back then. I picked up the washin' from Lee's for you. I just left it on the back porch."

His sister's head bobbed her thanks and he continued. "I have something to ask you."

"What's that Jakeb? Can you ask me while we walk back to Pearl's, or is it private?" Jo stood up and Jakeb reached out his hand to carry the basket for her.

"It ain't, we can walk. I was just wondering how much you'd ssaved, in gold I mean." He hoped he sounded casual and that his voice didn't reveal the panic he felt inside. He searched Jolian's face for any sign that she'd noticed.

"Oh I don't know," His sister looked like she didn't suspect a thing as she stooped to pick a handful of tiny blue flowers. "Pearl gives me mostly nuggets, which are fetching what... about sixteen dollars an ounce?"

Jakeb nodded his reply and tried not to look too eager as his sister calculated the amount.

"A couple hundred, maybe," Jolian stated. "Not much really when you figure a barrel of flour is fetching two hundred dollars at your store."

"Two hundred and twenty-five."

"Two hundred and tweny-five?" Jolian whistled under her breath. "Well, we must remember we've got Pearl to thank for our room and board as well. Why do you ask, Jakeb? Was there something you were needing?"

Jakeb gazed into the honest blue eyes of his little sister and changed his mind about the lie he was about to tell her. He just couldn't ask her to give him her savings. "I was thinking of a marker for Ma and Pa's graves. Maybe I oughtta just make one up myself."

"Oh, Jakeb." He suddenly found himself being hugged about the neck and pecked on the cheek. " You are a dear. I was thinking about a marker as well. I just didn't know how we'd afford it. Something you made yourself would be so much more, well, meaningful. I'm sure it's what they would have wanted."

Jakeb could see tears glistening in his sisters' eyes. He felt like a louse. She turned her back to him and knelt on the ground to add a white flower with heart shaped leaves, to her makeshift bouquet.

"Sometimes it's hard to believe they're gone." Her voice was choked with emotion. "And then at times, it's so real, it's frightening."

"Don't worry about a thing." Jakeb placed his hand on her shoulder and gave her a reassuring squeeze. "We'll make out just fine. As a matter-of-fact, I ssspoke to Angus earlier about taking another partner in on our claim."

"Oh. Are there money troubles again, Jakeb?"

"No, it's not that," Jakeb lied easily. "It's just with me working at the store part time to pay for lumber and sssupplies... Well, I just don't get much time to be down in the ssshaft. Angus has been working down there night and day. He's determined to find the lead. His feet are bad though—Doc sssays he's ripe for gumboot gout."

68

"Oh, Jakeb, that's horrible!" Jolian exclaimed. She turned to face her brother and he nodded in agreement. It looked as though he was just trying to pacify her with his compliance. Yes, he definitely looked like he had something to hide. She'd not be silent about this! She'd disapproved of her brother's mining in the first place, and now—Gumboot gout was serious! Even though they'd all planned to work their claim once they'd arrived in the Cariboo, her family had been blinded by the thought of the gold. They'd known nothing about the day in day out aspects of mining when they began their journey.

The stories she'd heard and the facts she'd acquired in the past six months had only confirmed her beliefs. Mining was extremely dangerous both physically and financially. She'd all but begged Jakeb to sell his share of the claim. She hoped that was what he may be thinking now. She'd have to move cautiously into the conversation though, or there was sure to be an argument. "You've given some thought to my suggestion of selling out then?" Jolian ventured.

"I'm not ssselling my share!"

Too late, Jakeb's face was already turning red. Still, she had to say it, "Well if Angus can't mine and you're busy at the store..."

"I can't believe you'd bring this up again. Damn it, Jolian! We've been over and over this. I only took that lousy job at the ssstore because of that whoreson who ssstole all of our money when he murdered our pppparents! Who, may I remind you, died on their way here in sssearch of gold! I am going to find gold, Jolian, if only to prove their deaths weren't for nothing. Gold is why we came here and I'm not ssselling out!" Jakeb dropped the basket of vegetables he was carrying and stomped angrily past her.

"Well!" Jolian said out loud as she stooped to pick up the basket and slung it into the crook of her arm. One little suggestion and he practically explodes! *Need I remind you that our parents died on their way here in search for gold?* She was there. No one ever had to remind her of that horrible day! How dare he speak to her like, like she was some naïve, silly girl! She was the responsible one here. She was the one looking out for his welfare. If he was going to be so horrid, well then he... he deserved to be a miner!

"Go ahead and mine then!" Jolian yelled into the trees. "But if you go and get yourself killed—don't come running to me about it." Jolian had to smile at her lousy attempt at argumentation. She was always right in her own head; it's just when she spoke, her point in the conversation sometimes eluded her. She was, after all, only trying to warn him. Why, just last week she'd read in the *Cariboo Sentinel* the average age a miner lived to was only thirty-two!

~ * ~

Pearl was not her usual, jovial self. She snapped at the girls to quit "lolly-gagging about" and get ready for the evening. Jo kept to herself in the kitchen. The last thing she needed was another debate. Pearl's probably just nervous at seeing her old beau again, Jolian reasoned. She didn't want to speak with Pearl when her mood was so foul but it looked as if she was going to town. If Pearl could pick up a few things at the mercantile it would save her the dreaded trip. If only she hadn't argued with Jakeb then he could have made the purchases for her. Ah well, it looked as though she was destined to be yelled at today.

Jolian raised her head, took a deep breath and asked the favor of Pearl. She only barked at her for not organizing her situation better. A small price to pay for having her shopping done for her. Pearl would be back in time for dinner, so Jolian set a place at the table for her. Maybe the ride would bump the grumping out of her.

Six

Alone in one of Pearl's upstairs sleeping rooms; she sat before an oval oak framed mirror brushing her hair, slowly, luxuriously, from root to tip. Its length fell to her waist and its thickness nearly covered her naked, seated body. She turned quickly as the door to the room flung open.

He hesitated in the doorway and then rushed forward. She turned to meet him and his hands gripped her shoulders, pulling her bare body close in a rough embrace. His lips crushed hers with the hunger of his kiss. His bold hands explored her flesh, touching her in places no man had ever even seen...

~ * ~

Jolian sat upright in bed, gasping for breath. She kicked off her covers and breathed easier as the crisp morning air hit her sweat-soaked nightshirt.

"This is absurd!" she told herself. Why did she keep dreaming about him? And in that way! Her dreams had started the night Cooper left and were becoming more vivid and detailed with each passing day. "This is absurd," she scolded out loud this time as if to convince herself. She hardly knew the man. Still, there was something about him. Something that made her feel all woman. Something that made her want to be a woman when she was with him.

~ * ~

Cooper stepped out of the door of the log house into the bright July morning. Squinting his eyes against the yellow fireball just peeking over the mountain in the east, his fingers absentmindedly scratched at the week old growth of whiskers on his chin. He bent to tie his bootstraps then lifted a suspender over each shoulder as he

71

stood. A long narrow path led him to the campfire where Guy sat holding a steaming tin cup.

"Morning." He nodded to his friend as he reached for the pot of coffee Guy had made.

"Looks like it is going to be another day of heat," Guy said.

"Umm."

"Something on your mind, *Mon ami*? You were up and down all night."

Cooper stared at the snow-capped peaks in the distance as he sampled some of the steaming brew from his cup. "Yup."

"Is it Lorna again?" Guy prodded.

Cooper ignored the question and hoped Guy might let it drop. He wasn't one to spill his can of beans just cause someone poked it with a pocketknife. Of course, Guy had never been one to open up too easily either. Cooper always pushed and pushed until Guy had had enough and conversation would flow like the Fraser River. It was a technique Guy had turned back on him in recent months. Cooper knew the reasoning behind it, too. He was determined to keep Cooper sober and talking, rather than whiskey soaked and brooding. Guy had let it go for almost a week, giving him some space to sort things out for himself. Obviously his friend had had enough of his moodiness and felt it was time to get out his pocketknife.

"That is it. No more we play the mouse and cat, Cooper. You have something on your mind and you need to speak up before you start drinking to bury it."

Cooper flashed him a sour expression. "I'm not going to start drinking again, Guy. I promised you, and myself that."

"Still there is something on your mind, no?"

Cooper relented and spoke about the woman he'd seen bathing at the giant steps. It felt good to unburden himself of the guilt. "I guess it's just rattling me that Ts'kaw was right about the boy being—well, her. I can't believe I could've made a mistake like that. I was so certain she was a boy!"

"I do not think it is your mistake that has you rattled. I think you are rattled more by how you can get to see her naked again." Guy looked like the cat that'd swallowed the canary! Pretty pleased at how he'd got to the heart of Cooper's brooding.

72

"You are probably right!" Cooper laughed. Although he had to admit, if only to himself, there was a certain amount of guilt attached to the thought. He'd put a young girl to work in a brothel! Pearl was as good a woman as you could find in these parts, but she was still a woman of business. He'd have to start visiting her place on a more regular basis. Yup, that would take care of the guilt. He'd keep a close watch on Joe and make sure nobody came too close to her. It was the least he could do.

"Ah, you are a normal healthy man Coop. We all have certain physical needs that must be fulfilled."

"Yeah, I guess it's been a while since..." Cooper's thoughts stayed with Joe as he pondered Guy's words.

"A while! It's been close to a year since Lorna er... since Lorna, and there has not been anything warmer in your bed than a brick!"

He must have visibly recoiled at the mention of the name, because Guy added, "I am sorry, *Mon ami*, I didn't mean to re-open a wound to make my point."

"It's all right, Guy. I've had plenty of opportunity to put my time with Lorna into perspective. I know I messed up with her. I should have committed her to the hospital when Doc Rawley suggested. I just thought I could handle her on my own."

"You 'andled 'er fine." Guy reassured his long time friend with a pat to his back. "You could not see into the future and know she would follow Ts'kaw up 'ere. Where Ts'kaw was concern, Lorna had ze idee fixe. Who would have thought anyone would be so captivated by 'is ugly mug, eh?"

Cooper smiled at his friend's attempt to lighten his mood. Ts'kaw was the type of man who turned heads wherever he went, but Lorna had not just taken a look at him, she'd become fascinated by everything he did. An unsettling situation for a man—to find his wife infatuated with one of his best friends.

"You have a sense of duty that is bigger than your brain, *Mon ami*. It's one of ze reasons I keep you around!" Guy faked a punch to Cooper's shoulder.

"Ha-ha-ha." Cooper laughed sarcastically and punched Guy back. "Keep me around, eh? I've been trying to shake you off my coat tails for years!"

The two joked lightheartedly as they made sure their fire was out and then returned to the log house to load up their gear. The new prism they'd ordered by mail and recently picked up at Fort Alexandria was wrapped in several layers of cotton, then leather and secured in the pouch of Cooper's saddlebag. He wasn't going to take any chances this one might break, too. They couldn't waste any more time waiting for another one to arrive. With the summer upon them, miners were lured back to the goldfields like spawning salmon. They'd need to get busy if they were to keep on top of surveying the claims.

"How many claims do you figure we have left?" Cooper asked tying his bedroll securely behind the saddle on his horse.

"Fifty to one hundred, I am supposing." Guy shrugged. "Two weeks, three at ze outside and we could have it done. Then again, ze weather could change as many times as I have fingers, and with more and more miners arriving, we could have work until ze first snowfall. You never know."

"Yeah, the first snowfall could be tomorrow!" Cooper laughed at their age-old joke about the changeability of Cariboo weather. He was enjoying this easy light feeling that had settled over him. He couldn't remember the last time he'd actually looked forward to the future. It felt good, real good. He re-checked the straps holding his personal belongings and survey equipment. He rubbed his horse on the nose and whispered in his ear.

"Hey, Storm, one last day of this dusty trail and its time off for good behavior for you." Cooper swung himself into the saddle with ease and settled in behind Guy and his mare on the trail. One more day and he could see Joe again, too. Now, *that* was going to be a complicated situation. He couldn't very well come out and accuse her of concealing her true identity without explaining how he knew. It would never do for her to find out that he'd spied on her, as accidental as it was. No, that little gem of information would have to remain between him and Guy.

A smile played across his lips as he thought about her masquerade. He had to give her credit for her disguise. She'd certainly fooled him, and a lot of other people. She had obviously gone to quite a bit of trouble to keep her gender hidden, so who was he to expose her to the world? As much as a part of him wanted to tell her he knew she was a woman, the other part of him knew he had to keep that piece of knowledge to himself, for now anyway.

Cooper thought about Guy's comment earlier. Sometimes his ethics *were* bigger than his brain. That had absolutely been the case with Lorna. His own personal code of ethics had been the force that drove him to marry her. It was the standard his father had set and one of the ways Cooper measured himself as a man. You took care of women. It didn't matter if it was your mother, a family friend, or a whore. If a woman needed help, you gave it. Up until Lorna had come into his life, Cooper had never questioned his father's reasoning, or his own behavior in that regard.

He could still picture the first time he'd seen Lorna. She was standing on the outside deck of a Cunard liner docking in Victoria harbor. Her ebony hair piled high on her tiny head; barely fitting underneath the parasol that shielded her from the sun. She looked just like one of those porcelain figurines his mother collected.

He remembered like it was yesterday... how he'd thought, between the size of the umbrella, her tiny form, and her enormous hooped skirts, that a good strong gust of wind could've sent her flying overboard. It almost would have made sense to see her floating down the river on her own skirts, like Hamlet's Ophelia. For the two were of the same mind. Not that he would have ever wished that upon her. For as crazy as she'd been, and for all of the hell she'd put him through, she'd been fragile too, and needed his protection.

"Cavaliers!" Guy called back over his shoulder and interrupted Cooper's thoughts. Cooper pulled Storm to stand next to Guy's mare just as the two riders came into his view. The men were members of the Royal Engineers and they were moving at such speed that once they spotted Guy and Cooper, they barely had time to rein their horses. The riders introduced themselves with name and rank. Cooper stated Guy's name, his own and then he asked, "Is there a problem, Captain?"

"Yes indeed." The older of the two men responded. "There's been another murder on the Harrison-Lillooet trail. Found by one of our survey parties. Three men this time. Miners by looks of it."

Cooper cursed under his breath and Guy removed his hat and mopped his brow with his sleeve.

"Did you say Guy Renault and Cooper Holt?" The Captain asked and Cooper nodded. "The same Renault and Holt survey crew who came upon the scene of the Grayson murders earlier this year, I presume."

"*Oui*." Guy answered. "Ze luck of our profession, eh? It 'as been a surveyor that 'as come upon each of ze 'orrible crimes."

"Yes, quite." The Captain looked solemn.

"Is there any reason to think the two murders are connected?" Cooper queried.

"Plenty of suspicion and a few similarities." The other man, a sapper by the name of Fox, answered the question.

"Yes," the captain agreed. "There was also another murder a week ago of a young lad in Yale. It seems all three incidents are likely connected. We've been mapping out the area for the new Cariboo road and brought the information to the Constable in Richfield. We're heading back to Yale by way of Fort Alexandria now. We wanted to pass on the information at the Fort, if they had not yet heard."

Cooper shook his head. "We left the Fort yesterday and there was no mention of it yet. Are there any suspects?"

"Not yet in custody." The captain looked grave. "The only witnesses so far are the two boys you gentlemen came upon. The Constable gave us a copy of a sketch they're circulating, based on the descriptions from the lads." He took a paper out of his saddlebag, unfolded it and held it up for Cooper to view.

"As you can see, this could be any one of a dozen men. There's been such a rush of miners to this area and more than half of them could fit the description of dark coloring and bushy beards. Still, it is likely the man in this picture here is unaware that the one boy survived." He passed the picture over to Guy and continued.

"And then there is the other lad, the one who saw him leaving the scene, the murderer doesn't even know about him. That's about the only thing I can figure the law has on its side right now, the element of surprise. This ruffian's thinking he's getting away with these murders and leaving no witnesses. Those boys' testimonies will be key as soon as the scoundrel is caught."

Cooper's thoughts drifted to Joe and how she would feel about this news. The poor girl, hadn't she been through enough? "Does the Constable have any leads to his whereabouts?"

The sapper spoke this time. "Only by the bloody trail he's leaving. It looks as though he could be in this vicinity, but then again, he may have doubled back. I don't think any of us really want to speculate as to his reasoning. We don't want to alarm folks, but at the same time I think it's wise that all men in the area keep their wits about them."

The captain nodded his agreement and added, "Judge Begbie's circuit is due within a few weeks, so they'll be on the lookout for this madman. We've started our work on the new Cariboo road, and we're obliged to help the local law in any way we can as well. Are you men armed?"

"*Oui*, ah, yes sir." Guy patted the revolver he kept in his saddlebag.

"It's my sworn duty to remind you it's still unlawful to carry firearms or Bowie's knife within the townships of this colony, but here on the trail, I wouldn't hesitate to keep those weapons handy." The captain motioned to his subordinate then tipped the brim of his cap down. "We'd best be off then. Keep your heads, aim level, and good day to you."

"*Bonjour*," Guy replied. Both Guy and Cooper took the lieutenant's advice and removed their guns from their saddlebags. Cooper tucked his into the rear waistband of his trousers and nudged Storm with his heels.

The two friends rode side by side at an easy pace. "It is unsettling," Cooper responded to a remark Guy made about a murderer in their midst.

"It sure as 'ell is!" Guy half shouted. "Up until now we 'aven't even 'ad a chicken thief in these parts. It's that damn gold! People are so greedy for it. It makes them—*avoir perdu la tete*—ah, senseless. Gold fever is correct, they are all sick with it!"

"Hey, Guy," Cooper placed his hand on Guy's forearm to calm him and slowed their horses' gait even further. "You can't judge all people by one man's actions."

"I know." Guy still seemed agitated. "It's just... ah *sacre*, Coop. This used to be such a quiet stretch of country. Peaceful, you know? The last few years it's just more people and more people. We 'ave already surveyed close to twenty-five hundred claims! And it's not just ze miners. Ze people they are settling in, building 'omesteads. Before you know it, ze whole Cariboo will be like Victoria. So damn jam packed full of ze people, you 'ave to lay flat on your back just to see ze sky!"

"Did you just come up with that one or have you been rehearsing it?" Cooper felt himself chuckle at his friend's expression. "You *can* exaggerate Guy. But, you've got nothing to worry about, my hermit pal. Sure, people are settling in here once they've had a taste. This is the most beautiful country I've ever seen. But the miners won't stay. Well, a handful maybe. The majority will pack up and head out as soon as the next big strike is found, you know that."

"*Oui*, I suppose. I'm no 'ermit though. I have Po and Ts'kaw living with me."

"Those two are more reclusive than you are!"

"I just like my privacy."

"I know it, and so does everyone else around here. Which, come to think of it, is probably why *you've* not yet found a wife." Cooper knew the joking and needling would take Guy's mind off the murder and would help to keep the anger at bay.

"Don't look at me like that, Guy, you know I'm right. You've had yourself holed up on that mountain of yours for years. Coming to town for supplies and working occasionally. I think the miners have been good for you." Cooper looked Guy straight in the eye. "Being overworked this past year has kept you with people, and that's a good thing."

"I see people."

"You see Doralynn for "your needs" as you put it. I mean everyday talking and socializing. Yup, the miners have done you a lot of good."

"I see Doralynn for more than my needs," Guy mumbled.

"Sweet on her are you?"

"She's a real nice girl Coop, *petite amie gentille*."

"For a while there I thought you had something going with Po."

"Po?" Guy's mouth was agape. "You know she only stays with me because she feels obligated. I tell 'er that I paid 'er debt to get 'er away from that Johnny Huang, not to 'ave her for a servant, but she says, where would she go? She likes living on the mountain, I can't just throw 'er out to ze streets."

"And you talk about my sense of duty! I hope Doralynn's not the jealous type."

Guy's cheeks flushed and he nudged his mare to a trot past Cooper on the path. *Guy and Doralynn, hey?* He could see it. She was a quiet sensible girl, from what he'd seen of her. He knew she hadn't been with Pearl all that long. She'd be a fine partner for Guy if she chose. Cooper envied Guy's feelings. For although he'd felt bound to Lorna, Cooper knew their marriage had never been an ideal one.

He had always envisioned the union of two people to be just that. An equal joining of hearts and minds, a partnership of sorts. He wanted the kind of marriage his parents had. A giving and receiving love, not an all-consuming madness that doused any spark of true happiness. He'd come to the conclusion his parents had something that happened once in a lifetime and it wasn't going to happen for him. His heart and soul had gone into making things work with Lorna, but his best effort had been disastrous.

What more evidence did a man need? Nope, he was not the marrying kind. He'd sworn to keep his distance from that situation and it was one vow he planned to keep. Still, there was no harm in fantasies.

His thoughts drifted once again to his favorite daydream. Maybe once they were back in Barkerville he'd see her again. Maybe he'd ride up to the "giant steps" for a swim after dinner. Cooper smiled at the thought. He didn't have to admit anything to anyone in his fantasies. The girl in the lake could be whoever he wanted her to be. And in his fantasies, she could be his.

~ * ~

It was mid-afternoon when they finally arrived at Guy's homestead on Pinkerton Mountain. After a week on the trail the two-story farmhouse looked more inviting than the swankiest hotel.

"I feel like I could eat a moose!" Guy joked as he dismounted and stretched his limbs.

"I'm thinking about a dip in the lake myself," Cooper said more to himself than anyone.

"Looking for a certain, ah... young boy?" Guy half whispered as he saw Ts'kaw come out onto the porch. "Come on in for a bite to eat first. It'll build up your strength for your—ah, swim."

Cooper ignored the jibe. "Now that you mention food... is that salmon I smell?"

"Probably. Ts'kaw said 'e'd be bringing a catch by this week. 'E was going to smoke some and make some jerky. Po wanted to pickle some."

"No wonder you don't have a wife yet, with those two keeping you in food!" Cooper dismounted and walked his horse toward the barn.

Ts'kaw was the last person he felt like seeing right now. Although they'd been friends since Cooper's father had first moved his family from England, he couldn't think of a thing to say to him at this particular moment. It was strange to feel animosity between them. Despite the difference in their cultures, they'd been fast friends from the start. They had been lads, hunting together, the first time they'd met Guy.

He and Ts'kaw had been tracking a rabbit through the fresh fallen snow. He could see the tracks in his mind's eye as if it were yesterday. Suddenly, something jumped the boys from above! They'd screamed and flailed their arms about, trying desperately to beat off the wild creature. Which had, of course, turned out to be Guy. Layered in pelts and missing his two front teeth, the wild trapper's son... Those were the days! The carefree times in the woods, sleeping out beneath the stars... Maybe one day he'd relive them with a son of his own.

The thought was there before he'd had a chance to stop it. He'd never have that chance. It wasn't in the cards for him. Not anymore. He forced his thoughts to concentrate on the brushing of his horse. He forked fresh hay into the stall, slipped the leather strap over the post to hold the railing in place and closed the barn doors behind him.

Seven

Jakeb's hands rummaged through the box of underclothes in the back room of the Barkerville Mercantile. He found a cotton undershirt and a pair of knee length cotton drawers he figured would fit Jolian. He folded them neatly, placed them on the shelf by the back door and took one last drag off his cigar before extinguishing it. He slipped through the curtain separating the storage room from the general purchasing area and began to unload the new shipment of Mason jars onto a shelf. The bell above the front door chimed and he turned to greet the customer.

"Good afternoon, Mr. MacDonald." He recognized the local postman as he entered. "How have you been kkkeeping?"

"Ah, fair to middlin' lad, fair to middlin'." The Scotsman placed a bundle of letters and two packages on the counter. "And yourself?"

"I'm fine, thank you, sssir." Jakeb made sure he caught and held the man's eyes for a moment. He'd noticed MacDonald glanced at the few accessories for women the store held, so he put on a look of genuine concern as he moved to stand near the table of jewelry and toiletries. "Is there anything I can help you with today, sssir?"

"My sister in Vancouver is coming up to a birthday. Thought I'd see if there was anything here she'd fancy. Maybe a handbag?"

"I have just the thing." Jakeb felt a thrill surge through his body as he reached for an embroidered reticule. He would make this sale; he knew it already. "This one here has a fine gold thread running through it. Makes it practical and a bit fancy at the sssame time. Any woman would be pleased to carry such a feminine piece of handiwork."

"You're quite the salesman lad!" MacDonald chuckled. "Wrap it up then and add it to my account."

"Yes, sssir, thank you, sssir." Jakeb smirked at the man's back as he turned to the counter. He hadn't even asked the price, and as always, Jakeb had not been forthcoming with the information. He presented the parcel to the postman and bid him good day. He carefully added the purchase to the books. Adding one full dollar for his trouble, and then removing the extra cash from the till. A dollar here and two bits there, it wasn't much to each individual but it added up for him. In the few short months he'd been at the store, he'd pocketed several hundred dollars, he was sure of it.

Jakeb thought of the Scotsman. He'd been pleased with his purchase and the service he'd received. No one was being harmed with his little addition. Of course his sister with her holier than thou attitude would surely find fault with it. He thought of his own purchase for her, sitting on the shelf in the storeroom. He walked back over to the table he'd shown McDonald and picked up another reticule; identical to the one he'd just sold. Practical and fancy, that was a good line. On impulse he took the handbag back to the storage room to take home for Jolian.

"Since you can't dress like a woman, I thought this might help you feel like one." That's what he'd tell her. She'd like the gifts and be in a better mood for his news that way. Jakeb's hand reached to his breast pocket and took out the letter he'd received last week from their Uncle. Maybe he should just show it to her and be done with everything. No, no, he needed a plan. Jolian had her hopes pinned on going back to San Francisco and he wasn't going to be the one to... Nope he needed a plan. He put the letter back in his pocket and picked up a broom. In a town full of gold miners there had to be a way to make some fast money.

~ * ~

Although it seemed hard to imagine, Pearl was even grumpier than she had been the day before. She had all of her girls in the parlor scrubbing walls, washing floors and polishing tables, while she barked out orders like a staff sergeant.

"This place's gotta be sparklin'," Pearl demanded. "Y'all have been taking things a might too easy since Jo's been here. Elspeth, those windows are streaky—do 'em again."

Jo took the cornbread out of the oven and set it near the window to cool as Pearl came into the kitchen.

"Anymore coffee in that pot?"

"I'll pour you a cup," Jo answered as Pearl settled herself at the big pine table. She carried a steaming cup and set it down before her employer. Pearl seemed to have something on her mind and from her experience, Jo found sometimes just being available and a good listener, helped people to trust and confide in you. She kept her back to Pearl but answered her queries with care and concern and in no time Pearl conveyed her grievances.

"Maybe I'm too old for this." Pearl sighed and let her head drop down towards her chest. Jo turned from wiping the hot stove and stretched out her hand to touch Pearl's arm. As Pearl raised her head and looked up towards the ceiling, Jo could see tears glistening in her eyes. Now it was time to speak. "What is it, Pearl?"

"Ya gots a big heart to care about the likes of me, Jo. I shouldn't burden you..."

"Nonsense. Sometimes talking about things is what clears it up for you. Keeping it inside only makes the problems feel too big for one person to handle. Believe me, I know." Jo sat down beside Pearl and gave her hand an affectionate squeeze.

"Last night some customers were talking about Billy Barker comin' back." She sighed heavily. "One of 'em said it won't be the same now that he's gone and got himself hitched."

"Oh Pearl... Maybe they're wrong—"

"Nope, I asked around. 'Pears as though my blue eyed Billy found himself a lonely widder woman this winter." Pearl's high-pitched wail could have been comedic under other circumstances. Her bottom lip trembled with emotion and Jo felt her own heart sink in response.

"Pearl, I'm so sorry."

"Yore right, Jo. Saying it out loud makes me look at things a might differently. A course he'd get married. And not to the likes of me. My first instincts were right. His proposal to me, was only the liquor talking after all." Pearl blew her nose into a lace handkerchief and took another from her pocket. She mopped at the tears that tumbled down her cheeks and tried to force a smile.

"I'm thinking maybe its time I moved on, Jo. Pack it up and head to Victoria or New Westminster. Folks don't know me there and I could set myself up in a boarding house or something. Maybe make a fresh start."

"Is that really what you want, Pearl, or are you just running from things you don't want to face here?"

Pearl looked taken aback by her comments and for a moment Jolian thought maybe she'd overstepped the boundaries. She didn't want to offend the woman who had given her so much kindness.

"I'll have to think on that, child." Pearl fixed her gaze just above Jo's head.

Jolian didn't know what to say, so she just wrapped her arms around Pearl and hugged tightly.

Pearl let Jolian hug her for one full minute before she seemed to get embarrassed and mumbled something about dusting the upstairs rooms. Jolian released her from the embrace and watched her hold her head high as she walked towards the parlor.

Her heart went out to Pearl. She knew about broken dreams, too. Perhaps the answer was not to hope for the future but to live in the present. Just to take each day as it was offered and be thankful for that. She was glad she had held her tongue and not gone ranting on about the selfishness of miners. But really, couldn't Pearl see that she was better off than to have married such an inconsiderate man?

He'd even proposed! Drunk or not, a proposal was a proposal. And a Madame or not, Pearl was still a woman with feelings. She hoped she'd meet this Billy Barker the next time she went into town. Just because he had the place named for him, it didn't give him the right to treat Pearl the way he did—not even the decency to tell her in person. She'd been right all along! Miners were about as sorry a lot as you could ever hope to find! She never wanted to have anything to do with any of them again ever!

Of course, living so close to a town teaming with them, it wasn't going to be easy to just eliminate them from her life. Oh, and then there was Jakeb. Her own brother the miner. She couldn't very well not have anything to do with him. She supposed certain miners would be all right... She was just making excuses and she knew why. It was because of Cooper! She was trying to get her mind around the fact that she was a tiny bit—yes, just a tiny bit—infatuated with a miner. She was weak; she admitted it and cursed herself for it.

Jo stayed lost in her thoughts as she lay out a supper of cold pheasant and warm cornbread for the girls. She sandwiched a few slices of meat between some bread and wrapped it in a cloth for Jakeb.

As she walked to her cabin a thought hit her so hard she stopped dead in her tracks. Maybe her plans for the future, of going back to San Francisco, maybe that was just running away. Maybe she was thinking about herself and not Pearl when she'd doled out her advice. She had such big plans for returning to San Francisco— to what? To her lessons with Jean Pierre?

He had told her when she left it was for the best anyway, she was ready to move on, learn new things. What else was there for her back home? An uncle who hadn't cared a whit for her family? Jolian shivered when she thought of him. He was her only kin, save for Jakeb. He hadn't even responded to the letter Jakeb had written months ago, telling him of his own sister's death. Why was she in such an all fired hurry to go back?

Because she wanted things the way they had been. Of course, nothing could bring her parents back, but nothing good could come from being in a town full of miners either. It might be a flawed plan, but it was her plan nonetheless. She would continue to save her money until she had enough for her and Jakeb to go home. She needed to be strong. Strong enough for both of them. She'd think of a way to make Jakeb understand. Mining wasn't the life for them. There was no future here for Jakeb. When and if he struck the lead, he'd still have to leave eventually.

She wanted a home. Whether it was her old one or not, she wanted something of her own. A place that would always be hers, not Pearl's or Jakeb's or her Uncle's although *she* would always welcome family staying with *her*. Yup, a big home filled to the rafters with family. Kind of a strange wish for someone who planned a life of spinsterhood. Well, there were always nieces and nephews, if Jakeb ever settled down.

Miners never provided their family with a stable home. All they ever did was move from town to town following the next rush. You'd just get settled, plant a few crops and off they'd go to follow their dreams of gold. Even if she had little or no chance at ever having children of her own, she'd never do that to them, never. She wanted stability, roots, that's what was important. That's where she was heading, that was her future.

There was definitely no future here for her working in a "house", even if she was only cooking and not the other. She needed to finish this phase of her life so she could get on with living. Just like Aklu'ut had told her. Biscuits! Even a miner wouldn't have much to do with her if she stayed working at Pearl's. If only her father hadn't had that tiny bit of luck in '49, maybe they never would have attempted this trip in the first place.

~ * ~

Cooper woke with a start. Why was it dark? Where was he? The ropes holding the mattress on the bed moaned their response as he sat up and let his eyes adjust to the dark.

Oh, Guy's house, his bed at Guy's house that's where he was. But why was it dark and why was he still fully dressed? Slowly, his brain, thick with a dead man's sleep, began to sort out the details. After a huge meal of salmon and rice he'd come to lie down for a nap. Some nap! Cooper parted the curtains and lifted the sash on the window. From the second story room he looked out at the night sky. Not a star in sight. The moon was only a hazy glow through the thick layer of clouds.

Something tugged at the corner of his memory. The lake. He'd planned to go to giant steps after dinner for a swim and... And what? What were the chances that he'd see her again anyway? *There's always a chance,* the optimist in him challenged. *Tomorrow you could...* No, tomorrow he and Guy and Ts'kaw needed to get back to work.

The sooner the surveying work was done, the sooner he could spend more time on his claim. Cooper smiled at the thought. Just the thought of gold could make you smile. You couldn't say that for too many other things in this life. Oh sure, he'd make his fortune eventually in surveying; Victoria was booming with development and desperate for surveyors. But, the thought of a lifetime's worth of earnings struck all at once, just lying below the surface, begging to be found... Now that was exciting! He could feel his heart begin to hammer in his chest at the thought.

The only other thing that had elicited such a response in him lately had been the sight of his golden haired angel in her sunset pool. Cooper stretched his arms and laced his fingers behind his head. Now that would be perfect, a fortune in gold and an angel to spend it on!

86

Of course, he was nothing if he wasn't a realist. He knew the odds were against him, probably on both counts. There were thousands of men flocking to this part of the colony with the same dreams. The chances that he'd strike gold were no better than any of theirs. But they were no worse either, and a man without a dream, was a man who turned to whiskey.

Besides, he needed the money more than most. He knew if his angel ever came to have feelings for him, he'd have to tell her the whole sordid story. It was probably best to keep his hopes more realistic. He'd spend his free time in his mine and his nose to the grindstone. Either way, he'd have the money he needed before the summer was over, and that was a promise.

He'd spent the better part of last year and nearly all of this year on the road and more than half of that time he'd been drunk. No wonder it took him a few minutes to figure out where he was when he woke up. This is the last of it, Cooper decided. He'd already sworn off the whiskey, now it was time to plant some roots. He pulled out the papers he'd received more than a month prior. This was it, it was final. He had made his decision about going back to Victoria. Cooper signed his name to the documents before he could change his mind. Yes, it was time to stop running. Time to stop searching. Time to have a home again.

He'd send a letter to his parents this week announcing his intentions. One thing he'd learned when he'd stopped drinking, the more people you pledged an oath to, the more likely you were to keep it. Lies came easy to yourself. Never mind this week, he'd write to his parents tomorrow. That way everyone would know.

Cooper stripped himself naked and climbed between the fresh cotton sheets of his bed. Amazing how clear your life could become in the middle of the night. He didn't think he could still be tired after his long nap, but after sleeping on the ground for a week, the cool sheets and soft feather pillow felt like a little piece of heaven to his trail weary body.

"Heaven," he sighed aloud. With golden haired angels, swimming in the clouds.

Eight

A bright flash of light jarred Jolian out of a fitful sleep. Thunder rolled in the sky outside her cabin. She pulled the patchwork quilt up under her chin. The light flashed again and Jolian began to count without consciously deciding to do so.

One... two... three, thunder! Jolian strained to hear Jakeb in the next room. Flash! One... two... th. Thunder! So loud it shook the walls of her tiny cabin and seemed to threaten entrance. "Jakeb?" Jolian whispered as if by speaking loudly the storm may truly find her.

Skies split open and rain pounded on the rooftop. Another flash and Jolian screamed as she saw a figure at the foot of her bed.

"Hush," Jakeb's voice cooed to her. "It's only me. I know how much you hate storms. I thought I'd check and make sure you were all right."

"Thank you, Jakeb." The storm and her quilt muffling her voice.

"Did you want me to stay?" Jakeb sounded like he wanted to go back to his own bed.

"No, no that's all right." Her own voice shook as she spoke.

"Are you sure? I'll stay if you want."

"No, really. I'm fine. Just knowing there's someone nearby, in case. Thank you." Jolian watched as Jakeb returned to his spot behind the curtain. She pulled the quilt right over her head and squeezed her eyes shut.

~ * ~

Drumming in a soothing hum, the rain that had eventually lulled her to sleep, still fell steadily on the rooftop as she awoke. Jolian could hear the drip... drip... drip... like a metronome and her eyes searched for the leak she was certain was somewhere in her bedroom. She finally spotted the droplets falling in the corner of the room right into her china basin! *What a thoughtful little leak!* She smiled. It felt good to smile; she should make a point of doing it more often. The grin left her face when she thought of having to climb up on the roof to fix the thoughtful little leak.

Reluctant to leave her cozy cocoon, her eyes roamed about her room once more. This time settling on the cotton underwear folded upon her ottoman. She smiled again. It had been so considerate of Jakeb to bring her the gift last night. She loved the reticule. She'd promptly opened the bottom drawer of her dresser, taken out the old woolen sock where she kept her hoarded pay, and transferred the money into the pouch. She felt her smile widen as she thought of how Jakeb had blushed when she'd thanked him with a kiss.

She looked again at the new underwear she'd set out to wear today. The weather here was as unpredictable as where gold would be found next! She reluctantly left the warmth of her bed and pulled on her old woolen unionsuit. Gray skies and driving rain waited beyond her window but her sunny mood wasn't threatened. She dressed quickly, ran a brush through her hair, washed her face and wiped her teeth. Feeling somewhat awake, she walked around the blanket separating the beds to wake Jakeb.

"I'll start a pot of coffee for you before I go to Pearl's if you like."

She felt herself smile again at his muffled response. She could get used to this feeling of lightness in the pit of her being. She caught herself humming as she lit the stove and put the coffee on to brew. A week, she thought to herself. It's been a week. Cooper Holt should be back in town. Even the downpour of rain couldn't dampen her spirits as she ran the distance between her cabin in the woods and Pearl's back door.

~ * ~

"Oh!" Jolian was startled as she entered the kitchen to see Pearl sitting at the table, hugging a cup in her hands. "I didn't expect to see anyone up and about yet."

"I cain't sleep." Pearl moaned and took a sip from her cup.

"If that's my day old coffee in your cup I shouldn't wonder!"

Pearl cocked her eyebrow at Jolian. "I bin up half the night."

"Did the storm wake you as well?"

"That started it, yup. But then I gots ta thinkin' on what you said yesterday and—"

"Oh, Pearl, I do apologize to you about that. I think I may have been out of line. I never meant to imply you are the type of person who would run from your troubles." Jolian half held her breath at the response she might get from Pearl.

Pearl scratched her head and tilted her head. "I knows ya meant well by what you said about runnin' from my troubles." I didn't get my back up to ya or nothing. Truth be told, it was mighty refreshin' ta have someone tellin' me their honest thoughts. 'Course I do get an earful of what's on Vera's mind as regular as sun up. But folks ain't usually frank with me like you was."

"You came to a decision then?" Jolian scooted on to the wood bench opposite Pearl.

"Well, I came to one of sorts. I thought I'd stay put till summer is up. Face up ta Billy an' well, hell! I ain't lettin' some broken liquored up promises run me off! Especially when business promises to be as good as it looks fer this summer!" Pearl laughed a little and rose from the table. "Who knows, by Suptumber I jist may have enough money to re-tire on."

"Maybe." Jo smiled at Pearl's off beat sense of humor. "I'm glad you decided to stay put for a while."

"What's been putting the smile on yore face and the bounce in yore step this mornin'?"

"Hmm?" Jolian pretended not to hear the half question as she rose from the table and began to brew a fresh pot of coffee.

"Hmm?" Pearl mocked her. "Here I am pourin' my heart out to ya and y'all are setting there smilin'! Ya've smiled more in the last ten minutes than I've seen in the past six months.

"I have? I didn't mean to make light—"

"Don't be apologizin'! It looks good on ya." Pearl gave her a friendly pat on her bottom. "Now, Miss cheerful, if ya don't mind, I think I'll go back upstairs and try and git some shuteye. Don't work yoreself too hard." She shook one chubby finger at Jolian and then padded out of the room.

Jolian spent the morning canning raspberries. She'd been picking the berries all week cursing the heat of the sun and now it seemed it might never show its face again. She couldn't see ten feet out of the window through this rain. She couldn't see the trail leading up the hillside to Pearl's either, though she caught herself checking in that direction every now and then in hopes that a certain miner might soon cross her path.

~ * ~

Cooper adjusted the flipped up collar on his duster to stop the rain from dripping down the back of his neck. *Miserable day.* He dreaded the task before him. Normally he thoroughly enjoyed his chosen profession, out mixing with nature, setting his own pace. But here, surveying the claims, helping to settle disputes, it was the same thing day in and day out. The sooner they were caught up the better it would be with him. Then he could begin to work on those promises he'd written his parents about this morning.

Today marked the beginning of getting back to work and a new beginning in him. It felt good to have one's life in order. He supposed Joe could be having the very same thought... and he was about to turn the lives of Joe and her brother completely upside down. Having to tell the Grayson's about the murderer being in these parts would be distressing for them, to say the least.

He'd already decided to speak with Joe. While Jakeb, the older brother, was the one he should speak to according to propriety, there was something in him Cooper just didn't trust. The few times he'd run in to him at the general store in town, Jakeb had put on quite a sales pitch. Cooper had the feeling he was a bit of a shyster, or at the very least, not what he appeared to be.

Of course, the younger one wasn't exactly what she appeared to be either, but Cooper did have the feeling she was the one with whom he should speak. He'd thought her to be awkward and shy when he'd thought *she* was a *he*. He realized now she was probably just trying to make herself less noticeable. The thought of what she had been through in the past six months was remarkable enough for a young lad, extraordinary for a young woman.

Not that Cooper believed any myths about the fairer sex, for his mother was stronger in spirit than most men he knew, but the physical hardships of traveling through the Cariboo in the middle of winter would have stopped many grown men in their tracks. Joe had dealt with that and all of the emotional pain, and done it all while masquerading as a young boy!

Cooper felt something different when he thought of her now. A feeling he simply couldn't pin down. Respect, admiration? Neither seemed to adequately sum it up. He did have a high regard for her courage. Yes, that, along with the respect and admiration... that's how he'd explain it to Guy anyway. That's the reason he was going to visit Joe. Oh yeah, and he didn't trust the brother. Good reasons, both, yet neither that he could tell Joe. Hell, he'd think of something.

~ * ~

Jolian was just putting the jars in the pantry when she swore she heard a rider. *Don't be silly*, she chided herself. *It's just your wishful thinking.* She'd done such a good job of convincing herself, the knock at the kitchen door actually startled her. *It must just be Jakeb,* she told herself as she made her way to the door. *No one uses the kitchen door but us.*

"Mr. Holt!" Jo blurted as she opened the door. She didn't know if she felt more surprised or elated as Cooper stood before her, as if she'd summoned him up out of her daydreams. She reached her hand up to pull her ever-present shako cap lower on her head.

"Mornin', Joe." Cooper flashed his dimples at her while his hat shed water like a roof. "I thought I'd come straight to the back door as it was you I came to see."

"Me?" Jo felt tongue-tied.

"Yes... ah... I know I'm as wet as a rat on a sinking ship but would you mind if I came in for a bit?"

"Oh." Jo shook her head as if to clear it and then consciously lowered her voice. "No, not at all. Um, I apologize for that... ah, come on in."

"Thanks." Cooper smiled a grin full of overwhelming charm, flustering her even further.

"I've got stove on the coffee. Ah, I mean... that is..." Jo fumbled.

"Coffee sounds great." Cooper chuckled as he shrugged off his wet outerwear and hung them on a peg by the door.

Jo thankfully turned her back to Cooper and busied herself with pouring the coffee. She reached for the pot and forgot to protect her hand with a cloth.

"Biscuits!" She cursed under her breath. It was so inconvenient to not wear her apron whilst in the kitchen. She didn't want Cooper to think she was clumsy or that his visit had rattled her, so when he inquired as to what she'd said she fudged with "Cream and sugar?"

With her back to him she examined her burned hand. It would be fine, just a little pink. She pumped some water into the sink on the pretense that the coffee mugs needed rinsing.

"Black's fine." Cooper called from the table.

Jo took a few extra minutes to slice some fresh cornmeal biscuits to serve with the coffee. It gave her a chance to settle down her thumping heart and to let her throbbing hand return to normal. Acting like Jo the young boy was getting more and more difficult lately. She took a deep breath and turned to face him.

Cooper sat on the bench, elbows resting on the table. His long fingers folded around his large hands. As she moved toward him he unfolded his fingers and reached one hand out for the steaming cup. She handed it to him and his fingertips brushed the back of her hand. The sensation of his touch traveled from her fingers to the center of her being. The hair on her arm stood up and tingles ran down her spine.

She needed to keep her guard up. For some reason, around this man, her head took a holiday and her senses took control of her body. Maybe she should come right out and tell him who she was. She had no reason to fear him or to think he wouldn't keep her secret. But then again, what would he think of her for being untruthful? What possible reason could she give him for wanting to reveal the truth now, after all this time?

"I want you to know that I'm really a woman and the way the wave of your hair resting on your collar is beckoning me to run my fingers through it." Nope that sounded too bold and unrefined. How about *"I know you think I'm a boy but I'm not. And more than anything I want to feel your lips on mine, your hands on my flesh."* Oh yes, that was the epitome of sophistication and culture! That's it; she had officially lost her sanity!

She noticed herself swallow. Heat began to rush through her body and towards her face, yet a smile played at the corner of her mouth.

"Help yourself to the biscuits if you like, they're fresh." She spoke slowly, trying to keep her voice low but even to her own ears it sounded wanton.

"Fresh biscuits, ummm. How is it a boy like you knows so much about cooking, Joe?" Cooper reached for a biscuit and pulled it open, the steam rose between them.

This was her chance! She could tell him now, she could tell him the truth. The words wouldn't come. Every reason, every thought was muddled. She'd have to keep her charade for now. At least until she could think clearly enough around him to explain herself. Jo shrugged in response to his question and pushed the raspberry preserves towards him.

She'd focus on what she knew. Cooking, yes, she knew cooking. At least she could be truthful about something. She kept her eyes focused on her hands, as she sat across the table from Cooper.

"Back in San Francisco, we lived in a fine hotel, run by my Uncle Julian. We all worked, to help out and for our keep. I spent most of my time in the kitchen. My Uncle's chef, Jean Pierre, was from Nice, France. He made the best food I ever tasted. Different things, not like my Ma. His pastries would melt in your mouth. I plan to open my own restaurant someday. My share of the gold was going to pay... that's what I'd planned, anyway."

Jo raised her eyes to Cooper's now. She looked into their blue green depths and saw he understood. She saw something else there, too. It gave her a sense of well being. As if his eyes were telling hers it would all work out for her someday.

She was grateful she hadn't needed to fib or find an excuse not to answer his question. She valued honesty and wished she wasn't living a lie. As soon as her heart stopped ruling her brain, she would think of a way to tell him the truth. There was something in this man sitting before her, his mustached mouth full of her biscuits, his strong hands holding a cup of her coffee. She knew the 'something' she was searching for would never be found if she continued to live as a boy.

"A restaurant?" Cooper swallowed his bite and took another mouthful of coffee. "Well that's not so far fetched. Sounds like you've apprenticed some. If the rest of your cooking is half as fine as these biscuits, you'll be mighty successful! Don't give up on your dreams, Joe. Dreams are important. Especially for a boy of... what age are you? About fourteen?"

"I'm eigh—eh-yup fourteen." *Dang! Another lie.* Yet, it's better he think she was younger. Why at eighteen, a boy would have whiskers already and she surely couldn't feign whiskers. Better to stop daydreaming and remember to keep her guard up.

"Fourteen. Well then there's plenty of time for you to work and save up the money to start your own business."

If Cooper had noticed her stumble, he didn't show it.

"And speaking of business, I guess I should come to the reason for my visit. I'm afraid I have some troubling news." He explained about running into the Royal Engineers and all of the information he'd gleaned. "While I don't want to worry you and your brother unnecessarily, I thought it best that you know. Your brother would be wise to keep his wits about him. If the murderer's in these parts there is always the chance he could run into him. He may recognize Jakeb and if that's the case, he'd be a sure target."

Jolian's hands were shaking as she stood and turned to the stove. She shoved them into the pockets of her trousers and stared out of the window.

Cooper continued. "As I said, there's the Constable's office in Richfield if you have any concerns or questions. Though the Constable himself spends most of his time in Barkerville these days." He hesitated like he wanted to tell her something else. "If either you or Jakeb feel Guy or I can be of any help in any way, I want you to feel free to call on us. We'd be more than happy to do what's needed. We'll be down at the claims for the next week or so anyway. Most of the miners know us and can steer you in our direction if need be."

Jolian felt his words more than she heard them. It was almost as if she knew this day would come. Anger surged up inside her. *"Anger is only one letter away from danger";* she heard her mother's voice in her head. Only a moment prior, her heart beat fully with thoughts of love and now it pounded with a fury and rage, she never knew existed within her. Now she understood the "danger" in her mother's warning. With anger like this, she believed she was capable of killing, too. What right did that horrible beast of a man have to live anyway? How many lives had he taken? And how may others, like hers, had he destroyed?

Cooper spoke and brought her thoughts to the present. "The captain mentioned testifying once they catch him."

Jo spun her body around to face Cooper. "Oh I'll testify all right." She could feel the anger burning her cheeks as she hissed the words out through clenched teeth. "I'll do anything to make sure he gets exactly what he deserves!"

Cooper's eyes widened and he pulled his head back as if she were about to strike him. She had a right to be angry, damn angry. If it shocked him, well, too bad!

"I'm glad you're comfortable with testifying, Joe, but don't go and do anything foolish. The law is just and fair and it would be best to let it work its proper course." He paused as if to give her time to calm down. "That man is dangerous, I don't have to tell you that. Let the law handle this, Joe. You can do your part in court." Genuine concern for her and her brother shone from his eyes and calmed her. "As soon as the roads are safe to travel, I promise I'll take you and Jakeb to your parents graves."

Jo felt her anger begin to subside slightly. "Once again I find myself in the position to thank you, Mr. Holt."

"None needed." Cooper shook her offered hand.

"May I take a look at the sketch the officers are circulating?" She wanted to make sure it accurately reflected her memory.

Cooper gave her a quizzical look.

"When Jakeb and I first reported the crime to the Constable, I found him to be—I guess the word would be contrary. He didn't seem inclined to believe us. Jakeb insisted a sketch be drawn from our descriptions and the Constable informed us he would take care of the matter. I just think it's rather odd he'd be distributing a picture without asking for our final approval."

Cooper fished the folded paper out of his shirt pocket and held it between his fore and middle finger as he passed it to her. She opened it, placed it on the table and smoothed the creases with her hands.

"Why this could be anyone... anyone at all!" She could feel the anger begin to burn inside her again. She took a deep breath and let it pass. It wasn't Cooper's fault the Constable was as thick as porridge.

"If it isn't a good likeness then there's not a lot of use for it is there?" Cooper sounded frustrated.

"Just a moment." Jolian excused herself from the kitchen and hurried to Pearl's office. Finding her needed instruments among Pearl's precisely efficient desk, she carefully carried the ink, pen and blotting pad back to the kitchen. "Is it acceptable to draw over this sketch?"

"If it will improve the likeness, then by all means!"

Jolian dipped her pen in the pot, blotted the tip carefully and began to portray the image permanently fixed in her mind's eye.

~ * ~

Cooper watched in awe as a nondescript sketch began to take on character. The face had shape, the nose was distinct and the eyes, it felt as though they were truly watching you from the paper. "Joe, you are a wo... wonder of hidden talents!" *Good cover!* He'd almost admitted to knowing she was a woman! And what a remarkable woman she was! She possessed such a unique array of abilities. Joe beamed with the compliment and the room took on a glow of its own. "Now this is what I call a sketch! If this were circulated amongst the Royal Engineers in the colony, I'm sure the law would have much more luck in finding the man."

"I'd do anything to make that happen." He watched her smile fade as the reality hit her. They may never see justice for her parents' murder. He hated that he was the one to cause her grief. He wanted to lift her chin with his finger and look into her eyes that were as blue as the Cariboo sky after the rain. He wanted to kiss away her fears and doubts and promise her everything would be fine. But who was he to promise such dreams? He'd better stick to the present. He could at least turn her attention to something more positive.

"Joe, could you make a few more copies of this for me?"

"I'd be happy to draw some more if it would be helpful but I'm not sure if there is paper. I'd have to ask Pearl."

"I could pick them up later in the week." *And give me an excuse to come back to see you again,* he added to himself. She agreed, with his words anyway. "Speaking of Pearl, is she around?" He hoped he sounded casual.

"Actually she's still in bed." Jolian lowered her eyes as her cheeks began to take on a rosy hue. "Ah—She was up real early when I first came in, that is, and—"

"No need to wake her then," He interrupted to ease her discomfort. "I'll speak to her another time. It was nothing important really, but could you mention I wanted to speak to her if she's planning to come to town?" He finished buttoning his coat and reached for his hat. He'd better make his escape now, while he still could. If he stayed a moment longer he'd pull her into his arms and put some proper colour into those cheeks.

"I'll do that," Jo called through the door after him as he ran through the driving rain to the barn.

Nine

The rain stopped as suddenly as it began. A westerly wind came up and blew the sky free of clouds, just as Cooper, Guy and Ts'kaw were packing up their gear for the evening. Cooper cursed under his breath as he began the task of carefully peeling open the rain-soaked pages of field notes in his survey book.

Impossible! Taking notes and making calculations in the rain! He could barely read what he'd written. Frustrated, he laid the book to dry against the rocks, which bordered the fire.

Cooper stretched his leg muscles near the warmth of the campfire and felt the drying canvas separate from his thighs like a second skin. They'd decided to make a camp near the creek until the rest of their fieldwork was finished. It would save the long ride to and from Guy's each day, and with days like today; they'd need all of the extra time they could fit in before sundown. Maybe staying in town he'd get in a chance or two to work on his own claim. He could easily mine by lamplight. And of course, it kept him closer to Joe.

He wished he could think of a reason to visit her again tomorrow as she likely wouldn't have time to complete the sketches yet. Where had that thought come from? He hadn't wanted to find an excuse to be near anyone in a long time. It was probably for her cooking, he thought to himself, as he stared at the plate of "whattheheckisthisstuff?" Guy handed him.

"It tastes better if you use ze fork."

"Somehow I doubt that." Cooper knew he could get away with teasing his lifelong friend about his cooking. He dug into his meal like it was his last and emptied his plate in no time.

"I see, it is so bad that you want ze number two now, eh?"

"Seconds, Guy, its called seconds. And yeah, I guess I'll take you up on it."

"See, you make fun of my cooking and that was just ze leftovers."

"Ya, but leftover what?" Cooper got one last jibe in before Guy walked away shaking his head. He finished his seconds and set the plate by his side. He stretched his arms above his head and then patted his slightly rounded belly.

He inhaled a deep breath and exhaled the difficulties of the day. Mostly warm and comfortable with his side to the fire, he thought about the old trick his father had taught him about camping out during fieldwork. You never faced a fire, or looked directly into the flame. You couldn't know what danger lurked in the night, surveying among the wilds of the colony, and it was best not to give your opponents the lag time of having your eyes re-adjust to the darkness.

While the opponents his father had spoken of were usually kept at bay by the fire itself, occasionally, an animal, crazed with hunger or rabies would brave the blazes. Here, in 'civilization', the opponents were more dangerous than any animal he could ever face, but Cooper was relatively relaxed among the miners. The strict laws governing mining in the colony made things like claim jumping practically non-existent. As far as the murderer went, Cooper felt certain he would never try anything here, even if he were in the vicinity. Not with all of the miners about at all times of the day and night.

As a surveyor, Cooper was respected and even looked up to in the mining towns. Often called upon to make decisions or to settle minor disputes, that really had nothing at all to do with surveying, made him feel valued. It felt great to be good at something and to have the admiration of people you respected.

Yup, he was in a good place right now, both physically and professionally. He had a place in the community, was a partner in a great company that was making money, had life long friends at his side and he had prospects. *What more could a man ask for?*

Cooper laced his fingers behind his head and shifted against the boulder supporting his upper torso. His mind wandered over his visit with Joe earlier. She was a fine looking woman, even dressed as a boy. Now that he knew her secret and looked at her with that knowledge, he couldn't believe her disguise had ever fooled him. Her features were fine and delicate. Her skin smooth and soft looking. It almost had the sheen of satin. How could he have *ever* thought her a boy?

What an extraordinary young woman she was, maintaining her disguise while working where she did. She worked hard and quite skillfully, according to Pearl. Joe's salary supported the brother, Cooper figured. She had a rare quality about her. It kept his thoughts coming back to her time and again. A freshness, a glow, a sense of wonder within her very being, was that what drew him to her? He had never known a woman quite like her. Maybe he couldn't put his finger on the reason she was constantly on his mind but he had to admit, he could get used to having her in more than his thoughts.

~ * ~

Jakeb let the rocks slip through his fingers. *Nothing!* This claim was turning out to be a humbug! Everywhere, all around him, men were striking unbelievable fortunes. Only last week, the Lazy-dazy claim right next to his had hit their lead. They were pulling out a thousand a foot! Lucky bastards!

He had to do something, and he had to do it soon. *Where the hell was Angus anyway?* He was supposed to meet him at six and it was nearly seven. Jakeb fished in his pocket for the last of his gold; twenty-five, maybe thirty dollars worth. Still, it'd buy him a night of comfort with Hog-Judy. She didn't have half the class of any of Pearl's girl's but he couldn't take advantage of their services. Not with his sister working there.

Besides, why should he pay three or four times as much for the same thing anyway? Maybe Hog-Judy didn't dress as fancy or smell as pretty, he laughed out loud, but she was willing. Hell, she may even be willing for a shared bottle of whiskey—Now that was a fine idea!

~ * ~

Cooper put aside his copy of *Moby Dick* and checked his fieldbook to see if it was dry. Good enough, he'd separate the pages again tomorrow. The fire was too low to read by, so he let his gaze drift upwards. The rain clouds had dissipated and the night was a brilliant black canvas dotted with millions of minute fireballs.

Expertly, his eyes sought out the Great Bear, then shifted to the blue hue of Vega and his invaluable guide, Polaris. The opaque prominence of the Milky Way spanned the sky from Capella through Cassiopeia. Cassiopeia the proud queen, mother to the beautiful Andromeda. Studies in astronomy and mythology collided in his thoughts. Yes, Andromeda, so lovely bragged her mother, her beauty bested anything Neptune had to offer. Then again, Cassiopeia hadn't seen *his* golden angel.

Cooper chuckled at his thoughts. He lowered his eyes and let them half close as he thought of her once again... emerging from the water... tiny droplets glistening on creamy skin... the sunset reflecting her golden curls... He shifted uncomfortably then rose and made his way to the canvas tent. He would have to think of something else if he wanted to get any sleep at all tonight!

~ * ~

Jolian let herself into the kitchen and went straight to work cooking breakfast. Fresh eggs and dried mushrooms mixed with a few chives and served on top of sourdough biscuits. She wished she could get her hands on some oranges. She missed the fresh squeezed juice she used to have in San Francisco.

"What smells so divine?" Doralynn asked as she yawned sleepily and sat herself at the table. "Um, Joe, this looks wonderful!" her smile full of encouragement. "Pearl sure was smart to hire you on as our cook."

"Thank you." Jo couldn't help smiling, too. It felt good to hear compliments about her cooking. Jean Pierre had been kind, but firm and not too free with praise. It made her feel special to think people enjoyed her food. Jo basked in the glow of her feelings for a moment and then the rush of girls into the kitchen soon took up any time she had for such fanciful thoughts.

As the girls finished their meal and began to file out of the eating area, Jo tried to catch Pearl's eye.

"Did Mr. Holt catch up to you yet?"

"No, was he lookin' fer me?"

Jo explained about Cooper's visit the day before and that her parents' murderer may be in the area.

"Are ya feeling safe in that old cabin out back?" Pearl had a look of genuine concern on her face.

"Normally I do, but, well, Jakeb didn't come home last night."

Pearl popped a biscuit into her mouth and spoke around it. "It sounds like yore worried about him."

Jo nodded as she wrung her hands through a cloth. "He doesn't know about the murderer, and Cooper, I mean Mr. Holt, was sure he'd be a target if he was recognized."

"I suppose he would be at that," Pearl agreed. "Still, I reckon he's most likely just fine. Yore brother's spent the night in town before ain't he?"

"Yes. You're right. I shouldn't get myself worked up. It was just being all alone out there that did it I guess." Jo turned to the stove and lifted off the heavy pot of water warmed enough for washing dishes.

"Well if yore ever frightened, for any reason, all ya have ta do is come up here. Hell, there's sure ta be at least one man around here most nights what could protect us." Pearl laughed and Jolian felt her tension melt a bit. She poured the warm water into the dish bucket and then picked up her paring knife to shave in tiny slivers of soap. Pearl moved closer and patted her on the back.

"Yore always welcome ta sleep in one of the upstairs rooms. If it's one thing we gots plenty of around here it's beds!" Pearl laughed at her own joke until tears formed in her eyes. Jolian laughed, too. The more Pearl snorted, the harder Jolian giggled. And that just seemed to make Pearl laugh more and more. Pearl held her sides with her hands and her belly shook. Jolian put her hands to her cheeks. Her face hurt, it actually hurt from the laughter!

Jolian squeezed her cheeks with her fingers to relieve the tension in them. Pearl walloped her across the back and wobbled into the parlor still chuckling to herself. It was a release, pure and simple. A welcome release after the fitful night of sleep she'd spent with her gun under her pillow. Customers or not, maybe she would sleep at Pearl's tonight.

~ * ~

Jolian pulled her shako cap low on her head and stared the horse straight in the eyes. Her relationship with these animals had always been tentative at best, but it would never do to see a boy riding into town, alone, in Pearl's fancy buggy. No, a boy would definitely ride on a horse.

"Well, Star, it's you and me." Jolian took a deep breath, held the reins tight on the saddle-horn and hoisted herself up onto the sizeable horse. She settled her feet firmly into the stirrups, and let her breath exhale. "Ya just haf ta let em know whose in charge," Jolian mimicked Pearl's words out loud.

"Gid'yup!" Jo shouted with more assurance than she felt as she put her heels to the chestnut mare. It wasn't just the horse that set her nerves on edge, but the ride into town by herself. Not only did she have the town to worry about, what with all its rush and scuttle, people bumping into you, and the like, but now she had to worry about the trail as well. *If only you'd come home last night Jakeb.*

Jo tried to let her shoulders and the muscles of her forearms relax a bit. She could keep a firm hold on the reins without keeping every muscle in her body tensed. It was that dammed murderer's fault. That beast! Here it was a beautiful summer's day; she should be enjoying the time by herself. *You're by yourself on the trail.* Jo wound the reins around her left hand freeing her right hand to feel for her Colt revolver. Her fingers encircled the cold metal of the gun. Maybe she'd keep it in her hand, just in case.

No! That was letting him win; letting her fear rule her life and she had worked too hard to let that happen again. She forced her fingers to release their grip and she brought her hand out of her pocket to let it rest upon her thigh. She would enjoy this ride, she would. If only to prove to herself that *he* wouldn't win. He had killed her parents, but *she* was alive. Biscuits! She wasn't going to live a half-life!

Jolian puffed her chest up with her next breath and decided to take notice of everything around her. The air smelled sweet today. There, one simple thought and she felt better already. She let her gaze drift upwards past the tall cedars and towering pines, above the Cariboo Mountains in the distance to the powder blue sky, dotted with sheep's wool clouds. From the rising temperature, the day promised to be a scorcher. This was beautiful, wild, untamed country. How she wished her Ma could've lived to see its beauty.

Star moved along at a leisurely pace and Jo's hips settled into the swing of the walk. She made a mental list of the items she wished to purchase in town, once she'd found Jakeb and told him the news. She figured she might as well do her shopping and kill two birds with one stone. *Jakeb, Jakeb, where could you be?* The trill of a chickadee sounded in the woods off the trail and she felt herself relax somewhat. Maybe there'd be a new shipment of food at the mercantile. Maybe she'd even find oranges. Now that was a hopeful, positive thought!

Once she reached the town of Richfield, she began to see other riders regularly on the path. This both calmed and aggravated her. While she felt safe with other people around, she didn't want these people to get too close, lest they discover her secret. She kept her cap low on her head and her greetings to a nod.

The office of the gold commissioner, Thomas Elwyn, was located in Richfield, but the gold to be found beyond the canyon was evidenced by the well-worn mile long path between Richfield and Barkerville. Jolian reasoned to herself if the success of the mines in Barkerville continued that eventually the commissioner would have to move his office.

She followed William's creek along the dusty trail out of Richfield and past Conklin Gulch until she reached the town of Barkerville. The settlement consisted mainly of two parallel streets. The main street of town, called Front Street, was actually the natural path of William's creek. The miner's had built a huge bulkhead, which diverted the creek to the east, so they could mine the gold that ran beneath the ground where the water had previously run. The town of Barkerville had sprung up along the main street, built around the claims and mine shafts. The bulk of the new claims springing up now were along Back Street, which ran the length of the relocated creek.

Jolian's gaze drifted to the hillsides surrounding the town. They were slowly being stripped of all of their trees, most likely for use in the shafts, sluiceboxes and cabins. She could also see huge tanks that had been dug and cribbed into the hillside. From these tanks, three main flumes ran over the tops of the buildings into the town and then into barrels and troughs. This method supplied the town with fresh water. Jakeb had explained the relatively new system to her and it fascinated her to see it up close.

Her last time in town had been briefly in the spring, when the main street had been impassable. The miners had not considered the spring run off from the surrounding mountains would not only push through their carefully constructed bulkhead, but also fill the main street of their new town with over two feet of mud! Everyone had been frantically trying to raise their buildings and drain the water and mud out of their structures. No one had taken notice of a young boy in their midst. She hoped the same would be true this time.

She remembered thinking the bulkhead on the creek had been extremely ill planned. *That's what those fools got for trying to outwit Mother Nature! What was it about being a miner that took away all of your sensibilities? Couldn't one of those miners have foreseen the melting snow would fill the banks of the creek to overflowing and the creek would again run on its natural path? Of course not. Miners' only thoughts were of the immediate future and of what could be gained today.* Hadn't that been evidenced in her family?

Her father's rush to the goldfields had certainly been poorly timed. One only had to look at the town of Barkerville to see hundreds of miners had made it here safely by waiting for the spring. Oh biscuits! She'd better just find Jakeb.

But where would she begin to look? The town had changed so much! Jolian sat atop Star at the entrance to Front Street and felt her jaw go slack in disbelief. There weren't just hundreds of people here... there were thousands. This wasn't just a mining camp but truly a bustling city!

Front Street was narrower than she remembered, but still a muddy mess. Flanked on both sides by boardwalks, haphazardly built and looking quite precarious in some sections. The buildings, some with false fronts, were cramped and poorly spaced. Obviously there had been less planning given to the town than to the construction of the bulkhead. She nudged Star onto the main street and into the section of Barkerville known as Chinatown.

A wonderful smell of ginger and something else she couldn't put her finger on, assaulted her nostrils. *Could it be? Oranges!* It had been so long since she smelled them, but she was sure nonetheless.

She dismounted and immediately sunk ankle deep in mud. "Biscuits!" she mumbled her curse. Trying not to look dismayed, she led Star to a nearby hitching post, secured the reins and hoisted herself up onto the boardwalk. As she followed the glorious smell, her eyes caught a glimpse of green on the hillside between the buildings. Was it? Yes, it was a garden and the most curious looking one she had ever seen. Terraced and sectioned, she had never thought of a garden as a work of art, but this was truly beautiful. Lush green leaves mixed with all of the colors of the rainbow, in neat rows and patterned clumps.

"You like?" A Chinese woman dressed in a navy silk wrap embroidered with red dragons engaged her in conversation.

"Yes, oh yes. It is very... ah, beautiful." Jolian tried to make her voice deep.

The woman nodded her head and smiled. "I grow in sections. Make most of short time to grow here."

"How very clever of you!"

"You come to store. I show you."

"Thank you." Honestly interested in the types of crops that grew well here, Jolian followed the woman down the boardwalk. Her own garden, a kitchen garden really, was not doing nearly as well as she would have hoped. It would be helpful to get some tips.

Besides, finding Jakeb didn't seem quite so urgent now that she'd seen how large the town had grown. Even if their parents' murderer was in town, what were the chances of him spotting and recognizing her brother? She was always making mountains out of molehills with her worrying. She reminded herself about her decision to live a full life and followed the Chinese woman into the store.

Inside the store, Jolian could hardly believe her eyes and her nose! Everywhere she looked there were baskets and containers of fresh and dried vegetables, fruit, spices and rice. She recognized gingerroot and wild carrot, dried figs, peanuts, mushrooms and sesame seeds. The aroma of oranges wafted throughout the store.

"I smell oranges."

"It is tea. Dry oranges cooking in tea. Oranges for cake, tea for drink. You like?"

"I would, yes, thank you."

This was wonderful. Recipes and new combinations of foods began to form in her mind. The woman had dried oranges! Jolian chatted with the woman, whose name was Kwan Loo Fan, for what felt like hours. It seemed to Jolian that she had met a kindred spirit. It felt so good to just sit and chat about gardening and recipes as if neither of them had a care in the world. Either Kwan Loo Fan had guessed she was a woman, or she didn't find it odd that a boy would be so interested in the subjects. When the time finally came for Jolian to say goodbye, she had several new recipes, two small pouches of spices and a generous bag of the dried oranges.

Pearl wouldn't mind the expense once she tasted the dishes. For Pearl had a love of food like no one else she'd met and it was wonderful to cook for someone who really enjoyed eating.

~ * ~

Jolian secured the food in her saddlebags and mounted Star. She carefully navigated her way down Front Street and then crossed near the Barker claim, over toward Back Street. She had never even been to see Jakeb's claim, but he had told her how to find it if she ever needed him. What did he call the method of mining he was using? Some kind of animal... dogging? No, coyoteing —yes, that was it, coyoteing! The miners dug a shaft deep into the bedrock and then tunneled out in all directions trying to find the richest vein of gold. They called it coyoteing; that's what Jakeb had told her.

As she neared the spot Jakeb had described, she cold see a large crowd beginning to gather. She dismounted and hobbled her horse. The growing crowd made her feel anxious. Wondering what all of the commotion was about, she tried to make herself inconspicuous as she eavesdropped on several conversations at one time.

"Seems like it happened last night."

"Sounds like he's down there, too."

"Here comes one of those fellers. He's been lookin' it over and he ortta know how best ta goes about it."

Jolian pushed her way through the crowd and her heart began to thump hard in her chest. Dread filled her veins as she heard the words 'cave-in' and 'somebody down there' time and again. She looked to see whom the miners were waiting for and found Cooper Holt walking towards her.

"Joe." He seemed startled to see her. "I didn't think someone could've been to Pearl's and back already."

"What for? I mean, I was in town... I am looking for my brother."

"No one came to get you then?"

Jolian didn't want anyone to voice the words reforming in her mind, so it startled her when it was *she* who asked "Has there been some kind of accident?"

"Yes, Joe. It seems there has been a cave in at your brother's mine here, and by the sound of it, I'd say he's down there."

Cooper's words hit her like gunfire. She had chatted about recipes while her brother was struggling for his life down a caved-in mine shaft? Jolian's knees wanted to buckle and she locked them in place lest her body crumple beneath it's own weight. Cooper was still talking, and she just stood there staring into the mineshaft trying to make sense of what he was saying.

"I figure if we go down into the shaft on the Lazy-dazy claim next to this one, we can probably tunnel through without too much difficulty."

Jolian turned to face Cooper, her knees barely able to keep their lock and hold her body upright. Cooper reached out a hand to help steady her and his touch seemed to energize her and force her back to reality. Thoughts began to race through her head at breakneck speed and she began to talk just as quickly.

"You mean to tell me that Jakeb's down there in that shaft, blocked by rocks and everyone is just milling about up here!" Jolian half screamed into the crowd. "Well I am not going to stand here while my brother runs out of air. I, for one, am going to do something!"

Jo began to lower herself down into the shaft. Suddenly two strong arms enveloped her and pulled her out.

"Don't be a fool, Joe!" Cooper yelled at her. "We already have one person trapped in there, we certainly don't need a second. I know how you must be feeling, but we have to be rational about this. That mine is far too unstable for anyone to enter!"

"How could you know how I'm feeling?" Jolian knew he was right, but she couldn't let it go. "Is it your only family member trapped down there while the only people who can help him are milling about deciding what route to take? Why don't you all just order a pot of tea, and while you're at it my brother's headstone!"

Jolian knew she'd gone too far. She was behaving rudely to people who were just trying to help. She was frustrated, embarrassed and angry all at the same time. She didn't know how to help Jakeb and now she'd been horrid to those who did. She knew she was going to cry and that would make everything even worse, so she pushed her way through the crowd and began to run up the creek bed.

As the creek turned sharply and hid her from view, Jolian fell to her knees behind a shrub and let her tears come. Why had she spent all of that time talking with Kwan Loo Fan? She couldn't survive another death of a family member, she couldn't! Jakeb had to be alive. She lifted her eyes toward the heavens and prayed from her heart. She offered God her own life to let her brother live. It was a selfish thought to leave her brother with her death to deal with, so she quickly rephrased her offer to the Lord: she'd do anything to save her brother... anything.

Suddenly she realized she was doing just what she'd accused the men at the shaft of doing—nothing. She dried her eyes on the sleeve of her flannel shirt and rose to her feet. She said she'd do anything and she would prove it!

Jolian walked back to the shaft. The crowd had moved to the Lazy-dazy mineshaft one claim over. She supposed they had taken Cooper's suggestion and were going to tunnel through from there. She glanced about, saw that no one was paying attention and lowered herself down the ladder into the shaft of her brother's claim.

The lower she climbed the darker it became. She reached the bottom of the shaft and the dust from the cave in diffused what little light was left. The particles of dust hung in the air like a dense gray fog and Jolian coughed and wheezed as it irritated her throat. What was that? She'd heard a noise.

"Jakeb?" She yelled between coughing fits. "Jakeb, is that you?"

A muffled response was her only reply. It's him! She knew it! He was alive and she planned to keep him that way. She began to pry at the rocks with her hands. How foolish to not have thought of tools! She needed to start thinking with her brain and not her heart. Should she climb back out to get tools now? No. Cooper, or one of the other men might see her and try to stop her again. She'd just have to work with her hands.

There! One big rock gave way and Jolian let it roll past her. There were several smaller rocks and she found that if she could halt her coughing long enough, she could move them quite easily. She stopped for a moment and buttoned the collar up on her shirt. Then she flipped the collar up and pulled the shirt up between her mouth and her nose. That was much better. Now that she could breathe through her mouth without coughing, moving the rocks would go much faster.

~ * ~

Jolian had lost track of time. Muscles ached over her entire body. She had no idea how long she'd been moving rock around in the tunnel. It could've been thirty minutes or three hours. The way her arms and back were screaming it had to be closer to the latter. The air was still and thick with dust. Shuffling under the weight of the rocks, as she moved them, didn't help matters any. But she wasn't about to stop. She hadn't heard the muffled sound for a long time now. Concern about the lack of air for Jakeb kept her aching body moving. Maybe he'd lost consciousness.

That thought gave her the renewed energy she needed to continue. She reached for another rock and as she lifted it, the rocks beneath it fell forward instead of backward. She'd done it! There was a tiny hole through to where Jakeb was!

"Jakeb! Jakeb, can you hear me? Jakeb, are you able to talk to me?" There, she hadn't imagined it had she? She'd heard something. Jolian climbed up on the rocks and put her mouth then her ear close to the opening.

"Jakeb, it's Jo, are you all right?"

"It's Angus." It was barely a whisper but she'd heard it just the same.

"Angus, oh dear Lord. Angus, are you injured? Is Jakeb there, too?"

His voice must be hoarse from the dust she thought, as she could barely make out his words.

"It's my leg, in the rocks... No Jakeb today... just me. The lumber too thin... just gave away."

"Don't worry about anything now Angus." Jolian spoke with more sureness than she felt, and hoped her voice didn't reveal the relief in her heart. Relief mixed with guilt. It had never even occurred to her that Angus might have been in the shaft.

"There's a party of men tunneling through to you Angus. They're coming in from the claim downstream. They should be there soon."

"How long?"

"How long? I couldn't say Angus. Are you in a lot of pain?"

"Ain't... pain... its water. Pump smashed... water is rising..."

Jolian didn't stay to hear the rest. She ran as fast as her legs would carry her over the rocks she'd moved, then, to the rickety ladder leading out of the shaft. Back in the daylight, she gave her eyes no time to adjust as she sped in the direction she'd seen Cooper head earlier.

"Cooper, Cooper Holt! Cooper Holt come quickly!" She tried to yell but her throat was sore and dry from the dust. Some of the men at the top of the Lazy-dazy blocked her way down into the mineshaft. She tried to squeeze through the crowd.

"What are you hollerin' about, lad?" A Scotsman grabbed onto her shirt and held fast. She struggled to free herself, but he held her firm. "Hey, hey what's this all about then?"

"It's that shaft," Jolian spoke hoarsely as she gestured toward the hole in the ground leading to the trapped man, "Angus is down there and his pump is broken. I dug through but only..."

The man let go of her shirt at the mention of the broken pump. He turned and half-dove down the Lazy-dazy shaft where Cooper and the others were digging.

Jolian kept talking, between coughing fits, and the other men around her listened in earnest.

"Angus, my brother's partner, is down there and he's hurt his leg."

"Is yore brother with him?"

"No, Angus was alone. The shaft is full of dust and it's hard to breathe."

Jolian croaked out the last of her words as the men moved toward where Angus was trapped. There was nothing for her to do now. She gave into her trembling legs and sat down right there.

Within minutes, the Scotsman who had held her shirt climbed out of the Lazy-dazy mine, followed by a herd of men. They had lanterns and tools as they rushed by her to the other shaft. Cooper led the pack, but didn't appear to notice her as he passed.

Jolian's hands hurt. She looked down at them and found blood. Her fingernails were ripped below the quick and her hands were a mass of dirt, blood and blisters. She rose from her spot on the ground and looked up and down Back Street. Her eyes finally rested upon a livery not too far away.

The creek itself was often the dumping spot for the garbage of the town and the water there seemed less than hygienic to Jolian. Half dazed, she walked over to the livery, spoke to the owner and then went to the water trough to wash.

Slowly she immersed her hands into the water and tried not to cringe as it stung in every split and scrape. She focused on the coolness and tried to relax her hands. When the water felt bearable she reached for the soap. This was going to sting but better a twinge now than an infection later! She rubbed the soap gently between her palms until she worked up a good lather. In between each finger, under what was left of some her nails, she washed until her hands were clean enough to have passed her mother's inspection.

She wished she could bandage them. That was out of the question though. Not only did she have nothing to bandage them with but a boy would probably just tough it out.

She borrowed two buckets and filled them with water. Before she left for the mineshaft, she asked one of the stable hands to try and find a doctor. The town had no formal hospital, but there were several doctors who were mining for gold. Angus would need medical help as soon as they rescued him from the shaft and she wanted to make sure it could be provided.

After she left the water by the opening of the shaft, Jolian asked around town, as much as she dared, trying to discover the whereabouts of her brother. Jakeb had become fairly well known in Barkerville, as were most people who worked in the stores, but no one had seen him. She told those she'd asked, that if they did happen to see Jakeb, to tell him that she'd be waiting at the mine. After that, there was nothing to do but wait. She returned to the mine and found a tiny bit of shade in which to sit.

Jolian slumped to the ground under the fledgling oak, surprised no one had yet used the puny tree for something. Lumber seemed to be in such demand. If she had the money she'd open up a lumber mill. The real money to be made in this town was not from mining gold, but mining the miners. Cautiously, she leaned back against the trunk of the tree. It gave a bit, but seemed to hold her weight. She positioned herself so her face was mostly in the speckled shade. Then she adjusted her cap to cover the areas the shade missed. Her skin would never be the same.

~ * ~

Hooting and hollering stirred Jolian. She'd half dozed as she waited beside the mine. She scrambled to her feet and awaited the emergence of Angus from the shaft. The men who were helping to dig him out had put another pump in the tunnel, giving them more time to remove the rock and debris. Still, whether from water or perspiration, the men exiting the shaft were drenched. Finally they pulled Angus out into the daylight, with the doctor at his side.

Her heart pounded with joy despite the fact she barely knew Angus. She just felt so elated he'd made it out alive. It was like a ray of hope in a place where death appeared to dominate life.

Jolian rushed toward him, the smell of rotting flesh nearly overwhelmed her as she approached. Jakeb had mentioned gumboot gout, but Jo had no idea it would be as bad as this. His gnarled foot was a mass of blood and infection.

"His leg was crushed in the cave-in." The doctor explained to her. "I've already told Angus it'll have to come off. The foot is so badly infected as it is... I'll take it at the knee. If I wait, it may mean taking it higher later, or worse."

Jolian swallowed hard and tried not to show her shock and disgust. It wasn't unusual for miners to lose limbs or their lives, for that matter. She had just never seen it up close. Angus moaned and rolled his eyes.

"Is there anything you want me to do for you?" Jo tried to breathe shallow and slowly through her mouth, so the smell wouldn't make her retch.

"Naw, I'm thankful y'all found me when you did." Angus barely whispered. "Yore brother was supposed ta meet me last night, Joe. I don't know what became of him. I'm livin' on borrowed time. I cain't mine with one leg... so, with all here as witness, my share in the mine is yours."

She wanted to comfort him, despite the smell. She wanted to reassure him, despite how bad it looked. But those were womanly feelings so she just nodded and thanked him. Men had killed for less than a share in a mineshaft, prosperous or not. She had no use for the share, but she'd deal with that later.

She thanked all of the men who were emerging from the shaft as she shook their hands individually. Her own battered hands screamed in response, but it was the right thing to do, nonetheless. The last man to exit the shaft, was Cooper. She held her hand to him like she had all the other men. He took her hand more gently than those before him and shook it with a tenderness that made her search his eyes for a hint of knowing.

His eyes met hers briefly but she couldn't read his thoughts. She wanted to talk to him but could think of no reason to start a private conversation. She just nodded her thanks and turned her eyes back to the doctor.

"I'll take care of the fee, just let me know." She spoke with her ear close to the doctor's so as not to disturb Angus, but she needn't have, as he had lost consciousness.

~ * ~

Jolian walked away feeling lost. After the odd exhilaration of finding Angus and then the anticipation of his rescue, it seemed so unfair he may lose his leg, *and* his ability to mine. Even though she didn't approve of it, mining was obviously his whole life, as he'd continued even with the seriousness of his foot condition.

Gumboot gout was common among miners, she'd heard. The problem with the kind of mining they did here was they were always working in water. Jakeb and Angus had the pump in their tunnel but even when it worked properly it couldn't keep the shaft as dry as it should be. The miner's feet got wet inside their gumboots. They worked such long hours most miners never had a chance for their socks, feet, or boots to dry properly. Top that off with poor hygiene, and the conditions were ripe for the foot fungus that infected Angus's leg.

In her mind's eye she pictured Cooper rising up out of the mineshaft. His hair had been plastered to his head with dampness and his face streaked with grime yet Jolian thought she had never known a more attractive man. He was more than handsome in appearance, but it was the quality of him that drew her admiration. A natural leader, a man to whom others looked to, for guidance and direction, if Cooper said it was so, no one questioned his authority. Well, no one but her. She hoped it wasn't anger she'd seen in his eyes when he'd so calmly accepted her handshake. It couldn't have been. He didn't seem to be the type who couldn't admit to being wrong, or to hold it against her that she'd gone down the shaft despite his warnings.

The sight of Angus's rotten leg flashed in front of her and she shuddered involuntarily. Jolian said a silent prayer for him. Losing a leg was unthinkable to her, but at least he was alive. Life had never been as fragile as it seemed this past year. She wouldn't let this latest brush with mortality go unnoticed. She would use it as an opportunity to affirm the life in her. Yes, she would take this experience and do something positive. She couldn't let his experience roll off her, it had to matter, for Angus' sake if not her own.

Start living life to the fullest, that's exactly what she would do. No half-baked promises like before. Life was far too fragile, far too precious. This was her life and she needed to make the most of it. And Jolian Caroline Grayson was nothing if not determined!

~ * ~

The tinkling of the bell caught her attention as she pushed open the heavy cedar door to the Barkerville Mercantile.

"Be right with you." She knew Mr. Duke's voice even though she hadn't spent much time at all in his store. He was an exacting man with a voice to match. A bit of nasal pitch to it, just enough to make one think he may be coming down with something. Jolian's eyes roamed the neatly ordered shelves stacked to the ceiling with canned goods, dried goods, staples and luxuries. The selection had certainly grown since her last visit to town!

114

She tried to unclench the muscles of her stomach. It would be fine, just fine. She had probably passed Jakeb like a ship in the night. He was most likely waiting for her back at Pearl's right now. She exhaled audibly and clasped her hands behind her back. How would a boy act in her situation? Probably not with as much emotion showing as she felt right now. Kicking her feet out a bit as she walked, she tried to appear casual and relaxed for Mr. Duke. She neared the cash register and leaned an elbow against the counter.

Mr. Duke had several glass jars of candy lined up on his counter. How odd. She couldn't remember seeing many children in town. Not as many as would support the selection of sweets the Mercantile boasted.

"Got a hankering for a sweet?" Suddenly, Mr. Duke was behind the counter as if he'd appeared out of thin air. He peered down at her from over his spectacles, which were perched on the tip of his nose.

"I must admit, I do have a weakness for salt water taffy." If she chewed on a taffy it would prevent her from having to start a lengthy chitchat. While she enjoyed the extensive conversation they'd had the last time she visited his shop, Jo hoped she could be in and out quickly this time.

"I have a fresh batch behind the counter Joe. I'll fix you a scoop."

"Thank you, Mr. Duke." Jolian took the cone shaped waxed brown paper he offered to her. She felt like a little kid as she peered inside and chose a neatly wrapped red and white taffy. She took it out and offered the cone to Mr. Duke before putting its point in her pocket.

"No thanks, son, you go on ahead. I have an entire sack full of those delicious little morsels. Had them shipped in all the way from back east. Must admit, I've always had a taste for sweets myself." He smiled as he dug a piece of taffy out from behind the counter and popped it into his mouth. There was a bit of an awkward silence with them both chewing on their taffys and neither wanting to speak with his mouth full.

Jolian finished first and tried to sound nonchalant as she inquired after her brother. "Seen Jakeb?"

"Nope, I haven't seen him yet today, Joe. As a matter-of-fact, he didn't show up for his shift last night either. When I heard about the cave-in I assumed he was down there and that was the reason he'd missed his scheduled time. One of the men came by and told me it wasn't Jakeb after all but Angus! Damn shame that. As for Jakeb, I suppose he just forgot."

Jolian tried to swallow her fear and keep her erratic pulse from bursting through her veins. He'd be waiting for her at home surely. She obviously must not have done a very good job of disguising her rising panic. Mr. Duke's features changed to reflect her apprehension.

"I wouldn't worry yourself about it, Joe. Jakeb's forgotten many a thing since he's been in my employ. A shift or two, now and then, an order here and there, his mind's not really on this job. He's thinking of his claim morning, noon and night. But I understand and I'm just thankful for the help. It's so difficult to find any kind of help these days. Most of the capable young men in this town came to mine and can't see themselves doing anything else."

Jolian nodded and thanked him for the information. She didn't want to appear rude but she had a foreboding image filling her mind and she just needed to find her brother quickly. She asked Mr. Duke to add the taffy to her account and he dismissed her with a wave.

"Taffy's on me, son," he hollered after her as she exited the store. "Anything for a fellow sweet tooth!"

~ * ~

Jakeb seemed to have vanished. Her brother had always been a bit of a loner, needing more space and time by himself than the other members of her family. Jolian swallowed hard at the thought. Jakeb was the *only* other member of her family, now. She wasn't about to let negative thoughts overtake her. Jolian walked with purpose through the mud and mire of Front Street toward her horse.

"Hey, Kid!" Jolian turned at the shout not realizing it was directed at her until she saw a giant of a man charging toward her. She pointed a finger at her own chest and when the man nodded she stopped and waited for him to catch up to her.

"William Gilbert, Overlander." The man held his hand out to Jo.

"Jo Grayson." The man's grip was firm as she took his hand and shook it resolutely. As soon as she'd heard the word 'Overlander', Jolian couldn't help but be impressed. The Overlanders had made their journey to the gold fields from back east by way of land—hence their title. The journey had been terribly treacherous, had taken four months and seven people had died. The title of 'Overlander' was in honor

116

of that journey and each member of the party used it following his name to pay tribute to his fellow traveler.

After her own difficult journey to the goldfields, Jolian felt a kind of instant kinship with the Overlander. Jolian looked at the large, stalwart man and mentally added "one" to the "life" side of the tally board.

"What can I do for you, Mr. Gilbert, Overlander?"

"It's what I can do for you, I believe, son." He slapped her hard on the back as he spoke.

"Oh?"

"I heard you was asking about fer your brother Jakeb. Would that be the same Jakeb that works at the mercantile?"

Jolian tried not to appear too hopeful. "It would be, yes. Have you seen him?"

The giant scratched at his bearded chin and smiled. "I did, in fact. Last night I saw him and Hog-Judy heading toward Back street. They were singing and a-carrying on. I believe the whiskey had something to do with it!"

"Hog-Judy?" She couldn't believe it!

"I thought everyone'd heard of her." Again with the backslapping.

"Oh, I know who she is, I'm just surprised that Jakeb would... ah..."

"Your brother's a man ain't he?" The Overlander laughed.

Thinking she may have sounded prudish, Jolian cleared her throat and deepened her voice as she added "Hell ya, I just thought he was broke, that's all."

This time the man ruffled her cap on her head as he bellowed. "Well, son, that's why they call her 'hog'. She doesn't fetch much more than a shilling!"

Jolian tried to laugh heartily like the big man and hoped she didn't appear too pathetic. "You said they were heading to Back Street?"

"Hog-Judy's place I reckoned. I'm walking over that way myself, I can show you if you like."

"I'd be obliged."

"You know, son, you shouldn't be too hard on your brother. Just about every man in this town will go for a ride on the "Hog" eventually. I heard you work up at Pearl's and I'm sure you're partial to the company you keep there. The gals at Pearl's are sweet and fine but old Hog-Judy's cheap and willing. She's just the thing for a man who's broke and 'hard-up', if you know what I mean." Jolian hoped her ribs wouldn't bruise from his elbowing as she tried not to gape at his bluntness. Men were so crude amid their own.

"Here we are." The Overlander said as he rapped on the rickety door of a lean-to. "Hog-Judy, hey, is Jakeb still in there?"

Jolian felt the hairs on her neck begin to rise. The chill of dead silence surrounded them. Something felt terribly wrong here. She couldn't put her finger on it, but as the man rapped again on the door, Jo involuntarily took a step backwards.

"Ain't nothing to be shy about, son." He laughed again as he pulled the door open. "Old Hoggy's probably just sleeping off that whiskey I told you about. She won't mind if we go on in and wake her up. Especially if you've got a hog for her!" His laughter stopped with his expletive.

"Shit! Holy Key-rye-st! What the hell?" The man stepped back from the open door and looked at Jolian with such horror that she knew even before he spoke.

"Someone's killed her! Dad Almighty! They split her wide open or something... There's blood everywhere! Shit!"

The man turned from her and began to heave. Jolian turned as well, and began to walk away. She couldn't look at that, and she didn't have the strength to run. *Jakeb, my God, where was Jakeb?* She didn't want to believe there was any way Jakeb could be involved in this.

Once again death pulled into the lead. What had she been thinking earlier? That she had some control over fate? She had no more control over her life than Angus had about the mine caving in. Her life was caving in. Soon it would all fall in on her and there'd be no more air to breathe.

She had to focus her mind on something. She would concentrate on getting her horse back to Pearl's as soon as possible. Maybe Jakeb would be waiting there for her. Maybe she'd wake up in her cabin and find that this whole horrid day was just a sick demented dream.

Jolian found her horse and mounted. She turned Star toward home and put her heels to the horse's flanks. She felt removed from the whole situation, as if she watched herself from above. She'd felt like this before but she couldn't put her finger on just when or where. She saw the townspeople rushing about and she heard them shouting "Murder! Murder!" but she just rode on toward home.

Ten

Jolian led Star to the barn. She couldn't see anyone right now, not even Jakeb... even if he was here. She took off the saddle, saddle blanket and bridle. She took her time and brushed Star thoroughly. She used the pitchfork to add fresh hay to the stall, filled a manger with oats, led Star in and closed the gate. She took Star's water bucket to the well and filled it with fresh water. She did everything she could think of to do in the barn.

An hour or so later, the barn was as clean as most houses and Jolian no longer had any excuse to avoid people. She should go to her cabin. Jakeb must be there. Or, she could go to Pearl's and deal with all of the questions. There were always so many questions after a murder. What did she see, smell, hear? Who was present? What did the scene look like? What did the murderer look like? How long since she had last seen them alive? Where would she go now that she was an orphan?

Jolian shook her head, to clear her thoughts and walked over to the well. She brought up a bucket of fresh water, removed her cap and dumped the water on her own head. Its coldness was like a slap in the face, soaking her scalp and most of her torso. Just what she needed to bring her back to her senses. This was *not* her parents' murder all over again! She could deal with this, and she *would* deal with it now! That Overlander had linked Jakeb to the murder but it was only his way of thinking. It didn't mean everyone thought that way... did it?

Jolian practically marched all the way to her cabin. The semi-darkness lengthened shadows and quickened her steps until she was all but running. If Jakeb was at the cabin she would deal with that, if he wasn't... She opened the cabin door and a quick survey told her he was not. She let herself in and called his name anyway as she walked through to the back porch, but found herself alone. She'd go back to Pearl's then, maybe he was... there, over there. She knew it! Beside his crumpled bed-sheets were the clothes he'd worn yesterday. She was certain. Jolian picked up the clothes and examined them. They reeked of whiskey, but had not a speck of blood on them! She knew Jakeb could never have committed a crime so, so heinous! She knew it in her heart, but was relieved to find the proof of it nonetheless. She would focus on finding Jakeb and clearing his name. For it was inevitable he'd been linked with the crime in town. She shuddered at the thought. *Put the image of the woman in that lean-to out of your mind.* She couldn't think about it anymore or her sanity really would crumble like the walls of the mine.

Jolian gave her head a shake and stared at Jakeb's dirty clothes on the floor in front of her. She was missing something. Of course! The dirty clothes were also proof Jakeb had been home sometime since last night. He was alive and safe and likely on his way to work at the mercantile right now. Probably he had passed right by her while she had been in the barn.

Jolian smiled to herself as she began to undress. She needed to get out of her sweat-soaked clothing. She had no energy for bathing at the lake tonight. None even for a cloth bath. Tiredness was overtaking her usual fastidiousness around cleanliness. She'd just lie down for a moment on her bed. It was so comfortable.

Oh! The spices, she'd completely forgotten them in her haste to find Jakeb. They'd be safe in her saddlebags. They could wait until tomorrow. Why did her mind always turn to the inane at times like this? *Better inane than insane.* She used what was left of her energy for a half smile.

She supposed she should go and check in at Pearl's. She didn't want to worry Pearl like Jake had worried her. In a moment, she'd lie here for moment longer.

~ * ~

Jakeb sat at a small wooden table in the back of Sassafras Jack's Saloon. Smoke lingered like fingers in the thick, stale air. The smell of old beer wafted through the air, mixed with the scent of beans and urine and clung to his nose hairs. The piano was three tables down and the man who sat before it had been playing the same song over and over for the last half-hour, maybe longer. Still, Jakeb had no idea exactly what song it was supposed to be. Maybe it was a cock-eyed version of Barbry Allen. Not that he was here for the music anyway.

Jakeb took another sip of his whiskey, not too much, just enough to calm his nerves. Damn, it tasted good! Much better than that watered down jug of hooch he'd shared with old Hoggy last night. He felt good. Better than he'd felt in a long time in fact. Last night's encounter had been just what he needed to make him feel like a man again.

Hog-Judy had given him her all for the shared bottle of moonshine just like he'd anticipated. She'd turned out to be a bit feistier than he'd bargained for, but he'd handled it fine. He was beginning to think there was just about nothing he couldn't handle. Then he thought about the letter in his coat. His miserly Uncle! The bastard! Who did he think he was anyway? Sitting up there in his office, in his fancy hotel in San Francisco. Telling him how to run his life. Telling him what he should do and how he should think. He was just his uncle, for Dad's sake. He had no right to try and mess with his life. He'd show him. He'd show them all. They'd learn not to mess with him.

Jakeb tried to keep his gaze moving casually, all the while watching, waiting, deciding. He'd just needed the gold up-front was all. Now he had a plan, he just had to pick out a victim. He'd have to be careful though. Drunken miners could turn ugly quick. He knew that one from experience. Best not to dwell on the past. Especially when the future looked so promising. He'd have to use his best judgment and pick out just the right one. Then, he'd set the trap and wait.

He knew Jolian was going to wonder where he'd gone off to, but he couldn't worry about that now. She was such a goody two shoes she'd probably side with their Uncle. After all, she had something to go back to in San Francisco. That French chef would probably have married her if she'd asked him. *He* knew what Frenchie had been thinking when he offered to give Jolian cooking lessons. The only one who didn't see it was Jo. She'd actually taken him seriously. The joke was on Frenchie in the end too, for Jo had not only learned to cook, but she'd up and left the entire country! Jakeb couldn't help smiling.

He put the glass to his lips and let the last of his whiskey swirl in his mouth before it slipped down to burn in his belly. Yup, he could feel it in his bones; luck was riding in his hip pocket tonight.

~ * ~

Jolian woke with her nose in her armpit. Yuck! She needed to bathe. But first she needed to move! Never in her entire life had her muscles been this stiff! It was as if there was an invisible giant sitting on her body as she tried to lift herself. Every muscle screamed its resentment as she inched her legs over the side of her bed. The air felt as thick as oatmeal and her limbs seemed to be made of a substance resembling cast iron.

As she slowly went about her morning routine, she realized that she never had made it to Pearl's the night before. She'd slept alone in the cabin and hadn't felt nervous at all. *Exhaustion, what a way to relieve fear.* She winced as she lowered her hands into a basin of water. These were definitely no longer the hands of a young lady. How unthoughtful, at least she still had all of her limbs. She thought of Angus and wondered how he was faring this morning. A shiver coursed through her and she hoped the surgery had gone well.

Then there was the other fact she'd completely put out of her mind. She was half owner in a mine. She knew from Jakeb, he and Angus each took fifty percent of the mine. A fair split down the middle, he'd said. Well now, like it or not, her brother had a new partner. Maybe she could finally convince him to sell. If Angus losing his leg didn't bring home the dangers of mining to Jakeb, nothing would.

Jolian dressed at a snail's pace and then reached for her ever-present shako cap. It was becoming such a habit Jolian doubted if she would ever get use to wearing a bonnet again. She tucked her hair up into the cap's band and stared at her reflection. With a heavy sigh she shook her head and left her cabin.

~ * ~

Cooper peered through the transit and noted the angle in his fieldbook. Someone was cooking bacon and his mouth was watering. They'd been surveying the claims for the past three days and the going was slower than they imagined. At this rate he'd not get much time for his own claim.

He decided it was time for a coffee break, that bacon smelled too good. He raised his fists into the air, touched his thumbs together and then snapped his fists apart. Ts'kaw recognized the 'break' sign and repeated it back to him, for confirmation, and began to roll up the chain they used to measure distance. Cooper took the transit down and placed it in its case. He collapsed the tripod stand and hoisted it onto his shoulder. By the time his gear was packed, Ts'kaw had closed the distance between them. The two friends carried their equipment back to their camp by the creek. Cooper was pleased to see it was Guy cooking the bacon.

"Smells good."

"You are not yet tired of bacon, *Mon ami*?"

"Nope." Cooper grinned as he used a fork to scoop several slices of sizzling bacon onto his plate. "Those biscuits done?"

"Help yourself." Guy gestured to the other pan full of pan-fried cakes.

Cooper picked out a biscuit, pulled it partway open and made a face at Guy. "Are these biscuits, or weapons?"

"You have been eating too much of your woman's cooking."

"She's not my woman." Cooper pushed the bacon into the half- opened biscuit and pulled off a bite with his teeth. He exaggerated his chewing, placing a hand on his jaw, as if in pain. "I still say you should go into the catapult business."

"The man who cannot boil water should not judge the man who cannot bake biscuits." Ts'kaw smiled, bit into a biscuit and feigned a broken tooth.

Cooper laughed as he walked away to sit on a boulder by the creek and Guy threw a biscuit at Ts'kaw. "I told you... weapons." He hollered back over his shoulder.

"You are lucky to be out of my range, *Mon ami!*"

Cooper finished chewing his breakfast. Guy's cooking left a lot to be desired, but Ts'kaw was right, he couldn't cook either. Joe's biscuits were like biting into a soft cloud. His woman, hah, just because he liked the way she cooked... and he thought about her all the time... and he'd seen her naked... that still didn't make her his woman.

He hadn't thought about making any woman his again, for a long time. It was a good thought though. He had to admit, he was definitely attracted to her. It was more than Guy had said about wanting to see her naked again, although to be honest with himself, that would be just fine with him.

The way she had looked at him yesterday, when he'd pulled her from the mineshaft and called her a fool. He admired the pluckiness in her eyes. He'd been completely stunned when the Scotsman hollered to him the little brother had dug through the rocks and found Angus. She had spunk; he'd give her that. And stamina!

That was extremely physical work, even for a man. His muscles were aching today. He could only imagine how Joe must feel. He wondered what Joe was short for... probably Josephine. That sounded like such a big formal name for his little angel.

He'd wanted to speak with her after they'd brought Angus up, but he'd felt too ashamed at the time. He should have made certain she was safe at all times. He felt responsible for her; he'd admit that. He'd thought long and hard about his feelings last night, and he knew he only felt shame because she was a woman. He'd have been fine with a boy or a man going into the mineshaft and risking his life. He should have taken her suggestion and put men in that shaft to dig as well, but it had seemed too unstable at the time. She had been right about going down into her brother's mineshaft and he should have at least told her as much.

Damn, he was thankful the mine had held up to Joe's diggings. He'd have to be more careful in the future. Now that he knew her nature, maybe he'd be able to predict her actions more easily. He couldn't just expect she'd be the obedient little woman when he asked her to not do something and, to be honest, that fact made him all the more attracted to her.

He'd never liked weak and submissive women. He needed the woman in his life to be strong in mind and spirit. He wanted interesting and stimulating conversation, someone who had her own opinions and could think for herself. He enjoyed the moments they spent together. Joe was a capable young woman and he revered her courage. He should have told her so the day before. Wouldn't he have said as much if any of the men had risked their lives like she had?

"Back in an hour," Cooper yelled to Ts'kaw, and his friend nodded. He knew he should be getting back to work, but now that he'd started to think about her again, well it wasn't like he was going to be getting a whole lot of work done anyway. He'd ride up to Pearl's place. He'd speak to Pearl first and then to Joe. Pearl knew women much better than he did and if anyone could advise him it would definitely be Pearl.

~ * ~

There was a horse she didn't recognize tied at the post in front of Pearl's. Not that *that* was such an unusual thing; there were always strange horses tied to Pearl's hitching post. The unusual part was that it was still early in the morning. Would Pearl even be awake at this hour? Maybe the fellow, for it was almost certainly a man, had just stayed the night over. Jolian shrugged it off and let herself in the kitchen door.

"Morning, Jo. The Constable here is looking to speak to you abouts yore brother."

The officer of the law, taller than a barber's pole and just as skinny, stood and extended his hand to Jo as Pearl spoke. "Morning."

"Good morning." Jo shook his hand and supposed she should have expected it really. No one else knew about Jakeb's clothes. They were probably still thinking Jakeb had something to do with the murder. She'd have this cleared up in no time. "I know just why you're here."

The Constable cleared his throat and spoke with a nasal whine. "You do?"

"Of course. I'm sure the Overlander told you I was there when he found that woman. I am also sure, he told you he saw my brother with her the night before. But, what you may not know, is I have proof of my brother's innocence."

"You do, do you?" The constable lifted one eyebrow at her. Jolian wasn't sure she approved of this man's tone. He seemed to be mocking her. The man was as unpleasant to her now as he'd been the first time she'd met him. She was certain he had taken an unfounded dislike to her.

"Yes, I do have evidence. It's back at my cabin, although I'm sure once you find Jakeb he'll put your suspicions to rest."

"We have your brother in custody, son."

"You what?"

"Your brother has been arrested for the murder of Hog-Judy, a common street prostitute. If you have some specific evidence that you are withholding as some sort of surprise for the Judge, I'd strongly advise you against it. Judge Begbie will be in town later this week and I can assure you, he is not one for surprises. I will be happy to examine and take into my possession any item you may believe to be relevant to the innocence of your brother. You have my word of honor as an officer of the law and a gentleman the item will be kept in the same condition in which you presented it to me and that it will be accessible as evidence at the trial of your brother."

Jolian opened her mouth to comment and then closed it again. What could she say? This man seemed to think Jakeb was guilty and nothing she could do or say was going to change things. He was unbending and irrational in his dislike for her and her brother. Jolian felt his prejudice marred his judgment but it seemed Jakeb, like it or not, was in for a few nights in the local jail. At least now she knew for certain he was safe, from the murderer at least. She blew at a delinquent curl that had escaped her cap and dangled into her lashes.

"I don't claim to know a whole lot about the law, Constable Towers, but I'm thinkin' that yore way of speaking to Jo ain't right. Y'all don't need to be treatin' Jo like he's the one that done somethin' wrong." Pearl shook a chubby finger in the Constable's face.

"I do not believe that was my intent. If that was the impression you perceived, then it is you who are in error... ahem... Madam." The constable turned to stare hard at Jo. "I do, however, wish to make it clear, as his closest relative, you will most likely be called as a character witness."

"Jo, I thinks you and I need to have a discussion over in the hall for a moment." Pearl spoke so sweetly that Jo immediately assumed the worse and followed her to the hall between the kitchen and the parlor.

"Jo, did ya hears him?"

"Yes, he thinks I might have to testify for Jakeb. That's fine with me."

"You cain't." Pearl looked about and mopped her brow with her hanky.

"Why not?"

"You cain't testify yore tellin' the truth about yore brother, when you ain't tellin' the truth about yoreself." Pearl indicated Jo's boyish clothes with a sideways glance up and down the length of her.

"Biscuits! I hadn't even thought about that. I don't think I want to discuss that with the Constable either. He seems to have taken a dislike to me right from the start." Jo twisted her fingers into a knot.

"Yore right about that. Although I wouldn't be worryin' yerself too much about him. From what I've heard, he talks high-falutin' but he's purty much bacon-brained. Let's just get him outta here and we'll think on what to do." Jolian smiled at Pearl's colorful description, nodded and followed her back into the kitchen.

As luck would have it, the Constable was waiting at the door, hat in hand. "I must take my leave, unless you wish to present me with that evidence you spoke of earlier."

She wished she had more definitive proof of Jakeb's innocence but she wouldn't let the Constable see her uncertainty. "I will bring it with me, Constable Towers, sir, as I will be coming to Richfield shortly to visit my brother. I assume you're holding him in the jail there?"

"We are. Visiting allowed from noon until two." The Constable spoke out of the side of his mouth as he puffed his chest up and ran his finger and thumb along the brim of his hat.

"I will be there at noon then."

The Constable put on his hat and with a curt nod, left by the back door.

Jo watched out the window as the Constable rode away, then she turned to speak with Pearl.

"I guess I'm going to have to stop the charade of being a boy now."

"It does seem like its yore only choice. It'da be against the law fer ya to testify as a boy, I'm shore."

"Yes, they could charge me with perjury."

"I ain't the one ta talk to about juries. I've avoided the law all my life. Or paid to have them avoid me as the case may be."

"Pearl." Jolian couldn't help but smile at her friend's confusion of the words. "Pearl, I need to ask you to keep my secret, for now at least. I'm going to soak some of this stiffness out in a warm bath. Then, I'm going back to my cabin and get Jakeb's clothes and my savings for a lawyer. I hope you can manage without me today. I'll decide what I'm going to do after I speak with Jakeb."

Pearl helped Jolian set the heavy cast iron pot onto the stove to heat water for her bath. "My word is my word, Jo. Until you tell me different, I ain't tellin' no one that youse a girl."

Eleven

Cooper slowed his horse and steered him toward the barn. Storm may as well get out of the heat and enjoy some of Pearl's hay while he attended to this business. If everything went the way he was planning he should be back to work before Ts'kaw really needed him.

Cooper took off his hat and slapped it against his thigh to rid it of trail dust. He ran his fingers through his hair and placed the hat back on his head. One more deep breath and he'd go and face the music. She'd probably be angry. She hadn't looked angry yesterday, but if the roles were reversed, he certainly would be.

His footsteps echoed on the hollow of the back porch, knuckles decisively rapping the wooden door. Cooper exhaled the breath he unwillingly held. He couldn't believe guilt could have such a big effect on his mind and body.

Pearl answered his knock and filled the doorway. "Howdy, stranger. Heard ya was lookin' fer me yesterday."

"Morning, Pearl. Yes, I was. And I do want to speak with you but first, or actually maybe I should... Is Joe here?"

"What's got yore gut in a knot?" Pearl laughed heartily as she walloped him on the back. "Nothing that warnt be fixed by some a Jo's cookin' I reckon?"

"Now that you mention it, I could use a bite." Cooper relaxed and let his anxiety slip to the back burner. There was no rush, really. Guy could work the transit if he was late getting back. He might as well take advantage of the opportunity to eat properly. After all, a man had to keep up his strength, working out in this heat.

"Jo was here earlier on, but ah, *he's* gone back to his cabin to git a few things. D'ya hear the Constable arrested Jakeb fer that murder?"

"Jakeb? For murdering Hog-Judy? The boy hasn't really amounted to much, but I wouldn't think he'd be capable of murder."

Pearl nodded, setting her chins a flapping. "Jo agrees with ya. He told the Constable he kin prove it, too."

Cooper looked the woman square in the eyes. "What do you mean prove it? Jo's isn't about to do anything unsafe?"

"Naw, Jo's got some evidence fer them. Some of Jakeb's clothes or something." Pearl poured him a cup of coffee and handed him a slice of cornbread smothered in raspberry preserves.

"Thank you." Cooper breathed a sigh of relief. "Well I guess that couldn't do any harm. Do you have a minute, Pearl? I could really use some advice."

Cooper stared into his coffee and let his mind go back in time. He shared his secret of how he'd spied on Joe, and that he knew she was really a woman. "The thing is, Pearl, I just can't see a way to tell her without embarrassing her." Cooper looked up from his coffee cup when Pearl didn't respond.

"Jo is out back at the cabin. I think y'all better have a talk. And that's all I's saying."

"I could use your help, Pearl."

"I knows it. Don't think I don't. Yore my friend, Cooper Holt. Ya've helped me more times than I could count. But when you brought Jo here I made a promise. I might be nothin' but an old whore, but when I give my word I stick to it."

"Pearl, I—"

"Git yerself to the cabin."

~ * ~

Jo knelt at the foot of her bed and sobbed into the crook of her elbow. It was gone, all of it! She had nothing left now. What was she going to do? Who could have taken it? She couldn't believe it was Jakeb, but no one else knew where she kept her gold. Jakeb had watched her transfer the nuggets into the new reticule; he was the only one who knew where the gold was hidden. It was their future, it was going to pay for their tickets home. Roots, it was going to buy her roots. For the first time in her life she was going to have a home that no one could take away from her but now, someone had.

"Oh, Jakeb, how could you?" Her house... and his lawyer, it was going to pay for his lawyer. How could he have done it? How could he?

"Joe?"

Cooper? What the...? He was knocking on her cabin door! Jo sat up quickly and tried to dry her eyes. She glanced in the mirror but it was no use, her eyes were swollen and red, he'd know she'd been crying. Maybe if she stayed quiet he'd just go.

A sob racked her body and the sound escaped her lips. She put her hand to her mouth to try and hide the noise.

"Joe? I know you're inside. Can I please come in? I'm sure you must be angry, I'd like to talk to you about it."

Angry? You bet she'd be angry, just as soon as she could get over this feeling of utter hopelessness. The sobs were becoming irrepressible now, and she just let them come. What difference did it make anyway? She was going to have to start all over. All those months of scraping and saving her pay—for what? For nothing! She couldn't ask anyone for help. They all knew she'd been saving her money. How could she explain why she needed money now? She was mortified that her own brother had stolen from her. She couldn't tell people the truth. What was she going to do?

She couldn't hear Cooper at her door any more. He'd probably left. Her breath came in shudders as her tears fell uncontrollably. She didn't care who heard her. She had nothing, nothing left but tears.

Then suddenly, he was there, the man from her dreams. Holding her, kissing her neck, nuzzling her with words of comfort. It felt so good to be held by someone. His arms were stronger than she'd imagined. She needed the strength of him. Her body formed to his as he pulled her closer. He lifted her chin to study her face and she was struck again by the splendor of the green flecks in his blue eyes. He bent his head and touched his lips to her so gently, that at first, she believed it really was a dream. She raised her lips to meet his and felt his arms tighten about her. Feelings of sadness were irrevocably erased.

The musky scent of him filled her nostrils as she reveled in the sweet taste of his kiss and the tingle of his moustache on her skin. He slid one hand to the nape of her neck and cradled her head in his palm. His lips were gentle upon hers; barely kissing, then biting, tempting, teasing. A moan of pure pleasure escaped her lips and seemed to incite him. His other hand ran down the length of her forearm and around to the small of her back. His fingers caressed her neck while his other hand massaged and squeezed and lowered to her bottom. "Joe, Joe," he murmured as he pulled her hips to his and she pressed her hand against the rock wall of his chest.

Her lips parted under the pressure of his and a new kind of shudder ran through her. His tongue touched hers and she melted into the sensation. His hands roamed her back while his lips explored her mouth. A shiver coursed through the length of her. His breath, hot on her neck... She wanted more.

His lips, his hands, his tongue, all were leaving her breathless but she didn't care. Her hands moved against his chest, seeking to explore more of him. She felt alive and free as though a part of her was awakening. As if she had come out of herself and was a different person. A woman like the one from her dreams.

But even her dreams could not compare to what she was feeling now. She wrapped her hands around his neck and let her fingers spread through the thickness of hair at the base of his neck. Oh, how she'd longed to do this! His hair, substantial and lustrous in her fingers, was just as she'd imagined it would be. He moaned in response and she felt the shiver cascade down her body again. Could it be her touch, caused him to feel the same way?

Cooper cupped her buttocks and pulled her body towards his. A sigh escaped her and he growled a response. Gently, he eased her back onto the bed and lay beside her, cradling her in his arms. She could feel the hard length of him against her soft abdomen and it caused her pulse to quicken, her breath to become ragged. This was all so new, so thrilling! Her body's actions raced ahead of her thoughts. His lips left hers and traveled again to the base of her neck, blazing a path of kisses that stirred fires in the center of her being.

"Don't stop..." her voice pleaded with husky passion.

Her words seemed to break the spell and he pushed her to arm's length. Jolian was dazed. Did he think she had asked him *to* stop?

"Damn!" Cooper swore under his breath. "What am I doing?"

Cooper rose from the bed and raked his hair with his fingers. He stood with his back to the bed as if he was loathe to look at her. Jolian didn't understand. Had she moved too fast? Maybe he felt she was too forward. Should she have been more reserved? Thinking back on her behavior caused a blush to rise in her cheeks, she could feel it. She'd even moaned in pleasure! He must be disgusted with her actions. She'd behaved like... like a whore! She sat up on the bed and folded her hands in her lap. What was she doing? What had happened to her vows of chastity and to keep away from miners? Was she so soft in principle that a few kisses could sway her moral fortitude? And why was Cooper kissing someone he believed to be a boy?

"Cooper, I mean, Mr. Holt, I apologize for the way I behaved..."

"You?" Cooper spun around to face her and in one fluid motion he pulled her from the bed into his arms. He stared fully in to her eyes as if beseeching her to believe him. "You have nothing to apologize for. I am the one who should be apologizing, for taking advantage when you were in such a state. I am sorry, Joe, I've just wanted this for a while, imagined it even... and then seeing you like this—"

"I never fooled you then? My disguise was so transparent?"

"No..." He relaxed his hold on her and lowered his chin.

"I suppose all of the others know as well."

"Ts'kaw knew from the start, and Guy—"

"You all must think I'm such a fool, dressing as a boy."

"No, Joe. Nobody thinks you're a fool. Nobody could ever think that about you." He pulled her close and pressed his cheek against her hair.

"Was that coffee I smelled when I came in?" He pulled away from her and walked towards the kitchen, then, as he reached the doorway, he turned an uneasy look back on her.

"I can easily make a pot, if you'd like."

"Thanks, Joe, but no, I'll pass."

Jo nodded like she understood but really she couldn't make sense at all of what had just occurred. Coffee and kisses and confusion. The men knew all along that she was a woman and yet they brought her to work at a house of prostitution? She thought they were fooled by her masquerade. Why hadn't someone said something earlier? And then Cooper had apologized for the kisses. If he didn't think she was brazen then why should he be ashamed of holding her?

Biscuits! Why did she have to keep second-guessing herself? The result of years of strict upbringing she supposed. Society's rules once more. She wouldn't let that ruin this moment. She'd just had her first kiss! She was going to let herself savor the memory not scrutinize it to death. Right now she didn't care if the whole world thought she was a whore. Right now all that she cared about was the man of her dreams had kissed her and it felt good. She'd enjoyed his kisses and the way he'd held her. She needed his strength. She would particularly need it now, that she had so much of the outside world to face. She pushed the negative thoughts from her mind for good.

"Joe? Say, what is Joe short for anyway?" He'd moved to her side again and she wanted to be in his arms. She needed to be held by him. She moved closer and whispered her name in his ear.

"Jolian."

His arms encircled her waist and he whispered back "Jolian? That's an unusual name."

"Yes, it's my mother's creation, half of my father's name and half of my Uncle's." Jolian wound her fingers into the hair on his neck. "She always told me she wanted a strong name for me. One that would serve me well when times were tough and when times were tender. I never really knew what she meant by that."

"Jolian..."

Her name on his lips sounded like a seduction and she offered her mouth to his. Now she knew what her mother had meant about tender times as she felt herself sink into his embrace. His touch was gentle, almost exasperatingly so. She wanted more of him. She wanted him to touch more of her. His lips on hers, his hands on her body, they were driving her wild with desire. He kept whispering her name, softly, over and over. And she answered 'yes' to his every advance. His lips left hers and brushed the hair at the nape of her neck. He cradled her cheeks in his palms and gazed into her eyes.

"You were crying, Jolian, when I came in. Is it your brother?"

He knew about Jakeb's arrest. She answered his questions about Jakeb and told him of the evidence she had.

"The clothes aren't really going to be much proof, I'm afraid. You see, Jolian, you could be bringing the Constable any old set of clothes and saying Jakeb wore them on the night of her murder. You have no proof he was wearing that shirt and those pants." Cooper moved his arms to hug her waist.

"Well, Jakeb only has two sets of clothes and he's wearing the other set in jail!" She hadn't meant to shout, but he had taken away her only hope. Pitiful though it may be.

"I know," he whispered to her like she was a child. He reached for her hand and stroked the back of it with his thumb.

"Don't worry, angel, Jakeb will be fine. Judge Begbie may be called 'the hanging judge', but he would never sentence a man unjustly. He'll get to the bottom of this. Let's put our trust in the law." She nodded her response.

"Are you going to visit Jakeb?" He pulled back to look into her eyes.

"Yes, I had planned to..."

"Could I come by later then? To see what the Constable had to say I mean."

"Of course. Oh, I've told Pearl I'm spending the night at the big house tonight. With Jakeb away and all, I'd just feel safer there." His eyes were magnificent. She could spend forever gazing into them.

"I could meet you there. At say, nine o'clock?"

"That would be fine." She suddenly felt awkward. What exactly had happened here? He'd kissed her and she didn't know what to do next. What did his kisses mean really? He'd called her 'Angel' and said he'd waited a while to kiss her. She must mean something to him if he'd given her a pet name. Were their kisses special or did everyone kiss like they had? If everyone did, how did anything ever get done in the world? How she wished she'd had more experience with men.

Cooper was leaning forward. Did he mean to kiss her again? Jolian raised her lips and closed her eyes. She felt his kiss—on her cheek!

"Take care of yourself, Jolian."

She just stood there like a fool; her lips puckered in the air, watching him leave. Cooper closed the door without looking back and Jo raised her eyes to the roof of her bedroom. A groan escaped her lips. She wanted to crawl into bed and never get out again. Embarrassment filled her from head to toe!

She turned her mind to his kisses and felt her face begin to redden further. Her first kiss... her first real kiss. She'd never imagined anything as wonderful in all of her fantasies. He'd kissed her; he'd really kissed her!

Jolian hugged herself and then let her arms open wide. She spun in circle after circle and giggled to herself as she fell onto the bed. She squeezed her own shoulders and pressed her hand to her lips. The memory of his lips was still warm on hers. His were not just kisses, they were *kisses*!

~ * ~

Cooper walked away from the cabin with long purposeful strides. He'd barely made it out of there. He couldn't even look back because if he did, he knew he'd turn around. God help her if he turned around. No, he'd continue on without looking back. Caution was the word; he was going to have to be more cautious. This wasn't one of Pearl's experienced girls he was dealing with, this was Jolian.

He loved her name! Jolian. He would never shorten it again. Her mother had been right when she said what she had about the name. He suddenly wished he'd had the opportunity to meet Jolian's mother, if only to give him a glimpse of Jolian in the future. He was anxious to know her in every way he could. She was so beautiful, even with her eyes puffy from her tears and her lips pouting from his kisses. She smelled good, too. Her hair had felt like fine silk against his skin and her response to his advances had thrilled him. He'd been with her like that so many times in his fantasies. Oh, he was going to get himself in trouble again.

He should've told her the truth, of how he saw her. But, then again, he didn't want to embarrass her. She seemed embarrassed enough with what he'd done. Her cheeks were even glowing with his shame. Could he not have come in here and comforted her without taking advantage of her? Did he have no honor left at all where women were concerned?

Cooper put haste in his step and tried to push the image of her pouting lips from his mind. Too late. Just the thought of her lips filled his mind with their tenderness, their sweet response to his. His moustache had reddened the skin around her mouth and neck. He vowed then and there to stay clean shaven. He would never hurt her, even unintentionally. He was going to have to keep his desires in check. He had almost no self-control back in that cabin and that simply couldn't happen again. He'd have to start thinking of something other than those soft pouting lips that wanted kissing.

He rubbed the whiskers forming on his chin and tried to focus his mind on the task at hand. There were some serious allegations to disprove and he had his work cut out for him. He'd start with passing around the picture of the suspected murderer that the Royal engineer had given him and Jolian had improved. If anyone in town could identify the man, his guilt in the murder of Hog-Judy would practically be a certainty and Jakeb could be set free.

From the time that he'd heard about the murder of Hog-Judy, he'd had an ugly thought forming in the back of his mind. He had a feeling that the man who had murdered Jolian's parents had struck again. It wasn't anything he wanted to alarm Jolian about and the thought, it seemed, had not yet occurred to her. She was probably too worried about getting her brother out of jail. That was good. If she could keep on that train of thought she'd be less likely to do something foolish. Jakeb was safe, for the time being and as long as she was at Pearl's, Jolian should be out of harm's way as well.

~ * ~

He was lying face down on the cot in the corner trying to get some sleep. When the guard at the door announced his *brother's* presence, Jakeb mumbled his response.

"I don't want to see him. Tell him I'm sleeping."

"I am already here, Jakeb."

"I don't feel like talking right now, Jo." *What was she doing here?* He could handle this on his own.

"So it seems. You may not have anything to say to me Jakeb, but I surely have a thing or two to say to you."

"Keep your voice down!" Jakeb sat up and hissed out his whisper. "Do you want the Constable to hear everything?"

"I don't care who hears it now, Jakeb! What difference does any of it make now that you've taken my savings?"

"I—How did you find out?" Damn! Now guilt edged his thoughts. How would he ever figure a way out of this situation if he had guilt gnawing at his mind?

"We need money for a lawyer." Her honest face peered through the bars at him.

"They'll provide one if I don't have the money."

"Well that's good because you don't have it and now, neither do I. What on earth were you thinking? What could be so important that you would have to steal from your own sis... from me?" There was anger in her voice and he couldn't bear it.

He couldn't answer her. He had no response to her questions. She was right to blame him because he was guilty. It didn't make any difference now. He would have to show her the letter from their Uncle and come clean, it was the only way. She had a right to know why he'd taken her money, especially now there was no chance of him winning it back.

He stood, pulled the letter from his pocket and turned it over in his handcuffed hands. He looked up at his sister. She stood before him with her hands on her hips; her hat pulled so low on her head he almost missed the look in her eyes. Her silence demanded a response. She had guts and strength and stamina. She would never steal *his* savings.

He was a loser. He always had been. The past two years had been entirely his fault. He saw that now, everything was so clear. Jolian had a right to know the truth but he didn't think he could tell her. She still loved him; he could see it in her eyes. Yes, it was still there, under all of her anger and determination. The only other people who had ever loved him like that were his parents. The guilt of their death pushed Jakeb to sit back down on the bed. If he were to be hanged, he'd go to his grave with one person loving him. That ought to count for something at the pearly gates. Nope, he wouldn't tell her. He couldn't lose the only person in the whole world who still cared about him, he couldn't. He lay down and rolled back over on his cot.

"Go home, Jo, I can't talk to you now."

"What were you going to give me just then? Was it a note from that Hog-Judy or something? Could we use it for your defense? Jakeb, Jakeb, will you roll over and talk to me please?"

"Go home, Jo."

"Jakeb Adam Grayson, sit up and speak to me! I cannot help you if you won't help yourself!"

He buried his head into the moth-eaten wool blanket as he stared at the wall.

"Go home, Jo."

~ * ~

Jolian turned and stomped her foot. It was a girlish thing to do but she didn't care. His behavior was so frustrating! She stood there with her back to the cell trying to think of a way to make him talk to her. How could she help him if she didn't know what was going on? What reason could he possibly have for not wanting to speak with her? That was childish. He was simply being childish.

Maybe, he was afraid of her anger over the theft of the money. She probably should have stuck to her original plan of forgiveness, instead of blaming him straight away like she'd done. No wonder he didn't want to speak to her. She turned to face the cell. Jakeb still lay close to the wall, his body curled into itself. He was scared and alone, and had she been the least bit supportive?

"Jakeb, I'm sorry I was so angry. Jakeb? Look, we'll forget all about the money. I won't even mention it again. I want to help, Jakeb. Please talk to me."

He hadn't even moved. Jolian dropped her shoulders and turned to leave. She'd come back tomorrow. Give him the night to think it over. She was sure Jakeb would talk to her once her apology sunk in through his thick head.

Stiff with dignity and purpose, Jolian walked down the hall toward the Constable's office. The man stood at the edge of his desk looking in her direction as if he were waiting for her, knowing she would have no luck with Jakeb.

Jo liked most people straight off, but there was something about the Constable she didn't trust. Still, he was the only law in the area, until that Judge arrived, and so it seemed he was also her only hope. Since she couldn't use any of her feminine wiles to charm him, (not that she had any anyway) she would have to come directly to the point.

"What do you think about those clothes then?"

"I am afraid they don't mean much to the law, kid. Good try though. You sure you weren't *with* your brother at the time of the murder?"

The tin of his thin laughter stung her ears. He mocked her attempts to save her brother? What kind of lawman was he? As if convicting her brother before his trial wasn't enough, now the man was trying to crush her self-esteem in the process. She was more of a man than he was, and she'd prove it!

She swallowed her disgust and smiled at him.

"I wasn't *with* my brother at the time of the murder, but I am sure I will find the evidence needed to clear Jakeb of the crime."

The constable snorted. "Judge Begbie should be in town tomorrow, so your brother's trial will most likely be set for the day after that. They call him the 'hanging judge' you know."

Jolian wanted to slap the snide look off of his face. She wanted to tell him exactly what she thought of his sarcastic grin and antagonizing attitude. Instead she raised her chin and looked directly into his eyes. "I am certain, that to be made a Judge in this country you must be not only a fair man but a man with great knowledge of the law. I feel confident Judge Begbie will find my brother to be innocent because I am sure his vast intellect will allow him to see the obvious. I believe he will be very interested to hear just how much help *you* have been in seeking justice. Good day, sir."

Her speech complete, she turned on her heel and exited the building. She had no idea what the 'obvious' thing was that she spoke of but she was sure the Constable didn't either and it would give him something to ponder. Better for him to think about the fact he may have imprisoned the wrong man, than to think of ways to irritate her and Jakeb.

She wished there was an 'obvious' to discover and that she was clever enough to find it. The only thing she could surmise was that Jakeb had been seen around town with Hog-Judy, and why would someone who planned to commit murder let himself be seen with his victim. No doubt the prosecutor would argue he had never planned to kill her, or that he killed in a fit of rage. From what the Overlander had described of the scene, it certainly sounded like someone had fury in his heart.

A deep sense of despair overwhelmed the proud carriage she'd put on for the Constable and her shoulders slumped their response. She hoisted herself onto Star's saddle with what little strength she had left and steered the reins towards home.

Twelve

Jolian sat in front of the oval mirror in her bedroom. She scrubbed her face with a wet cloth until her skin was red and rosy looking. In her heart she knew she wanted to make herself look nice for Cooper, but there was no use in trying to pretty herself up when she still had to dress as boy. Jakeb would stand trial for murder in two days and the world would have to know her identity then. Meanwhile, she'd continue her charade. She didn't need anything more to handle at the moment.

But, to be honest, she just wanted to put on a dress, march over to Pearl's and throw herself into Cooper's arms. The memories of his lips on hers would have to sustain her until they could meet in private again. A sigh escaped her, loud enough to be heard at Pearl's she was certain.

Jolian carefully bound her breasts in muslin and put on her clothing. She may have to look like a boy, but she didn't have to smell like one. She'd dab a little lavender behind her ears. That would set Vera's brain a buzzin'!

Darkness began to surround the tiny cabin, so Jo lit a candle to brighten her spirit. She took her revolver out of its special pocket in her trousers, checked the bullets in the barrel and then returned it. She had half an hour or so before she needed to meet Cooper and her weary body begged her to lie down. She couldn't understand her tiredness. Since Jakeb's arrest she had felt more lethargic with each passing hour it seemed. Just when she should be using all of her extra time to come up with some sort of plan, her body betrayed her and forced her to rest. Maybe she'd just lie down for a few minutes before her meeting with Cooper.

~ * ~

Jolian woke with a start. It was pitch black outside her window and the candle had burned almost half way down! She sat up quickly and had to pause for her eyes to focus. She was going to be late. Quickly, she ran a brush through her hair and shoved her cap on her head. She licked her fingers, extinguished the candle and let herself out the door.

A shiver of moon hung high in the night sky and the air was heavy with the musty scent of the last of the raspberries. Her feet knew the path so well she felt sure she could make the distance to Pearl's with her eyes closed. As her feet slipped into the darkness, the old fear began to rear its ugly head and Jolian wished she had brought the candle from her cabin. Even the crickets had stopped their usual twitter.

She stopped and let her eyes adjust to the surrounding blackness, pricking her ears for any sound that should or shouldn't be heard. Her own breathing gave answer and so she concentrated on slowing it while trying to convince herself of the fatuity of her fear. Slowly, she began to breathe normally. Her eyes focused on objects and her fear of the dark left with her emerging perceptibility. While the moon's thinness hardly contributed to the visibility, there were thousands upon thousands of stars. She focused on them and it gave her an odd sense of belonging to feel the presence of the night sky.

As a child, when she had first learned of Heaven, her mother had looked up into the vast darkness with her, and spoke of the stars. She told Jolian the stars were made from the glorious light of Heaven shining through pinholes in the night sky. She told her once you departed this life you could forever watch over those you left behind on Earth by peaking through a star at night. Funny how she'd suddenly remembered a childhood conversation, she hadn't thought of it in years. Jolian gazed at the stars above her and wondered if her mother watched over her now. It was a comforting thought.

Confident she wouldn't trip in the darkness now her eyes had adjusted, she began to hurry her steps until she was almost at a run. She stopped herself. She wasn't so late she had to get herself in a panic and arrive perspiring and all out of breath. Jolian took several deep breaths and slowed the beating of her heart. The last thing she wanted was to appear frantic to see him. She'd already got things off to a dodgey start, according to the principles her mother had advocated.

The kiss they had shared would have been saved for a wedding night, if her mother had still been alive (or if she could wield any power over the living from her place in the stars). There was one thing about growing up with a mother with such a strict sense of morality; you had enough guilt to last you a lifetime! But then again, thanks to her mother's imagination and encouragement, she had enough dreams to last her a lifetime, too.

As she neared Pearl's she could see the lanterns on the front porch had been lit. A sign to all, that Pearl's Place was open for business. Jolian naturally turned to towards the back door where the darkness would conceal her arrival. Halfway between the front and back porches were the large glass windows of the parlor. The windows were framed like pictures with their velvet green swag curtains. The lamps from the parlor cast their luminescence out into night like a beacon calling to her. She stayed her course and walked closer.

There he was, his feet planted firmly on the hard wood floor. His head was thrown back in laughter over something in his conversation with Doralynn. Jolian felt a twinge in her chest as she stopped in her tracks.

Staying put, lest he think she was spying on him, which, of course, she was, she willed the moment to last forever and knew she would always remember this night. She watched Cooper through the huge paned glass window and it felt as though he were a dream come to life. He emptied the glass he held and Doralynn placed her hand over his as she took it from him. Again with the twinge in her chest. *Was it jealousy?* It didn't seem to describe the feeling.

Her eyes stayed focused on him as he moved a few steps over to whisper something in Pearl's ear. The movement stirred the memory of his lips near her own ear and a warm feeling flowed through her. Could she be falling for this man? Her, the 'boy' who had sworn herself to spinsterhood? Of course, she had made that decision without ever letting a man get close to her.

Maybe she'd been too hasty with her condemnation of men. They weren't all the same and even those with the foulest of qualities had some good points as well. Her Uncle, for example, had always been exceedingly kind to her Mother, regardless of the cruelty he had inflicted on the other members of her family.

Her family. Some of the people she stared at now were just as much 'family', if not more so, than her Uncle. Pearl had taken her in and given her work, shelter and kindness. Doralynn always had a kind word of encouragement for her. And Cooper, was there anything that man hadn't done for her in the past six months?

It seemed odd that she could feel so close yet at the same time so distant. The distance was because of her charade. She needed to tell everyone the truth about her gender. There was no use hiding it any longer. Given Jakeb's trial and the fact Pearl and Cooper knew, what *was* the point of keeping it from the others now?

Jolian started for the front porch. She might as well go straight in the front door and tell everyone without hesitation. The trouble was finding the right words. She just couldn't blurt out to the girls that for the entire time she'd known them she'd lied to them. That was the problem with lies; you could slip into one as smooth as satin but getting out of it was tougher than untangling a double-knotted corset.

The snort of a horse jolted her attention to a rider who approached the front porch as well. Too lost in her thoughts to notice earlier, Jolian now had no way of getting around him without a greeting. Keeping her voice low and scrunching as far down into the collar of her flannel shirt as she could manage, Jo let out a muffled "Evening" and turned toward the back entrance once more.

"Hang on there boy—" The man's voice boomed and commanded her compliance.

Jo halted in her spot and shrunk down further into her flannel. She dreaded this, the meeting of a customer. Stupid! Now she would have to have a conversation with this man.

"This here Pearl's Place?" He jerked his thumb towards the building.

"That's what the sign above the door says." She couldn't keep the annoyance at her own stupidity out of her voice. It made her speak with an insolence that shocked even her. "Or can't you read?"

The minute the words left her mouth she wanted to apologize, but then the man's laughter echoed in her ears.

"Yore quite an upstart fer a runt!"

He put his hand to his belly as he laughed again. Then he stopped abruptly and leaned forward on his horse, peering at Jolian in the darkness. So close, she could smell the whiskey on his breath. He sneered at her, an odd glint in his black eyes. Saliva shot through a hole in his leer where a tooth should have been.

"Is thar a red head inside?"

Jolian's skin crawled up her arm and choked in her throat, strangling the air to her lungs. She forced her hand to creep into her trouser pocket for her revolver. That laugh... it was... oh dear Lord! *Him... not just a customer... him...*

"Answer me runt or yule be wearing my slap!"

"W-what?" She managed to choke out.

"A redhead, dammit! I fancy some fire tonight an' I wanna git me a redhead."

She tried to focus on what he said but her gun wasn't in her pocket! How could she have been so careless? She'd had it earlier.

"Runt! I'm askin' ya a question. Do ya or don't ya know if'n I kin find a redheaded whore inside?"

Jolian bobbed her head up and down and hoped he'd just leave her alone. The last thing she wanted to do was make this man angry.

"The cat got yer tongue boy? Gimme her name. The name of the whore, runt! *Or caint you speak?*" He mimicked Jo's earlier tone.

"VVVera."

"Vera, you say, hey?" He sat upright on his horse and slowly licked his lips. "Vera the redhead, yore in fer the ride of yore life!" He hollered his promise out into the night as he dismounted and flung the horse's reins about the hitching post.

Move feet! She felt like she'd been rooted to her spot. The murderer of her parents was walking right towards her and she was frozen. No gun, where was her gun?

Move feet! Run! Her heart beat inside her chest like the living would beat inside a coffin. He stood before her now. So close she could stab him with her knife, put a shot in his belly. But she had no weapon, she had nothing.

"You still here?" Spittle ran down his bearded chin as hissed at her. "Git!"

Jolian spun around and ran, as fast as her wobbling legs would carry her, down the length of the building. She could feel his breath on her neck, racing behind her, but it was only her fear pushing her away from him. Laughter ringing with the din of death echoed in the air. She ran until she reached the back porch and turned the corner to hide herself from his view. Not that he would care about the likes of her now. He seemed pretty intent on getting his hands on Vera.

Jolian leaned her back against the wood siding and let her breath catch up to her. She had sent him in there to Vera! But really, what else could she have done? She dared a peak around the corner. He was climbing the steps, nearing the front door. She'd let that monster walk right by her, into the place where only moments earlier she had concluded her "new" family dwelled. He'd already killed her family once and she wasn't going to let him do it again. He was in there now with Pearl, Doralynn and Cooper! And Vera, poor Vera. She had to do something.

Jolian sprinted to her cabin. It was her only chance. She knew who he was but *he* didn't know that. Which is precisely what would give her the upper hand. She entered the cabin and wasted no time in lighting a candle and finding her gun, which was lying on the floor a few feet from her bed. It must have fallen out when she'd napped earlier. How could she have been so careless? She just hoped she wasn't too late.

Jolian stuffed the gun into her waistband and opened the bureau drawer where she kept the extra bullets. She dumped the whole box into the pocket of her trousers and began to run back to Pearl's. She was halfway there when she stopped short. She needed a plan. What could she do? She couldn't just waltz right in there and shoot the man. She had the nerve to do it; at least she thought she could. But what if when it came right down to it her hand hesitated? A split second could mean life or death for any one of the people in Pearl's Place right now and that was a chance that Jo was not willing to take. She needed a plan and she needed it fast.

She walked towards Pearl's with her mind racing. What could she do? What did *she* know? Cooking, she knew cooking inside and out. And vegetation, thanks to Aklu'ut. Edible, non-edible... That was it, her only chance at a quick and sure-fire plan. She would have to work fast and she would have to work accurately.

~ * ~

Cooper recognized the man from Jolian's drawing as soon as he entered Pearl's. Pearl had approached the louse, welcomed him and supplied him with a tumbler of whiskey, as he had requested. Cooper heard him bellowing about a redhead while Pearl spoke to him about the basic "rules" of the house. Furtively, Cooper made his way up the stairs towards Vera's room. He slipped inside and put his finger to his lips as a startled Vera began to speak.

"Vera," he spoke in hushed tones "There's a fellow downstairs that's asking for you and you need to know more about him than he's going to reveal."

"Oh, honey, aren't you the most! All I needs ta know about any man is what theys most certainly is gonna reveal ta me! After all I gets paid for them ta reveal it!" She laughed at her own joke, sat back down on her ottoman and continued applying rouge to her cheeks. "Y'all are sweet, but tell him I'll be down shortly."

"Vera, this is serious. He's the man who murdered Jo's parents and if I'm not mistaken, Hog-Judy as well."

"Hoggy?" Vera's eyes widened. "But she was split open from arse to teakettle!"

"That's why I am here to warn you Vera."

"Warn me? What the hell good does that do me?" Panic lit her eyes.

"That ma—" the words came through clenched teeth, "downstairs, is determined to find you and he's asking for you by name. I want to send one of the girls off for the Constable and I'll stay close by you. You have my word, Vera, he won't harm one little red hair, but you have to do *everything* I say."

A glint replaced the fear in her eyes as Vera sauced, "Oh, honey, I been waiting my whole life to hear them words from you!"

~ * ~

Jolian slipped silently through the back door and reached for her mortar and pestle in the dark. She knew her way around the kitchen; there was no need for candlelight, not yet anyway. She found what she needed in a sealed jar on the top shelf of the pantry. Now she had to prepare it properly. Aklu'ut had told her one day her cooking would serve her well; she just never imagined it would be like this!

Carefully, she shook the chunks out of the jar and into the marble bowl. She crushed it with a turning motion of the pestle until it broke into a fine powder. She hoped her plan would work; their lives were dependent upon it. Usually, the concoction she was mixing took at least an hour to prepare, but she just didn't have that kind of time. She'd have to make it extra strong, just to be sure.

Jolian reached to the shelf above her counter where she kept her cooking supplies. Thankfully she hadn't added all of the whiskey to the deer roast she had marinating for tomorrow. She poured what was left of the whiskey into a tumbler, similar to the ones in the parlor. She added the powder from her mortar and then lit a candle. She had to be meticulous with her mixing. She was betting his senses were deadened by his previous consumption of whiskey and he wouldn't notice the slight change in flavor.

Jolian prepared a plate of sliced meat and bread in an instant. Checking her pistol one last time and placing into her secret pocket, she inhaled deeply and exhaled slowly. For this to work, she needed Pearl to play along with her. One more deep breath and Jolian raised her head and puffed up her chest.

She walked with more confidence than she possessed, tray of food in the air, whiskey behind her back, hoping she presented an air of servitude that wouldn't be questioned by anyone in the parlor. From the hallway Jolian could see the man was beginning to walk toward the stairs that led to the bedrooms. She had to move quickly if she was going to do this.

"Here ya are, Mum." She said with flare. "The food ya requested all ready for ya." She caught Pearl's astonished gaze and held it securely. Jolian backed towards a table with ease and placed the whiskey down beside Pearl's hand. She turned her back to the murderer and while it appeared she held the plate for Pearl's inspection, she signaled to Pearl with her eyes. Pearl seemed to follow her unspoken request, or was at least willing to play along for the time being.

"Thank you, Jo." Pearl moved to the whiskey decanter and made it look as though she had just refreshed the man's drink.

"Keep yore pants on now!" She cajoled the man as she expertly steered him away from the staircase. "Vera will be down in a minute. Now have another drink and a bite to eat. I want ya to keep yore strength up, big boy. Ya want ta get yore money's worth! No one leaves Pearl's without getting' thar money's worth I always say."

She slapped the man on the back, put her arm around his shoulder and handed him Jo's whiskey.

"That's it, drink it all down now. Want another?"

Jo left Pearl to the deed and whispered the word "kitchen" to Doralynn as she walked by her, casually checking to ensure they were not followed.

"What's going on?" Doralynn talked in hushed tones as she followed Jo into the kitchen.

"It's a long story, Doralynn, but the man in there murdered my family and I am trying to keep him from doing the same to Vera and, well, everyone in there is pretty much in danger. I have a plan, but I can't explain it now. I need you to go and get help. Cooper told me he was camped down at the claims with Guy and Ts'kaw. Could you go there, Doralynn? Can you ride for Guy and Ts'kaw?"

"Of course I will." Jolian could see the realization hit Doralynn like boulder. All of their lives were in danger here and time was a factor.

"Thank you, Doralynn. If you see the Constable I suppose it wouldn't hurt to have him come as well. Be careful."

Doralynn left, and Jolian realized she should have inquired as to Cooper's whereabouts. She had expected to see him in the parlor when she took the food in, but a quick glance around the room had confirmed her biggest fears. She needed Cooper as back up for her plan. Hopefully, he hadn't left yet. Jolian wanted to go back into the parlor but she couldn't think of a reason for the hired help to be socializing with the 'girls'. She wanted to sneak up the backstairs to warn Vera, too, but she had to keep her eyes on the outhouse. If everything was going to work according to her plan, she had to keep her eyes on the outhouse.

When she had begun to believe she couldn't wait a moment longer, she saw the man dash outside. She waited until he went inside the privy and then she ran into the parlor.

"Where's Cooper?" She half shouted at Pearl.

"What in tarnations is going on around here Jo? I know yore up ta somethin'. I am willin' to go along with a practical joke, but ya've gots ta let me in on the gag."

"It's no gag, Pearl." Jo spoke quickly "The man who just ran outside is the same man who murdered my parents. We haven't got much time. Please find Cooper and send him out to the outhouse. I'll keep the man out there as long as I can."

"Jo, wait..."

"Just get Cooper, trust me."

Jo left Pearl with her mouth hanging open and hoped she would do her bidding. She ran outside then slowed her pace as she neared the outhouse and hoped the man was too "otherwise occupied" to hear her approach. As silently as she could she crept around the small wooden structure to where she'd hidden the piece of lumber. She hoisted it into her arms, carried it around to the front of the outhouse and dropped it into the metal hangers she had nailed on earlier. The moment the board slammed into place, holding the outhouse door firmly shut, the hollering started from inside.

"What the—?" She could hear the man try to open the door. "What the hell is going on? Open this door!"

He must not be as drunk as she'd hoped. Jolian took several steps backwards and removed the revolver from her pocket. She cocked it and held her finger steadfast on the trigger. If that door so much as opened a crack she was going to fire her gun. The man was yelling loudly now and it seemed as though he was slamming his body against the door. The whole outhouse shook with each jolt. Jolian knelt to the ground and dug her feet in firmly. She wished Cooper was here, this was part she most afraid of and she could use his help. She steadied her trembling hand by placing her elbow on her knee and then she grasped the handle of the colt with both hands.

Another jolt and another. Each time the man hit the outhouse it felt as if he was hitting her. Jolian concentrated her vision on the door. It opened wider with each jolt. She swallowed hard and renewed her resolve. She could do this; if she had to, she could kill the man. She could fire her gun and protect those she loved from this horrible beast of a man.

"Who's out there!" He yelled. "Who's done this? It ain't funny! Open this door now or I'll kill ya!"

Jolian could see he was trying to get his gun through the opening he'd created in the doorway! She edged her body to the left and kept her gun trained on the door. More hollering and cursing and more slamming on the door. The lumber was holding, but the nails were not! A few more jolts and the beast would be free from the cage she had made.

The terror of the situation froze Jolian in her spot. The time she dreaded had come and everything seemed to be slowing down. It was like her parents' death all over again. Everything moved at half speed, each fraction of movement burning into her memory. She heard Cooper's voice behind her in the distance. Yelling, but she couldn't make out his words. She wouldn't turn her head now, she couldn't. The nails gave way and the door came open. The man stumbled out into the night. Time crawled, each action taking minutes to complete. Jolian aimed her gun and fired. Only the bullet traveled at regular speed. The force of the gun knocked her back a bit. She steadied her aim and fired again.

Suddenly, Cooper was there and so was Pearl. Pearl pried the gun from her hands and Cooper fell on top of the man slamming his fist into him. Had her aim not been as true as she believed? Again and again knuckles connected with nose until Pearl hollered, "Coop, he's out cold!"

Time resumed its normal speed and Jolian exhaled the breath she'd been holding. Pearl stood over Cooper and the murderer, the revolver in a death grip in her hands. Cooper tied up the man with a rope. Only then did Jolian take a good look at the beast from the outhouse. Cooper had flipped him over when he'd hog tied him and the bloodied brute lay face down on the ground, his pants still about his ankles. Apparently, the choke cherry laxative she'd slipped into his whiskey had done its job too well. Jolian turned her head from the sight.

She didn't know if the man was dead or alive and she honestly didn't care. He was unresponsive and restrained and he would hold until the law came for him. She turned to walk back toward the house as the rest of Pearl's girls came rushing out into the night. She needed to sit down and have a cup of coffee, or maybe a stiff drink of some kind. She felt numb inside. She didn't know what she should be feeling. She assumed she'd feel satisfaction, or at least relief, not this hollow sort of nothingness.

"Jo!" Cooper's words halted her in her tracks. She turned to face him and he put his hands on her shoulders. A hug, yes that's what she needed. More than coffee or a drink, she needed a hug. But Cooper didn't take her in his arms as she expected. Instead he kept his hands on her shoulders and began to shake her.

"What were you thinking? You could have been killed! Don't you ever do anything like that again do you hear me?"

"I could hear you better if you weren't shaking me!" Jolian managed to blurt as her head rocked back and forth.

"I'm sorry, I'm sorry." Cooper hugged the stuffing out of her. "I should have stayed by you. The minute I recognized him I should have found you and stayed by you. I'm sorry, Lorna, I let you down, I'm so sorry."

Jolian didn't know what he was talking about or whom Lorna was, but she wasn't about to push away the comfort. She'd needed a hug like this. It felt good to be in his strong, secure arms. She closed her eyes and tried to breathe normally.

Cooper held her as if his life depended upon it. She could hear people chattering in the background and thought she'd heard Doralynn's voice. She had probably brought the Constable after all. Jo didn't care; nothing could make her move from the embrace of the man she loved.

Yes, there was no use in hiding it any longer. There was no use in hiding anything. She was a woman and she loved a man. She didn't even care that he was a miner. They'd work something out. If she always felt the way she did now, she'd follow him from claim to claim if he so much as suggested it. Yes, she was most surely in love! Who could blame her with a man like Cooper Holt around?

The chattering became louder and she focused in on some of the comments.

"I don't know why he's hugging the boy..."

"Jo's the one who captured him. Gived him some kind a tonic what gived him the runs. And boy did he run!"

"Cooper said he figured that man kilt Hog-Judy as well, better lock him up tight, Constable."

Reluctantly Jo peeked up from Cooper's embrace. Ts'kaw and Guy had lifted the tied man up onto his horse and they were fastening the rope to the saddle horn. Another man, who she assumed was a doctor, tended to the murderer's leg. Maybe she'd shot him after all.

Jo had heard right. It was Doralynn's voice and she had brought the Constable. Jo broke from Cooper's embrace, walked over to him now, took off her cap, and extended her hand.

"Constable Towers, I have a confession to make."

"Is that so?" He shook her hand reluctantly like she had some kind of contagious disease.

"Yes, sir. I shot at the man that's tied up on the horse there. I don't know if I hit him, but I intended to. He's the man who murdered my parents. Jakeb will attest to the same." A self-confidence and sense of closure she had never felt before were slowly replacing the numbness she had felt earlier. She held her head high and looked the Constable in the eyes. She would be honest and take what was coming to her.

The Constable cleared his throat and then raised his voice for all to hear, "This man has a minor wound on his thigh. It's a good thing I brought the doctor from Richfield along with me. I think it's *you* who I should be taking into custody. And as for your brother—he would say anything to get off on a murder charge."

"That's the other thing,'' Jolian stated with ease. "Jakeb is my brother, but I'm not his."

"What do you mean, he's yurs but ya ain't his? Are ya kin or ain't ya?" Vera's loud bellow made everyone present turn to look at Jo. Jo swallowed hard and continued.

"Jakeb is my brother, but I am his *sister*." Jo stated matter-of-factly. "My full name is Jolian Caroline Grayson. I am Jakeb's younger sister. I'm eighteen." She answered the question that hung on Doralynn's lips before she could ask it.

"YORE A WOMAN?!" Vera shouted so loudly that Ts'kaw and Guy looked their way and began to lead the horse, with the murderer atop it, toward the Constable. Vera tossed her head in apparent disgust. She held her chin and skirts high as she strode past the crowd and into the night.

"I guess all those times she fancied you are coming back to haunt her." Doralynn couldn't keep the giggle from her voice and the others joined her laughter. All but Cooper and the Constable. The former was nowhere to be seen and the latter commanded all of her attention.

"I do not see the humor in deception of any kind." The Constable's voice was firm with no vestige of tolerance.

"Ah, come on, Bert. Ya can smile, it won't crack yore face!" Pearl's voice bubbled with laughter.

"We'll see who's laughing when the Judge hears this story. As for you," he looked at Jolian with such contempt she could feel his coldness through to her bones. "Don't leave town, I may still decide to arrest you, for attempted murder, in the very least."

"You'll do what you have to do I'm sure." Jolian spoke with the confidence of justice on her side.

The Constable snorted a reply, mounted his horse and led the other, with the still unconscious man tied to it, towards Richfield. The Doctor walked towards Jolian.

"The wound is shallow and just grazed the surface. He should recover without incident," he said.

"Can you spend ze night at ze jail?" Guy pulled the doctor aside and spoke with him privately. They walked towards the barn and moments later the doctor raced past them towards Richfield. Jolian wondered what was going on and turned to ask Guy as he approached.

Just as she opened her mouth to speak, Pearl interrupted. "Yore too brave for words, honey! I am so proud of you."

Once again Jo found herself in an embrace that would rival a bear's.

"Don't worry yourself about the Constable, Jo." Doralynn reached over and patted her arm while Pearl continued to hug her. "He's just making bricks out of straw. The doctor will stay in the jail overnight until the circuit Judge arrives in the morning. Judge Begbie will see the truth of the situation." Guy slipped his arm around Doralynn's shoulders.

Jolian couldn't hide her smile from Doralynn. She had been so afraid the girls would feel betrayed by her ruse, and with the exception of Vera, they all seemed to be treating her as if they'd known that she was a woman all along.

Everyone seemed to want to know all about her, now the truth was out. Jolian found herself being pushed and prodded into the parlor along with Guy, Ts'kaw, and the rest of the girls. Someone pressed a drink into her hands and everyone seemed to be talking at once. There was only one person with whom she really wanted to speak and he was nowhere to be found.

~ * ~

Cooper couldn't stop shaking his head. What was wrong with him? Here he had a chance to start over, with Jolian, his angel, and he was blowing it. He had no right to hold her in his arms or think of her as his. She had faced the man who murdered her parents, stayed calm and planned for his capture while he... what had he done? Nothing. Nothing except let her down and then call her Lorna!

That was going to take a bit of explaining, to himself, too. He thought he had put Lorna out of his life forever, and yet she kept popping into his mind. He thought he'd dealt with this. He had, he had dealt with this. Then why couldn't he shake the feeling he needed a drink? He needed to talk to someone. He needed to talk to Jolian and to try and explain.

Cooper turned and walked back to Pearl's. He wasn't going to let anything stop him. Jolian was his angel and he'd show everyone he deserved to have her. As he neared Pearl's place, Cooper could see Guy in the parlor with his arm around Doralynn. They made a nice looking couple. Was that a pang of jealousy he felt? It was so easy for Guy and Doralynn. They loved each other right out in the open and let the chips fall where they may. He wanted that.

153

As he turned to make his way towards the front door, Cooper saw something out of the corner of his eye that halted him in his tracks. It was Jolian. She was laughing and drinking and talking with Ts'kaw. Anger rumbled like thunder inside him. As he tried to rationalize it away, Jolian stood on her tiptoes and kissed Ts'kaw on the cheek. No wonder he had called her Lorna, she was just like her!

The anger was back full force and he had no will to stop it this time. Why hadn't he seen it before? It was happening again and he wasn't going to be made a fool of this time! Cooper turned for the barn, led Storm from his stall, mounted and rode off into the blackness.

Thirteen

Everyone had long since disappeared from the parlor, the conversations buzzing like bees. Some were upstairs; some had gone home leaving the parlor dark and silent. Jolian sat in the dark and sipped her drink. The whiskey she'd been handed earlier had gone straight to her head and she'd quickly made the switch to lemonade. The sweet and sour drink felt good on her scratchy throat. She'd talked more tonight than she had in the past year!

By morning it would be known from Richfield Mountain to Quesnelle that she was a woman. The thought was overwhelming to say the least. She'd surely have more explaining to do and that meant more talking. She cleared her throat and took another sip of her lemonade. Time for bed. What was she waiting for anyway? It was well past midnight. It wasn't like *he* was going to show up now.

She couldn't keep her thoughts from Cooper. Where could he be and why wasn't he here? It had been a triumphant evening and everyone had been in a celebratory mood. She wanted to celebrate too but she couldn't. The name Lorna kept flashing in her mind's eye. Who was she and what made her so important to Cooper that he would call her that name?

Reluctantly, she rose from her spot on the settee and pulled her weary body up the stairs. She'd sleep at Pearl's tonight like she'd planned originally. It was too late and she was too worn out to walk to her own cabin for her belongings. She entered the spare room, slipped off her shirt and unbound her breasts. She slipped her shirt back on and pulled off her trousers. Sliding between the sheets, she felt herself drifting into sleep before her head even touched the pillow.

~ * ~

Cooper scratched at the whiskers beginning to develop on his cheeks. His fingers stroked his moustache with pride. He couldn't believe he'd been so blinded by her he'd almost shaved it off! He'd look like a baby without it. Besides, he was already one of the most clean-shaven miners in town.

The water began to flow through the sluice box. Now he'd see what treasures his sleepless night had wrought! Cooper rocked the box to separate the heavier gold from the dirt. The sun was rising fast and Cooper worked quickly. He wanted to test his metal by first light. Dawn chased the shadows across his claim. Brightness sped towards him as he reached his hand to the bottom of the rocker. He grabbed hold of a rock, wet and dripping, he pulled it free of its hiding spot and raised it to the sun.

Was it the light playing tricks on his tired eyes? He gazed at the nugget, for that's what it was. A greenish-yellow nugget nestled securely in his fist. He'd done it! There was gold in his claim and from the looks of it, he, Cooper Holt was a rich man indeed.

Of course he was no fool. Many a time had miners found nuggets, thought they'd hit the mother lode, cashed it all in and started a frenzy. He wasn't about to tell anyone. He knew exactly what he had to do. His heart hammered in his chest as he began to collect all of the nuggets he could find. He washed the dirt again and again until the last of the gold dust was safely stored away.

He chose a hiding spot down one of the first canals he'd dug in his shaft. It hadn't panned out and he'd filled it in with rock from another tunnel. At least that's how it would look to anyone who may enter his mineshaft looking for gold and a charge of theft.

Cooper knew he had to dig deeper. Nuggets like this only meant the vein, the lead, the evasive ribbon of gold that was his true fortune was down deeper yet. Pick in hand, he began the painstaking process of excavating rock. He couldn't use dynamite now, not when he was so close to the lead. He tunneled and dug and burrowed until exhaustion threatened to stop him. He took a break and sipped some water from his canteen. Guy would be expecting him, but he didn't care. He'd worked harder than two men in the last week and he was taking today for himself. If he was truthful with himself, he knew he was avoiding a run in with Ts'kaw. He just wasn't up to that yet.

If he was going to confront his friend for the second time in as many years about stealing his girl, he was going to do it as a wealthy man. That way, regardless of what Jolian did with Ts'kaw, he'd appear to have won. He would have won. That's what he'd come for, the gold, not some woman. And that's what he would leave with—gold!

Cooper put his canteen away and grabbed his pick once more. He'd be damned if he would let thoughts of her into his head again! They were all alike and he was staying away from the lot of them. He knew what he was here for and he would concentrate on gold, only the gold.

~ * ~

"Come in." Her voice squeaked dryly, so Jolian cleared her throat and repeated herself a bit louder.

Doralynn poked her head around the door. "I thought you might like a bite to eat, seeing as how you have been cooking for all of us for so long, it only seemed right that I bring a tray up to you."

"Is it that late?" Jolian tried to sit up but her head pounded and begged to stay imbedded in the pillow.

"Almost midday."

"Oh my! I never sleep—I can't believe it!"

"Pearl insisted that you were not to be disturbed. I made a meal for the girls, nothing fancy, just hotcakes. Most of the others are just retiring for their afternoon nap. I thought it might be a nice time for you to rise leisurely and maybe even have a chance for a hot bath." Doralynn had bent to retrieve the tray she promised and Jolian felt overwhelmed by the attention.

She lifted her chin to look straight into Doralynn's green eyes. "What a kind, thoughtful gesture. Thank you, I would love a bath."

Doralynn settled the tray in front of Jolian. Coffee and hotcakes with a tea rose in a crystal vase adorned the platter. "This looks absolutely delicious! It's been a long time since anyone cooked for me. Thank you, again."

"Don't you mention it." Doralynn smiled sweetly as she left the room. "I'll start to heat the water for your bath." She called through the closed door.

Jolian couldn't keep the smile from her face. It felt wonderful to be treated so kindly. She sat a bit more upright and rubbed an aching temple. No wonder she had a headache! She hadn't eaten in almost twenty-four hours and then, there was the glass of whiskey she'd downed like water last night. Jolian soaked her hotcakes with butter and syrup. Her first bite was warm and sweet and melted in her mouth. Doralynn was a good cook. She'd have to remember to compliment on the breakfast the next time she saw her.

As the food fuelled her brain, her mind began to work as fast as ten wild horses. There was so much to think about, so much had happened! Jakeb would surely be back at their cabin by now. Regardless of his ornery disposition, the Constable couldn't hold her brother when the true murderer of Hog-Judy was so obvious. Yes, Jakeb would have to be free this morning.

She'd have to think about getting some new clothes. Now that her secret was out, she couldn't very well keep wearing men's clothing. She would most certainly have her virtue questioned if she did. She audibly groaned at the thought of wearing a corset again. She'd become used to the freedom trousers allowed. Maybe she'd shock everyone and take to wearing bloomers like that English woman!

It felt so good to have carefree thoughts and humor inside. That was one of the things she loved about Cooper. He seemed to have a lively sense of humor. People were just naturally comfortable around his easy, relaxed personality. She could think that on one hand, but then on the other there was the powerful, passionate side of him. That side fascinated and terrified her.

The way he'd looked at her when they'd kissed, it had an intensity she'd never felt before. She'd felt as if he was branding her or claiming her for his own. And then again, last night as he shook her and then held her so tight. Strange feeling, this belonging to someone, even if she was the only one who felt like there was a 'belonging'. She felt complete, like a part of her had been missing, and not just because he brought out qualities in her she longed to possess. It just felt right to be with him. He was the one she had been looking for without even knowing she'd been looking.

She didn't even entertain the thought he might have feelings for her that could measure up to her own. He had some feelings, she was sure, because you didn't kiss someone the way he had without having feelings for her. At least she didn't think you could. She knew she couldn't.

Jolian finished up the last of her hotcakes and dressed in a robe from the armoire in the corner. If the girls were napping, no one would be about to see her sneak down the stairs half clothed. She peeked out the window to see it was indeed midday and sunny and warm. She felt sunny herself as she half-hopped down the stairs and into the kitchen.

The door to the bath was ajar and there were swirls of steam sneaking out. Jolian felt a giggle rise in her still scratchy throat as she inhaled the fragrance of rose. Rose! How long had it been since she'd smelled that fragrance on her body? She pushed open the door and could hardly believe her eyes.

Beside the tub on the long cedar bench lay a willow green bodice and skirt. The bodice sported a cream-colored lace inset and had the tiniest pearl buttons all down the front. The same lace cinched the waist and was stitched in scallops on the skirt. It was certainly the most attractive outfit she'd ever seen! Surely Doralynn couldn't have meant for her to wear it?

"Don't you like it?"

"Oh, Doralynn..." Jolian croaked as she turned to see her standing in the kitchen. "It's beautiful."

"It's yours if you'd like, I am sure it will fit." Doralynn held her hand up in protest as Jo began to speak. "I won't take no for an answer, Jo. I haven't worn it in over a year. And besides, even if it did still fit, it's just not my style anymore."

"But if you leave Pearl's..."

"To be with Guy you mean?" Jo nodded and she continued. "If I decide to marry Guy, I have more than enough money saved to buy myself ten new outfits, with hats and shoes to match!"

Jolian laughed along with her new friend. "Then I will accept it if you will accept my heartfelt gratitude."

"Done."

~ * ~

Jakeb rubbed his swollen jaw. It hurt like the devil and the stuff that so called dentist had given him wasn't even taking the edge off the pain. Still, it was more than he deserved. He'd have to hurry if he were going to accomplish everything he had set out for himself and still get to Pearl's before nightfall. He'd made himself a promise and this was the beginning of keeping it.

The news was all over town about Jolian. Everywhere he went people were stopping him and wanting to know the story first hand. What could he tell them? It's not like he'd been there. He couldn't believe how fast news could travel in a town as big as Barkerville.

Jakeb reached the claim and looked around. Someone had been busy and recently, too. There were piles of rocks and bits of lumber everywhere. He could hear the steady tap-tap-tap of a pick on the rocks and knew where to find the claim's owner.

"Hello?" He called down the shaft. "Cooper? Hey, Cooper Holt, is that you down there?"

The tapping noise ceased, but no voice rang out.

"Hey, Cooper, I know you're down there. It's Jakeb Grayson." Nothing. "Cooper, I understand you may not hold me in the highest regard in light of what's happened, but I really need to speak to you."

"What is it then?" Said a voice from so close behind him Jakeb visibly jumped into the air.

"I thought you were down *there*."

"I was. There are two openings."

Jakeb felt uncomfortable under Cooper's intense stare. He couldn't help but notice Cooper never even gestured as to the other opening of the mine, like he couldn't be trusted or something. Jakeb shifted his weight from one foot to the other and tried to figure out the best way to broach the subject.

"I er... that is I... is your claim doing well?"

"Why?"

"What do you mean, why?"

"Why do you want to know how my claim is doing? I'm not interested in taking on a partner."

"Just making polite conversation. It looks as though someone's been doing a lot of digging. As a matter-of-fact, your claim looks just like the Lazy dazy did right after they hit their lead. Say..."

"Like I said, I am not interested in taking on a partner."

"Hey," Jakeb raised his hands as if to surrender. For whatever reason, Cooper was never overly enthusiastic about talking with him, but he was usually at least cordial. "I could care less what you're bringing up, I just thought it might make my offer a bit more attractive if you'd hit."

"What offer?"

"I want to sell my claim. The Lazy dazy on the other side of me was pulling out a thousand a foot. Now it looks as though you've got something going on this side. Damn! I told Jo this spot was ripe! Anyway, that's neither here nor there now, cause I'm looking to sell. I thought I'd give you first crack at it, seeing as how I'm indebted to you, for everything you've done. That don't mean I'm selling it cheap, mind."

"It's not all yours to sell. I heard Angus swear in front of at least a dozen men, that he was giving his share of the mine to your sister."

"He what?"

"Well, she did save his life."

"Har-har-har! Well that's fine, that's real fine! Jolian a part owner in a mine! If that don't beat all!"

Cooper just stared at the boy. He was slapping his thigh with one hand and holding his jaw with the other. The laughter had a bite to it, if Cooper wasn't mistaken. He couldn't see the humor in it himself. Jolian had saved Angus's life and he'd repaid her with the only thing he had that was worth anything. It was poignant, sad even. But funny? He didn't see it.

"Don't you get it?" Jakeb half shouted. "Jo's been on my back ever since I staked that claim. Sell the mine; sell your share, that's all she ever talks to me about. Now I'm selling and she owns the other half! It's killing me it's so damned ironic! Especially now that you've hit. All the signs are there—oh you can deny it all you want. My claim is right in the middle of the Lazy dazy and yours. Both of you have just hit, my site is practically a sure thing. Are you buying or not?"

"Nothing is a sure thing when it comes to mining" Cooper laid his pick on the ground and scratched t the whiskers on his chin. "What'd you call it?"

"Our claim? Angel's gold."

"Wwwhat?" Cooper stammered. He couldn't have heard right.

"I said 'Angel's gold'. I sent Angus to register the claim. It was supposed to be 'Ang-Jak's Gold' but Angus can't spell. He called it Angek's and the Assay office copied it out as Angel's. Sounded better, so we stuck with it. Does it matter?"

"No, not really. How much are you asking for your share?"

He settled on a fair price and arranged to meet Jakeb at the assay office in the morning. If what Jakeb said about Jolian not wanting to mine was true, then Cooper felt certain he'd have no difficulty in acquiring her portion. He didn't bother to ask Jakeb his reasons for selling. He didn't want to know. Didn't want to know why the kids face was swollen either, probably a fight in the jail. He hoped Jakeb would put the money to good use. Cooper grabbed his pick and headed back to the mineshaft. He needed to get back to work. He needed to stop thinking about the "Angel" he would have named the claim for. The less he had to do with the Grayson "boys" the more it suited him.

~ * ~

Jolian lazed in her bath until the water cooled. The steam had helped the scratchiness in her throat. She took her time in dressing and pinning up her hair. Thank goodness she hadn't cut it again! It was just long enough to lift off her neck and pin in place. A proper hat would hide the fact she was practically bald in comparison to most of the women she knew. She smiled at the thought. Fancy that she could have the pretense of long hair and not the bother of it! Rather like the situation with the corset.

Doralynn's dress was just large enough that she didn't need to lace herself into one. It felt truly fabulous to wear a dress without a corset and she pledged, albeit privately, she would never wear the horrid contraption again. With that thought, she lifted her skirts and removed a petticoat.

She hadn't been out of her bath for more than half an hour and already the heat penetrated her layers of skirts. That would never do. If she could go without a corset she could do without the petticoats, too. She lifted her skirts again and stripped off the second underskirt. She'd keep the wire cage; at least it allowed air to circulate.

Jolian used a washcloth to wipe off the condensation accumulating on the mirror. Her metamorphosis complete, she stepped back until her full-length reflection was visible in the oval glass. So much had happened in her life since she'd last worn women's clothing. Tears began to fill her eyes and Jolian brushed them away with the back of her hand.

Her father's face in her memory roused her tears. He'd promised her the first thing he'd buy with his share of the gold was a new dress for her, in the latest style.

She'd promised him the first dance in that dress. Staring at her reflection, she could see her father's face in the mirror, as if he stood beside her in the bathing room off Pearl's kitchen. Jolian watched in horror as the image of her father's smiling face began to fade and the face of the man with a bullet in his forehead appeared in his place. She pulled herself from her trance by shaking her head and clearing the thoughts of her father.

It was getting harder and harder to remember him in any other way except how she'd found him that day, lying in the snow. But at least she could still see him briefly in her mind's eye. She didn't even try to summon up a picture of her mother; the blood was too vivid, even in her memory. She could feel the tears pooling in her eyes and she forced her mind to turn to a new thought.

Jolian finished tidying up the bath and left the room intent on carrying her old clothes upstairs. She felt the cool wooden floor through her stockinged feet. It was embarrassing, but she was going to have to ask Doralynn if she could borrow a pair of proper highshoes. She couldn't wear a dress again and clomp about in her old work boots, which currently, were the only pieces of footwear that she owned. What a spectacle she'd be!

~ * ~

Less than an hour later, in her borrowed highshoes and Pearl's buggy, Jolian bounced along the trail to Barkerville. It felt very strange to be heading into town and actually looking forward to it. She could hardly remember the last time she'd strolled through a town in a dress. A vision of San Francisco popped into her mind. Oh biscuits! Why did she have to have a memory anyway? She consciously shifted the picture in her head to something more pleasant.

An image of Cooper flashed before her. He was definitely a pleasant image and so easy on the eyes. A fancy little hum escaped her and she put her hand to her mouth in an attempt to silence herself. She was riding into town in hopes of seeing him, even if she had told everyone she was off to search for her brother, who hadn't been at their cabin after all. She needed to see Jakeb, but she wanted to see Cooper. She didn't understand why he'd stayed away last night.

She left her buggy in town and walked the short distance to Back Street and Jakeb's claim. If she knew Jakeb, he'd be at his mine. It seemed nothing was more important to him lately. Despite the heat of the day, the street was still mucky and

Jolian had to be careful of where she chose to step. Doralynn's highshoes were loose on her feet and it made walking quite an art.

"Jo? I hardly recognized you."

"Jakeb—" She raised her head, her hand shadowing the sun from her eyes, and saw her brother walking towards her. His face was swollen and bruised and she immediately hurried to his side. She gingerly touched his bruised cheek and he winced in pain.

"Jakeb what on earth has happened to you?"

"Oh that? It's nothing really, Jolian. Look at you! You are quite lovely little sssister."

"A compliment? Why do I find that suspicious?" Jolian half laughed. "You need to get some witch hazel on that cheek before the bruising gets any worse. Don't tell me you've been in some kind of fight?"

"You and your Indian remedies! It's nothing, but I will tell you all about it if you'll accompany me to the coffeehouse and bakeshop."

"I guess I could use a nice pot of tea." Her curiosity just got the better of her. She certainly hoped Jakeb's injuries were not a result of his time in jail. Jakeb held his elbow out for her and she graciously accepted. He could be such a charmer when the mood struck him.

"I was planning to check in on Angus—"

"Actually, I Just came from ssseeing him. He wouldn't want to sssee you, Jo, trust me. He's not taking the loss of his leg like I thought he would. I mean it's not like it was a big sssurprise. If the cave-in hadn't happened the gout would've taken it eventually."

"I guess nobody's ever ready to loose a limb."

"I guess."

They walked the rest of way to the bakeshop in silence. Once inside, Jakeb chose a window table with a view of the main street and even pulled out a chair for her.

"The cinnamon buns are good, but not as good as yours."

"Why do I have the suspicion that you're going to try to sell me something, Jakeb?" Jolian peeked over her menu card to catch his eye.

"Me?"

164

"Don't look at me with those puppy dog eyes, Jakeb!" Jolian giggled as she swatted at her brother with the list of daily specials.

"Ouch! Hey watch it! I'm already injured enough." Jakeb feigned an injury and Jolian laughed a little more. He'd forgotten what a pretty young woman his sister was. It was good to see her in a dress again. He was glad that he'd bumped into her in town and convinced her to come to the restaurant. She was right on the mark with her intuition. He'd wanted her in a public place when he told her. Besides, she'd be less likely to make a scene in public.

"Injured or not, I think you've got something up your sleeve."

"I am sssure you have more than enough reason to be leery of me, Jo." Jakeb didn't let her look sway him. He ordered a cinnamon bun for himself and a scone for his sister. He had to come clean with her now; he owed her that much. He watched as she removed her gloves and the thought struck him that his tiny, feisty little sister had pretty much single-handedly captured the most wanted criminal in the colony. He hoped to have half her courage in the days to come.

"I'm leaving, Jo."

"Leaving? What do you mean, leaving Pearl's?"

"No, I'm leaving for home, Sssan Francisco, tomorrow morning."

"What? I don't understand."

"Just take a breath and keep your voice down. I was going to leave you a note—"

"A note? Jakeb, you're killing me! I can't... You can't—"

"Breathe, Jolian. I have a lot to tell you. Ssstarting with, I've made up my mind to leave." Her look changed from shock to worry as she took a deep breath.

"Let me ssstart by sssaying how proud I am of you, Jo, for everything you did last night. It's your courage that's given me the mind to do this."

"Well then I take it back! I'm not courageous, Jakeb. You of all people should know that! I can't even stand a little summer storm."

"You are courageous, Jolian. And you sssell yourself ssshort too often. I have taken advantage of your kind heart more than once and I'm not willing to live that way anymore. No, don't interrupt me. Just let me get it out before I lose my nerve." She acquiesced, albeit reluctantly and her face looked pale as she folded her hands in her lap. He wouldn't let it stop him; she deserved to know.

"All right. I need to sssay these things and tell you how it is, Jo. Sssome of these things ain't easy to tell and sssome of them ain't going to be easy to hear. First off, I am the one who's responsible for us being orphaned and being here in the Cariboo. I know you've always thought it was Pa that talked the family into coming, and he did. But it was on my behalf that he did it." He took a sip of his coffee and continued without looking his sister in the eyes.

"I was up to my eyeballs in gambling debts in Sssan Francisco. Uncle Julian had bailed me out ssso many times before and finally he just put his foot down. Pa didn't have a choice and neither did Ma. They did it for me, Jolian. They're lying in the cold ground because I can't resist a poker game." He raised his eyes to look at her then and could see she didn't blame him. She looked as if she was going to try and convince him that somehow, someway it hadn't been his fault. He wanted the whole truth between them now, once and for all.

"I am a gambler, Jo, and I'm not good at it. I risk more than I can ssstand to lose and I lose all the time. I stole your sssavings. I needed a poker stake. All those nuggets you earned with your hard work, I ssstole them and I gambled them away. That's not all I've been lying about either." He paused as the waiter brought their requests and he was thankful for the respite. He needed to get a hold of his emotions.

He hadn't cried since he was six years old and he wasn't going to start now. He took a long drink of the coffee. The hot liquid stung like the dickens when it hit the back part of his mouth. He focused on the pain and let his emotions return to normal. He hadn't thought this would be so difficult.

"Jakeb, you may be a gambler but lots of men like to gamble. If you aren't any good at it, then I agree; you'd best stop. But if you're worried about the money you took, that's already forgotten. I'll just start over that's all. I saved it once, and I can do it again. You don't need to leave, Jakeb, and you aren't responsible for Ma and Pa—"

"You're kind, Jolian, you always have been. You're like Ma that way. Maybe I didn't pull the trigger that killed her, but I am to blame nonetheless. Ssshe stood up to her own brother for me. Ssshe begged him to pay my debts. I was a constant sssource of ssshame to our family and I intend to change all of that, ssstarting today." Jakeb held his hand up to stop further interruptions.

"I know you think badly of Uncle Julian because he never responded to my letter telling him about the murder. The truth is, he did respond, Jo, and he blames me for the death as much as I do, if not more. He also wrote to tell me that President Lincoln has brought in a conscription law as of July 13th. It ssstates, all able-bodied men are to be drafted into ssservice unless they can pay three hundred dollars to furnish a sssubstitute. He intends to let them know that I am trying to escape the draft—that is, unless I report for ssservice as of August 21st. Which, as of today, gives me nineteen days to report for duty."

Jolian was thankful Jakeb kept talking because she was truly dumbfounded with the news he provided.

"I know it's no excuse, Jo, but that's why I stole your sssavings. I was trying to make enough to pay sssomeone else to join the Union forces in my place. After everything that's happened sssince yesterday morning, what you did, without a thought for your own sssafety... I, well, I've taken ssstock. I'm joining up with the North to fight the good fight. I may be late but I think it's a battle worth fighting. I've written to the 72nd Illinois regiment as they are offering a three hundred and two dollar bounty to join. I've told them to sssend the money here to you and that any other funds could be sssent here in your name as well."

The war? Her brother was going off to war? Just when her life was beginning to show a bit of hope he was going to war? She hadn't paid much attention to what had been going on back in her homeland but they'd heard bits and pieces about the war all of the time. It was horrible! So many people were dying everyday. She agreed the cause was a just one but he was all the family she had left. She couldn't just sit back and let him walk out of her life. But before she could form a thought he was going on, telling her of his plans.

"I've arranged to sssell my share of the mine to Cooper Holt. I think he may have a sssurprise for you by the way, and no, I wasn't in a fight. I sssold two teeth this morning. That'll give me enough money for a horse, a few sssupplies and passage back to San Francisco on a ssssternwheeler. There was also the matter of a sssmall debt to Mr. Duke at the mercantile, but I won't go into all of that now. I have a few more things to sssettle up in town, I'll ssstay there tonight, and I'll leave directly after the trial tomorrow."

Jolian felt as though *she'd* been kicked by a mule. She couldn't believe everything being told to her. How could her Uncle be so cruel? She couldn't agree with a law that said the wealthy could pay for someone to fight in his place, but at the same time she couldn't stand the thought of her brother going to war. *He'd sold his teeth?* Biscuits! She despised her uncle more than ever now. She finally was able to put her thoughts together and she expressed all of her feelings to Jakeb. He stood his ground. With no other recourse she decided begging was not beneath her where her brother's safety was concerned.

"Jakeb, I... don't go. Please, I beg you, Jakeb. I can't lose you, too."

Jakeb looked at her like he was seeing her for the first time in ages.

"You're a bit of a thing, even back in your big hooped skirts again. But you have more strength than I do. I know it feels like I'm letting you down again, but this time I know I'll make it right. This is my last chance to make something out of myself, Jolian. I owe it to Ma and Pa and to you, too. Mostly though, I owe it to myself and I intend to do it right. You've had a hard life so far, Jolian. It's not the life you deserve. I hope you can understand why I have to go, why I need to go."

"I do, Jakeb, I do understand. I just hate the thought of you in the war. I couldn't bear it if anything ever happened..." Her throat constricted.

"Hey," Jakeb reached across the table and took her hand in his. "I will be back before you know it, Jo. Yep, before you know it you'll be begging me to leave and find a good job. You know, your cinnamon buns are ten times as tasty as the one's in this shop. I'll have to come back for those alone."

Jolian tried to smile as she squeezed the hand that held Jakeb's. "You promise me you'll come back, Jakeb?"

"I promise I'll come back, Jolian."

"Then God speed." She could barely choke out the words. It felt as though they were stuck in her throat but she had to bless his journey. He'd made a decision about his life. He hadn't gone off haphazardly. He'd put honest thought into his choice. Who was she to squelch his ideas and diminish his dreams? He paid their bill and they rose in awkward silence. She kissed his cheek, the unswollen one, and watched as he hoisted his canvas pack to his back and wiggled his hat into place on his head.

"Want me to ride back to Pearl's with you?" Jakeb offered.

"Oh no, I still have a few things I need to do in town and you said you wanted to spend the night here."

"Ya, I want to say goodbye to some friends and whatnot. I guess I'll see you tomorrow at the trial."

Jolian nodded and then with a flash of his typical 'I could charm the Devil out of his pitchfork' smile, her brother walked out the front door of the restaurant. Even though she'd see him in the morning, Jolian felt as though they had truly said their goodbyes.

Jolian sat back down at their table and finished her pot of tea. She felt like she could use more than just tea to steady her nerves. What was to become of her now that her brother was leaving and her secret was out? She couldn't stay working for Pearl now, could she? Not without her brother as her chaperone, unless she really wanted no reputation other than a bad one. Maybe she should leave for San Francisco with Jakeb. But somehow, the idea of leaving made her feel even worse. *Oh, Jakeb!* It wouldn't do to start sobbing in public. That surely wouldn't help her reputation either.

She decided she wasn't going to care what people thought of her. She knew the kind of person she was, and when and if she chose to make a life with someone, he'd have to love *her* not her standing in the community. If she wanted to remain in Barkerville without a chaperone then that was a choice she would make. She wouldn't leave because of some silly rule of society's.

Oh why couldn't she just be honest with herself? The reason this was forefront in her mind was just because of him. Cooper Holt. The reason she was ready to throw all of her good upbringing and moral standards out the window. So much for leading a chaste life as a spinster. She was even contemplating lying with the man. There, she'd let the thought that had been lurking about in her mind since their first kiss, come to the forefront.

Her mother had told her *never* before marriage. Jakeb had told her he hadn't waited (and neither had Sally Redmont). The thought caused a giggle. When she'd first thought of leading a life alone, it had been based on the fact of the insurmountable injustices between men and women.

When she really stopped and thought about it, she was giving in to the injustices by taking that route. The road to pursue was one of "do as the men do". That was how she could even up the tally. Who was it that made the "rules" anyway? Little old blue haired ladies who knew nothing of her and her life. Her mother would be turning in her grave if she were privy to her thoughts! Oh, how quickly could wicked thoughts over take her sensibilities. Still, if it was all right for a man...

Jolian kept mulling over the reasons for and against in her mind. She decided despite what her mother had told her and despite what society ruled, her heart would be her judge. It had never failed her in the past and she knew she would make a decision that was right for her when the time came.

She left the restaurant and walked leisurely towards the claims on Back Street. Jakeb had said he sold his share in the mine to Cooper. The thought still had her shaking her head. All the times she'd begged with him, pleaded with him to sell. All of the arguments they'd had in the past six months. Then he up and sells it to join the army! She'd never figure out men, never.

She reached the border of Jakeb's claim—well her and Cooper's claim now. She let her eyes drift over to the shaft from where they had pulled out Angus. One moment he had been working on his life's dream and the next... She shuddered at the thought. She *would* seize the moment. She would live *her* life and she'd live it how she chose. Not by some antiquated rules of society. This was 1863, not the dark ages!

Her resolve and self-esteem strengthened, Jolian half marched to the adjoining claim belonging to Cooper alone. It looked as if someone had been very busy around here lately. She wondered if this was the surprise Jakeb had spoke of earlier. Had Cooper hit the lead? That would be wonderful for him! Oh, how her heart could use some good news!

"Cooper?" The sun was beginning to set; she really needed to be getting on her way. "Cooper, are you down there? It's me, Jolian." She waited a few moments longer and when she still had no response she began to make her way back to her buggy in town.

~ * ~

She'd left it too late; it was going to be pitch black by the time she was only halfway home. Her stomach tightened at the thought. She focused on inhaling slowly and pushing the fear out with her breath. She had nothing to be afraid of now, the murderer was behind bars. She could get herself home. Star knew the way blindfolded. In no time at all the moon and stars would peek out from behind the clouds and the night wouldn't be half as terrifying.

She led Star to the trail and urged her to a steady gait. *Inhale calmness, exhale fear, inhale calmness, and exhale fear.* It'd work; she just needed a few more... What was that? Something moving in the copse of trees to her left. *No, come on, Jolian, it's just your overactive imagination. Inhale, exhale...* There! She saw it again. She didn't know if the buggy would stand up to the beating it was about to get but she didn't much care!

"Yah! Yah! Gid'yup there!" She cracked the reins as hard as she dared and let Star have her head. She squeezed the leather until her fingers were white knuckled and prayed whatever she'd seen in the bushes wasn't as fast as Star. She wasn't looking back, not for anything! Childhood fears and adulthood realities mingled in her mind. All of her nightmares as a child had proven minimal compared to some of the things she'd seen in the past year. The thought made her holler at Star and snap the reins again.

"Gid'yup!! Yah, yah!!"

The wind whipped her face and tugged at her hatpins. She should reach a hand up to hold her borrowed straw bonnet in place but she couldn't pry her fingers from the reins. Cedars and pines blurred in her peripheral vision as she focused all her energy into reaching her destination.

She rounded a bend in the road and had to force her weight to one side of the buggy to keep it from rolling over. She should slow down. Crashing the buggy would only let whatever was in the bushes catch up to her. In an instant she made her choice; slow the buggy she'd be caught for sure, if she crashed... she'd handle it then. Right now she was going to get back to Pearl's as fast as the buggy and Star would take her.

"Yah! Yah! Gid'yup!" She hollered as her hat flew off into the night and Star pulled her closer and closer to her target. She could see the light above Pearl's flickering through the trees and fixed her gaze upon it. It acted as a guidepost, a beacon to her sanctuary; if she could reach the porch light she'd be safe. She bounced and jostled, bobbed and bucked as she raced against the faceless monster to the finish line. When Pearl's place came fully into view she pulled hard at the reins and the wagon slowed on the rut-filled trail.

She may have arrived in one piece although she had her doubts as to the safety of the buggy's wheels after such a wild ride. Jolian breathed her fear out in a sigh. Now that she was back among things familiar, it all seemed so foolish. Maybe, probably, the monster was just a deer or a moose, some harmless creature more afraid of her than she should have been of it. Star snorted and caught her attention.

Oh she'd done it there hadn't she? Star would need an extra long brush and some fresh hay and water. She was beginning to have some feelings for this animal despite herself. After all, the horse was a heroine! Had she not just saved her lady, from the dreaded tree creature?

Jolian chuckled to herself as she pulled the horse around to the barn and made it ready for the evening. She led the Star into her stall and tossed a few carrots on the pile of fresh hay.

"Thanks friend." She rubbed her hand down the length of the horse's nose.

~ * ~

Perspiration dripped from Cooper's brow every time he lowered his head. He supposed he should have answered Jolian when she'd called out, even if it was just to tell her to leave him alone. He put a hand to the small of his back and arched backwards as he stretched. This was back breaking work, but it was the best work he'd done in a long time. This wasn't furthering his business or helping out someone else, this was for him and his family. He didn't care if his muscles ever felt normal again; it was worth it. Lorna would live a comfortable life and the money from this claim would make sure of that.

Cooper stopped for a moment, took a swig form his canteen and mopped his brow with a handkerchief. He'd christened his claim the "Blue Moon" when he'd set the first stick of dynamite. He had no mining experience, only what he'd read in books. He figured he'd see more blue moons in his lifetime than gold. Boy had he been wrong! His studies in geography had helped, too. He figured if any spot were going to hit it would be where his claim was staked. Odd, he always thought he'd feel pure joy if he ever struck gold. Now that he had, it wasn't what he'd imagined it would be.

The gold he'd found today alone would pay for that fancy hospital to care for Lorna for a few years at the very least. He hadn't seen his wife in over a year. He didn't know if he would ever see her again, but at least now he could keep his promise to her.

Suddenly his shoulders seemed free of the weight that had been dragging him lower and lower. Was that why she kept popping into his mind? Could it be as simple as that? Was the reason he couldn't let go of her memory because he hadn't kept his promise to her? It sure made sense. He had promised her "Until death do we part" and then at the first sign of trouble he'd packed it in, let her down.

All right, it wasn't the first sign of trouble. If he *had* packed it in then, he never would have married her. But that was a whole different scenario. He had married her and he had promised to take care of her. Well, he would definitely be able to keep that part of his promise now. He would take care of Lorna until the day she died.

He felt so much better! Why hadn't he thought of it before? Guy had even ribbed him about his personal code of ethics and still he hadn't seen the light. He was probably just too close to the situation. Yeah, that was it. He was just too close to it. He could see it for what it was now and everything seemed to be falling into place.

Still, there was the anger he'd felt. Where had that come from? Like an epiphany the answer rang in his brain. He was angry with himself. He felt things for Jolian he'd never even known were possible for him to feel. Just looking at her made him glad he was a man, but it was more than that, so much more. There was an ache that filled him whenever he thought of a life without her. And it wasn't just loneliness or a desire. He could fill those with any woman. He didn't want just any woman, he wanted Jolian. He'd never felt the need to unite with Lorna. He'd never felt anything except obligation for Lorna.

The anger had been misdirected. He was angry, but it was with himself for the way he'd managed his life so far. This wasn't the way he'd wanted things to turn out. He never should have married Lorna, never. He could have helped her without marrying her. He was angry he'd wasted so many years of his life, first in the marriage and then with the drinking. He needed to whip himself into shape before he could start fresh in this new direction. Lightness began to fill his body. It seeped into every pore until he wanted to scream with the feeling. He wanted to jump up and down like a schoolboy. Finally, he knew what he wanted and what he had to do to get it.

~ * ~

Pearl had told her to take the time off, as much as she needed, and Jolian had taken her up on her offer. She would have the next three days to do as she wished, but right now she'd give anything for a meal to prepare. Without the never-ending chores of cooking and dishes there were no mind numbing tasks to keep her hands busy. She wasn't used to a life of leisure; it gave one too much time for thinking. She tried to read, but her mind wandered. She tried to sleep, but she tossed and turned. Even writing out some new recipes she'd recently perfected couldn't hold her attention.

Pearl's place was hopping busy tonight! She couldn't even sneak down the stairs for a glass of water. News was out that 'Little Jo' was a woman and everyone wanted to come and see for themselves it seemed. Thankfully, Pearl handled it all with her usual style and a flare for the dramatic. Through paper thin walls, she listened as Pearl seemed to bloom more colorful with each telling of how her "tiny cook' outwitted a murderer even the law couldn't touch. Jolian stayed hidden away in her upstairs room like a disgraced family member, not feeling at all like the heroine Pearl was making her out to be.

When she wasn't thinking about Jakeb and his upcoming journey, or the trial and all that entailed, she was thinking about Cooper and wondering why she hadn't seen him since the night before. It seemed odd he hadn't even stopped in to see how she was faring. Half of the town had inquired after her today, but the one she wanted most to see had stayed away.

She'd felt sure he'd had feelings for her. Maybe he didn't have feelings as strong as hers, but she felt sure there was more than just a passing interest in the kisses they'd shared. Yet, if he did care for her then what could be keeping him away? Of course there were a hundred things that could have demanded his attention and right now Jolian felt jealous of every single one of them. She'd just discovered kissing and she wanted more practice! *That was a completely selfish thought, Jolian Grayson.* But it made her smile nonetheless.

She'd just have to wait for tomorrow to see Cooper. If she'd have a chance to see him before the trial started, that was. Of course, according to Pearl, the way the Judge held court would make that nearly impossible.

He'd gather a jury in the morning, hear testimony by noon and pronounce a sentence before nightfall. He'd beleaguer the jury until they reached a verdict and Pearl said he had no patience for people who couldn't make up their minds. She'd said she'd heard of cases where night began to fall and the jury had yet to come to a decision. The Judge would just waltz into the jury room and tell them that if they hadn't come to a conclusion in ten minutes he'd sentence *them* for the crime!

Pearl said he was a no nonsense type of man and he could seem very overwhelming, but he really just had justice in his heart. She said he was impatient only when others couldn't see the truth as clearly as he could. She reassured Jolian everything was going to work out just fine and a good night's sleep would be the best thing for her now.

Jolian supposed Pearl was right and she decided to give sleep another chance. Even though she'd spent the day doing nothing more strenuous than engaging in her fantasy chase home, she felt tired and overwhelmed by her life's events. She stripped down to her chemise and drawers and slipped beneath the sheets of the bed. Being up on the second story of the house she'd felt quite comfortable with leaving her curtains open and her window ajar. Once she'd checked outside her window to make sure no one could enter by climbing a trellis and secured the bolt on her bedroom door, that is.

Now tucked beneath her quilts, her head on a soft feather pillow, she gazed out at the star filled sky and imagined being in Cooper's arms again. Despite all the horrific events and life changes of the past year, there was one thing she was more and more grateful for: Cooper. Her burdened spirit craved the tonic that was he. When her thoughts turned to him, peace enveloped her. She could find solace at last, from the buzzing of her mind, just by imagining his arms about her. It was a wonderful feeling, although not nearly as wonderful as the real thing. She would let this comfort settle over her. She would let his touch, albeit imagined, be the strength she needed now. She'd let her dreams expand the truth of her memory.

Fourteen

The day of the trial dawned rainy and cold. Like the murderer had brought winter back by the sheer coldness of his soul. Jolian dreaded the day that lay before her and wished she had Cooper or even her brother to lean upon for support. But even as the thought crossed her mind she chastised herself for having it. She didn't want to be that kind of a woman. Just because her heart had found a love she wasn't going to turn to mush and helplessness.

Last night she'd dreamed of her mother and had seen her face again, as it had been in life, so beautiful and full of the joy of living. She had woken with a renewed sense of purpose. She wanted to be every bit the woman her mother was, as well as the woman she knew she could be. She wanted to possess all of her mother's traits of commitment and compassion and yet keep her convictions to be true to herself. That was who she was going to become and Cooper could choose to be with her or not.

Of course she desperately hoped his absence was due to something other than him choosing not to be with her. But somewhere inside an intuitive voice told her there was something wrong. If she had learned anything since she left San Francisco, it was that she should listen to her intuition. What had happened between them since they'd shared those kisses?

Everyone knew she wasn't a boy and she'd assisted Cooper with capturing the murderer. Or rather he'd assisted her... Could that be the reason for his absence? Was it some kind of foolish pride or manly ego keeping him away? She hadn't thought of Cooper as that kind of man, but she supposed every man wanted to feel like a hero to his woman.

Listen to her! She was going on like they were some old married couple! For heaven's sake, they'd only shared a few kisses. Just because she thought about him day and night didn't mean he felt the same way. That was the crux of it, really. The little voice inside of her warned her of just that. She was afraid that Cooper Holt stayed away not because his feelings had changed, but because they were never there in the first place. Oh biscuits! She couldn't think about this now, not with all that was happening today.

She dressed in yet another outfit from Doralynn. Despite Jo's protests, Doralynn had insisted upon giving her a beautiful navy suit. She'd have to wear Doralynn's "too big" highshoes again as well as borrow a cloak from someone. She felt apprehension crawl up her spine. It was absolutely freezing in her room. How could it be this cold on August the fourth? Jolian moved to close the window and could not believe the sight that met her eyes. Hail! It was hailing in August! The murderer truly had brought winter back.

~ * ~

Cooper scratched at the whiskers on his chin. He should shave before the trial. *And before you kiss her again.* The thought brought a smile to his lips. He took one last swig of his cold coffee and looked around the Hotel Richfield's restaurant. Everyone looked the same as they always had. He had thought things would look different once he was wealthy, but everything was pretty much the same. He glanced at his watch and motioned to the waiter to bring him some more coffee. He'd give the Grayson kid five more minutes and then he had to leave.

Deep inside he supposed he felt a pang of guilt for buying the kid out. He'd told him there were no certainties in mining and he honestly did believe that. Then again there were the sacks upon sacks of nuggets he'd just validated at the assay office. He knew the owners of the Lazy dazy had done the same. He felt like a kid with enough money to buy his first horse.

Getting Jakeb's share of the mine was pure bonus. It was as close to a sure thing as you could get in this business. Only a matter of time before the lead from his claim exceeded its boundaries into "Angel's Gold". How long it would last or how pure the gold was; now that was another matter all together. And since the cave in, it would take a lot longer to re-dig and excavate Jakeb's mine, but there was gold in Jakeb's claim and any minute now he'd own it.

Just as the waiter began to pour his coffee, Cooper spied Jakeb entering the assay office across the street. Cooper placed a nugget, worth more than the table itself, beside his coffee cup.

"Find me a room with a hot bath and you can have this."

"Yes, sir!" The boy's eyes bugged at the sight of the nugget.

"Could you also arrange for my coffee to be taken up? I'll be back shortly. Oh, I'll need a razor as well."

"Yes, sir, right away, sir!"

Cooper smiled under his stern façade as he walked across the street. Hail fell steadily, collecting in the tiny main street like snow. It bounced off his hat and slicker. Still, he walked slowly, deliberately toward the assay office. He didn't want to appear too eager to Jakeb.

The assay office was a small hastily constructed building. The walls were thin and had shook with the wind when Cooper visited earlier in the day. The walls shook again as he closed the door. Gold Commissioner, Thomas Elwyn, had his official office next door. They'd go there next to transfer the title of the claim.

"Jakeb."

"Morning, Cooper."

"Still want to sell it?"

"Yup."

"Speak to your sister about it?"

"Yup."

"Does she have any complaints?"

"Nope."

"Then let's do it."

The assayer weighed out the gold and attested to the purity of it. Cooper paid Jakeb a fair price and then at the last minute included another four hundred dollars.

"What the...?"

"You were right Jakeb. I did hit on my claim. I guess that makes yours a bit more valuable, that's all."

"I knew it! I hope you make a bundle, Cooper. I hope 'Angel's Gold' hits for you too and that my sister gets rich beyond her wildest dreams. She deserves it, you know."

"Hmm."

"Thanks for the extra loot, too." Cooper did a double take as the boy weighed out half of the extra and handed it back to him.

"Give this to Jolian for me will ya? I don't plan on sticking around for the end of the trial. I spoke to the judge and he agreed to let me testify first off so I can head out early."

"In a hurry, eh?" *The kid probably had some scam cooked up.*

"I'm joining up with the 72nd Illinois regiment. They'll be expecting me to arrive on time."

"You're what?" Cooper half shouted.

"I've joined the army, leaving today." Cooper watched a grin break out on the boy's bruised face. It was as if he enjoyed the look of astonishment Cooper knew was prevalent on his own face. He couldn't help it. He was shocked.

"I'll shake your hand then, son." Cooper had a new respect for the boy, guarded though it may be. He was off to a good start, and he seemed to have the right attitude. But Cooper knew only too well that when push came to shove, it was easy to fall back on old habits. It was the day in day out ability to keep your life on track and resist temptation that was the true test of a man. He'd wait for time to show the boy's true character.

Their business complete at the commissioner's office, Cooper left Jakeb for his warm bath at the hotel. Entering the specified room, Cooper found not only the steaming tub, soap, brush and razor but also a box of cigars and a bottle of Glenlivet Scotch. Ah, the life of a wealthy man had its rewards after all! What had he just been thinking about temptation?

He opened the box of cigars and inhaled deeply. There was nothing as fine as the smell of a first-class cigar, unless it was a select bottle of single malt whiskey, or the love of a good woman. He opened the hallway door to place the unopened bottle of scotch whiskey outside, just as the waiter was bringing up a pot of coffee. He handed the bottle directly to the boy with the statement "I don't drink". He slipped another nugget into the boy's hand and turned back into his room. The liquor he would resist, the cigars he would smoke and the woman he would ponder.

~ * ~

Try as she might, the navy suit was not going to fit without a corset. Jolian gave up trying to fasten the button on the waistband, and began to strip herself down to her chemise and drawers. Reluctantly she cracked open her bedroom door and called for the help Pearl had offered earlier.

Pearl pushed her way in through the bedroom door. "I told ya so. If thars one thin' I know it's bodies. I could tell from looking, yours weren't gonna fit into that suit. You may be tiny, Jolian, but that suit is itsy and you just ain't itsy."

Jolian exhaled as Pearl cinched the waist tighter. Thank goodness she had no appetite for breakfast this morning. Pearl chattered away and Jolian knew it as a ploy to help keep her mind off of the day. She could sense tension in the house and knew most of it was due to worry over how she was going to handle the trial.

She wished she could ease everyone's minds and tell them everything would be fine. However, the truth was, she was worried sick about the lot of it. But, best if she didn't bother Pearl or the girls with her worries. Yes, it was better to let Pearl talk nineteen to the dozen than to face the baker with no dough.

Pearl finished her lacing and her prattles and left Jolian to dress in private. Jo tied a petticoat at her waist and then another on top of that. She added the navy shirt and was still able to button the waistband easily. Even though she never wanted to wear one again, she had to begrudgingly admit, corsets where good for one thing; they gave you a waist no woman could naturally achieve.

Jolian put her arms through the elegant lace inset sleeves and felt a proper young lady as she secured the neck-high buttons. Thankfully, she had coifed her hair into its simulated chignon before she got dressed. The tightness of the corset hardly left room for breathing let alone the stretching movements of pinning up one's hair. The young woman staring at her from the mirror was definitely not the same one who'd tumbled out of bed an hour earlier. This one looked much more composed and rehearsed than she felt.

With one last stern glance at her reflection and her resolve to keep her composure firmly in place, Jolian headed down the stairs to meet the girls in Pearl's parlor. Pearl continued to chatter away about the weather and other idle bits while she handed her a cloak and gloves, borrowed from one of the girls, she imagined.

Jolian felt as though she watched herself step up into the covered carriage Pearl had hired for the day. Surely it must be someone else heading to Richfield to testify in the murder trial of her parents. How had it come to this? How had she? It was like a dream she couldn't wake from. *Where was Jakeb? And Cooper?* She wished she could take a deep breath and calm herself with thoughts of him again.

~ * ~

As their carriage pulled into Richfield, the rain plummeted the ground with such intensity the mud actually looked like it was boiling. Jolian stepped out of the coach and felt a strong pair of arms whisk her up onto the boardwalk that ran down the main street of Richfield.

"Oh, Jakeb! Thank you."

"My pleasure, miss." He winked at his sister and tipped his hat as he let go of her waist and reached for another girl. "I am glad I got the chance to see you again, Jolian. If I had known I... never mind. There are plenty of people here already. The Judge has set up the trial in that building yonder." Jakeb motioned with a nod of his head, as his arms were busy helping yet another girl out of Pearl's coach. "Go on ahead if you want, Jolian. I'm going have a moment with Pearl before I enter the building. Oh, and Jo?"

Jolian turned her head towards her brother.

"I just wanted to say thank you, on behalf of Ma and Pa. I think they're resting easier today because of you."

Jolian couldn't speak for fear that she'd burst into tears, so she simply nodded her silent reply. Jakeb must have sensed her uneasiness and he nodded back, gave her another wink and then turned from her to walk towards Pearl.

Jolian took as big a breath as she dared and held her chin parallel to the ground as she walked straight for the building Jakeb had indicated. She *would* keep her composure if it were the last thing she did today. She fastened her eyes to the building to help steady her resolve. Really, all she wanted to do was to search the crowd for Cooper. However, frantically scanning the crowd may send a message of uncertainty to the potential jurors who may be among her and the last thing she wanted was to appear unsure of her testimony.

Jolian entered the building that would serve as the courtroom. It was ordinary enough in structure. Rough whitewashed lumber paneled the inside walls and reflected the eerie glow of lanterns lit, she supposed, in attempt to brighten the dreary day. The one-room edifice was more square than rectangular and had been prepared as an office of the court. At the door where she entered there was a wooden pew being used as a makeshift cloakroom. Jolian discarded her borrowed cloak in a vacant spot, and then immediately regretted not bringing a wrap of some kind. The room had a chill despite the wool of her suit and the iron potbelly at the end of the cloakroom pew.

She forced herself to take in the rest of her surroundings. Concentrating on the aspects of the courtroom would help calm her and would furnish her mind with a steadiness her hands sorely lacked. Jolian faced the court and the large table set in the center of the room. A pitcher of water, a tin cup, a bible and a tiny hammer sat atop it; surely this was where Judge Begbie would sit, though, perhaps not.

"Does the Judge stand to preside over the court?" Jolian asked Pearl.

"Oh, honey, ain't ya never heard about his chair? It's rightly as famous as the man himself. He carries it with him on his circuit. Begbie's a big man and a big man needs a big commanding chair. Wait till you see it, it's like a throne for the king. Now move along darlin', yore holdin' up the line."

Pearl bonked her gently with a sway of her hips and turned her attention to a man in line behind her. Jolian turned to face forward once more, placing one foot in front of the other, dread filling her further with each step.

In front of the Judge's table were two smaller tables each with a chair facing the Judge. She deducted the lawyers would occupy that station. To her left there were two wooden pews, one behind the other; the jury's destination, she was almost positive. To her right was an elevated platform, fenced in by a whitewashed banister. She had to force herself to look at that area. She held the picture so long she could see it still, even as she slowly closed her eyes. That was where *he* would stand.

Jolian felt as though *she* were on trial as she moved down the aisle set between what looked to be about fifty chairs. She made her way to the front and sat on the chair furthest away from the whitewashed box *he* would occupy. She sat with her back erect and her eyes looking straight ahead.

It seemed to take hours for the room to fill up with spectators, when really it was only a matter of minutes. Jolian concentrated on breathing in and out, as deeply as she could despite the tightness of her chest. She could hear the shuffling of feet and the whispers of the audience.

She kept her gaze focused on a knothole in the paneling. The whitewash had obviously been hastily applied and they hadn't taken the time to completely fill the hole. The result was a pattern resembling a crooked faced elf with a long pointed chin. The more she focused on the spot of missed paint the more obvious the face became.

As Constable Towers entered, the crowd became hushed and the jury filed in to their seats. He would act as an officer of the court while it was in session, Pearl explained to her. Jolian sat, transfixed by her little elf and paid little attention to the scraping of chairs and clearing of throats. She closed her eyes and tried to remember the story her mother had read to her about a peasant girl who spun straw into gold. She could hear the chains dragging on the floor as the prisoner was put in his spot. She heard the shifting of wood on the floor and assumed someone placed the Judge's chair in position at his table. Her eyes opened, found and never left their mark. The image of the little evil elf on the wall, his name was Rumpelstilzchen. Why she should think of that now? Surely, she was losing her senses.

The Constable had said something but she hadn't listened. She needed to concentrate on what was happening. She didn't want to make a foolish mistake like the peasant girl in her fairy tale.

"All rise!"

She did what was asked and found the man who entered the room could easily keep her gaze from the elf in the corner. He was a commanding figure in a powdered wig and regal robes. He picked up his tiny hammer and banged it twice on the table.

"Sit!" His voice commanded authority over the crowd even more than his royal appearance had done. Whether it was the high-backed plainly carved wooden chair he sat upon, or simply his attitude and bearing, the man became more than a man and all eyes focused on him as an uneasy stillness filled the room.

Jolian focused on the timbre of his voice and noticed how the words seemed to sink into her body through the pores of her skin rather than just enter through her ears. She jumped as he punctuated a statement with a pounding of his fist on the table. She trembled as his next sentence came in hushed tones. Listening to this man was more terrifying than facing the murderer head on!

"I will have calm and quiet proceedings in my court. If at anytime you are required to leave my presence, you must first rise and bow to the court. Should I determine your reason for leaving inconsequential, you will find yourself in contempt of court and be availed of a night's stay in the local jail." Judge Begbie paused, only slightly, then boomed his voice so loud, Jolian swore the windows rattled in their panes. "I invite anyone who feels they cannot hold up for the entire trial to leave now and make room for another spectator from the rabble that gathers about the doorways and windows." He turned then to the lawyers, hardly giving anyone time to take a breath and commanded, "Proceed."

Each lawyer spoke his turn, telling the jury of how he would proceed and what verdict he expected from them. Neither of the men had half of the command of the room the Judge had demanded.

Then the prosecuting attorney began to call his witnesses. Jakeb took the stand first. Jolian knew he had spoken to the Judge about being the first to testify. He wanted to get an early start for San Francisco as soon as his testimony ended. This may very well be the last time she saw Jakeb before he left. Despite all of her anxiety and apprehension she looked Jakeb in the eyes and smiled the most carefree, loving smile she could muster.

If he left directly after his testimony, she wanted him to remember her with ease. She couldn't show him the fear that threatened to overtake her, not now when he was heading off to war. She wanted his mind to be free to fight the battles he would face, not to be thinking about the sister he left behind and wondering if he had done right by her.

Jolian tried to listen carefully to everything her brother said, but truth be told, her mind wandered. She knew it was her built in safety shield, sparing her from hearing the details of the murder over and over again. It was simply too much for her heart to endure.

Jakeb showed the court the scar over his left temple where he'd been kicked by the mule. Jolian flashed her smile at him again and let her eyes wander about whilst keeping her back to the jury. They wouldn't be able to form any opinion of her if they couldn't see her face. She slowly began to shift her body sideways and she caught a glimpse of something on one of the attorneys' tables. It looked like a chain of some kind poking out of a sack.

Just as she searched her mind for why it looked so familiar, the attorney walked over to the table and opened the sack. He produced her father's watch and held it up for the whole crowd to see. Jolian couldn't hide her gasp of astonishment. She quickly raised her hand to her mouth in attempt to hide her surprise and realized she still wore her gloves.

The prosecutor queried Jakeb about the watch and Jolian slipped the gloves off her hands. Her fingers trembled so badly she felt thankful to have something to do with her hands if only for a minute or two. The attorney told the court the contents of the sack had been found on the person who now stood trial before them. He asked Jakeb if he had seen the watch before. She heard Jakeb state the watch was the one her father always carried. He told the court their mother had given it to their father as a wedding gift and he had not seen the watch since the day his parents were murdered.

"How can you be certain this watch is the same one, which belonged to your father? Surely there must have been many watches made similar in appearances and style." The prosecutor faced the jury as he questioned Jakeb.

"My father's watch was indented on the bottom, just as that watch is there." Jakeb spoke directly to the jury as well. "I was fond of playing with it when I was a child and I'm afraid I wasn't always as careful as I sh-sh-should have been."

"Still, there are many reasons why a watch might have become damaged in such a way." The prosecutor paused for a sip of water and continued. "How can you be certain this is your father's watch and not someone else's?"

"Well, there's the inscription..."

"An inscription you say?"

"Yes."

"Could you tell the court now, before you examine this watch, what the inscription on your father's watch read?"

"Of course. It sssaid 'I promise. March 10, 1841.' Which was my parent's wedding day."

"Sir, I present this watch to you now, which I remind the jury was taken from the person who now stands trial before you. Sir, I pray you, open the watch and read the inscription for this court."

Jolian closed her eyes and felt the tears strike her cheeks as Jakeb read her mother's vow. It was the one thing she had longed for during all these months of missing her parents: a belonging, or a memento. It seemed a trifle, but if she only had a keepsake of some kind she knew it would help to ease the pain. She had wished for something to help her hang onto the memory of her parents, but she had never voiced that wish, as it seemed inconsiderate somehow, as if her own memories weren't enough to keep them with her.

If she was thrilled and overwhelmed to see her father's watch, it was nothing compared to the feelings that smothered her when the attorney pulled her mother's wedding ring from the sack. She felt revolted and relieved all at the same time. That ring had meant so much to her mother. It had been the symbol of her troth to her husband and she had never taken it off. Jolian felt pleased it had been recovered but her stomach churned to think it been pulled from her mother's finger after her death. Jolian knew for a fact that was the only way her mother would have ever relinquished her wedding ring.

She also knew the ring had been engraved with her parents' wedding date. It had been such an extravagance to keep pieces of jewelry when they had lost their farm in California. Her mother had cried and cried and swore they should sell them. Her father had tried to convince her mother they were not prideful people just because they wanted to keep their wedding gifts to each other. He had said their children would gain more from the love of their parents than the trifle of food, their jewelry would purchase. He vowed he would keep his watch with him until his death and her mother had promised to wear the ring to her grave. The conversation could have occurred yesterday, it was that vivid in her memory. Only a short while later they'd moved into her uncle's hotel.

Jolian snapped her attention to the present as the attorney who questioned Jakeb walked towards her. Did he mean to ask a question of her? Had he already and she had missed it? Her heart began to pound and she could feel the heat rising in her face. The man came closer. She could see the wedding ring in his hand. He held it out as if he wanted her to take it from him. Then at the last minute, he walked right by her and gave the ring to the man behind her, the foreman of the jury.

Jolian rounded in her seat to see each member of the jury examine the ring in turn. Jolian felt sure her mother would disapprove somehow. To have all of these strange men examining her personal belongings seemed at the very least, inappropriate. She turned to look at her brother and could see the concern in his eyes. She remembered her pledge to keep Jakeb free from worry and she tried to smile a little for him. He smiled back and seemed to be telling her it was okay, Ma would understand. She knew he was right. The most important thing was to see the murderer pay for his crimes.

Jakeb had been dismissed as a witness once the defense had asked their questions of him. She hoped the Judge would break for a few minutes, enabling her to say goodbye. He didn't and the best she could do was to hold Jakeb's eyes with her own until he reached the door. She didn't have the nerve to leave the courtroom, not even to say another goodbye to her brother. Jakeb winked at her, smiled his happy-go-lucky grin and disappeared from her life like the setting sun.

As she watched him leave she felt an odd sense of peace settle over her. Unusual, to say the least. The last thing she thought she'd feel at her brother's departure was peace, but she felt it just the same. Maybe it was a sign all would be well with him and he would return safely from war. That's what she would take it for regardless.

"God bless Jakeb and keep him safe." She whispered to herself.

"What's that?" Pearl whispered from beside her.

"Nothing."

"Ya holding up okay? Do ya wants a drink or somethin'?" Pearl exposed a silver flask by lifting her skirts to reveal her snuggly-fitting garter.

"No, no I'm fine, thank you."

"Ya don't look it."

"Well thank you very much." Jolian sarcastically whispered back. She knew Pearl was just trying to lighten her spirit. She watched as her friend nonchalantly removed the bottle and then unscrewed its lid. She tipped her head slowly, swallowed deeply and turned to grin at Jolian. Jolian smiled back and hoped Pearl felt some warmth from her apathetic attempt.

She watched as Guy took the stand and then Ts'kaw. She held her breath as the Constable called Cooper. She hadn't seen him in the courtroom but then again; she hadn't looked about as much as she could have. She closed her eyes now and tried to pretend nothing had come between them since the afternoon of their kisses. For even though she had no idea of what could have changed, she knew something was different. Such a tangible tension hung in the air, that even with her eyes closed; she knew the moment Cooper walked by her.

A chair scraped on the wooden floor, the Constable asked for his oath and then she heard it, Cooper's voice. The sound resonated through her being and shuddered in her soul. She'd missed its richness, the melodic cadence that was his and his alone. She knew his voice as she knew her own. She'd dreamt of it. He'd whispered into her ear and branded her heart forever. She didn't know what had come between them but at that moment, she hoped nothing ever would again. She would do everything within her power to fix it and make it right.

She opened her eyes and they immediately focused on Cooper. She drank him in, slowly and deeply like Pearl had drunk from her silver flask. Her body began to fill with the familiar heat only Cooper could bring her. He looked exceptionally dashing today in a dark blue suit and crisp white shirt. He focused directly on the jury and spoke unhurriedly, with calm, precise words.

~ * ~

He kept his gaze on the twelve men until his testimony ended. The attorneys discharged him and then, only then did he allow himself the luxury of looking at her. As he moved his eyes he caught her staring and he held her gaze intently. He could see a blush beginning to rise in her cheeks but still he didn't back down. She was beautiful, simply beautiful. He'd known all along that he was in error really. He'd been a fool to deprive himself of her for even a few days and he wasn't too proud to admit it.

Jolian's blush deepened and she bowed her head slightly, lowering her lashes only for a moment. She looked to him, like a fresh blooming rose just waiting to be picked. To think he had let his own past overshadow a chance at life with this woman was so ludicrous; he wanted to laugh out loud. He pushed back the chair and rose to go to her. He would ask for her forgiveness and tell her everything, if only he could see her face first thing each morning and last thing every night for the rest of his life. The way she looked at him with those eyes as blue as the sky itself... Damn! He had to kiss her.

"The court calls Jolian Caroline Grayson to the stand." The Constable's voice boomed in the makeshift court.

Damn. Now that he'd made up his mind to speak with her, he didn't want to have to wait another moment. Suddenly, the man on trial began to hiss and shout.

"That's the runt! A danged split-tail! I shoulda seen her comin' a mile back and ett her up fer breakie!" He spit as he shouted and then laughed a gruesome, strident wail.

The women in the room seemed to all inhale together. Some of the men instinctively reached to their belts for the weapons, which, by law they had left at home. Cooper had stopped in his tracks at the sound of the man. His gut instinct was to put himself between Jolian and the crazed lunatic. He needn't have worried though as he could see the man was thoroughly shackled to the railings surrounding him.

"Outbursts will not be tolerated in this court!" The voice of the Judge exploded like gunfire and knocked the grin off the murderer's face.

Cooper let his breath out slowly as he turned his back on the man and strode toward Jolian. The blush had disappeared from her cheeks and her eyes took on a glazed quality as her head tilted sideways. Cooper ran as fast as legs would go, and grabbed her just in time to keep her from fainting onto the courtroom floor. As his arms filled with her limp form, he never felt more emotion surge through his body.

~ * ~

Jolian woke to see four faces and eight eyes staring intently at her. She blinked several times and shook her head slightly trying to clear her mind. They were in a small room, which held a davenport, desk and a few personal items. From her quick glance she surmised it must have been the private room of the Judge.

"Ya fainted," Pearl stated as she pushed her nose ever closer to Jolian's. "But yer color's starting to come back now. She'll be fine." Pearl backed off and Jolian focused on the other people still staring at her.

"Of course she will." Doralynn flashed her a calm smile and pressed a mug of water into her hand.

The Judge snorted and stood to his full height giving Jolian a feeling of vertigo she feared would pitch her into the blackness again. She'd done the very thing he'd cautioned against; she'd disrupted his courtroom. She feared his wrath and it took all of her nerve to hold his gaze steady with her own. To her surprise, she saw compassion reflecting back at her. The Judge smiled for her eyes only.

"Take all the time you need, Miss, as long as you're back in ten minutes," his whisper barely audible above the discussion the others were having.

Jolian could hear the concern in his voice and wondered if the fainting spell had caused her mind to be playing tricks on her. The Judge moved out of her range of vision and Cooper's face came into focus before her. She smiled at him and felt his hand encircle hers.

"How are you?"

"I... I'm fine, I think. I can't believe I fainted."

Pearl jostled for a position in front of Jolian. "Ain't no surprise to me, what with that screamin' idiot out there. Thank God that dungferbrains Constable chained him in like he did or he'd be a dead man now fer sure. Even without their weapons, mosta the men out thar would a beat him to a pulp! Could'a saved us all a whole lotta heartache if we'd a just had ourselves a linchin' instead of a trial."

"Miss Tuttle!" The Judge's voice boomed and then quieted. "I'll have no such talk in my court, or my chambers for that matter. The best course of action is always the lawful course. There is no room in this colony for vigilante justice. I believe everyone here concurs with me and will abide by the laws that govern this land. That said, I shall take my leave of you and return to my bench. I fear the prisoner's outburst has caused some disquiet amongst the masses. They will look to *me* now, for solace." He exhaled as he spoke with such pomposity, Jolian would have laughed had she not been so terrified of him.

Even Pearl looked humbled beneath the Judge's admonishment; although she was the first to turn on him once he left the room.

"He might talk big, but under it all he's as soft as a baby's arse!" Pearl laughed at her own vulgarity. "Ya sure yer okay?"

"I am." Jolian had sat upright and sipped from her mug of water. She had never fainted before and felt quite ashamed at having done so. Fainting was for the gentry, not for a working girl like her. Probably it could be blamed upon the corset, and the fact she hadn't eaten anything today. She finished her water and accepted Cooper's arm as she slowly came to standing. She must have imagined the rift between them for he was nothing if not attentive and caring. She thanked everyone for their concern and assured them all she was well enough to continue.

"We'll leave the two of youse then. But remember, his honor said *ten* minutes." Pearl grabbed Doralynn's elbow and half pushed her out of the Judge's chambers.

Jolian turned to face Cooper, lifting her chin to look at him directly.

"I need to speak with you." Cooper's eyes seemed to be pleading with her. Had there been no problem after all? He seemed torn, as if he couldn't bring himself to say something that had to be said. He opened his mouth and shut it again.

Cooper pulled her shoulders to his chest. He held her suspended on her tiptoes while his hand encircled her waist and his lips brushed hers. So close, yet not quite a kiss. His eyes searched hers, as if he looked for an answer to an unspoken question. He brushed her lips with his own again. It was his own brand of torture, this playing with her senses. She wanted to scream at him to kiss her, to take her the way a man should take a woman. His head moved closer, his fingers searing through her suit as one hand moved to the nape of her neck. He turned her head with the slightest pressure from his hand and his lips were upon hers.

She had waited for this; dreamed about this. His tongue sought hers. She could feel his heart hammering in his chest as he claimed her for his own. Again and again their mouths drank of each other until she could see the evidence of her desire reflected in his eyes. He relaxed his hold and nuzzled her earlobe.

"We really need to sit down and talk." He said as he nibbled on her neck. His words said one thing but his eyes, hands and lips were saying something quite different.

"Um-hum."

"Shall I meet you outside after the trial? Are you really feeling up to going back into the courtroom?"

"Yes..."Jolian cleared her throat and smoothed the bodice of her suit as he released her to arms length. "Yes, I'll be fine and yes I will meet you afterwards. I want to do my duty; I want to testify." *I want to make love with you.* The last words were in her own head but she wasn't shocked in the least with her thoughts. She'd known for a long time now she'd lay with him if the opportunity presented itself. The only thing that did shock her was her body's ability to melt into his with the slightest touch, even in a Judge's chambers!

~ * ~

Jolian went back into the courtroom and faced her fears head on. She pointed out the man, and identified him as the murderer that he was. She was calm and clear. She spoke from her heart but with her head. At times, tears fell unchecked down her cheeks. Other times, statements brought anger and disgust to her voice. Through it all Cooper felt amazement, wonder, and an overwhelming love for the petite angel addressing the court. How could he have ever thought her like Lorna in anyway at all? She was courageous, candid, determined and beautiful, everything he'd always wanted and never thought he would have. She was amazing and he was in love with her. Everything seemed to be falling into place for him. Now that her true identity was out in the open, nothing stopped him from letting the whole colony know how he felt about her.

Cooper couldn't help but smile at the thought of all those little old ladies back home in Victoria. He could actually picture the looks on their faces as he scooped the boy-clad Jo into his arms and kissed her the way he had back in the Judge's chambers. They really need to have that talk that he'd alluded to earlier.

Fifteen

"Have the right-honorable men of the jury come to a resolution in the Crown's case against Frederick Brewer?"

"We have."

"What say you?"

"We find the defendant, Frederick Brewer, guilty as charged."

The applause and hoots and hollers generated by the crowd in the makeshift courtroom in Richfield were nearly loud enough to be heard in Barkerville.

"Come to order! Come to order at once or I shall clear this court!" The Judge's thunderous voice produced the silence he demanded. He turned to face the man who stood chained before the court.

"It has been proven that you carried on your person, private items belonging to Mr. and Mrs. Joseph Grayson. It has been witnessed that you were with the deceased at the time of their deaths and that you left the scene with their belongings. As you had no prior introduction to the deceased, or credible reason to be in possession of their belongings, it is therefore concluded your crime was committed solely for the purpose of monetary gain." He paused, more likely for the effect than the need to actually breathe, and looked about the courtroom.

"It has been displayed by the prosecutor that you were arrested with weapons matching the style and caliber of those used in the Grayson murders. While we have not heard direct evidence to place you with the other murdered victims recently discovered from Yale to Barker's ville, suffice it to say I have no doubts as to the perpetrator of those crimes." The silence in the courtroom was palpable as the judge turned to face the accused.

"As you have shown no remorse or for that matter professed your innocence, it is my conclusion to side with the jury and find you guilty of the murders of Caroline and Joseph Grayson. You are flagitious down to the pit of your very existence. As ye reap, so shall ye sow. You have lived your life full of contempt for the law and indeed without thought for your fellow man. I pray those in this court to mourn your passing with as much concern. It is my deepest regret that the law will only allow me to sentence you but once for your crimes. I hereby declare sentence upon *you* Frederick Brewer. You are to be hanged by the neck until you are dead. May the good Lord, in all his wisdom, take mercy upon your soul."

The Judge punctuated his decree with the pounding of his gavel and again the crowd cheered their approval. This time he let them have their way and indeed seemed to revel in their ovation. His chest puffed broader with each shout of approval, his chin raised higher and higher with the growing rhythm of applause.

Two of the Constable's men entered and led the prisoner away. The rumblings of discussions began as the crowd began to disperse. Pearl informed Jolian that men would begin work on the gallows the next day, but the execution would likely take a bit longer. The Judge had to send the official documents by approved carrier back to Victoria. He would then await the Crown's approval for the proclaimed execution. Pearl told her the last time she'd attended a trial it took about six weeks from sentencing to hanging. They reached the pews where their cloaks were waiting and Jolian quickly spied the one she'd worn.

"If they have already had a hanging here, why are there no gallows? Was the last hanging that long ago?" Jolian queried. She could hardly believe it was over.

"Thar ain't any gallows 'cause it's in the law that they gots ta be taken down after a hangin'. And the last time I was at a hangin' was... oh let me think. I remembers it. It were just after Cooper left with his wife, about three years ago."

"His wife?" Jolian could actually feel the color draining from her cheeks.

"Yup, that was the last time I seen him. They honeymooned up here, stayed at Guy's place. 'Course Guy, Ts'kaw and that ol' hag Po weren't around at that time, they had the place all to themselves. I gots to know Cooper real well then."

Jolian wasn't listening to anything Pearl had to say. How could she when she'd just found out that the man she was in love with... the man who had just kissed her defenses away in a room not twelve feet from here... the same man who waited to speak with her with this very moment *was married*! How could he? How could she? What was she going to do? She'd given her heart. She loved him. What on earth could she do now?

Her head spun with the news. Could she not just bask in the victory of the trial for a few minutes before her entire future came caving in on her like some faulty old mine shaft? Mine shaft? She groaned audibly. Not only had she kissed a married man and planned to give him her innocence, she was also a partner in Jakeb's mine with the louse. What kind of a man was he, that he would take advantage of her like he had? A miner. A self-serving *miner*!

"Did ya say somethin'?"

"No." But she needn't have answered. Pearl chattered away about something Jolian wasn't listening to in the least. Thank goodness Doralynn seemed to be paying attention. At least that way she could slip away to their carriage without going through the front doors where Cooper would surely be waiting. She needed a few minutes alone to put her thoughts in order.

"Pearl, excuse me, I am sorry to interrupt you, but I really wanted to have a moment alone with the Judge. If you would just excuse me, I'll meet up with you at the carriage." She couldn't believe how calm her own voice sounded. How could everyone be carrying on like nothing had happened? Her heart was breaking. Slowly shriveling into the tiny dried up heart of the spinster she had planned to become. She should have maintained her itinerary, steadied her course. How had she strayed so far from her chosen path?

"All right, Jo, see ya there."

"Congratulations on the victory," Doralynn managed to sneak into the conversation before Pearl continued with her ramblings.

Jolian wondered if she had actually smiled for her friends. She hoped she had. Better they think that everything was right as rain. She pushed her way through the remains of the crowd toward the Judge's chambers.

"Hello? Is there anyone here?"

"If you've come for the items belonging to your parents, they'll be returned to you once the court receives its official notice from Victoria that the sentence will be carried out. They have to be held as evidence until then." The Constable sat behind the desk, his nose buried in paperwork. The Judge, thank goodness, was nowhere to be seen.

"Actually I came to—"

"See the Judge? He has left for the evening ah... Ma'am." There was a definite sound of contempt in the man's voice.

Better to let him think what he wanted than to have to engage him in conversation further. "Oh, I see, thank you."

He grunted a reply. Not much, but it was a more civil discussion than she'd ever had with Constable Towers.

"Would it be all right if I just left by this back door then?" There was too much hope in her voice. He'd say 'no' just to spite her now.

"If it'll make you leave more quickly, then by all means."

Jolian didn't wait for him to change his mind, or to look up from his paperwork. She hurried across the room to the door and let herself out. She'd make her way around the back of the building and to the carriage, before Cooper could see her.

"Jolian!"

"Biscuits!" Cooper had spied her from across the street and was pushing his way through the crowds. She needed a moment to get her bearings. Just where had Pearl's carriage dropped her off? She couldn't speak to him now, not now! She raised her chin and pretended not to hear his shouts. She tried looking over the heads of those on the boardwalk, but the crowd was too plentiful. She craned her neck from left to right but she could only see a river of faces, hats and bonnets coming towards her. She floundered, like a salmon swimming upstream. She daren't glance backwards but she sensed Cooper gaining on her position. She raised herself up on her tiptoes to try one last time.

At that very moment the crowd dispersed slightly and she had a clear view of Cooper crossing the street towards her. Her heart began to pound and her face became hot. So shamed, she desperately wanted to flee his approach. She swiveled her hips about in an attempt to turn tail and run but before she knew it, she landed flat on her bottom in the mud of Main Street.

The hustle and bustle came to an immediate stand still. It felt as though the entire town stopped to stare at the fool sitting red-faced in the mud. Jolian scraped the bottom of the barrel for what little dignity she could find and rolled over onto her

196

knees. In her lovely hooped skirt with its two layers of petticoats, there was no other way for her to get into a standing position.

After what felt like an eternity, a man who stood close by moved to her side to offer his hand. Jolian accepted his offer by placing her hand in his. Without raising her head, she leaned her entire weight onto his hand as she tried to free herself of the muck. She murmured a 'Thank you' to the man, whilst still maintaining her focus on the ground.

"My pleasure, Ma'am" The man courteously kept his voice low as he retained his firm hold on her hand and put his other hand on her elbow in an attempt to usher her back to the boardwalk. A gallant gesture, thwarted only by the errant highshoe that stayed behind as Jolian took a step forward.

The man turned to pick it up but Jolian urged him forward with a tug on his arm.

"Just let it lie." She whispered through clenched teeth, her chin practically resting on her chest. Her step hardly faltered as she firmly set her stocking clad foot onto the wood of the boardwalk. If only her sure-footedness had come a moment sooner.

Jolian raised her mud soaked skirts, as well as her chin, puffed up her chest and pulled back her shoulders. Click, fwap, click, fwap—her one remaining highshoe and other sludge saturated, stocking-clad foot alternated down the boardwalk. Her high-low limp evidencing her clumsiness, for any who may have missed the spectacle of her fall.

She reached Pearl's carriage and climbed aboard. Doralynn averted her eyes and Pearl sat slack-jawed. It was a first, truly a first. So ungainly, she'd rendered the garrulous Pearl silent. Jolian rapped on the ceiling of the carriage signaling the driver to make haste. She'd gone out of her way to avoid Cooper and she wasn't about to let a little awkwardness stop her now. The rest of Pearl's girls would have to find their own way back. She wasn't about to sit here in the carriage and wait for anyone!

~ * ~

Jolian had never heard the quiet as she did on that ride home. Still, she was thankful Doralynn and Pearl weren't trying to compete with the voices in her own head that were driving her half-mad. *Its not enough that the whole town is buzzing with the knowledge that you're a woman, no, you had to up and faint in the courtroom to give them a bit more gossip. But you didn't stop there did you? Let's see what could possibly be more embarrassing than that? Hmm? Ah yes, how about a swim... in front of everyone... IN A MUD PUDDLE!*

Her only saving grace was the people of the town could not see the contents of her heart. The humiliation of being in love with a married man, of being the 'other' woman, was almost more than she was able to bear. They would, of course, begin to comment about her working at Pearl's like she did and then there'd be speculation of what exactly she did there. She would have gladly executed a swan dive into the puddle if she could've avoided the pain she felt now. Why, oh why, hadn't she heeded her mother's advice about virtue? Jolian groaned out loud. She didn't care who heard her; she'd earned the right to groan.

"It wasn't that bad, honey," Doralynn whispered as she reached over to pat Jolian's lap. She had no sooner touched her than she recoiled and turned up her nose at the mud stuck to her hand from Jolian's knee. "I said that you could keep that suit didn't I?"

Jolian just rolled her eyes to the roof of the carriage and groaned again. She'd let them think she was upset about the mud, the less people who knew what a true fool she was the better.

"Really, honey, one day you'll look back at that moment with laughter. I mean, after all, it was awfully funny..."

Jolian could see the laughter in Doralynn's eyes as her friend turned her head toward the window and pursed her lips to keep from laughing. Is that why Pearl was silent? Jolian had thought it was out of sympathy for her, but was it because she was hiding her laughter?

"Pearl?" Jolian commanded Pearl to turn and face her. Pearl turned her head slowly and seemed unable to contain herself any longer. Her laughter bubbled up like an over stuffed pie. Doralynn joined her and the carriage rocked and pitched with laughter on the rut filled trail.

Jolian kept her gaze focused on the window and tried to keep her mouth from tilting down at the corners. The only women friends she had in the whole world were laughing at her "gaucherie". She shuddered as she recalled the word her uncle had used when describing her. He had said her cooking was beyond compare but her gaucherie would always prove her true status in life. He said she would never fit into fashionable society if she couldn't learn the art of grace.

Of course she couldn't very well have practiced it lately, what with having to contend with her "masquerade". She didn't know very many young boys who had grace. She had a sinking feeling in her chest. She thought she'd learned a bit of refinement, but obviously not. She had never set her sights on the upper class, but she thought she at least fit in with her friends. Now they were laughing at her. What did it matter really? Nothing seemed to matter anymore. She wished she'd never met Cooper Holt.

"Oh, Jo, we ain't laughin' at ya. We's laughing with you."

"In case you hadn't noticed, I'm not laughing." Jolian barely contained her sobs as she choked out the words. Maybe she was overreacting. Maybe she should just let the incident roll off her.

Cooper obviously had just been toying with her. He couldn't have serious feelings for her when he was already *married*! She should've known better than to have become involved with a miner. She had no one to blame in this but herself. Who knew better than she that a miner never thought about anything but gold? Hadn't every man in her life been that way? Her father and her brother both had sacrificed everything, including their moral standards, for gold. Her uncle's love of money had taken precedence over the love of family time and time again. She knew she would never have Cooper's heart because miners had no room left in their hearts. Every ounce of space had been taken up with the love of gold, gold, gold!

She was making excuses for him. Just like she did for her father and her brother. She was trying to find a reason for his lies and his hurtfulness, something that would help her understand. She wanted to be able to find a motive so she could persuade herself he could overcome it and truly love her. She fooled no one but herself. If he couldn't stay committed to his wife, a woman that he'd pledged himself to before God, then he would never stay committed to her.

What had happened between them had seemed special and beautiful to her, a once in a lifetime kind of feeling. But what did she know? After all, it had been her first kiss. He had played her like a pianist tinkles the ivories. He must have known she was naïve the minute he'd laid eyes on her. He'd used her. Either for his own silly little game or for a cheap thrill. She didn't know which was worse; that she'd let him kiss her and touch her the way he had or that she'd believed in him. Either way he'd broken her heart. She felt betrayed, completely betrayed!

She stared out the window and pretended she couldn't hear Doralynn and Pearl whispering about her. When the carriage dropped them off, she wouldn't stay at Pearl's. She'd walk the distance to her cabin and sleep there tonight. She had nothing to be afraid of now the murderer was convicted and safely in jail. Besides, the laughter at Pearl's would just keep her awake.

~ * ~

The Carriage dropped them at the front door to Pearl's. Jolian informed them of her decision and Pearl disparaged her. She said that Jolian was "making fires out of sparks" and she should let it go.

"You're probably right, but nevertheless, I wish to be alone tonight." Jolian jutted her chin upwards and stared towards the front steps of Pearl's Place.

"Well, I suppose thar's no harm in it," Pear acquiesced.

Jolian walked through the parlor to the kitchen and packed herself a light meal. She took off the remaining highshoe and foolish looking or not, put on her old work boots. What did she care about the way she looked now anyway? Her clothes were saturated with mud and her foot was numb with the wet. She had half a mind to take Pearl up on her offer and have a long soak in her big bathtub. No, she needed to be alone.

Jolian walked the trail to her cabin holding her skirts with one hand and her dinner in the other. Once inside her tiny home she finally let everything fall, her skirts and her tears. They were tears that needed shedding, rational or not. She cried for her embarrassment, for her brother, her parents. She cried for her foolish dreams about Cooper and for the perfect future they'd never have now. She even cried for the man they were about to hang for the murder of her parents. That one puzzled even her.

She wanted to see him pay for his crimes but now he was going to, it didn't seem right that yet another life would be lost. Her parents had always taught her what they themselves believed: an eye for an eye was true justice. Now it was coming to pass, she thought somehow it would be better to leave the judgment up to God.

Jolian stripped off her mud soaked clothing and bundled it together. Her eyes were finally dry; there were just no tears left to cry. She stared at the food she'd carried to her cabin and her stomach growled its response. She hadn't eaten all day but she couldn't bring herself to consider even taking a bite. Her head ached and she simply wanted to crawl into bed and sleep for a hundred years.

In just her chemise and drawers she walked through to the wash porch at the back of the house and dumped her bundle of clothing into a pile. She stood and stared at the half barrel she used to wash her dainties. There was no way she was going to fit even the skirt of her new suit in there! Now what would she do? She couldn't just leave the clothing saturated in mud, the stains would never come out, not to mention the smell. Exhausted or not, she would have to clean it.

She supposed she could try to rinse the mud out of it section by section... biscuits! She'd take the whole lot of it down to the lake. This was too fine a suit to see ruined by her clumsiness. If she hurried, she'd have enough light to launder her clothing before sunset.

Dressed in her old stand-by flannel shirt and trousers, Jolian carried her bundle to the lake. It felt right somehow that she should be there, alone. It was as if all the events in her life had conspired against her, to push her towards the thing she feared most. The truth was as clear to her as the lake itself. She was terrified of being alone. Not just for an hour or more, for she valued her own company and the peace of mind she found in solitude. Her fear lay in the true aloneness that lay before her now. Strange how she had thought to choose a life of spinsterhood, as if somewhere deep inside, she'd known one day she would have to face her fear and deal with it all by herself.

The same feeling terrified her during the stormy nights as a child and well into her adult years. The kind of isolation that presently enveloped her was the root of all her fears. What with her parents gone, Jakeb off to war and Cooper... She couldn't even think about him going home to a wife, it was too painful to bear. She was truly alone now, truly alone.

Now she knew why her mother had followed her father to California and then here to British Columbia. Her mother hadn't been weak; she had been in love. She'd made sacrifices in her life not because she'd pledged obedience but because she'd felt love.

"Oh, Ma," Jolian spoke aloud to the heavens. "I've made such a mess of things. Please, if you can hear me, show me the way." Her heart sunk in her chest as she lay her washing by the shore of the lake. This was true heartache. Would the pain in her chest ever leave her?

The shallowest part of the lake was the best spot for washing. She separated each piece of clothing as she lay it out in the water. Taking off her boots and work socks, she rolled her trousers up to her knees. Ankle deep in the water with her trusty bar of soap, she scrubbed and rubbed and twisted and rinsed until she was too tired to feel anything.

Funny, the air was chilly enough that her feet were actually warmer in the water than her shins on the surface. The weeks of continued hot weather had warmed the lake considerably since the last time she had bathed in it. The thought of washing the smell of the mud off her body, cemented a decision. Without a second thought, Jolian pulled her washing out of the lake and lay it on the surrounding rocks.

She walked around to the deeper part of the lake, stripped herself of her clothing and then on a whim climbed up onto the highest platform she could reach. She turned to face the lake as naked as the day she was born. She stood tall and raised her face towards the heavens. If she were meant to be alone, then alone she would be. She would do it with her own brand of grace and style. She spread her arms out and inhaled until her lungs wanted to burst with the breath. She edged her toes to the rim of the rock bent her knees and dove into the water.

Her last vision before she hit the water was of Cooper standing at the perimeter of the lake holding her lost highshoe in his hand. She inhaled before she should have and took a glug of water in through her nose. It burned in her throat and she coughed and sputtered her way to the surface. *Some brand of grace! What was he doing here!* Was he looking for her? How could he have known where she'd be? He'd seen her naked!

"Jolian!" He shouted from the side of the lake.

Jolian coughed and choked and tried to speak but she couldn't seem to clear her lungs of the water. Of course, it didn't help that she was in the deepest part of the lake, treading water and attempting to keep her chin at water level whilst trying! She kept her eyes focused on Cooper and her body safely hidden beneath the surface as she grappled for a clear breath. What was he doing? She tried to yell out to him but her words were scarce and struggling.

"No... Help! I... no... help... don't..."

But it was too late. She watched horrified, as he removed his hat and boots, tossed the shoe he held aside and waded into the water towards her. She tried to turn and swim away from him but her strength had been compromised by the coughing fit, which was only now beginning to subside.

~ * ~

Cooper ran into the water until he was up to his knees and then dove towards Jolian. A few fast and sure strokes brought him to her side. He'd seen this kind of thing before when someone was drowning. The way they thrashed about, refusing assistance, even swimming away from their rescuer the way she was now. He knew just what to do. He approached her from behind and slipped his arm around her waist. He held her tight to him as he turned his body to the shoreline and raised his arm up under her breasts, securing her head above the water. Her bare buttocks rested against his hip and he was ever conscious of the silkiness of her skin in the water, even though his mind was focused on her rescue.

It was his fault, all his fault and he'd make it up to her somehow. The poor thing, as if she hadn't been humiliated enough in Richfield today, now this. He should have called out to her the moment he'd seen her. He had missed her at Pearl's and again at her cabin. He'd arrived at the lake in time to see her bare bottom walking towards the craggy peaks surrounding the lake. He was honestly speechless as he watched her tiny naked form climb the rock face, with the elegance of a dancer.

Then, as she turned and faced him and the setting sun wrapped her in its embrace; he was dazzled, bewitched and entranced. So pure and lovely, a true angel. He could only watch in awe of her poise and beauty as she dove into the lake. She must have seen him staring and startled on her way into the water. It was all his fault; if she wasn't all right he'd never forgive himself, never!

~ * ~

His right hand was touching her left breast! The man was squeezing her bare breast! She wanted to shout at him to let go of her. She wanted to wiggle out of his grasp. Her brain screamed at her to be free of him. But her heart had stopped aching with his touch. Her body trembled with desire for more of him. She was wicked and wanton there was no denying it now. Here was a man, a married man, honestly trying to save her from drowning. She was an excellent swimmer and no more in need of saving than he, yet she let him "save" her. She had no right to blame him anymore, for any action he may take towards her. She was fully aware of his marital status and yet here she was, contemplating the best way of turning so she could kiss him.

She had to think about his wife. Yes, that was what would bring her to her senses again. How would she feel if *her* husband had left her to go off and earn a living and some other woman was with him, like this, right now? The thought gave her all the ammunition she needed. She ceased her wriggling and calmly requested that he let her go.

"Are you sure you'll be all right?"

"Just fine."

He relaxed his grip and she turned towards him and pushed herself free. She kept her body below the surface as she traveled to a safe distance and then turned to tread water while facing him. He just stared at her with an odd look in his eyes. She had no idea of where to begin or what she could even say.

"How did you know where to find me?"

"I stopped at Pearl's and she said you'd gone to your cabin. When you weren't there I assumed you'd taken a trail to the lake, what with all the mud and everything..."

"Ah, yes, the mud. Well that really is the least of my worries."

"I apologize, Jolian, I should have tried to catch you before you slipped, there were just so many people in the street I couldn't get there in time."

"It was just as well you didn't, Cooper, er... "Mr." Holt."

"Mr. Holt?"

"Mr. Holt. That is the correct way of addressing a married man is it not?"

"You know about my wife..."

"Yes I know. Did you not think that was something I should have been privy to before you kissed me? Don't you agree I should have been told that you had a wife before you put your hands on my... on my..." She couldn't finish. It was just too painful.

"You're right, Jolian. Everything you said. I should have told you long ago, I don't know what has stopped me. The kiss was so, well, unplanned and I'm sorry."

He hadn't even denied it or tried to make an excuse! Her last shred of hope shriveled before her very eyes. Somewhere in the back of her mind she'd dared to hope that Pearl had been mistaken, but now she could see the truth. He *had* been toying with her. She was an effortless diversion from his old routine, a temporary easy target at which he could aim his desires.

She summoned all the will in her and spoke, "Then I guess there's nothing left to say but, goodbye." Would there ever be another happy moment in her life? Her heart shattered and she was helpless to stop it. She couldn't stay in the water, with him, like this. She also couldn't leave until he turned his back.

"Goodbye? You'd give up so easily?"

Cooper swam closer, grabbed her by the shoulders and squeezed her flesh until she cried out her anguish and pushed herself away. "Of course I'm giving up! Do you honestly think I am the kind of woman who would carry on with a married man?"

"I said I had a wife, not that I was married."

"You... what?"

"I said that I *had* a wife. I *was* married, Jolian, but my divorce papers came through the same day I kissed you in the cabin. I had come to tell you everything but you were upset and I couldn't find the words. I'm sorry."

Jolian consciously closed her gaping mouth. "Your divorce papers?"

"I'm divorced."

"Is she... was she, I mean..."

"She lives in Victoria. It's complicated—I want to tell you everything but the short version is I had her committed to an institution. She's insane, Jolian." He answered the question before she could voice it. "She probably was when I married her, she just hid it better then. Hell, who knows, the doctor said she could have been that way since birth."

"Oh Cooper! Oh Cooper, I'm so sorry I didn't know." Instantly she felt the repairs begin on her heart and she started to swim towards him. *Divorced? Who'd ever heard of such a thing?* He wasn't married now, that's all that mattered. He hadn't been married when they'd kissed either. She wasn't a wanton temptress; she was just a woman in love!

Jolian swam to him and Cooper swept her weightlessness into his open arms. She wrapped her legs around his waist and her arms around his neck. She pushed her breasts into his chest and felt a sensation shiver from their tips to her toes. His moustache glistened with tiny droplets of water and his lips parted as if he were about to speak.

She ran her fingers up the back of his neck and pulled his head towards her. She freely gave her lips to him and he kissed and nibbled until her insides boiled with desire. She wanted to free him of his clothing. She needed to feel his skin against her own. She pulled and tugged at his shirt managing to loosen it from the waistband of his trousers.

"Jolian," the roughness of his voice heightened her need for him. For all too quickly that's what it was becoming, a pulsating desperate need. She felt the craving for fulfillment more acutely than she had ever felt before. There was emptiness in her and his touch was the only relief that could satisfy her want. The longing she felt for him consumed her. His hands on her waist and on the bare flesh of her bottom, she felt she would go mad with the desire rising in her.

"Jolian, we have to leave the water."

She kissed his neck and let her hands roam freely over his chest. She could feel him moving beneath her and the sensation tormented her. She lowered her mouth to his shoulder and felt the primitive urge to bite his flesh. She wanted him in every way she could have him.

He had swum them in close enough to the shore and she could feel the water level lowering on her body. It ebbed her desire slightly and she buried her face into the hollow of his neck. She suddenly felt exposed and shy. She hugged her body to him and he wrapped his open shirt about her, covering her nakedness. He spoke no words, but carried her in his arms, the distance to her cabin.

"I want this to be right for you. If only I had some measure of restraint, I would wait and take you to the finest hotel in town—"

"I can't wait either. I don't want to."

Cooper carried her through the cabin's front door and kicked it closed behind him. Within seconds he set her onto the bed and removed the wet shirt from his body. She shivered slightly; he kissed her shoulder and then stood up and lit the candle in her bedside glass.

He turned back towards her and unfastened his waistband. Jolian felt as though she should avert her gaze but instead she sat up, looked him straight in the eyes and reached her hand to his bare hip. She felt herself swallow and she took a deep breath.

She slid her palm down his hip, pushing the trousers down his leg on one side. His thigh was hard, solid. She felt the heat of him and it seared through the flesh of her hand to burn deep, low in her being. Cooper pushed the pants down his other leg as anticipation whispered down her spine. Within seconds he stood naked before her. Her eyes left his and traveled down the length of his body.

She watched his pulse beating out a tattoo in his neck. His broad shoulders and muscled arms framed a bare, well-formed chest. She could see the defined ridges of his stomach that led to narrow hips and the part that made him a man. That part held her gaze until she began to think he would chastise her for staring. How could something so... well... well, generous be hidden in his trousers everyday? She began to feel nervous and unsure of her situation.

As if he could read her thoughts, Cooper knelt on the bed beside her. He pulled her into his arms and held her, flesh to flesh. His body touched hers in parts she'd never thought a man would ever even see, let alone feel. His hands roamed her back, his fingers working magic to relax her inhibitions.

"Are you sure, Jolian?" he whispered into her hair.

"Yes—"

"Look into my eyes and say it again."

"I'm certain." His eyes seemed to deepen in color as she stared into them. She had spoken the truth. Never had she wanted anything more.

She lowered her lashes and kissed him fully on the lips. She let her tongue dart into his mouth and felt a thrill as his reached out for hers at the same time. His kisses had urgency, spurring on the desire that swirled in her senses. His mouth left hers, as he kissed her neck and down to her shoulder. She felt as though she was made of ice and his fiery touch melted her, turning her insides to liquid. She placed her hands on his hips and drew him to her as she lay back on the bed. The heat from his body sped the fuse of her passion.

Cooper lowered his head and took her breast into his mouth. His teeth pulled on her nipple and she arched her back in response, giving him full access to her body. He brought his hands up under her breasts, rubbing his thumbs back and forth just under her nipples. Kisses so soft, then biting and teasing... Torture, exquisite torture. Just when she thought she could endure it no longer, he moved one hand to slide down her hip across her thigh and his fingers slipped inside her.

The sensation startled her. This was want; pure and simple. He built a steady stream of desire within in her. How could this ever be wrong? She needed more of this. He moved his kisses to her stomach, her hipbone and her inner thigh. Captivated by his touch, she offered herself to him, to do with as he may. As his fingers moved within her, his other hand reached beneath her to squeeze her buttocks. He lifted her towards him and nuzzled his mouth into a spot just slightly higher than where his fingers caused a tide of vibrations to flood through her. She half sat up at the touch of his mouth but his hand reached up from underneath her, caressing her breast and she was lost to the passion.

His lips and tongue were agonizingly tender. She couldn't stand it, she couldn't. She didn't know what to expect or what it was she was anticipating, but the wait was excruciatingly wonderful. Wildness enveloped her and she arched into him again, demanding more of the gentle torture. His hands and his mouth, the sensations he built within her. He caressed and teased and pushed, until wave after wave of delectation rolled through her being.

She couldn't move. Surely something that powerful would render her motionless for all time. Her breathing was ragged and she inhaled deeply trying to bring herself back from the cloud she floated upon.

Her eyes held his as he raised his head upward. She saw a look there she'd never forget. He wanted her in the most basic sense. It caused a thrill to serge through her being. How could she have thought she'd never move again? He was only beginning to pleasure her! He took her bottom lip between his teeth. Her fingers gripped his shoulders and she felt him slowly push inside her. He lifted her hip to help guide him inside. She could tell he was being cautious, holding back, trying to be gentle.

"Jolian." His voice was gruff and came from somewhere deep inside his chest. "I am sorry, my angel, but this will hurt only for a moment."

The building of her own need reflected in his eyes, she nodded her head in understanding and pushed her hips to his. He broke through the last barrier of her innocence and they were truly one. She shuddered with the fullness of the sensation. It felt so right; the perfect expression of her desire and love for him.

She could feel the length of him moving within her, filling her, completing her. She moved her hips to match his dance. He whispered in her ear, the words a blur but his breath, hot and huffing, sent tingles down her neck. His muscled shoulder flexed near her mouth, she kissed it, pushed her hand against his chest. His heart hammered. He rose up, shifted slightly and quickened his speed. His eyes held hers and she watched pleasure and possession build in them. She was his, she was his!

"Jolian... Jolian!" His release was hers as well.

~ * ~

The sun had set and darkness overtook the room. The candle flickered in the glass and cast a dancing light upon his shoulder. He nibbled her neck as she traced the light's path with her index finger. She was more than he ever could have imagined. She was a wondrous mixture of innocence and wildfire. He wanted to keep her like this, forever. He'd never tire of loving her. They'd lain in the afterglow of their lovemaking without the need for words.

He had to find some now. He had to tell her. He owed her the truth; should have told her long before. He kissed the top of her head and began to talk. He could tell her everything, as long as he didn't have to look her in the eyes. He couldn't stand to see the expression she would surely wear as he told her.

"I hardly know where to begin, so I guess the beginning is best. My family was friends with Lorna's, that's her name by the way—"

"The same name that you called me the night—"

"I know, I hope once I've told you everything that you'll understand."

"Go on."

He kept his chin near the top of her head and focused on the flickering light off the moss-chinked walls. "Before we left England, my father and Lorna's father— This is harder than I thought."

Jolian smiled and stroked his belly with her finger. "Do you really want to tell me, I mean right now?"

"There are plenty of things I'd rather do right now, Jolian, but this is something you need to know."

"Then just say it like it is in your mind. I'm not going to judge you, Cooper, I love you."

He moved his head to gaze into her eyes. Did he just hear what he thought he'd heard? A rosy blush glowed in her cheeks. "How did I ever get so lucky?"

"Shh, you." She put her finger to his lips. "Just tell me what you have to, so I can put your lips to better use."

"You are a wildcat! All right, all right!" He laughed as she growled and pretended to bite him. He felt more at ease to speak his mind with her than he ever had with anyone before. She was just right for him and he wasn't going to let her get away because of any more misunderstandings.

"My father and Lorna's father, Mr. Cummings, took their training as Royal engineers together. My family moved to Victoria but father kept in touch with Lorna's father. Almost three years ago Mr. Cummings wrote to ask my father for his help. Lorna had always been "spirited" they called it, I hardly realized that meant spirits actually inhabited her mind!"

Jolian smiled at his attempt at humor and he continued.

"It seemed that Lorna had got herself in "trouble" and she wouldn't name the father of the baby. They asked my family if we would take her in and help to a find a home for the baby once it was born. That way, Lorna could return home with no one being the wiser, I suppose. My family agreed, of course, and the Cummings sent her over. I really need a drink of water, Jolian. Is there—"

~ * ~

"I have some in a jug in the kitchen, I'll fetch it." She was glad for the distraction. She had a feeling that she could guess what came next. He'd fallen head over heels in love with the pregnant Lorna and asked her to be his wife. That had to be what he was going to say next. She didn't think she wanted to hear him talk about his love for another woman, not when he had never expressed those feelings for her, verbally at least. What they had just shared was beyond anything she could ever have imagined. She didn't want to think about him ever having that with anyone but her! She wrapped a dislodged cotton sheet about her body and meandered towards the kitchen.

She returned with his mug and one for herself. She sat at the end of the bed, facing him. It would just be easier to hear him profess his love for another if she weren't lying in his arms. He thanked her for the drink and if he noticed her repositioning, he didn't comment. In fact, he seemed to be lost in another world. She didn't know if her heart could stand what he was about to tell her. This was so new, so uncertain. She tried to read something, anything, in his eyes but he wouldn't look at her. He gulped the water down without stopping for a breath and then continued.

"Lorna arrived as scheduled by steamer in Victoria. She wasn't what I had expected. She was so terrified, at everything; it's hard to describe. I felt an obligation to assist her in any way I could. I was her only acquaintance in a strange country. In the beginning I wanted to befriend her. I thought it would make things easier. It's so hard to describe how she was..."

Here it comes, Jolian thought. *She was beautiful, radiant, glowing, oh and graceful, she'd most certainly have that quality.*

"If you ever meet her, you'll understand my dilemma in describing her. No one who looked at her would have any inclination there was anything amiss. Even to talk to her at a formal or for tea, none of the women in town suspected. It took me ages to recognize the depths of her insanity and even now I'm not sure I truly understand. She spun a web of stories, which were true to her but no one else. Before I knew I was trapped inside her web, believing her and feeling sorry for her. Jolian, I would spare you knowing this if I could, but I want you to understand the whole truth of it."

Jolian nodded and sipped from her cup and braced herself for what was about to come.

"She told me the name of the baby's father and the reason she could never return to England. Remember now, these were just her accusations. The party in question flatly denied the charges and considering everything, I am inclined to believe him now. It was her father, Jolian. Her own father was the one she accused of siring the child that grew within her!"

Jolian's couldn't believe what she'd just heard. "Her own father?"

"Yes. My father has known him for years and says he was more the type who would have killed any man that touched his daughter rather than to have touched her in that way himself. At the time though, with Lorna swearing it as the truth and trembling with fear at the thought of being sent home again—I hope you can understand why I believed her as I did."

"Of course." Was all she could say. *The woman's own father? How could she have even thought up such an accusation if it weren't true?*

"It gets worse from there I'm afraid. I, of course, offered her what protection I could and marriage seemed to be the best course of action. I thought in time we could make a life together; raise the child as our own. Lorna agreed it was a solution as good as any and we were wed on a Tuesday afternoon. Only Ts'kaw was present as a witness. My parents were completely against it and urged me to re-think my position. During the ceremony, I began to think maybe I should have heeded their warning. Lorna couldn't keep her eyes off of Ts'kaw. At first I took it to be nothing more than curiosity. She had never seen a native up close I told myself."

A coughing fit began to besiege him and Jolian handed him her cup of water. This was a story unlike any she'd ever heard! He hadn't admitted to loving the woman and she felt like her heart was perched on the edge of an abyss waiting, hoping...

"Thank you." He handed her back an empty mug and continued. "I told myself she just needed to be around more natives, it would help her to feel comfortable. I arranged for us to honeymoon up here at Guy's place. We traveled with Ts'kaw and stayed at the village of his people on the way. Lorna became, ah... obsessed, I guess is the best word for it. She talked about Ts'kaw constantly. Everything in her life began to focus on him."

"That must have been very difficult for you." She watched as he struggled with the words. She wanted to hold him and kiss away his uncertainties. He looked so alone.

"I thought it was my fault. I thought she must know I didn't love her and was just marrying her out of pity and maybe that was pushing her to seek comfort in the arms of another man. We left Ts'kaw's village and traveled up here. I tried to think of things to would bring us closer, make her feel more like my wife. Nothing worked. We had been at Guy's place for about a month when she went missing. I had left her to go into town for supplies and when I came back, she was gone."

There was anguish in his voice. Jolian's heart had leaped when he said he hadn't loved his wife, but now, she felt awful for her moment of joy. Cooper was in such pain! She didn't know what she could do to make it easier. She reached her hand out and touched his shoulder. He put his hand over hers and squeezed. The look he gave her held such raw, exposed pain that a lump formed in her throat and she felt as though she could cry at any moment. She couldn't stand to see him like this.

"I searched for ages. At first I assumed she'd become lost in the unfamiliar woods. The first day passed so slowly—searching and calling out her name. I couldn't believe she'd just run off . I held onto the idea that she was lost, which also meant she would have been unprepared for a journey in the Cariboo wilderness. I traipsed in circles, checking caves and old trappers' cabins. If only I'd hired the tracker right away, maybe... I destroyed all evidence of her tracks, I'm certain of it. Finally, after two days, I had to do something. I hired a whole team of men including a first rate tracker to look for her. He managed to find some tracks I hadn't obliterated, but they were difficult to follow. She seemed to have backtracked and gone in circles and then there was nothing. I left the men I'd hired to continue their search and I went on to Ts'kaw's village. I knew Ts'kaw was away for Aklu'ut's wedding, but Lorna didn't and so I clung to the hope I'd find her there."

~ * ~

Cooper looked to the ceiling and closed his eyes. Jolian moved closer to him and wrapped her arms around his neck. She held his head to her breast and didn't say a word. *Could it be, she might be able to understand?* Maybe to even—it was too much to hope for.

Thankful he didn't have to look her in the eyes for the rest of his confession, he took a deep breath and continued, this was the part that haunted his dreams. "I found her in the morning. I'd been traveling for days with little or no sleep. My horse needed to rest and I was half dozing as he walked into the village. There was fog, settled thick, on the ground. I've never seen the like since; it was, I guess 'eerie' is the best word for it. I don't know if I saw her first or if I heard her. She was sitting there on the ground rocking back and forth and humming. I got off my horse and the fog gave way as I neared her. I could see she held an infant. She'd given birth to a baby boy and it was dead. I don't know if it had been when it was born or if it had happened later. I'd estimate it had been about three days since the birth." Jolian's hand, which had been rubbing his shoulder suddenly stilled. He hated himself for having to bring any more ugly pictures into her head. But he had to get everything out in the open. Then, maybe, he'd be free to love her the way he wanted. He swallowed the lump of uncertainty in his throat and continued.

"The village had small pox. By the time she'd arrived the entire village was dead. It was horrible. She was sitting there among the bodies. Her hair was down; she'd always kept it up, it was full of leaves and twigs. The stench of the—the smell, it was... in her hair and on her clothes. I've never forgotten the smell. It was the end of her. She's never spoken since. She's never lost that look either, a vacant, deadness."

"Cooper, I... How awful—"

213

"You can't blame me anymore than I blame myself, I assure you. I know—" He stopped her before she had the chance to get the words out. He turned to look her straight in the eyes. "I apologize for not telling you sooner and will understand if you don't want to see me again."

"Cooper, how can you even think that? You can't honestly blame yourself! And what would that have to do with me not wanting to see you?"

"I failed at the most basic level, Jolian. I stood before God and promised to care for her and I let her down and then I divorced her. I know, there were many contributing factors, not just my negligence, but I still failed her... it was my fault." Would she turn from him now? He feared that more than anything! He didn't think he could live without this magical woman sitting before him. He searched her eyes for an answer.

"You are not even remotely responsible for what happened to Lorna. I think you did everything you possibly could to help her. It seems to me she was looking for something no one could have provided. I think the doctors were correct, Cooper. She must not have been right for a very long time. You can't blame yourself. You can't." She lifted his head and held his face in her hands as if she were beseeching him to agree with her.

She was incredible! He couldn't believe she didn't blame him. He'd wasted so much time in dwelling on the past. "I did. I blamed myself for a very long time. I drank myself into a stupor trying to forget the image of her with that baby but it didn't work. I think I have it licked now, the drinking anyway." He tried to smile and she ran her fingers through his hair. She was so good for him, so good. "Why couldn't I have met you years ago, Jolian?"

"I would have been much too young for you then." She worried her bottom lip with her teeth but Cooper could see a smile forming in the corner of her lips.

"And you're not now?"

"Nope, now I'm just right."

"You certainly are." Her smile warmed him like no fire ever could. She only had to look at him and he was aroused! He was going to have to get himself under control, at least until he could make an honest woman out of her. He knew the answer to his next question but he had to ask it nonetheless. "You still want me around then?"

"Just try and leave." She yawned her anwser.

He lay back on the bed and pulled her to him. There was so much to say but no words seemed to fit. He held her close and hoped she knew what his words couldn't convey. Her eyes closed and she laid her head into the crook of his arm. It was late, the middle of the night he was sure. Now everything was out in the open it felt so right; like a clean beginning. He should have known she'd react the way she had. She was the most loving, most understanding woman. Cooper reached his free arm around her and pulled the covers up. He fit his body next to hers and tucked the blankets in around them.

"Heaven."

"Um-hum."

Sixteen

She could feel Cooper trying to move his arm out from under her head without disturbing her. She'd slept like a log! His arm would surely be numb. She knew she should roll over but her stubborn side said 'make me, just try and make me leave this heaven'. She groaned in protest without opening her eyes and felt his lips brush hers. His moustache tickled her nose. She opened her eyes to see the man from her dreams lying beside her, his disheveled hair making him only more desirable.

"Good morning." She felt her smile come from the dreams of her childhood. She'd always wanted him, even before she knew it. She understood him completely now. She knew his reasons for waiting to tell her about Lorna and why he had needed to tell her last night. She could feel a new beginning, for both of them, taking shape in her mind.

"Good morning. Did you sleep well? I hope the thunder didn't wake you too often." His sleepy husky voice stirred her.

"There was thunder?" Jolian was astounded. She'd slept through thunder? She couldn't help but smile again. She thought she'd just had the best night's sleep of her life, and they'd had a storm? She couldn't remember the last time she'd slept through a storm, or indeed if she ever had. She stretched languidly and wrapped her arms around Cooper's neck. She could get used to this. Feeling so secure and wanted, enclosed in his embrace all night long. She nibbled at his earlobe and whispered intermittently.

"Umm-hmmm. Thunder and lightning."

"Really?"

"Really, almost as stormy outside as inside."

Jolian smiled her response.

"Coffee?"

"Umm."

"That feels good."

"Umm."

"Is there anywhere you need to be...?"

"Uh-uh."

"Me neither."

"Good."

A part of her screamed in protest. She couldn't lay with this man again! He hadn't declared his love for her like she had for him. He hadn't asked her to be his wife. It was only a temporary thought, for when she lifted her chin to look into his eyes, she saw everything she needed.

~ * ~

Her curls were tousled and her lips were swollen from their night of passion. Cooper swore he had never seen a more beautiful face. Just looking at her brought him fully awake in every sense. He took her lips hungrily and she responded in turn. He pulled her naked body close and wrapped his thigh possessively about hers.

Cooper lowered his head and took her breast into his mouth. "You even taste sweet," he growled into the space between her breasts. She moaned deep in her throat arousing his need further. Reluctantly, he left her breasts and with a sly grin, slipped his head under the covers. He covered her body with his, and then lowered his mouth to the succulent warmth between her thighs. A sigh of pure pleasure soon replaced her startled intake of breath. Breaths became ragged, shorter, faster and finally deep, moaning and satisfied.

Her powerful response caused a pulsating need to hammer within his groin. Desire, intense and all consuming, swarmed within him. He kissed his way up to her neck and lowered himself upon her until his hardness met her soft folds.

He moved in steady, even strokes as he felt her hips rising to match his rhythm. The walls around him pulsed and his release was swift and all consuming.

~ * ~

She felt absolutely, entirely idle. She could spend the rest of her life in this bed, naked, with Cooper. Of course there was food, she supposed they'd eventually need to find something to eat. And drink, she was beginning to feel a bit parched. They'd drained the last of her water jug an hour ago. They'd spend most of the morning in each other's arms and now she knew his body almost as well as her own. If there was one thing she could say for certain, it was he knew every inch of her. There wasn't a spot on her his kiss hadn't found.

She sat up on the bed and stared at Cooper's naked form. Oh, wantonness was so much better than spinsterhood! What had she been thinking? She could hardly suppress the giggle that bubbled up at the thought.

"What's so funny?" He opened one eye and lifted a brow to question her.

"Oh, I was just thinking of how I had dedicated myself to becoming a spinster with a proper chaste lifestyle. But with last night—and this morning, both those times—I guess I've wandered a bit off my chosen path."

"Chaste? I had no idea—but I'm glad you changed your mind." He growled low in his throat as he reached an arm across the bed and pawed for her like a lion hunting his prey. "Come here my little wildcat!"

She laughed at the game and pounced on top of him. He rolled her over and pinned her beneath him. "And to think I always called you 'Angel' in my thoughts."

"You think I'm not now?" She feigned a pout.

He interspersed his response with kisses. "I, think—you-are-a-wildcat-sent-from-Heaven."

"That's good?"

"The best." She kissed him full on the lips for his reply.

"Are you hungry?" She asked after several minutes of kissing and nibbling.

"Well, now that you mention it, I could eat something, but not if it means having to see other people. I know I'm being greedy, but I don't feel like sharing you with the world today."

"I could go to Pearl's and try to scare us up something." Her cheeks were burning even as she spoke. She felt a bit awkward about seeing Pearl this morning. Pearl had a sixth sense about such things and she would surely be grilled for all of the details.

Thankfully, Cooper took up the suggestion. "That's sweet of you to offer, Jolian, but I'll go. I wanted to pick up a few things in town anyway. Promise me you'll stay put? Like I said, today's just for us. I don't want to share you with anyone."

She nodded her head in response, which prompted him to add in a twangy teasing whisper, "I'd be obliged to you, Ma'am, if you'd stay just how ya are, in the buff and all."

They laughed and kissed some more before he was dressed and ready to go. Draped in a quilt from the bed, she walked him to the door of her cabin. She waved until he disappeared from her sight.

This was just too good to be true. She crawled back under the covers feeling absolutely decadent. She couldn't ever remember spending a whole day in bed, let alone in bed *and naked*! She stretched and yawned and then curled up in a ball and hugged her knees. Who ever thought that life could be so wonderful? Complete and utter contentment filled her from head to toe.

She giggled and hugged herself closer. Surely she must be living a dream and she pinched herself just to be sure. It was so unbelievable! She never would have imagined she could feel the way she did now. Yesterday everything had seemed so dark and gloomy, happiness far beyond her grasp and then, not twenty-four hours later, she was experiencing total unreserved bliss.

The knock at the door brought her back to reality. He was so sweet, feeling like he had to knock when they'd just shared what they had. She wrapped the quilt around her and hurried into the kitchen.

"Did you forget some—"

Constable Towers stood before her, his gaze traveling up and then back down her body. She instinctively pulled the quilt higher up her neck and took a step backwards.

"I wasn't expecting—"

"Obviously not."

She took offense at his tone. How dare he speak to her like that? This was her home he came to; he had no right to judge her behavior. She opened her mouth to tell him so but was cut off in mid thought by his words.

"I would suggest you dress before I take you in."

"In? What do you mean 'in'? I'm not going anywhere."

"Oh yes you are young lady. I am here on official business of the crown, to arrest you for the attempted murder of Frederick Brewer."

"Attempted murder? I thought the judge determined my shooting at him to be in self-defense?"

"The Judge did decide *that* incident did not warrant further investigation but it is to the attempt of *last* evening of which I currently direct my attentions."

"What are you talking about?" Jolian had never wanted to strike a human being as much as she wanted to slap the face of this man. His whole tone and manner was accusing. She was so thankful Judge Begbie had been appointed the law in the colony and not this man. She had half a mind to accuse the Constable of making up stories just to make himself look important.

"Frederick Brewer was poisoned last night and I am here to arrest you for attempted murder."

"That's just ludicrous! Why would I—"

"It is not ludicrous and I would suggest you put some clothes on, Ma'am, or I will be forced to take you to the jailhouse in your bedding."

Jolian knew he would most certainly do just as he had stated and he would take a certain pleasure in it as well. She told the Constable she would be a few moments and she closed the kitchen door. It would have been proper to ask him to step in but she didn't care what propriety suggested. The man was out to find her guilty of something and for no reason other than his own personal dislike.

The last thing in the world she wanted to do was to go with the Constable! She wished Cooper had waited a few minutes longer. Surely the Constable would have seen—They would have had to cross paths; there was no other way. Unless he had been at her cabin already, waiting for Cooper to leave. *But why on earth would he do such a thing?*

Jolian dressed slowly, methodically, trying to put the pieces together in her mind. He'd been so quick to arrest Jakeb for the murders, could he be involved somehow? No, that couldn't be it. There had only been one murderer of her family.

What was it that made him dislike her so? The heavy knock startled her and made her quicken her pace.

"Ma'am, are you dressed? I'm going to have to come in there if you're not out by the count of five. One... two... three... four..."

Jolian opened the door and stood before him. She had dressed in one of her old red flannels and trousers and she could see the distaste, like sour milk, on his face. If she had to go to jail, she wasn't about to do it in a dress! She only hoped Cooper would find her soon. She shivered at the thought of having to spend any time near the murderer, let alone in a jailhouse with him.

~ * ~

"Gid'yup!" Cooper urged his mount along the rough trail to Richfield. He couldn't stand to think of her at the jail, especially with that Brewer in there, even if he was behind bars! The murderer was too sly and the Constable too incompetent for his liking. Whatever could have possessed her to go with him?

At first when he'd arrived back at her cabin, he'd feared the worst. That maybe she'd had second thoughts and had decided to leave. He'd raced through the two rooms in seconds flat when she hadn't answered his call. For one horrible moment his past had flashed before him and he was paralyzed with the mere thought of it. Even before he'd found her note he'd chased the thought from his mind. Jolian wasn't the type to just up and leave. If she'd changed her mind about anything she'd come out and tell him.

He had been standing in the middle of the bedroom, arms akimbo, trying to figure out what had happened to her when he saw her note. A tiny scrap of paper wedged into the oval framed mirror on the dresser. Fine handwriting stood out from a hastily scratched list of what looked like to be an old grocery inventory.

His heart lurched again as he recalled her words "gone to jail with Const. Love, Jolian". She had abbreviated the word Constable but taken the time to write her feelings down. He'd picked up the note, folded it carefully and tucked it into his breast pocket. It was a treasure to keep, her first written declaration of her feelings for him.

He pulled the reins up sharply and slowed Storm to a trot. The town of Richfield sat around the next bend and he didn't want anyone to see him removing the gun from his saddlebag. He didn't care that he was breaking the hard and fast law of the town. He wasn't taking any chances where Jolian was concerned. He tucked the pistol into the back waistband of his trousers and continued into the town of Richfield. Main Street was unusually quiet for this time of day and immediately his guard went up. He tethered his mount to the post in front of the jailhouse and tried to appear nonchalant as he looked up and down the street and then entered the building.

Towers was seated with his hat over his eyes and his feet up on the desk, his chair tilted at a precarious angle. Cooper resisted the urge to kick it out from under him.

"Where is she?"

The Constable slowly tilted the brim of his hat back with his index finger. "Cooper Holt, what brings you into Richfield today?"

"Cut the small talk, Towers, and tell me where she is." Cooper kept his voice calm, steady. He knew how to handle the Constable and he had to play this right.

"Testy, testy!" Towers titched his tongue against his teeth. "I presume you are referring to Miss Grayson."

"You know I am."

"She's been arrested for attempted murder." Cooper wanted to punch the grin out of the man's teeth but he steadied his course.

"You don't say? Who'd she try to kill?"

"The same guy she tried to kill before—Brewer!" The sardonic whine of his voice grated Cooper's nerves.

"Have you got her in her own cell?"

"Of course!" The Constable snorted. "Besides, Brewer can't hurt no one today. He's real messed up from the attempt on his life. I had to call for one of the Doc's from Barkerville. Fact is, the Doc's still in there now. He ain't left Brewer's side all night."

Cooper nodded and tried to imitate the look of concern on the Constable's face, or was it frustration? "What, did she shoot at him again?"

"Poison."

"Poison? How do you know it was her?"

"She poisoned him before. I mean, before she tried to shoot him. Don't you remember? And besides, poison's a woman's crime. It's the sissy way out." The Constable stood and began to pace the room. "And like I said, she's got a history of it. She poisoned him with some concoction in his whiskey that sent him out to the john. That's why I figure it's her again. Brewer was sick something awful last night. He nearly died!"

Towers puffed up his chest and ran his thumbs along his belly in the waistband of his trousers. He probably thought it made him appear more confident but in reality he looked every bit the ham-fisted, bungling idiot that he was. Cooper just nodded like he agreed with the fool.

"By the way, is Begbie still in town?" Cooper looked out the window as if he expected the Judge to waltz in any minute.

"Left for New Westminster after the trial."

"I thought he might have. He's going to be... I guess the best word would be *irate*, when he has to come all the way back." Cooper kept just a hint of sympathy in his voice.

"Back? Who said he was coming back?" Towers actually glanced around the room and Cooper had to bite his cheek to keep from laughing. It was just as he expected; the man was terrified of the Judge.

"Well he'll most certainly have to come back for the trial, and he'll want to be notified straight away I'm sure. As a matter-of-fact, I rode into town with a friend who'd gladly start for the Judge now if I asked him—" The bluff slid off his tongue like butter off a hot cob of corn.

"Oh... oh that's all right, no need to rush. I have to assemble the evidence and it could take a few days—"

"But the Judge was leaving for New Westminster on vacation wasn't he?" Towers' nod came as no surprise to Cooper. "He'll want his slate cleared before he takes leave. You know the Judge."

"Yes, yes I do."

"I think I'd better send my friend—"

"No, no." The Constable moved to Cooper's side and placed a hand on his shoulder. In hushed tones he continued. "I'm not certain it was Miss Grayson who poisoned him, and the Judge likes things to be certain."

"Oh." Cooper nodded and kept his voice low as well. He wanted to shout at the good-for-nothing, negligent imbecile. If he had harmed one curl on her head..." Maybe I could help you with the details then."

"That would be great!" Towers half shouted, the relief evident on his face.

"All right, first off, have you questioned the suspect?"

"She'll just deny it. And I can prove she's a born liar."

Cooper began to lose his patience with the man. "What makes you think she would be untruthful?"

"She lied to the whole town Mr. Holt. She told everyone she was a boy!" Towers looked at him like *he* was the fool! "I can pretty much guarantee that she'll lie again."

Cooper wanted to just take the easy way out and tell the Constable he had spent the night with Jolian. But he couldn't do that to her. It would be all over town within days and he would hate to be the instrument of any embarrassment to her. No, if he could free her by any other means he would. Even if it meant solving the damn crime for the man! He took a deep breath and tried another approach.

"Did Brewer have any visitors last night?"

"Just Vera."

"Vera? From Pearl's?"

"Yup, she said she owed him something and I figured, the man's going to hang, why not let him have one last fling."

"Did Vera bring anything with her?"

"Yup, she brought some stew from Pearl's for his dinner. See? That's also how I know it was Miss. Grayson. Everyone knows she does all the cooking at Pearl's Place."

"Towers, did you ever think that Vera might have poisoned the food?"

"Vera? Hell no. She's just a stupid—"

A classic case of the pot calling the kettle, he'd just let the man think on it for a second or two. Towers stood slacked jawed and Cooper swore he could see the wheels turning in his mind. The Constable's eyebrows pinched together as if he were in deep deliberation. Cooper almost guffawed out loud at that thought. The lawman raised his eyebrows and turned his gaze back towards him.

"I think I'd better speak with Miss Grayson."

Finally, he could see her! Cooper waited impatiently as Towers fumbled for the keys to the cell and then hurried his gangly body down the hallway. It seemed to take forever for him to bring her up to the office. She finally arrived with her hands shackled in front of her. A quick glance told him she was fine but he'd have given anything to take her in his arms and kiss away the uncertainty in her eyes.

"Constable Towers tells me Brewer was poisoned last night." He was trying to comfort her with his eyes and not give away their more intimate knowledge of each other in front of the constable.

"Yes. He thinks I am responsible."

"Well, now, that's not completely true..." Towers fumbled for an excuse.

"What I think the Constable is trying to say is, he had to arrest you for your own safety until the real criminal could be brought to justice. We're thinking the case can probably proceed without the need for calling the Judge back from his holidays." Agreeing with Cooper's every word; the Constable was bobbing his head on his shoulders like a piece of driftwood in a storm.

Cooper hoped his wink to Jolian had conveyed everything was going to be just fine and that she should play along. He needn't have worried as she took the bait and clearly reveled in the moment.

Jolian sighed. "I am certainly glad to find out the truth. For a moment there, I was worried that I was going to have to call in my uncle's lawyer—"

Cooper couldn't resist interrupting. "Isn't he a good friend of Judge Begbie's cousin?"

"Poker pals." Jolian concurred.

"Oh now." The Constable forced a smile too big for his face. "I think everything will be cleared up fine, Mr. Holt. There won't be any reason to be calling Judge Begbie back from his vacation. He's worked so hard and has been looking forward to this vacation for so long."

"Well, I suppose I could refrain from contacting my lawyer if my name has been cleared..." Jolian rubbed at her still shackled wrists as she spoke.

"Clear as Jack of Clubs Lake!" The Constable nodded his head too eagerly.

"Then I see no reason to be hanging about." Cooper took the keys from the Constable and released the chains that held Jolian's slender wrists. If he saw so much as one bruise, he would have to return and give the Constable a piece of his fist.

"So you must have an idea as to who did perpetrate the crime then." Jolian directed her statement to the Constable.

"Yup and I intend to arrest her on my way back to dropping you at your cabin."

"My cabin? Surely you don't think it's someone from Pearl's place!" Jolian couldn't believe her ears.

"I don't think, I know! It's Vera!"

"Vera?" Cooper and Jolian chimed.

"Now hang on a minute there, Towers. Just because she brought Brewer some stew it doesn't mean that she poisoned him. I know I said it *might* have been her; I was just making a point, by way of example. Anyone could've had access to the food. It's going to be a very difficult thing to prove." Cooper put himself between Jolian and the Constable.

Towers scratched at his chin and looked thoughtfully at the ceiling.

"You'll definitely need to gather more evidence before you proceed. Think of it this way, how much evidence would the Judge need?" Cooper persuaded the Constable. "I can see Miss Grayson home. I need to ride out that way anyway."

The relief was all too evident on the Constable's face. "That would be fine with me as long as Miss Grayson here approves."

"Oh yes, Miss Grayson approves." Jolian smiled for only him and turned to leave the jailhouse.

~ * ~

He lifted Jolian into the saddle and climbed up behind her. A bit of a snug fit but he didn't mind one bit. He put his heels to Storm and headed for the back trails to Pearl's Place. As soon as they were a safe distance from town Cooper pulled Storm to a halt and placed his hands on her shoulders. She twisted in the saddle and offered her mouth up to him. A kiss so sweet he'd never tasted. She was the most delightful creature he'd ever known!

He wanted to pull her from the horse and take her right here on the path. The town be dammed! He didn't care who saw them. He loved this woman and he wanted the world to know it. He took a slow easy breath. He wanted to jump off of Storm and get down on his knees and beg her to spend the rest of her life with him. But he couldn't do it, not yet. She deserved more than that. She deserved a proposal she could re-tell to their grandchildren. He'd have to keep his desire in check.

She gave him a shy smile as their kiss ended and she turned back to face the path.

"I'm going to have to learn to hide my feelings a bit better or the whole town will be talking in no time!" Her shoulders bounced with her chuckle.

"Let them talk," he whispered into her neck.

Storm started off at an easy pace and Cooper tried to focus on anything, except the motion of the horse and the tight fit of the two of them in the saddle was making it damn difficult to keep his thoughts pure. Especially since his thoughts were evident to anyone who could see his trousers. He really needed to get things under control. There were serious issues he needed to discuss with her. Things best discussed while they were still clothed.

Her tight trouser-clad bottom bounced up and down along his groin and her floral scent filled his nostrils, taking away all-rational thought. He groaned audibly and snapped the reins.

"Ya! Giddyup!" Poor Storm, he was pushing it he knew, but he had no choice really. He could no longer control his need for her; not that he'd ever really had a firm grasp on those reins. He'd just have to face the facts; he was under her spell and only her refusal could stop him now.

He had originally intended to go back to her cabin but desire and spontaneity changed his mind. Not too far from where they were now was a secluded oasis he had to share with her. She turned a quizzical glance to him at the change in their course and he grinned his best "trust me it will be all right" smile. She did and his confidence doubled. She trusted him wholly.

"It's just through this grove and here... Ah the perfect spot! Just wait till you see it." Cooper dismounted and led Storm to a patch of tall sweet grass before he lifted his arms for Jolian. He placed his hands around her waist and let her body slide down his. He stopped her descent when her toes touched the ground and held her suspended as he kissed her fully.

"Why have we stopped here? And where exactly is here?"

"Here' is a spot I want us to call our own for all time."

"Ummm, I'm intrigued."

"Good. Then close your eyes and give me your hand."

Jolian did as she was bid and Cooper led her forward. She looked like a child who'd been given her first piece of candy. That was one of the things he loved most about her, the honesty of her emotions. Everything she felt was reflected on her face and indeed with her whole body. From the spring in her step to the bounce in her curls, he could see the anticipation flowing through her.

Cooper couldn't keep the smile from his face. Just one look at her and he felt as though he'd run head on into the side of a brick building. His heart pounded in his chest and he wanted to pick her up and hug the stuffing out of her. He chuckled quietly at the huge grin on her face and the way she crinkled her nose at the smell of sulfur.

"What's so funny?"

"You can open your eyes now." He waited for her to focus on him and then he kissed her nose and brushed a wayward curl out of her eyes. "The smell is from the Hot Springs."

"Hot Springs?"

"Yes. The water is heated beneath the earth's surface. They're warm as any bath and they stay that way year round."

"Oh, how lovely! We had them in California, but I've never been to one. I did hear talk, they had magical healing powers."

"I don't know about magic but folks claim to find them helpful for a multitude of ailments."

~ * ~

Jolian took in her surroundings and had to consciously close her mouth as it dropped open with awe. This had to be the most beautiful spot on earth! If all hot springs looked like this, she could understand why they had been associated with magic. The entire area looked as though it might be inhabited by faeries.

An emerald blanket of moss cushioned her steps as she crept towards the bubbly crater. Steam rose from its surface like a pot of soup simmering on the stove. Willow trees hugged the perimeter of their secluded hideaway, as did pines and cedars draped in sphagnum.

Tiny flowers and shrubbery filled in the underbrush and Jolian recognized the triangular white trillium and the tiny bell-shaped buds of the rosy twisted stalk. False Lily of the Valley stuffed any extra spot that had yet to be filled.

Next to the spring, she bent and dipped her hand into the water. Its effervescence startled her and she laughed spontaneously. Cooper was suddenly behind her, his arms about her waist. He spun her around slowly and caused Jolian to catch her breath at the look in his eyes, such emotion shone in their depths!

"Cooper, what is it?"

"It's you Jolian. My heart, my head, my entire body is taken up with you. You invade my thoughts constantly during the day... and my nights—" He inhaled a low whistle through his teeth. "Well, let's just say they're unbearable. Being with you has become a necessity for me. I wasted so much of my life before, and now, I can't believe this feeling. It's you. The way you look at everything with such wide-eyed wonder." He pleaded with his eyes as if he wanted her to read the thoughts he couldn't quite express. He took a breath and shook his head back and forth.

"Cooper...?"

He stared at the ground and Jolian began to feel she'd misinterpreted this whole encounter. Suddenly he raised his head and pushed back a lock of hair from her face. "I want to spend my lifetime brushing this stray curl from your eye and kissing your pouting lips. I love that no matter what life deals you, you approach each day with optimism. I love how you use food for cuss words... I love you, Jolian." He knelt on one knee before her.

Love for him filled her heart to bursting! Tears of pure joy spilled over her lashes to splash on her cheek. Despite her earlier intuition she was genuinely shocked at his words. He loved *her*, he loved her!

"Would you do me the honor of waking in my arms every morning for the rest of our lives? Jolian, will you marry me?"

Silently, she raised her face to the heavens. Her heart trembled with elation. He was the dream she never knew she even wanted, and he was real! She cupped his face in her hands and urged him to stand as she lowered her chin and her eyes met his. He looked terrified. What was wrong? She hadn't answered him yet!

"Yes, yes, yes! Cooper, I love you, too! I have for so long—" She spoke quickly to belie his worry. He kissed her neck and her lips, her cheeks and her eyebrows. He grabbed hold of her waist and lifted her into the air as he spun in circles.

"Jolian Grayson, you have just made me the happiest man in the world!"

"And I am the luckiest woman."

He set her down gently on the spongy moss and took her chin between his thumb and forefinger. His kiss, so tender, yet it breathed passion into her. Jolian knew he loved her enough for two lifetimes. Had happiness ever filled her like it did now? She didn't care if he was a miner. It seemed so trivial that she'd ever even worried about it. She'd go with him, anywhere. She laughed despite the tears on her cheeks. His arms held her to him and she could feel the pounding of his heart, steady and strong in his chest. His hands roamed her back and flickers of heat began to build within her.

Cooper peeled her clothing from her body, removed his own and wrapped his hands about her waist. She wound her arms about his neck and he carried her to the edge of the Hot Springs. Her eyes locked with his as he lowered her slowly into the heat of the water. As her skin met the steamy bath its warmth shocked her and she inhaled through her mouth.

"Is it too much?" He began to lift her back out but stopped when she smiled at him and shook her head.

"It's wonderful!"

Cooper released her and she lowered herself onto the smooth surface of a rock. A platform of rocks about two feet down into the pool made a perfect sitting spot.

He watched her position herself on the ledge and then he turned to retrieve something from his shirt pocket. When he turned back to face her there was an odd look in his eyes that aroused her suspicions. He lowered himself into the water.

"What are you up to?" Jolian felt an odd sense of knowing.

"When I left you this morning, I went into town."

"Yes..."

"And I bought you this." Cooper opened his palm to reveal a dainty gold band set with sapphires and diamonds. "I spotted this in the window of a shop in town a couple weeks ago. The sapphires reminded me of your eyes."

"Cooper it's beautiful! But it must have cost a fortune; it's too much!"

His expression became serious and his gaze deepened. "I have something to tell you."

"Not another wife hiding in the shadows?" Jolian teased him. He grinned a smile full of boyish charm. He leaned forward to whisper in her ear.

"We're rich."

"What?"

"We're rich."

"I don't understand—"

"I struck the lead on my claim and it's headed straight for the claim you and I own together. I've pulled out more gold than most people ever see, already, and the best is still yet to come." He looked like a little boy who'd found a stash of free taffy.

Jolian couldn't believe her ears! She studied his face and wanted to take it in her hands and kiss his lips forever. Still, there was a glint in his eye..." Don't joke with me like that."

"It's not a joke Jolian."

"Really?" She giggled.

"Really!" He slipped the ring onto her finger. "It suits you."

Jolian shook her head as if to help the news settle into place. She couldn't believe it. He couldn't be serious. "No more searching?"

"Nope, I've found it." She had a feeling he wasn't speaking of his claim. He slid closer to her in the steaming springs and kissed her cheek. "I'm going to have to hire some men in town to help with the excavation. It's become too much work for just me."

"There's really that much gold there?"

"You could open twenty restaurants and never have to work a day for the rest of your life!" Their laughter mixed with the rising steam and he hugged her body close.

"Oh, Cooper, I could have paid for Jakeb. I could have stopped him from having to go to war!"

"I thought of that. And Jolian, I almost did it to spare you the pain of saying goodbye to him but I honestly believe it would have done him not one ounce of good. Your brother was a changed man the day he told he he'd decided to go off to war. I think he needs this; he needed to make the decision to do something with his life. The choice was his to make and he made an honorable one. It'll be fine, trust me."

"I do, completely."

They shared a kiss of excitement and promise for their future. He searched her eyes and found that nothing had changed. He knew the money wouldn't make a difference to her, not in the way it mattered most.

"I don't really feel like I should have Angus's share of the mine. Especially now, it feels wrong somehow," Jolian said.

That was his Jolian. Never thinking of herself! Staring at him with those innocent blue eyes, beseeching him to agree with her. "I know, but I can't apologize for hitting the lead. That's why I was mining!"

Jolian smiled at him. "Could we use Angus's share to build a hospital?"

"Oh, Angel, I think the gold couldn't be put to better use." She was the most altruistic person he'd ever met. He wanted to spend the rest of his days finding new ways to tell her he loved her. "We'll not only build a hospital, we'll staff it with the best doctors this side of the Rockies!"

She laughed, the most melodic sound and wrapped her arms about his neck. "If this is the response I get for agreeing to build a hospital, I'll build one in every township in the colony! Heck I'll build so many buildings, you'll think you're back in San Francisco."

"Oh, Cooper, I can't believe it! Everything is all so incredible—I never, in all my dreams thought I could feel so, so... oh, Cooper! She squeezed him tight in her embrace and trailed kisses down his shoulder.

"Mmm, that feels great. Could you say my name like that again?"

Jolian licked her lips and whispered her breath on his cheek as she spoke his name.

"You are the most desirable woman!" He growled and kissed her neck.

A sigh escaped her lips. "Here in the open?"

"If you'll have me."

"I shall." She raised her lips and he collected them in a kiss. Her response was so full of passion it pulled him to the brink within seconds.

He ran his hands around her back and pulled her body towards his. Her breasts rose up out of the water and his mouth found one instantly. She wrapped her legs around him and the warmth of the water enabled him to slide into her with ease. She began to slide her hips up his belly and he grabbed her buttocks to assist the motion. Though steam swirled about them, it could not compare with the heat rising inside him. The buoyancy of the water created sensations all its own. They moved as one, in a rhythm born of their love and spurred by their passion.

Jolian caught his earlobe in her teeth and exhaled near his ear. "Cooper... Cooper!" her release was so powerful, so fervent, it pulsated in the center of his being until he could hold back no longer. His body shook with satisfaction and he exploded inside her.

Seventeen

Cooper pulled his shirt over Jolian's head. It fell halfway to her knees and she looked deliciously fetching in it. Would he ever get his fill of her? Somehow he knew the answer to that question already. He planned to spend every day of the rest of his life with this charming woman and still, he knew, it could never be enough.

He handed her his saddlebag. She emptied the contents and picked out a flat rock to lay the food upon.

"You must be starved, Jolian. I left for town hours ago and you'd wanted something to eat, then." He moved to help her unpack some of the provisions. He had jerked salmon, cucumber, tomatoes, a fresh loaf of sourdough and two bottles of sarsaparilla. Jolian squealed in delight as he pulled the bottles from the leather pouch.

"It's my favorite! How did you know?"

"I can't take any credit for that one, Angel; I'm partial to it myself." He didn't add this was a recent infatuation summoned by the absence of whiskey in his diet. He knew himself well enough to know his personality was the kind that quickly turned cravings to addictions. He had certainly found a better alternative to alcohol. Yup, he could quite easily live off of sarsaparilla and Jolian. He chuckled to himself. Jolian looked up and he felt adoration in her gaze. God, he loved her! He loved her more than he thought it was possible to love another human being.

"Did the Constable give you anything to eat while you were in his custody?"

"No, but I had a jug of water. Although I admit I spilled more than I drank. It was the chains he had about my wrists. I never realized they were so heavy!"

Cooper shook his head in disgust.

"You know, there's still something that has me a bit puzzled." Jolian took a long drink of her Sarsaparilla.

"What's that, Angel?"

"The Constable arrived at my cabin door not more than ten minutes after you left, but if you had seen him on the trail, I know you would have returned."

"Ten minutes?" Cooper almost choked on his salmon. "Of course I would have seen him. He must have been at the cabin already, before I left you."

"I don't understand, Cooper."

"Neither do I, not yet anyway. I have had a suspicion that's been floating around in my head for a while now. It's just the proof..."

"You don't think the Constable would have poisoned—"

"Yes I do."

"But why? He's a man of the law. Surely he wouldn't try to poison Brewer. And besides, why would the Constable want to poison a man condemned to hang? Why wouldn't he simply wait it out?"

"Maybe there's a reason he can't wait it out."

"You mean... You think he's involved with Brewer somehow?"

"It makes sense, Jolian. Why would Brewer risk coming to Barkerville? I know he wasn't aware Jakeb was alive and he thought he'd effectively covered his tracks by killing everyone he came across. Still, why would he risk coming into a huge city, on a trail dotted with Royal Engineers, who are practically the law in this colony? He must have had a reason to travel all this way. And Constable Towers must have a reason for wanting a condemned man dead sooner. I think they were working together somehow and the Constable is worried their collaboration will be revealed before Brewer hangs."

Jolian's face turned ashen. "If they're working together, the Constable could be persuaded to let Brewer go, couldn't he?"

"That's one of a number of possibilities." Cooper left his food, stood and paced the area around the Hot Springs. He rubbed his jaw in thought and then added, "I'm sorry, Jolian. I wanted this to be the perfect afternoon for us but I think we need to pack up and get to Pearl's place."

"I think you're right."

"Don't worry, my angel." Cooper pulled her to his arms and kissed her furrowed brow. "I'm not letting you out of my sight, ever again."

~ * ~

Less than an hour later Cooper and Jo stood around the big pine table in Pearl's kitchen. The girls, all five of them, had been summoned by Pearl and they were chatting all at once about the news they'd gleaned.

"I can't believe the Constable could—"

"He ain't so high and mighty as he pretends to be."

"To think of all of the times he—"

Pearl and her girls were shocked by the realization the Constable was very likely involved with the murderer but they had concurred with Cooper and Jo's reasoning. Vera had been outraged at the implication she may have poisoned the murderer. She had said it was she and not the Constable, who had insisted a Doctor be brought in from Barkerville.

Pearl confirmed the Constable had stopped by the day before and suggested Jo bring a plate of food to the jailhouse. Vera hadn't even thought up the idea of visiting the jail. Pearl had suggested Vera could bring the food, as it was Jo's day off. The Constable had agreed, begrudgingly. At the time, Pearl said she had thought nothing of it. The Constable was always asking for *favors* she had to comply with to keep him from shutting her place down.

"That's blackmail!" Jo gasped.

"And it's what goes on in all of the houses, in every town of this colony." Pearl snorted in disgust. "Just cause *they* say we's doin' somethin' ill-eagle."

"Regardless of what has gone on with the Constable in the past, I'd suggest you keep the curtains drawn and the doors barred." Cooper looked directly into Pearl's eyes when he spoke. "You and your girls are sitting targets here."

"I understands yore concerns, Coop, but I am more than comfortable protectin' my girls. Ain't nobody gonna git inta my house without my sez so. 'Sides that, Towers ain't never been the sharpest knife in the block."

Gracie-Rose and Elspeth put their heads together and giggled at Pearl's remarks. Cooper understood their need to release tension in laughter when they were probably so apprehensive about the law being untrustworthy. He smiled in a way he hoped conveyed his empathy but he still felt the need to caution them further.

"I know what you mean, Pearl. I, too, have had my doubts as to the mental capacity of the Constable. That in itself could be a problem. If he really *was* the one to poison his partner last night, it means he is feeling desperate and trapped."

Pearl nodded in agreement and Cooper looked at each one of the girls in the room.

"Maybe he'd made some kind of deal with Brewer and now Brewer has threatened to reveal the connection between them, I don't know, but either way I'd say the Constable is an impulsive, dangerous man right now. Desperate men don't think before they act. We all need to be very careful until this thing gets settled."

Pearl paid close attention to his words and nodded her head in agreement again. "I hear ya, Coop, and I reckon you's right. We orta all be on our guard. But how *is* this thin' gonna git settled?"

"That's a good question, Pearl." He hadn't had time yet to think about a plan of action. One thing he was certain of, he wasn't going to be able to do it alone. Pearl must have had the same thought as she interrupted just as he opened his mouth to speak.

"I think we's gonna need some help. You can't just ride inta Richfield with yore guns blazin'."

"Maybe if we could gather a posse of men from Barkerville?" Jolian interjected.

"I could go," Doralynn piped up. "The Constable has no grudge with me, even if I did run into him on the trail."

"She's right," Pearl agreed. "Doralynn knows where Guy's at, too. She kin get him to round up the men."

Cooper fingered his moustache as he thought over the idea. More than anything, he didn't want to leave Jolian's side but he couldn't put Doralynn in danger either. He carefully weighed both sides of the situation and decided Doralynn would be as safe on the trail today as she would be any other day.

Doralynn prepared herself with haste. Cooper could see no sign of anxiety or trepidation in her features. "You are a brave woman, Doralynn. Guy's a lucky man." Doralynn reached for her cape as a hushed anticipation blanketed the room.

"Guy ain't no luckier than Jo." Vera's voice wasn't much louder than a whisper, yet it filled the quiet with its envious tone.

"Ya, ya rub it in." Pearl snorted as she helped Doralynn don her cape. "First I lose Doralynn to Guy and now my male cook has up and landed herself the most eligible bachelor this side of the Rockies!" Cooper had to hand it to Pearl; she could always bring a spark of humor to tense situations. She practically pushed Doralynn out the door then closed and barred it behind her. She turned her ample form around and poked a finger in his chest.

"I should be furious with ya, Cooper. You up'n stole the best cook I's ever had! What in tarnations am I going to feed these girls once you marry her?" Pearl placed her hands on her hips and stared at Cooper like he was a misbehaving little child. Jo couldn't help but laugh when Pearl added, "Ya is plannin' on marryin' her, ain't ya?"

"Yes indeed, Ma'am," Cooper said his voice proud.

Jolian held out her hand to show Pearl her ring. "In my heart, we are already one and that's all that matters to me."

Vera groaned in protest. "C'mon Gracie-Rose, if we's closed for the night I might as well set your hair for ya."

Elspeth tagged along as well, leaving Pearl holding Jo's outstretched hand and staring at the ring on her finger.

"Oh honey." Pearl dabbed at her eyes with her lace handkerchief and then wrapped her arms impulsively about Jo's shoulders. "Don't ya know it ain't right ta make an old whore cry?" She sobbed and hugged until Cooper thought he was going to have to pry her off Jolian with a crow bar.

"I know, I know—" Jo's eyes were filled with tears now, too. "I can't believe it myself but I love him, Pearl, I really do."

Cooper felt his heart swell with her declaration. She loved him and she was going to marry him. He was one lucky guy. Before he knew what was happening, Pearl had let Jolian go and moved to throw her arms around him. She cried into his shoulder until, thankfully, Jolian gave him an excuse to push the woman to arms length.

"Cooper, I should begin preparing the evening meal, but I need a few things from the garden. Do you think you could accompany me?"

"A course he'll accompany ya." Pearl gave her nose a hearty blow into her handkerchief. "Do ya honestly think he's gonna let ya outta his sight with that crazed Constable about?"

Her tone was still teasing but her words rang all too true. "I can go to the garden for you," he volunteered.

"Could you pick rosemary and chive from the herb patch as well?" Jolian asked quite innocently.

"You have me there." Cooper caught Jo up in his arms and hugged her body to his own. "I guess I'll have to admit now— I don't know everything—and so soon in our relationship, too. I'd hoped to fool you a bit longer."

"What!" Jolian pushed him back playfully with her hands on his shoulders but her waist still tight in his grasp. "You don't know everything? Well that's it then, the wedding is off."

"Git outta this kitchen right now you two! Don't you tease an old woman that way. Git out ta that garden and pick something good fer dinner. Make us sumpthin' special, Jo, ta celebrate yore upcomin' nuptials and ta keep our mind off the good-fer-nuthin' varmint of a lawman."

"Something good? There's one thing we don't need to pick." Cooper couldn't resist the game.

"Oh, what's that?" Jolian took the bait he set.

"We don't need potatoes, not with this big sack right here!" He bent and picked Jolian up with her waist on his shoulder and her upper body hanging behind him. He held tight to her knees as she kicked and squirmed.

"Put me down, Cooper! I am not a sack of potatoes, Cooper, put me down!" She was laughing and he couldn't resist it. He carried her out the back door of the kitchen, leaving Pearl to shake her head with wonder.

Alone on the back porch he pulled her body to slide down his. He felt ripples of arousal pulsate through him and he tightened his arms to squeeze her body to his.

"I love you, Jolian Grayson."

"I don't think I'll ever tire of hearing those words." Jolian saw his smile deepen but she was not expecting his reaction.

"I love you, Jolian, I love this woman!" He called out for everyone to hear. He had publicly declared his feelings for her. Of course, the private declarations were the ones that mattered the most, but it suddenly seemed her magical faerie tale times with him were real. He honestly loved her and she was truly going to be his wife. She couldn't contain her joy and she shouted out loud as well.

"I love you, Cooper!" Those were the only words she could utter before his lips were fast upon her. She felt her body melting into his. Cooper's kisses robbed her of her senses and deprived her of the ability to think clearly. She could hardly believe only a day had passed since she had prepared herself to live the life of a single woman.

Jolian broke away from the kiss and stared deep into his eyes. What was it about him that caused her to feel the way she did? Everything felt different somehow. She felt invincible; she could face anything with Cooper's love on her side and yet life had never felt more precious. She wanted to savor every minute, make the most out of their time together. If there was one thing she'd learned in the past year, it was that life could end abruptly and dreams for the future would only ever be dreams.

She loved the way he looked at her, as if she were the only woman in the world for him. He leisurely laid his arm across her shoulders and she sighed with contentment as she fixed her body snug against him, one arm about his waist. They strolled through the tall grass towards the vegetable garden. There was no need for words. He seemed at ease with the speed at which their relationship had matured, as was she.

She stopped suddenly as she remembered. "Oh, biscuits! My clothes!"

"What's that?"

"My clothes. Oh Cooper, my lovely new suit from Doralynn. We left everything at the lake when we—" It was one thing to make love with a man, but quite another to talk about it out loud.

"We can go there right now." His tone was reassuring. They headed towards the lake on the path to her cabin. Once they reached the front door they naturally paused.

"I want to get a few things from my cabin while we're here. The vegetable basket, my gun—"

"I'll meet you on the back porch." He grinned. "If I come in, you know we'll never even make it to the lake."

Jolian felt herself blush from head to toe. She nodded her response and he threw his head back with laughter.

"You are such a contradiction, my wildcat-Angel!" ·

Jolian let the rag roll off her as she pushed open the door of her cabin. She closed the door behind her, watching Cooper all the way. She worried her bottom lip with her teeth as she smiled to herself. The view of him walking away was almost as good as the view of him walking towards her. Such thoughts! Maybe she *was* a wildcat. She slung the big basket she used for gathering her garden victuals into the crook of her arm and picked up her pace to retrieve the items she wanted from the bedroom. An odd smell in assaulted her nostrils upon entering the room. A stale smell. She couldn't put her finger on it.

A sweaty hand covered her mouth and a long arm wrapped around her midsection, pinning her arms to her sides and paralyzing her with fear. The Constable's words hissed into her ear. "Don't make a sound or I'll kill you."

Jolian nodded her understanding. Dread iced through her and the basket slipped from her fingers.

"It's all your fault! His voice reeked with desperation. What had Cooper said about him earlier? She must move very carefully. She could feel the spittle running down her cheek as hissed his words.

"I had myself a nice little business set up. He'd steal the stuff and I'd sell it. He just went a bit too far... he wasn't supposed to kill 'em. Then you and your brother came to town with your "description" and it changed everything. You know, you and I aren't all that different. You were willing to do anything for your brother and so am I. He may only be my half brother, but our ma raised us up together. He's all I got left and I had to poison him because of you! He woke up, you know. I guess I didn't give him enough of the stuff. He spilled his guts to that Doctor just like he said he'd do. The way I figure it, you're my only way out of here now. As long as I have you, they won't shoot me."

Jolian tried to wiggle her arms free but she only succeeded in angering him further. She couldn't believe the Constable and Brewer were brothers! She was in a lot of trouble here. What was she going to do? He yanked her back towards the kitchen, dragging her feet and slamming her skull on a flat-sawed log in the doorway between the two rooms. Pain sliced through her as white stars flashed before her and blackness narrowed her vision. She struggled to keep her wits about her. *Cooper,*

Cooper! She must warn him. The Constable would keep her alive to make his retreat but he had no reason not to shoot Cooper.

She wiggled again only to receive a low curse from the Constable as his fingers tightened their grip on her face, cutting her teeth into her upper lip. She could hardly breathe! She tried to force her mouth open for air but she gagged on the taste of his sweat mixed with her blood. Again her vision narrowed and blackness presented itself as an alternative.

"You can't bite me you little—"

The Constable muttered his deprecation and dragged her by her neck towards the kitchen. Jolian summoned all the strength she could muster and kicked her right foot out across her body. Her effort succeeded in knocking the coffeepot from its usual resting spot on the back of the stove. The clattering noise it made as it fell would certainly alert Cooper. Wouldn't it?

"What the hell are you trying to do? Want me to just kill you right now?" From the tone of his voice, Jolian suddenly realized it didn't matter what she did. Regardless of whether she fought or didn't fight, the Constable was going to kill her. Her only choice in this was how she was going die. She could choose to stay calm and let him use her as his shield to safety or she could stand her ground, push him to end it here and now and hopefully save Cooper in the process.

She knew her choice before she had even thought through all of her options. She felt an unexpected power surge through her body. This was her life! He had no right to do this! She began to twist her body to and fro. It was working. His arm about her waist loosened its grip!

Pain slammed into her skull on the exact spot that had been injured on the doorway. The room swam before her and the Constable's words sounded far away to her ears.

"Hold still bit—"

The shot thundered throughout the room and the Constable slumped to the ground. She fell with him, landing on top of his body. She had to hurry, to free herself from the grip of his arms.

"It's all right, it's all right." Cooper helped her to her feet and pulled her into his arms. "Hush now," he cooed to her as the sobs began to rack her body. His warm hands caressed her arms. She leaned against him and let her tears fall. The room was dark, then light again.

"He can't hurt you anymore." Cooper stroked her hair with one hand and checked the pulse of the lawman with the other.

She tried to speak but her words wouldn't come. She inhaled as deep as her chest would allow. Something heavy was pressing down upon her.

"I went around to the back porch to surprise you. I was sneaking through the back door and saw him drag you towards the kitchen. I had to shoot before he knew I was there, Jolian. I couldn't risk losing you. I waited for a clear shot and took it. It was my only choice."

Her words still wouldn't come so she raised her chin and kissed him through her tears. His voice sounded odd in her ears and she shook her head slightly to clear the ringing noise in the background. She should comfort him. Cooper needed reassuring. He'd just killed a man to save her!

"You're bleeding—my God, Jolian your head! What did he do to you? Come on." Cooper lifted her into his arms. "We need to get you to a doctor!"

Jolian didn't argue. She didn't have the strength for it. Cooper ran with her in his arms. *Were they heading back to Pearl's?* It seemed to take an awfully long time and then suddenly they were there and Pearl pushed a cloth to her head and shouted for the doctor. She opened her eyes to find she was in the parlor of Pearl's place. The Doctor was there too, how very odd; he'd got there so fast. He stared into her eyes and came far too close for her liking. She smelled something awful as her vision narrowed completely.

Eighteen

Again, a terrible smell accosted her senses. She turned her head to avoid the stench.

"Jolian?" It was Cooper's voice. She'd been dreaming about him. She smiled and turned her head towards him.

"Jolian? It's Cooper. Can you open your eyes? Angel? Open your eyes now." Open her eyes? Why would she want to do that? She was far too tired to obey his request. Couldn't he just talk to her like this, while she just rested a bit longer? Her eyelids were too heavy. She needed more sleep. Ah yes, sleep seemed like the best choice right now. She was sinking slowly into the void. The wonderful nothingness, it beckoned to her. Promising peace and rest and no pain at all.

"Jolian! Open your eyes!"

Cooper again and he sounded angry. Why was he angry with her? What had she done that had made him speak with her in that tone? She wasn't about to listen to him when he spoke like that. She'd go back to sleep now, that's what she'd do. Back to her own little land, where everything was peaceful...

"Jolian." Cooper again. This time his voice was soft and caressing her. It made the pain in her head seem much more bearable when he spoke softly. She smiled and spoke his name. At least she thought she had but no sound had come out.

"Jolian, I know you can hear me. I love you, Jolian, please, please wake up now." There was a pleading quality in his voice this time and Jolian couldn't resist. She tried to open her eyes.

"That's it, Angel, open your eyes now. You can do it Angel, I love you."

243

His voice was louder. He must have moved closer. If her eyes would only open, she could see who was rubbing her arm.

"Cooper?" Her voice sounded funny in her own ears and she struggled to bring him into focus.

"Jolian! Oh thank God! Jolian, you heard me. Thank God." There were tears in his eyes as he stared at her and then lowered his head on to her arm. *What had happened?*

"Doralynn, Guy! She's awake!" Pearl's voice rang out as loud as ever. What was the fuss about? And why was she in bed?

"You shore gived us a scare, honey." Pearl patted Cooper on the back as he stood, turned his back to Jolian and walked towards the bedroom window. Pearl took his spot beside her and propped another pillow under her head. "Are ya feelin' up ta sittin' up that much? Let me knows if ya needs ta lie back down again."

"Why is..." A coughing fit besieged her and Cooper turned abruptly from the window. Pearl offered her a mug of water as Cooper hurried over to her side.

"Take it easy, Jolian." Cooper took the mug from Pearl and eased it to her lips. The tepid water felt heavenly on her parched throat. She wanted to drink the whole cup but Cooper advised against it.

"You can have as much as you want, Angel, but take it slow. You've barely had anything in the past few days and gulping it now will only make you bring it all back up again."

"How long?" She managed to get out.

"Ya've been out fer almost four days." Pearl's voice came from somewhere behind Cooper. "The doc figured ya weren't gonna never wake up but we all knewed ya would, didn't we, Coop?"

"Um-hm." Cooper smiled at her and stroked her arm. It was the same feeling she'd had while she was 'sleeping' and she knew that he'd spent night and day at her side.

"Thank you." Her voice was barely above a whisper.

"He never left ya, Jo. I had ta drag him to the chair over in the corner ta gets sleep. Doralynn finally got him ta eat something yesterday. He weren't havin' nothin' but broth, the same as I was dribblin down yer throat. Said if you was gonna starve ta death then he didn't want ta live neither."

Cooper hushed Pearl with a look and turned back towards her. "But you woke up and now everything is going to be just fine."

~ * ~

The next few days saw Jolian become stronger and stronger. The doctor visited, checked her over thoroughly and gave her a clean bill of health. The wound on her head was healing nicely and by the end of the week she felt sturdy enough on her feet to take short walks out of doors, Cooper's hand ever present at her elbow. There were so many things she felt she had missed, being asleep for so long, but it wasn't until today she felt strong enough mentally to ask a certain question of Cooper.

"I have been wondering..." She let the thought trail away. Was she ready for this?

"What is it, Angel? Are you feeling weak? Do you want me to get Guy to go for the Doctor again?" Cooper spoke so quickly she hadn't time to interrupt.

"No, no I'm fine, really. It's Brewer. I wondered... I need to know—"

"I'm sorry, Jolian. I should have told you—He's dead."

Jolian breathed a sigh that took the weight off her shoulders. "How?"

Cooper led her to the shade of a giant cottonwood. He took off his coat and spread it on the ground for her to sit upon. A truly gallant gesture as her skirts were so big they covered his entire coat and then some. Cooper sat across from her and took her hands in his. "I'll tell you the whole story, but only if you promise me that if you're tiring you'll interrupt."

She nodded her promise.

"He was probably dead before the Constable ever attacked you." Cooper shook his head in disgust. "The doctor said Brewer had come to and told him everything but the Constable fled the jailhouse before he could be stopped. The doctor shouted for assistance and the men in the streets of Richfield had come running to the jail. Doc said he couldn't leave his patient and the men formed a posse to hunt down the Constable. He was at the end of the line by the time he got to your cabin. When I shot him, the men who were searching the woods came rushing towards the sound and saw me carrying you. You were in and out and fading fast. One of the men rode back for the doctor. The others dealt with the Constable's body. By the time I got you to Pearl's I was so worried about you." His voice broke and he stopped speaking to simply rub his thumb across the back of her hand.

"I know, I'm sorry I caused everyone so much grief." It hurt to see the tears in his eyes.

Cooper raised his eyes and stared into hers. "But what a beautiful nuisance you are."

Jolian felt a blush rising in her cheeks and Cooper chuckled. "Apparently, by the time the man got back to the jailhouse for the Doctor, Brewer had died. There is no one on this earth that is ever going to hurt you again Jolian. You are as safe as safe can be. I promise." Cooper moved to sit beside her and she rested her head against his chest. His arm slipped around her back and pulled her close to him. They sat for a few moments, content in their quiet time together.

"Our claim is doing well."

"Umm." Jolian gazed about at the rich green hillsides and powder blue sky. A gentle breeze played with the hair on her neck. This was the most beautiful country in the world, surely.

"Guy hired some men for me, some men he could trust and they've been pulling out fifteen hundred dollars a foot."

"Wwwhat?" She raised her head to look at him.

"I told you, Angel, it's going to be the richest claim in the area!"

"Cooper," Jolian shook her head in disbelief and then she smiled. "Does that mean we can make our home here, in the wilds of this colony?"

"Sure, Angel, we can live wherever your heart desires."

"I won't have to follow you around from gold town to gold town, will I?"

"Follow me around? I've only ever had these claims here—" Cooper stared at her like she spoke a foreign language.

"What are you saying... you're not a miner?" Jo was truly stunned.

Cooper shook his head. "Not by trade. I'm a surveyor. I thought you knew. Though, I suppose I'll give it all up now."

Jolian couldn't contain the laughter that bubbled up inside her.

"What's so funny?"

"All this time, I thought you were a miner and I've been struggling, wondering if I could follow you around like my ma followed my pa. Never having roots, always searching for the elusive strike. But then I fell in love with you, and I knew that I'd go wherever you asked. All this time, and you were a surveyor?"

"Yup," he whispered, staring at her lips. His mouth sought hers. The urgent need he always created within her began to build steadily. She was his, totally and completely. Oh, she'd follow him to the edge of the earth if he asked her! She thought she wanted nothing more than a home of her own. A place that was hers, something no one could ever take from her. She had finally found that place. As it turned out, she never would have found it on a map. For all the home she would ever want or could ever need, was right here, in the arms of the man she loved.

Meet

Camille Cavanagh

Camille's first memory of wanting to be a writer comes from her early teens. Her short story *"A Love To Remember"* had been gingerly passed to a friend. Unbeknownst to her, that friend shared it with another, and eventually circled it around the school, until one day a classmate thrust a well-worn copy back into her hands and said, "I don't know who wrote this, but you've *got* to read it!"

She has since written several novels, short stories and poems and is thrilled to see her first novel in print. Camille lives in British Columbia, Canada.

VISIT OUR WEBSITE
FOR THE FULL INVENTORY
OF QUALITY BOOKS:

http://www.wings-press.com

Quality trade paperbacks and downloads
in multiple formats,
in genres ranging from light romantic comedy
to general fiction and horror. Wings has something
for every reader's taste.
Visit the website, then bookmark it.
We add new titles each month!